T0356542

THE DEVIL'S KITCHEN

A MURDER IN YELLOWSTONE

MARK THIELMAN

SEVERN RIVER PUBLISHING

Severn River Publishing
www.SevernRiverBooks.com

Cover Image: Jackie Burkhart, The River, Grand Canyon Of Yellowstone National Park, USA , Wallpaper

ISBN: 978-1-64875-625-2 (Paperback)

ALSO BY MARK THIELMAN

The Johnson and Nance Mysteries

The Devil's Kitchen: A Murder in Yellowstone

The Hidden River: A Murder in the Everglades

The Firefall: A Murder in Yosemite

To find out more about Mark Thielman and his books, visit

severnriverbooks.com

To Betty
I couldn't do this without you. Nor would I want to.

1

Paris, France
January 1794

Jacques-Louis David watched as the prisoner began the slow march toward the guillotine. His companion, forced to wait, drummed his fingers against the bricks of the Hôtel de la Marine. Together they stood in the Place de la Révolution, the center of the rebellion in Paris.

As an artist, the images of death fascinated David. The condemned man shuffled to the stairs. A priest accompanied him. A National Guard member followed with a sharpened pike to prod him should the condemned man falter on these final steps. From where he stood, David could not hear the soft murmurings of the man's final prayers. He wondered if they were audible, even to the priest. David saw the man's dry, chapped lips. His hair, quickly barbered to reveal his neck, lay matted against his head. The crowd, accustomed to executions, continued their conversations during the prisoner's final walk. The exchange of Parisian gossip and talk of business drowned out the last rites.

David turned to his companion. "Who is this one?"

Maximilien Robespierre fluttered his hand. "If you wish to know, you must buy a program." He pointed his thin finger toward a hawker working his way through the crowd, selling the guides to the condemned. Other vendors sold bread and drinks.

David heard the heavy clang as the bascule swung into place. The prisoner's body, locked upright onto the board, slowly lowered like a drawbridge to horizontal. His lips moved faster, mouthing final prayers. David wondered if God heard. In the Place de la Révolution, the prayers were punctuated by the clack of the lunette securing the head and neck into position.

The crowd noise ceased. The executioner pulled the release handle. In the silence, David heard the rattling of the mouton sliding down the tracks. It clicked as it passed each seam in the wood. The sound always reminded him of snapping teeth. A heavy thud followed as the blade slammed into the block below the neck. A cheer arose from the witnesses, arms raised in triumph, liberty caps waved. Another traitor to the Republic had received his justice.

The executioner lifted the head from the basket and displayed it to the crowd. David watched the eyes flicker and widen as the head tried to understand what had transpired. The rumor traveling around Paris was that if someone witnessed the moment the head realized what had occurred, that person would receive good luck all that day. The eyes fixed. The executioner dropped the head back into the basket. He then set about the task of raising the blade with the heavy cotton rope. The Republic demanded that the executions stay on schedule.

Around the two men milled a throng of spectators. The group included a pair of working men dressed in dusty and tattered long coats. In contrast to Robespierre, both men had short, unpowdered haircuts. Liberty caps, faded red, covered their heads.

David thought of the condemned man and considered his coloring in those final moments. Color was one of David's tools to convey eternal virtues. Despite the day's chill, beads of sweat had dotted the man's pale forehead. His brow had worn a silvery sheen. His blanched face contrasted with his scarlet wrists, rubbed raw, David assumed, by the manacles he wore while imprisoned. His knuckles, pale white, gripped the priest who had pulled him up the stairs to the execution floor. The priest's florid face showed the strain. So much contrast within a small space. David had imagined a more serene look as the father guided a penitent into eternity, but the Republic had a schedule to keep. If the priest did not move this man along into the afterlife, the guardsman would. David pinched his eyes closed and tried to recreate the image of the condemned man and the priest struggling with beatific effort.

"Mark my words," a gruff voice beside him said. David looked. One of the men in the long coats spoke to his companion. "The next one will bow up his neck, thinking he can beat the machine. They all do."

"Can't help it," the other replied. "The head don't want to be split from the body. I've seen it with me chickens. Even if the priest tells him it will go easier on him, the body stiffens up."

David marveled at the artistry of the instrument. The angle of the guillotine's blade minimized the resistance, allowing the cutting edge to pass more efficiently through the neck. The weight of the mouton gave the blade heft and enabled the blade to sever the head of even the fattest of the royalists.

"Would we kill so many if we were not so damnably efficient at it?" David blurted, his unsettling thought expressed aloud.

"I am of two minds on the subject," Robespierre said. "We have developed the most democratic of all killing instruments. All are equal before the guillotine. The rich do not suffer less than the poor. It is the walk, not the death, that proves to be the fearsome part. The guillotine is an embodiment of the Revolution. Yet..." Here Robespierre paused before continuing. His face pursed as he continued to think on the subject. His eyes blinked constantly. "It is undeniable that the efficiency robs some of the terror. A bit more agony might be beneficial to the cause. If men and women knew that they would suffer more, they may offend less."

David wondered whether Robespierre had seen the face of the last soul to depart this earth. He had fear aplenty.

Robespierre nudged him forward. "I cannot stand here all day."

David fell into step alongside. Before they had gone far, the crowd became aware of the two men. Almost immediately, spectators surrounded them. Some merely wanted to touch the incorruptible Robespierre, others to offer suggestions about the direction of the Republic. Some shouted names of those whose fate should lead them to the guillotine. The crowds pressed against them. The small, frail Robespierre might easily be crushed. David stepped in front, drawing his elbows tightly to his chest, using his body as a battering ram to fight his way through the crowd before they were engulfed.

"Do not stop." In his ear, he could hear the nervous voice of Robespierre urging him forward.

Above the crowd, on the step of the guillotine, David saw a member of the National Guard looking in their direction. Pulling his arm from his chest, he gestured to the man. With a voice he could hardly recognize as his own, he yelled to the man. "This is Monsieur Robespierre. Come before we are killed!"

The guard moved to turn away. Crowds and vendors had been hallmarks of the carnival-like atmosphere surrounding the executions since the Reign of Terror had begun. Then, his head snapped back. His face registered a slow dawn of realization. He clapped a hand onto his fellow guard, and the two broad-shouldered men began fighting their way through the crowd.

The guards formed a protective cocoon around Robespierre, front and back, beefy arms flung wide, the small man sheltered in between. David twisted his way alongside and stayed close. Although he held immense power as a member of the Committee of General Security and the final judge of artistic merit in France, he knew that the guards would make no effort to preserve him until Robespierre's safety was secured. He pressed tightly and accompanied them through the crowd.

Safely free of the throng, Robespierre's green, almond-shaped eyes studied his two hulking benefactors. The guards looked down at the ground, unable or unwilling to make eye contact with the leader of the Revolution.

"Thank you for your service to the new France," Robespierre said.

The men mumbled a reply.

Snapping his jacket back into place and brushing a lock of hair behind his ear, Robespierre turned and set off on his way. David, his heart rate returning to normal, quickened his pace to catch up with the other man's brisk steps.

"Quite the morning," he said.

Robespierre glanced over, his face momentarily blank. "Oh, that," he said after the slight hesitation. "Another demonstration of the power of symbols."

David's eyes narrowed. He considered the remark.

"My artistic friend," Robespierre continued, squinting at him with his nearsighted eyes, "you of all people should recognize the symbols at work. The guillotine brings the crowd to a passionate frenzy. Then, into that mix steps a human symbol of the Revolution. Symbols incite passion, and crowds follow passion. The process is elementary and mechanical. We know the moral path; the crowd must be provoked to follow it. Symbols guide them."

"You and the guillotine, two symbols of the Revolution?"

"In peace, the advancement of virtue marks the purpose of government. In revolution, it is virtue and terror. Terror is swift justice, the embodiment of virtue. The guillotine is terror. I am virtue. We are inseparable." Robespierre stopped, turned, and, with his delicate finger, poked David in the chest. "You paint the images of the Revolution. The guillotine and I are its living incarnation." Dropping his hand, Robespierre spun on his heel and resumed his brisk, nervous pace down the Champs-Élysées. He had progressed little more than a dozen steps before he stopped again. "And that is why we must destroy the relics of the failed regime."

"But we have killed the king," David said.

Robespierre shook his head vehemently. "Lives are temporal. Let me ask you, if you want to darken the world, will it work alone to snuff out the candles? No." He pointed a finger to the sky. "The sun, our enduring source of light, that must be eliminated."

David spoke slowly, his voice wavering. "You want to blot out the sun?"

Robespierre dipped his head and looked down at his feet. David could only see the long, white, elegantly coiffed hair before the small man raised his face. Robespierre slowly shook his head. His eyes, rimmed with dark circles, continued to blink. Robespierre wore the ashen complexion of a man who slept little these days. "Sometimes," he began, "it is like speaking with a child. I do not wish to blot the sun." He closed his eyes and exhaled slowly before continuing. "I wish to eliminate the symbols that give the regents the belief in their own authority over the people." Robespierre turned in a slow circle, jabbing his frail arm into the air. "We convert the royal prisons into holding pens for enemies of the Revolution. We convert the palaces into public buildings. We turn their symbols into displays of our triumph." He stomped his foot. "But we must go further. The badges of authority. The jewels of the failed king must be melted down."

"We have done so, the crowns, the chalices, the cruets have all been dismantled and recast or sold. I sometimes pity the loss of such beauty," David said.

Robespierre paused. Reaching into his pocket, he withdrew his green-tinted spectacles. He adjusted them on his nose, his eyes now taking on a lizard-like quality. He appeared less human than he had moments before. The leader of the Committee of Public Safety, the man most responsible for deciding who lived and who died in France was stalling, struggling to regain his composure before he spoke. David felt fear in the pit of his stomach. His hand began to shake; had he held a paint brush, his canvas would be ruined. He began to stammer. "The Revolution is my life. I have sacrificed my marriage—"

"Come, my friend," Robespierre interrupted. "I am hungry. It is time for our noon repast."

David followed. He hated to eat in public. The old injury, a fencing scar from his youth, deep on the left side of his face, made chewing difficult. Yet, he could not refuse Robespierre. He allowed himself to be led to a small table at a café. Robespierre said little until the food arrived. Although the silence remained uncomfortable, David felt the tightness in his stomach relaxing.

When Robespierre spoke, his voice was cold, his eyes reptilian. "We must dig out the symbols of the ancien régime. If you are too rooted in your aesthetic to move this country forward, we will find another."

David's leg began to shake, banging against the bottom of the table. Though fearful of looking away, he could not face those twitching eyes.

"Purity is called for, Jacques-Louis. I trust you have the spirit to shape our beloved nation."

David nodded enthusiastically. He felt afraid to open his mouth for fear his voice would betray him.

As quickly as they had arrived, the inhuman eyes of Robespierre disappeared. "I never doubted for a moment that you were faithful, my friend. Still, such words have sent many citizens up the stairs of the guillotine. We who shape the nation must carefully preserve our tongues...to preserve our heads. Please, my friend, eat. You've hardly touched your food."

David took a small bite of bread and chewed deliberately. He concentrated on keeping his mouth closed. He hoped to soften the bread with his saliva. His mouth felt so dry that he did not know if he could swallow.

Robespierre watched him eat. He carefully put a hand into his pocket, then withdrew a clenched fist. Slowly, he extended his arm. "Jacques-Louis, give me your hand."

David laid his fist upon the table. Robespierre's hand hovered just above David's. Their eyes met, and Robespierre smiled, his thin lips pressed together. With a delicate, almost childlike index finger, he pried open David's fingers. When his hand was flat, David felt something fall into his palm. Robespierre withdrew his hand. David's eyes widened. He held three most exquisite jewels, a diamond, a ruby, and the largest, most iridescent pearl he had ever seen. His heart leapt at the fortune he held—a reward for his loyal service to France. The sum easily surpassed the money he had lost on commissions when he turned his back on wealthy royalist patrons and supported the Republican cause. The hours in meetings, the endless talk and haranguing fell away as he looked at the jewels.

He closed his hand to feel them. He needed to make sure that the rush of excitement after being trapped in the crowd had not befuddled his mind. He straightened his fingers.

The jewels remained. Their superb coloring dazzled his eyes. His heart pounded in his chest; his artist's soul sang. David clasped perfect beauty. He drew a short intake of breath.

"They are from the altar of Charles the Bald, part of the crown jewels kept in the Abbey of Saint-Denis. I pried them from the altar myself with the most common of peasant knives. I carry them around to remind myself constantly of the corruption of the royals. Do you find them exquisite?"

David's eyes darted about, from Robespierre to his own hand. His mind frantically thought about how to answer the question.

"Your eyes betray you, my friend. They are flawless jewels. You should see them in better light than this café offers."

David nearly leapt from the table to run outside. He willed himself to remain.

"Eat them, Jacques-Louis."

David's gaze snapped up from his palm. His eyes met Robespierre's. David saw only a cold and level stare.

"Eat them," he repeated. "Eat them now, and in a day or two, they will emerge covered in shit. One symbol will replace another."

David looked at the man across the table. His expression had not changed. He could feel his throat constrict, the muscles of his neck drawing together. His body involuntarily tightening at what would soon happen to it. He thought of the unnamed man at the guillotine.

David pinched the pearl between his thumb and forefinger. Slowly, he brought it to his mouth, placing it on his tongue. Then, picking up his wineglass, he washed down the jewel. Fighting back the urge to gag, his eyes returned to Robespierre, who made the slightest nod of approval. David swallowed first the ruby and then the diamond.

Robespierre leaned his head forward and began speaking in a soft voice. "You are the greatest painter in France, but I would keep this secret to yourself, or someone may slice you open to pillage your stomach contents. For the next few days, you are worth more dead than alive."

Robespierre removed his glasses and returned them to his pocket. He leaned back in his chair and began speaking, his tone matter-of-fact. "Gems have no value as food. They possess no taste. They are, for the meeting of human needs, worthless. Yet, many will kill for what they represent. Such is it with symbols. We must find the remaining crown jewels of the ancien régime and see that they are destroyed before they ruin our fledgling nation."

David's eyes returned to his empty palm. "But you said yourself that they have been destroyed."

"The Scepter of Dagobert remains, the oldest of the crown jewels."

"Every citizen knows that the scepter was stolen when Saint Denis was looted in the early days of the Revolution."

Robespierre shook his head. "Every citizen knows because we told them. We encouraged the story to circulate." He tapped his forehead with his index finger. "Control the story, control the mind.

"The scepter has been hidden by royalists. I feel certain it remains concealed near Paris. The guards will not allow it to leave the city. We will find it. We will turn over every hovel, every pigsty until this symbol of royal oppression is located.

"And when we find this public corruption, we will hold a ceremony. The people will melt down the earliest symbol of French aristocracy. Together, we shall destroy the tangible evidence that one man is better than his brother. And from it we shall cast a golden hammer. Or perhaps a guillotine blade. We will substitute our potent symbol for their symbol."

"And what shall be the fate of the man or woman who is found to have hidden it?" David asked.

"Her head will spend the last few seconds of her life disembodied."

2

Yellowstone National Park
June 2nd

"Good morning, welcome to Yellowstone National Park's Outdoor Classroom." Clarence Johnson projected his voice to be heard in the open space of the parking lot.

The replies varied in enthusiasm.

"You've come this morning for a short ranger-led hike on Uncle Tom's Trail. Anyone know what Uncle Tom did to get the trail named for him?" Clarence's eyes studied the children, seeking a volunteer.

"A guy with a cabin?" a boy said.

"Good try, but that's a different Uncle Tom. Anyone else?"

"In 1898, H.F. Richardson would ferry visitors across the Yellowstone River. These early tourists could then go down the South Rim of Yellowstone Canyon using a series of ropes and ladders," a teenage girl read, her eyes never departing from her phone.

"Good answer," Clarence said. "And for that trip, Uncle Tom Richardson would charge each person one dollar. He went out of business in 1906 after the Yellowstone Park administration built a set of wooden stairs down to the canyon floor."

Clarence's eyes scanned the crowd, this time focusing on the adults. The short man wearing the baseball cap and sunglasses gave an almost imperceptible headshake. Each trip, Clarence found at least one person who objected to the story of the government ruining an entrepreneur.

"I'm going to ask that you put your phones away while we are walking down," Johnson continued. "I do this for two reasons." As he spoke, he held up his right arm, the uniform tight against his bicep, and displayed two fingers. "First, the steps are no longer wooden. They are metal. Water from the Lower Falls will occasionally make them slippery. I want you to keep a hand on the rail as you go down. Second, I want you to keep track of the number of steps on the trail. We'll see what number you come up with at the bottom." Challenging the children to track the steps had proven the single best way to keep them focused.

"When we get to the base, I'd like you all to feel free to look around for a few minutes, and then we'll talk about a man without whom this park would not exist, the artist Thomas Moran." Clarence gestured toward the trailhead. He paused for a moment to stretch his right leg. Since he'd been shot, the leg took a little extra effort to wake up each morning.

The group crossed the parking lot to the South Rim Trail. From there, it was less than the length of a football field to the start of Uncle Tom's. Most of the teenagers raced ahead, seeking to separate themselves from their parents.

The walk, although short, was slow. A couple wearing matching red windbreakers with Canadian flags pinned to their collars paused to take in the landscape. A woman he recognized from the previous day's ranger hike waved. Clarence waved back.

"You'll like him. His talk is very good. Ask him about his dog," she said before hurrying on to catch up to the woman she hiked with.

The small crowd looked at him.

"Let's get to the bottom. The kids are pulling away." The group pressed ahead. Clarence took a step and massaged his quad muscle.

"Can't skip leg day," a voice said.

"Excuse me," Clarence said. He turned and faced the speaker.

The man, Clarence guessed he was in his late twenties, wore shorts, hiking boots, and a tight-fitting, long-sleeved shirt made from some wicking fabric. He looked like an ad for a high-end camping gear website. Alongside him stood a similarly dressed female.

"Your arms look swole, but your legs could use some work. You can't skip leg day," the man repeated. As he spoke, he twisted the ring on his left hand.

"I try to walk enough each day. You two here on a honeymoon?"

The man's eyes widened. "How'd you…"

Clarence stared at the man's hands, which had continued playing with his ring. The young woman made a short laugh, and the man dropped his hands to his sides.

"Three days," the woman answered.

"Thanks for spending your morning with me," Clarence said.

The man, unable to maintain the slow pace, paused to check the fitness tracker on his arm and then touched the woman on the elbow. "C'mon, honey." He strode on ahead.

She looked back briefly before moving to catch him. "See you at the bottom."

Clarence nodded and watched them go.

He soon came to the decline leading to the observation platform. Uncle Tom's Trail should have really been called Uncle Tom's Staircase. There was almost no trail to cover. The pathway was a series of steel stairs secured to the south canyon wall. Clarence grabbed the rail and began his descent. The first steps, he took gingerly. Small pains reverberated up his leg with each footfall. The recovery process, the doctors warned him, would take time. Clarence felt a hurt he associated with recovery and not an injury. He knew the difference, and ignoring the pain just required willpower. He took another step and continued down.

Small bits of morning mud fell through the metal grates of each step. The stairs made some people uneasy. But water couldn't pool on the metal grillwork. They also offered tourists the chance to see remnants of rope left behind from Uncle Tom's original business venture. Clarence didn't meet any of his group frozen with panic on the way down. Today had the makings of a good day. He paused briefly only twice when a flare of pain shot up through his thigh muscle.

The group gathered on the observation platform. The sound of tumbling water and the cooling mist off the falls made this a popular location.

Clarence slid the daypack from his shoulders. He withdrew his water bottle and took a quick drink. He put the bottle alongside his binoculars and the first aid kit he carried. Pulling out a laminated copy of Moran's painting of Lower Yellowstone Falls, he faced the group.

He passed his gaze over the children. "How many steps?"

"Three hundred and twenty-four," a boy said.

"Three hundred and fifty," the recently wedded man said, his eyes trained on his fitness tracker.

"Trust your eyes, not your technology," Clarence said. "Three-twenty-four it is."

The boy gave the man a victorious smile.

Clarence reached out and pointed toward the circling bird. "Did everyone see the turkey vulture?"

All eyes turned to see the bird.

"We can recognize a turkey vulture by the red head. Y'all will also notice that the feathers at the ends of its wings resemble fingertips. Likely, there is carrion in the area. The turkey vulture is a scavenger. It will find the remains of a dead animal and feed on that. They glide low to the ground and use their sense of smell to find a carcass."

A few of the children turned away from watching the bird.

"If you want to learn more, there is a ranger talk most nights in Hayden Valley about the birds and beasts of Yellowstone. Consult your Yellowstone directory for details, or talk to me after today's talk."

Clarence kept his voice loud to be heard over the tumbling waters.

"If you look up at the top of the Lower Yellowstone Falls, you will see what we call the green ribbon. Can everyone find what I'm talking about?"

His eyes roamed the group. Clarence saw craned necks and nodding heads.

"Geologists tell us that there is a deep channel beneath the falls. The water passing through there does not get frothy and full of air like the water coming off the rest of the falls. That's why it stays green and forms that band you can see. It's a detail that you need to be at Yellowstone to observe."

Here, he paused. Everyone always looked back up at the waterfall to see the green streak falling off the top.

"When you describe seeing the Lower Yellowstone Falls, I suspect that you'll always include the green ribbon. Listeners will know you have actually seen the falls because of the small details you include."

Most of the faces were focused upon him. He had lost the attention of a few children. Their eyes roamed ahead, looking for the next adventure rather than devoting any effort to where they were at the present. He knew, however, a technique to bring them back. He held up his copy of Thomas Moran's painting *The Grand Canyon of the Yellowstone*. Clarence had laminated his copy, the mist coming off the waterfall beaded upon the surface.

"Can you see the ribbon in this painting?"

Clarence walked in front of the group, holding the painting. Young arms extended, pointing to the overhang at the top of the waterfall.

"You see it, because the artist saw it. Thomas Moran receives the credit as one of the men most responsible for the establishment of Yellowstone National Park. His paintings such as this one, along with photographs by William Henry Jackson, grabbed the nation's attention far more than the written descriptions and diaries of the other members of the expedition sent to explore this area. They inspired Congress and President Ulysses Grant to create the first national park here at Yellowstone."

He walked the row of visitors again, showing the painting before handing it off to the newlyweds. Reaching into the backpack, Clarence withdrew a second copy.

"We will talk in a few minutes about where Thomas Moran set his easel to paint this picture, but I like to discuss the painting from this spot. We're too near the waterfalls for him to have painted it here. But look at the mist, the water droplets thrown off by the cascading water. Can anyone see a rainbow?"

Heads roamed the canyon, most nodded. A few people pointed. Where you saw a rainbow depended upon your location. One girl, Clarence noticed, looked behind her, searching for rainbows below the soaring turkey vulture. She had turned her back to the waterfall.

Good luck finding one, he thought.

"Thomas Moran," Clarence said, "came out of a group of painters known as the Hudson River School. They painted natural settings. The atmospherics show the debt the Hudson River painters owed to the English painter, J.M.W. Turner. I've always thought that standing here at this spot is a good place to get the sense of the moisture trapped in the air, obscuring the clear view, like smoke. It's also a good place to hang out on a hot day."

Here, the adults nodded.

"Do we have any painters in the group?" Clarence's eyes again surveyed the group. The Canadian woman raised her hand halfway and then pulled her arm back down.

"Don't be shy," Clarence said.

"A little," the woman said. "But nothing grand."

"I'd like to talk about technique. It's nice to have some painters in the group."

The girl whose back had been turned now faced Clarence and raised her hand.

"Are you a painter too?"

She shook her head. "No, but I have a question."

"What is it?"

"Is that vulture circling because that man down there is dead?" The girl turned and pointed.

3

Paris, France
November 1794

The guard walked the row of cells, banging his club against the bars. Citizen Guinyard, the jailer, always made as much noise as he could. He allowed no one to sleep when he was on duty. "After a prisoner goes to the Place de la Révolution, then he can rest," Guinyard would say.

David almost looked forward to Guinyard's rounds. Some talk with another fellow, even with a tormentor, was at least some talk. He thought of his students at the atelier, the painters who had studied under him. He wished more might summon the courage to visit. Usually, he was left with only his jailer.

Guinyard had a wiry frame and straggly hair, a dirty mix of brown and gray. He looked, David thought, like a mop that had been stood on end and then onto which a porridge had been poured. His thin build was masked partly by a stained tunic and baggy trousers tied at the waist with a rope. David considered mocking him but was dissuaded by the club the man carried.

"I've no word when they intend to execute you, Citizen David."

"You shall then have to feed me for at least another day."

"I would rather clean chamber pots than watch you eat. The way food sloshes out the side of your face. Pigs eat more delicately than you."

David's hand unconsciously touched the scar on his left cheek.

"Perhaps they will never execute you. Perhaps they exile you. Pack you off to Louisiana. An experiment to see if an artist can survive on the frontier."

"Guinyard," David began.

The guard rapped the bars heavily with his club. "Citizen Guinyard, you swine."

"Citizen Guinyard, you are aware that Louisiana is Spanish territory."

"Bah, their flag flies in the air, but on the ground our citizens walk. And one day, we will undo the foolish decisions the royals made. Rest assured, prisoner, we have the power to send you there."

David had not considered the idea that he might be banished.

"Tell me, Citizen David. Do you suppose that the bears and wild natives of the Louisiana Territory will sit still while you paint their portraits? Or will they eat you while you are setting up your easel?"

David, lost for an answer, shrugged his shoulders.

Guinyard banged his club against the bars of his cell and laughed.

David listened as the man made his way down the row of cells in the Luxembourg Palace. The government had turned the ransacked palace into a prison for opponents of the Revolution. He had been jailed in the cellar. The adjoining cells were vacant; only a few wretched souls found themselves remaining. He listened to the step and slide of Guinyard's footsteps against the floor grit. The man's left leg never worked as smoothly as the right.

Outside somewhere, through the small window near the ceiling of his cell, he heard a rooster from one of the poultry vendors. Crowing one moment, headless and sold for dinner shortly after.

He considered drawing a portrait. A few pages of foolscap remained. He rubbed his fingertips against his own face, felt the stone of scar tissue and his rough, crudely shaven skin. How far he was from the idealized faces of the Greeks and Romans.

David pictured a more appropriate subject. He thought of Charlotte, a face he knew better than his own.

Marguerite-Charlotte Pécoul had an egg-shaped face. Her eyes sat a bit too far apart, and her nose looked rather bulbous, her cheeks too florid. Charlotte's narrow lips thinned further when she smiled, which she often did. He missed the smile. She had never been the most beautiful woman in Paris, but he felt a longing for her. He marveled at the irony. The country's most famous painter of classical virtues—love, honor, devotion—had trampled those very virtues for a political cause. "Charlotte," he said her name to himself.

"Hey, Citizen David." Guinyard's call surprised him.

Wordlessly, he looked through the bars.

"Will you paint your Louisiana savages with feathers and war paints as we're told they wear? Or will you paint your bears dressed in the culottes of the nobles they have eaten?"

"Bring me colors and a decent canvas, and I will begin painting whatever you wish."

Guinyard shook his head, rejecting the suggestion. "In our new Republic, I hear that we do not call it Louisiana. Nothing is named for Louis anymore. The territory's name is Guillotina. She is the new ruler of France."

Guinyard lowered his voice and moved until his shoulder pressed against the bars. He cocked his head and gestured for David to move closer. Guinyard cast his glance up and down the corridor to confirm that they were alone. He gestured with his head again.

David slowly edged to the bars. He knew a beating would result from noncompliance. He felt Guinyard's wine-soured breath against his cheek and nose.

"Are you listening, Citizen David?"

He nodded. "Yes."

"Speak no more of this Charlotte. Guillotina is the only woman whose touch you shall feel upon your neck." Guinyard's hand shot between the bars and pinched his throat hard.

David jumped back; his face flushed with anger.

Guinyard racked his bat against the bars. He laughed as he swayed down the corridor. David heard the outer door bang shut. He grabbed his cell bars and shook them.

David could feel his heart pounding beneath his shirt. He opened his mouth and gulped deep breaths of air to calm himself. He breathed slowly, feeling the damp air traverse his nose and flow down the back of his throat. He exhaled and did it again, this time breathing through his mouth, that he might taste the fetid air. The sensation of breathing became a pleasurable act when it might be denied suddenly.

He closed his eyes, pursed his lips, and exhaled. David began planning a painting. He pictured a grand canvas. Grand messages required a large space. He thought of the Sistine Chapel. Then, he lost himself in the details, the exercise calming him. The front door of the Luxembourg Palace, the door through which the destruction poured, he saw this panel alive with color. He envisioned the frivolous and heady atmosphere of a carnival. The message clear to those who knew. The colors, bright and artificial, would be like the makeup of a clown or a harlot; they disguised the ugliness buried just below the surface.

Outside his window, the rooster crowed again. David thought of adding the bird to the painting. The barnyard animal served as a symbol of betrayal, reminding the audience of Peter's denial of Christ. He remembered the rituals at the Abbey of Saint-Denis before the building had been looted. The symbols moved people.

David turned his head so that his mind might look more clearly at the back door of the imagined painting. The rheumatoid pain made his neck creak. The prisoners shuffled in, bound and manacled, their shoulders slumped. Their stooped walks represented fading hope for the Revolution. He recognized some of the faces. He would paint them into the jail chain. Foremost among the beleaguered prisoners, David knew, the picture must contain Robespierre.

Maximilien Robespierre, who led the Revolution and began the purge, had ultimately fallen prey to it. Robespierre had been arrested at the National Convention and executed. David remembered yelling to his friend, "If you drink hemlock, I shall drink it with you."

David's imagination saw the men and women walking in the back door, the look of impending death upon them. He could paint death. His painting of Marat after death had become among his most celebrated.

Should he paint himself among the miserable in the line? He could not make an account of all he had lost for the Revolution. He need not count past Charlotte. He was like a debtor rotting in prison. He could easily have found himself in a handcart delivered to the executioner when the revolutionary winds had shifted. Instead, he had been imprisoned. Robespierre's suffering had ended, David's anguish continued.

He studied the bars. He might twist his shirt into a crude loop and end all of this. David had tried it before. When he failed to win the Prix de Rome, he had locked himself in his room and tried to starve himself. His friends intervened. His eyes went back to the bars. There would be no one here to pull him back. He fingered his shirt.

He stood up from his crude chair to retrieve some foolscap. The movement fired pains through the joints of his hips, knees, and ankles. He placed his hand against the stone wall of his cell and waited until the pain passed. The wall felt damp. The palace stood near the Seine. The water leaked into the lower cells. The cold moisture seeped into every part of his body. When the American revolutionary Thomas Paine had been imprisoned here, he had been given a large, upstairs room lined with windows. Paine had been locked in only at night. In that room, he had written his book *The Age of Reason*.

The idea of that room as a jail cell made David grunt.

"You have choices," the voice within him whispered.

He shook his head and chased the words away.

David hobbled to the small pallet of his bed. Taking up one of his precious sheets of foolscap, he drew with a crude piece of charcoal. He knew that the great work would remain undrawn. The painting would live only in his mind. David lacked the tools to make even a decent sketch. He closed his eyes and scraped the paint off his mind's canvas before it dried. He used the flat knife. Then, he set the easel aside for another day and opened his eyes.

He pinched the paper against his drawing board and began to sketch. The actual work must be far simpler than he had envisioned. Slowly, a black circle emerged. He stopped just before he closed the loop. David recognized what the paper intended to see.

His movements quickened once he held the picture in his mind. He drew the tail, the thin, serpent-like body of a leviathan rather than the bulkier physique of the tarasque, the mythological dragon of Provence. He sketched his fears for the entire nation rather than a cartoon for a single region. David gave the beast a great head and a wide, clawing mouth full of jagged teeth. He closed the circle and began to laboriously draw scales. The beast swallowed its own tail.

For a time, he forgot about the cold and dampness of the cell. Whether men died at the guillotine ceased to matter. David became absorbed by art. He studied the serpent, drawing musculature and the sheen of the scales as best he could.

He set the charcoal down on his pallet and slapped his hand against the leg of his pantaloons to knock the black charcoal dust free. David picked up the drawing and held it at arm's length, studying his work.

A dragon swallowing itself. The Greeks called it ouroboros. To some, it was a symbol of the continuing process of life, its cyclical nature. In ouroboros, David saw self-destruction. Perhaps that was the mystery inherent in metaphor, he thought. He could have a symbol mean one thing and most of the world would see something entirely different. He looked again at the picture of the self-digesting serpent. Ouroboros, his nation feeding upon itself. Another cheer came in through the small, high window. Guillotina enjoyed another meal.

4

Observation Deck, Uncle Tom's Trail
June 2nd

From the platform, Clarence watched the investigation.

A ranger worked his way around the perimeter, stringing up a barrier with plastic tape marked "Danger." The Park Service, apparently, didn't invest tax dollars in tape that said "Crime Scene." This tape probably worked better, anyway, Clarence thought. The words "crime scene" drew spectators.

He lifted his binoculars. The tape stretched wide, reaching from the wall of the canyon down to the water's edge, marking off an area downstream. Upstream, the plastic barricade closed off an area from the river back to the rock wall. Ropes, anchored up top, hung down Yellowstone Canyon. Two ropes supported a litter to remove the dead man when the investigators were ready. A photographer tethered to another line crawled about the rocky edge, documenting the crime scene. Obviously trained, the ranger moved easily. Johnson wondered why the Park Service didn't employ a drone for this sort of work. Perhaps the man enjoyed dangling like a spider and bounding among the rocks.

On the ledge above, portable lights were being erected. The search for evidence would likely be slow on this terrain. Clarence nodded; he liked to see law enforcement anticipating problems. The officer in charge had begun bringing in the necessary equipment. Yellowstone may not have correctly labeled crime scene tape, but the Park Service knew how to do rescue operations. They seemed well stocked with light bars and generators. If only they would do a few basic things differently.

Below, a woman stepped from rock to rock with a practiced ease. Trees occasionally shielded her from his view. She disappeared and then reappeared among the shadows, always keeping a discreet distance from the body. Her attention seemed to be focused everywhere but there. Maybe, Clarence thought, he should yell down and tell her that there was a corpse to her left.

The body lay splayed on the ground, arms cast out at odd angles, one leg folded underneath the other. The man looked as if he had been caught committing some hideous dance move. Clarence had no doubt that the man would readily trade his current situation for an embarrassing candid.

He lowered his field glasses. It felt strange standing out of the way, watching the action unfold. Clarence belonged at the center of these situations. The idleness felt awkward. He considered leaving. He had no business mucking around in the investigation. On the other hand, he did not have any real place to go. And he was interested in watching a death investigation in the wild. His lecture had ended abruptly. He gathered the names and cell phone numbers of everyone in the group. He had made a point to get the contact information for the girl who had first noticed the body. Then, he herded them up the staircase of Uncle Tom's Trail. The group pulled away from him on the climb, energized by more adrenaline and riding stouter legs. Once they had all made it safely to the top, he retraced his steps down to the observation deck.

A small amount of blood stained the rock where the man's head lay. It spread out and seemed distributed evenly. The head was turned, so Johnson could only see his profile. The one visible eye remained open, mouth gaped. His body canted slightly, as if the man died trying to turn onto his right shoulder. He wore a daypack. The pack's contents kept him from rolling completely onto his back. A camera lay behind the dead man, the strap still wrapped around his neck. The camera had a large zoom lens. He wore a water bottle clipped to his waist.

Through the binoculars, Clarence saw that the man had outfitted himself in technical clothing. He wore pants and a long-sleeved shirt made of nylon-like fabric. Clarence was sure that the fabric had some techie, exclusive-sounding name. The man had rolled up the sleeves and tied a rain jacket around his waist. He wore high-cut leather hiking boots. Good for ankle support, Clarence thought.

He may have died of a massive head wound, but at least he likely didn't suffer a sprained ankle during his fall.

A long wool sock, probably merino, lay exposed on his outside leg. The man had known to dress in fabrics that pulled moisture away from his body. Most of the people who visited Yellowstone rolled through the park in jeans and cotton T-shirts advertising some local eatery or 5K race. That clothing worked fine for traveling in an RV but proved dangerous for strenuous hiking. Experienced hikers had the saying that "cotton kills."

Not today it hadn't, Clarence thought.

He scanned the area around the body, running his eyes over the rocks. They bore the patterns of the lichens, slowly growing circles of colors, rust red, gray, black, and green. The lodgepole pines grew up around the rocks cleaved from Yellowstone Canyon. Johnson could see no other signs of gear.

The photographer continued picking his way, finding different angles to photograph the body. Clarence saw a collection of placards tucked in the photographer's belt. He knew the drill. If the photographer found items of interest, he would take two pictures, the first noting the scene as he found it and the second with a placard for ease of identification later. Johnson had yet to see him lay down a placard. Apparently, the team had not found much in the way of evidence.

Another ranger combed the brush and rocks for anything that might be deemed placard worthy. The investigator in charge had posted someone on each end of the crime scene tape, making sure that no hiker inadvertently stumbled into the investigation. A ranger slowly walked the river, scanning the bank for evidence.

Johnson's eyes returned to the woman. She stood away from the tree cover. She was dressed in a pair of jeans, although Johnson suspected she had not just leapt out of an RV. The jeans as well as her hiking boots looked scuffed and well worn. Beneath her baseball cap she sported a bobbed haircut. She had on a black, short-sleeved polo shirt. Both the shirt and the cap had the initials ISB prominently displayed. She worked for the National Park Service's Investigative Services Branch. Behind her and away from the body, she had hung her agency-issued windbreaker on a pine branch. It twisted lazily in the breeze, the large yellow letters announcing "Police Federal Agent" turning toward and then away from Clarence. Her eyes remained hidden behind sunglasses. They hid most of her face. He couldn't tell if the ISB issued designer eyewear. The woman had a badge and a semi-automatic pistol on her hip. As Clarence watched, she knelt for a closer look at something. She studied the ground. She picked up a handful of dirt and allowed it to sift between her fingers. Her head tilted first to one side and then the other. She stood up suddenly and motioned toward another man. Clarence wondered what, if anything, she had found. He looked down at his own waistband and silent radio. The investigators occupied a different frequency. He reached into the backpack to retrieve his water bottle.

"Keep your hands where I can see them," a voice behind him said.

Clarence kept his actions slow and deliberate. He pulled his hand from the backpack and rested both hands on the rail of the observation deck. He kept them relaxed.

"What are you doing up here?" the voice asked.

Clarence turned his head to the side. "A conversation would be easier if I wasn't facing the waterfall. May I turn around?"

The man paused. Johnson felt his body being surveyed.

"Turn slowly, and keep your hands where I can see them."

Clarence faced a ranger he didn't recognize. The man had drawn his gun and held it with both hands in the low ready position, the barrel of the firearm pointed downward. The pose was intended to make him feel less threatened. Clarence didn't like being on the other side of a firearm, even one pointed at the ground, especially since the ground consisted of a steel-rung observation platform. He had no idea where the bullet would ricochet if one were discharged.

He kept his voice calm. He could see the white knuckles on the ranger's hands. "My shirt has got all the same patches your shirt has. I think we're on the same team here. Why don't you put the gun down?"

"They've left half the park understaffed to send people here. And you're standing around secretly watching. Why don't you tell me what you're doing here?"

"I'd call what I'm doing observing," Clarence said. "I'm the guy who radioed in the report of the body. I thought you'd need me to stick around."

The ranger's eyes widened slightly, and he drew the barrel further away from Clarence's feet.

"You reported this?"

"The lengths I'll go to get out of a ranger talk."

"Identification?"

Unbuttoning the shirt pocket, Clarence withdrew his ID. The ranger studied it, his eyes flicking back and forth between Clarence and the card. The man's eyes wandered over him from toe to head. Clarence thought of commenting but elected to keep his mouth shut. The ranger's eyes blinked. He'd reached a conclusion. Clarence gave the ranger his most assuring smile. The ranger took a step back, lengthening the distance between them, and holstered his weapon. The smile had clinched the deal.

"I'm Ranger Wesley. I work out of the Mammoth station. Let's go up top."

Even though Wesley had put his gun away, Clarence could tell that he was not quite ready to become friends. He moved to the stairway. Wesley followed, keeping space between them.

"I'm obliged to say, no sudden movements," Ranger Wesley said.

Clarence grabbed the handrail and looked at the 324 steps above him. "Rest assured, there's going to be nothing sudden." He took a deep breath and started climbing.

"The Park Service really needs to think before they hire flatlanders."

At the top, Clarence paused to catch his breath. His heart beat hard beneath his ranger field shirt. Wesley turned slightly away and spoke into his radio. He then pointed along the South Rim Trail. Through the trees, Clarence could see the equipment brought in for the investigation. Spectators had gathered to glimpse the goings-on down below. A ranger stood stationed, keeping the public away from the rim. The Park Service did not need a slip and fall adding to the body count. Wesley spoke briefly to the ranger guarding the perimeter, then waved Clarence inside the tape.

A canopy had been strung up to shelter workers from the sun. A pair of rangers worked beneath it, one entering data into a tablet computer while the other looked at a clipboard and spoke into a radio. They paid little attention to another ranger in their midst.

"Safe for me to drink some water?" Clarence asked.

Wesley shook his head and barely looked his way. Johnson pulled the bottle from his backpack. He was, he decided, no longer the enemy.

Clarence surveyed the small crowd that had gathered to watch the criminal investigation. He recognized the newlyweds. Most observers loitered for a few minutes and then wandered off in search of a geyser. Tourists kept to a tight schedule of sightseeing in Yellowstone. They couldn't allow a murder to disrupt their plans for long. While most of the crowd drifted in and out, two men, one in a wheelchair, seemed content to stay.

Clarence withdrew his phone from his pocket. Setting it to record video, he captured the group of observers.

The woman he had watched through his binoculars crawled up from below the rim. She stood and dusted off her hands, then made her way toward them. She walked, Clarence thought, with surefooted confidence, like someone who hiked the rough terrain a great deal. She lifted her sunglasses and surveyed the area.

She looked to be a little younger than he was, perhaps in her early thirties. From what he could see, she wore little to no makeup. It did not appear that she needed to. The woman removed her hat and wiped her brow with her sleeve. She had sun-streaked hair and coffee-brown eyes. He would love to have her on his squad of investigators. Men would confess to those eyes. Even focused as they were, they still conveyed warmth.

She walked in his direction. She had to look up to make eye contact. Most people did. She extended her hand. "I'm Special Agent Alison Nance of—"

"Of the ISB, the Park Service's detectives," Clarence completed her sentence.

She stopped.

Johnson pointed his index finger toward her shirt and hat. "If your branch had a NASCAR team, they'd be dressed something like that. Especially with the jacket. You're wasting a lot of prime real estate the government could license for beer and firearm ads."

Nance didn't smile. Instead, she angled her head, narrowed her eyes, and studied Clarence. "And you are?"

"Seasonal Ranger Clarence Johnson of the National Park Service. Nothing special about me."

"Clearly. And why were you snooping on my crime scene, Nothing Special Johnson?"

"I prefer to say observing rather than snooping, Special Agent."

"I'll need a statement from you detailing what you saw."

"I can tell you now. I saw a guy hanging from a guide rope, taking pictures. It was like Cirque du Soleil...with guns."

Nance's expression didn't change. "I need you up at Gardner."

Clarence shrugged an acknowledgment. "Okay."

"I'm told you found the body and called it in."

"I give a ranger talk on Thomas Moran. A girl, one of the attendees, saw the body first. I called it in."

Nance rolled her eyes. "I don't suppose that you happened to get her name?"

Clarence heard the skepticism in her voice. He reached into the pocket of his shirt. "Here is a list of all the visitors I had at the talk this morning. I've included their home addresses and cell phone numbers. She is the top name on the list." He stretched his hand toward her.

Nance's eyes widened. She took the proffered list and examined it. "I'm impressed. When were you planning on bringing it over to us?"

"I knew someone would find me eventually. I was trying to stay out of the crime scene log."

Nance nodded. "Locard's Exchange Principle."

They were alone, the other rangers off, presumably in pursuit of their duties. No one to witness this game of forensic science trivia.

"If you mean Edmond Locard's maxim that everyone who enters a crime scene brings something into it and everyone who leaves a crime scene takes something from it, then yes, that theory."

Clarence paused. If Nance wanted to be the smartest cop in the trees, he could play that game.

"And if you're worried about people carrying things into and out of the crime scene, you need to start collecting names up here."

Nance's eyes took in the South Rim of Yellowstone Canyon.

"'Cause your victim was shot up here and fell or got pushed off the edge. Down there, that's your secondary crime scene. This is your primary. And you've parked lights, a tent, and a dozen tourists on top of any possible evidence."

5

Paris, France
December 1794

What would he do when he had used the last of the foolscap?

David imagined painting canvases, but it was not the same as feeling the creation emerge beneath his touch. He looked to his scant remaining pages. He closed his eyes and with his imagination stretched a canvas. David rested his hands in his lap. The advantage of painting within the mind—no preparatory work needed be done before the first stroke of the brush.

He would paint a heroic scene of Greece. David pictured the folds of tunics and robes, the exquisite detail and shadowing. His work would teach a lesson to the citizens through the greatest teachers of the ancients.

From down the passageway, he heard the crude lock and then the opening of the heavy door. Guinyard would soon begin his rounds. David kept his eyes closed and exhaled deeply, preparing himself for the verbal onslaught. Perhaps if he feigned sleep, the man would be content to bang the bars and awaken him. Even Guinyard knew that there was no sport to be had from a man recently pulled from the arms of Morpheus. David doubted Guinyard would recognize the Greek god of dreams.

He steadied his breathing. He pictured himself dabbing the colors to his painting as he awaited Guinyard's arrival. He heard small, light steps as the man crept down the hall. He did not bother the other prisoners. Guinyard's torment was a private game to be played only with him.

David returned to the canvas. Socrates taught in an Athenian garden. David focused on the tree alongside the great teacher. Wilting leaves on the tree spoke to the gardener's failure to tend the plant. Overripe fruit lay on the ground. David added a citizen turning away, refusing to heed the wisdom. The sun would be setting.

"Jacques-Louis, you cannot fool me. You are not asleep."

His eyes burst open in surprise.

"I have heard your breath as you sleep too many times to be so easily duped," the female voice continued.

"Charlotte." His painting instantly forgotten.

"Jacques-Louis, I am here."

She looked at him through the bars. His eyes swept over her. She remained exactly as he remembered. The dress she wore, simple. Her hair hung down on either side of her plain face, framing it. He could not take his eyes off her. His heart beat faster. David sat erect. His back pressed against the cold, damp wall of the cell. He was afraid to move to the bars. Impossible, he thought, that she might be here. Her standing here outside his door must be a trick of the mind. Yet, if this be madness, David sat unwilling, just yet, for sanity.

Reaching up with his hand, he brushed back his own hair, combing it as best he could with his fingers.

Her intelligent eyes watched his feeble efforts. "I should have sent word that I was coming, my husband. But I feared that if I aroused too much attention, I would be denied entrance."

"And here you are, Charlotte."

"A thousand years of royalty will not be eliminated regardless of the number of heads sacrificed to the blade."

David heard the veiled criticism in her voice. "At first, I thought you were an apparition. Instead, I see that you have come to gloat."

Charlotte's eyes flared momentarily. Then she closed them. He watched her chest rise and fall. When she opened them, her eyes held only pity.

"There is too much risk involved for gloating. This hole is too cold and too wet. The dampness would douse all self-satisfaction."

"Then why have you come?"

Charlotte put her hands into the cell, her forearms resting on the bars of the door. "To see you, husband."

He stood and stepped toward the cell door. Pain shot through his legs, and he groaned slightly. He limped quickly to her. Their hands embraced.

Neither spoke. David stood quietly, studying her face, reminding himself of every detail. He felt her thumbs tracing the outlines of his fingers.

"What are you looking at?" she asked.

"Your beauty."

He saw her cheeks redden.

Charlotte looked up at the small window. "This dim light has ruined your eyes. I am far from beautiful."

"Beauty has many measures," he said. "Many different types of paintings hang in the galleries. And it is tyranny to pronounce only one beautiful. Your eyes and your tongue demonstrate an intelligence which no accidental shaping of your nose may disguise."

Charlotte remained silent for some time. "You have the same soft hands. The only rough places are where you hold the brush. You possess the gentle hands of an artist."

His eyes broke from her face and looked at his hands. Her thumbs caressed the pads of his fingertips.

"These hands have been far from gentle. The pen they held has caused much destruction."

Charlotte, he noted, did not say anything to ease his self-remorse. He had signed his name on the king's death warrant.

David pushed forward until their joined hands rested outside the bars. He felt the cold iron of the cross bar on his forearms. "The twist of fate presents a farce worthy of Molière. I watched as my brothers jailed royalists. I cheered for their elimination. My brothers and sisters turned upon me. They became a mythical beast which fed upon itself. I sit now in the jail made from a palace, placed here by my allies. And I find my suffering eased by a royal."

Charlotte shook her head; her face held a frown. "I am not a royal motivated by virtue carrying out some mercy mission. Rather, I am a wife come to visit a long-absent husband."

"But we are divorced."

"Our marriage broke apart because the fires of your politics made it impossible for us to remain together. We stood divided by the extremes of the Revolution."

"I hoped to create a new France."

"You were politically blind."

David felt the anger surge. He bit back anything he might say.

"That never meant I cared less for Jacques-Louis, the man. I could not remain in the same house as Jacques-Louis, the politician."

He looked at the iron bars of the cell door. "And see the house I chose instead."

"Fortunes may change more than once."

"If what you say ever becomes true, know that I have abandoned politics. My path is only art."

He felt her eyes studying his face, searching for something. He returned the gaze.

"I have always loved you, Jacques-Louis."

"And I you, my Charlotte." He could not make eye contact. David turned away from her. The twist brought fresh pain to his leg. He winced.

"You are hurt, my love?" Charlotte asked. "Have they beaten you?"

He pinched his lips together and shook his head. "No," he said after the pain had passed. "It is the rheumatoid pain. I fear the cold and damp of this place takes a toll. The surroundings age a man before his time. Forgive me, I must sit down." He squeezed her hands gently before releasing them. He limped back across the floor and settled heavily on his bed.

Frowning, Charlotte watched his slow progress.

"Should you come to visit again, asking an apothecary to prepare a salve would be most appreciated."

"We should rub your legs with the Scepter of Dagobert. That would cure your ills."

"Being found with the royal scepter would indeed cure my leg problems. The guillotine would free my head of all my troubles."

She exhaled a burst of air. "All men remember about the scepter is that it is the symbol of French kings."

David hobbled back to the bars. He looked in both directions before speaking and lowered his voice to a whisper. "On the holy days, we went to the Abbey of Saint-Denis. We were in the audience when the king held the scepter. I remember that it was gold."

Charlotte's tone befitted a schoolteacher. She seemed unconcerned whether anyone else heard her. "Not just gold but the finest gold filigree and gorgeous gold enamel. It is beauty, and it is power. But it is so much more."

Charlotte paused. David leaned forward until his forehead touched the damp metal bars. He found himself breathlessly awaiting more details, waiting for the sound of her voice.

"You should also remember that the scepter was crafted a thousand years ago for King Dagobert by Saint Eligius. He is the patron saint of goldsmiths."

"I have spoken little of saints these last years."

"More talk and thought of saints and less of revolution, you might well find yourself at home, warm and dry."

David hung his head.

Charlotte's voice softened. "I am sorry, Jacques-Louis. We have been apart too long to begin arguing so quickly."

He nodded his agreement.

"Saint Eligius is also the patron saint for many who heal. He once came upon a horse that resisted being shod. He cut off the horse's leg, put the shoe on, and then attached the leg. Through this miracle, the horse neither toppled nor experienced pain."

"A prayer to him might benefit me were I only a horse."

"You have been an ass, which is close enough."

David smiled. "How I have missed you, Charlotte."

"And I you, Jacques-Louis."

He gathered Charlotte's hands once again. She squeezed back, pressing his hands tightly as if she were trying to wring moisture from them. He felt his mouth go dry. Something remained unsaid. Was she, he wondered, leaving him again, abandoning him here in this cell? Fear gripped him.

After a time, Charlotte broke the silence. "It is said that the scepter retains the force of Saint Eligius's touch."

He forced words, anything to continue the conversation. "It is gold, power, and magic wand?"

Charlotte stomped her foot. "Think less of your Republican foolishness and more about your great country before it descended into hell. Think of the scepter not as a magic wand but rather as the finger of God."

Her scolding startled him. He searched her face for some sign of jest.

"You believe that this gift from the saint could alleviate my pain?"

Charlotte nodded. She chewed on her lower lip. Her mouth opened as if to speak and then stopped. She clamped her mouth closed, but her teeth still scraped at the lip.

"Then I would like to rub the scepter on my knees and on my hips and on my back and..." David paused a moment and squeezed Charlotte's hands. "And on my heart, for that is where the greatest of my pains rests."

"Some aches may be healed without the intervention of God."

He looked into her eyes and smiled. "It is a legend to give strength to my soul. I have come to rue much of the last few years: my foolish notions that separated me from you, the death of so many, the chaos which we produced, and the needless destruction of so much art. So much beauty destroyed in the churches and palaces. Robespierre wanted desperately to find the scepter."

Charlotte sneered. "Only so that he might smash it and extinguish it as a symbol of royal authority."

David nodded. "Alas, it was carried off by thieves. Undoubtedly, its beauty was melted down and the lump of gold traded for wine and prostitutes." His eyes clouded.

Charlotte looked up and down the corridor. Her voice dropped to a whisper. "What if I knew where it was?"

6

Yellowstone National Park
June 2nd

Clarence excused himself from the Yellowstone Canyon crime scene and drove to the ranger station at Mammoth Hot Springs to write out his statement.

Or maybe he got dismissed and sent to the office, ordered to leave before he got fired for insubordination or arrested for interfering with a criminal investigation. Like much of life, this seemed a matter of perspective.

He'd suggested that Nance back up the perimeter of the crime scene. She had assured him that the investigation was in capable hands. He agreed that she knew what she was doing, if what she was doing was fucking up her case by polluting the crime scene with imbecilic methodology.

Then, she got mad.

Touchy, he thought.

Along the way to Mammoth, he stopped by his RV parked at the Canyon Campground. There were no towns close to Yellowstone. Some of the summer help stayed as far away as Livingston, Montana. Clarence had been lucky to land a parking spot with hookups for water and electricity. The space was cramped, barely room for a narrow bed, table, and efficiency kitchen. But he found he could work at the table, and he could not argue with the view. Outside his door, the northern Rockies opened. He also had room for the small dog bed just inside the door.

Tripod thumped her tail. Clarence bent down and scratched the dog behind the ears. Tripod began getting to her feet. Clarence scratched her again, trying to dissuade her. His three-legged dog moved remarkably well once she was standing, but getting there always proved a problem. Clarence saw that the dog was determined, so he picked her up and carried her down the two steps before placing her on the ground. The dog ran off in her own style to explore. Clarence sat on the step, opened his laptop, and watched her.

Clarence downloaded the video that he had taken of the crowd at the crime scene. He changed out of his ranger uniform. He had lost weight since his injury. Most of his civilian pants felt loose and ill-fitting. He settled on a pair of pressed khakis, cinched with a woven leather belt, and a blue chambray shirt. Clarence dressed comfortably; he wasn't sure how long they'd keep him at Mammoth. Then, he fixed himself a sandwich. After letting the dog back inside, he filled Tripod's water dish. The dog thumped her tail again as Clarence explained his afternoon plans. The Canyon Station personnel knew that Clarence was out for the day. If he had to spend the afternoon sitting in the Investigative Services Branch office, rehashing his story, he didn't want the dog to worry. Tripod had enough stress in her life.

If Nance ordered him to go give his statement, Clarence would comply. But he'd do it on his schedule. Clarence looked at his Fender Stratocaster leaning against the wall by the bed. He thought about playing—a guy should always make time to practice his art. He resisted the temptation; that was just being contrarian.

The ranger at the Mammoth Hot Springs station's front desk ignored Clarence, presumably because he'd been told to watch for a guy in an interpretive ranger uniform. The officer's name tag said "Philbrick." Clarence introduced himself. Ranger Philbrick's eyes swept over him, his mouth frowning.

"I don't like to wear the cape, too far to the dry cleaners," Clarence said.

Philbrick glanced at his phone and noted the time. "Don't like to wear a watch either."

He led Clarence to a small office at the back, confirmed that he had a pen, and showed him a folder with blank witness affidavit forms.

"Catch me when you're finished," Philbrick said and left him alone in the office.

He sat down and wrote his description of the events. The telling didn't take long. He penned a concise narrative about what he'd seen and heard, providing as much specificity as he could. The document ran nearly a page.

He turned in his affidavit and watched as Philbrick scanned the document. Philbrick's mouth returned to the frown.

"I waited around for this," the officer said.

"Sorry if it isn't the Rosie Moment you'd hoped for."

Philbrick's eyes showed no recognition.

"You've heard of the Rosetta Stone?"

Philbrick nodded.

"A decree from ancient Egypt written in hieroglyphics and Greek. The piece of rock became the key to deciphering ancient Egyptian writing. A Rosie Moment, the piece of the investigation that brings everything together."

Philbrick held up the affidavit. "This ain't it."

Clarence shrugged. "I tried to tell her that I didn't see much."

"I'll make sure Investigator Nance knows. But we don't get much murder here in the park. No one quite knows exactly what to look for," Philbrick said.

"You never do. Each one is unique."

Philbrick held out his hand, and Clarence shook it. Somewhere in the exchange, Philbrick's manner had softened. He had, there at the end, become almost conversational. Always good to make friends with a beat cop.

As he walked back to his car, a Porsche sped into the parking lot. The car flung gravel across the pavement as it came to an abrupt stop at one of the reserved parking spaces near the front of the visitor's building. Clarence looked but couldn't see the driver through the tinted side window. The Montana vanity plates read "Car-tel." The driver's door opened, and he watched Thor emerge. At least, that was whom Clarence thought of as the man with long blond hair and too many muscles stood. Thor's eyes, encased in wraparound sunglasses, swept the parking lot. Or perhaps he tossed his hair in slow motion, like an actor in a shampoo commercial. Then, Thor adjusted his sunglasses and disappeared inside the Mammoth Hot Springs ranger station.

Clarence paused outside his SUV. Thor reminded him of a linebacker he had known in college. He wondered whatever became of that guy. Then, he climbed in the cab and drove south toward Lake Yellowstone.

The colonial revival Lake Yellowstone Hotel overlooked the lake and was built to be approached from the water. Although packed with tourists, Clarence loved the view. During the summer, the lobby hosted a string quartet. He liked their version of Strauss, found the armchairs comfortable, the white wine palatable and not outrageously overpriced. He planned to sip a sauvignon blanc and think about his presentation on the artists of Yellowstone. Clarence believed that he gave a decent lecture on Thomas Moran, but he wanted to expand it, to educate visitors on Albert Bierstadt and Thomas Hill. He hoped eventually to show visitors contemporary interpretations of this marvelous landscape.

Soon, he hoped to outline his plans to Martinez. Although his boss had been at the park for so long that he had probably known Bierstadt, he still encouraged program development among his staff of interpretive rangers. The old man loved Yellowstone and tried to ensure that every visitor who came through the gates wrote their congressional representative to demand additional park funding.

The buzzing cell phone interrupted his thoughts about the lecture. Clarence stabbed the speaker button.

"Johnson," he said.

"This is Investigator Nance with the ISB."

"Thanks, that helps me keep all my Nances straight."

She paused for a moment before speaking. When she resumed, her voice sounded strained, as if she were struggling to keep the irritation from her tone. "I was hoping we might visit again."

"I love to visit," he said.

"Where are you?"

"I'm heading to the Yellowstone Hotel for a glass of wine."

"Kinda crowded, isn't it?"

"I'm a people person."

"Clearly. Mind if I join you?"

"You're people."

"Thanks for noticing. I'll get there as quickly as I can."

He hung up and found a parking space. In the lobby, he secured two chairs side by side overlooking the front desk. They weren't the best for viewing the water or listening to the strings. During the summer months, tourists quickly filled the prime seating. He considered himself fortunate that he could find two together. Clarence stretched himself across both chairs to hold the place.

A waitress approached. He read her name tag. Summer help arrived at Yellowstone from around the country, and the name tag detailed the point of origin. He enjoyed chatting them up; each kid working here had a story. Silently, she studied his contorted pose.

"Yoga," he said to Missy from Tucson. "The maharishi says that the recliner position is the surest path to enlightenment."

She nodded. "And the easiest way to keep the sweaty guy who has been hiking all day from sitting next to you."

"You're enlightened. I'll have a sauvignon blanc."

"And what about your friend?" Missy asked.

"She's in the restroom," Clarence said.

"I'll come back in a minute."

"Better make it two, the restroom is at the Canyon Visitor's Center."

Missy from Tucson smiled. "She might be a while. I hope nobody on the road sees a bear or a buffalo. Traffic will stop."

"Take your time putting in the order. And bring a breakfast menu just in case someone spots a jaywalking elk."

"Charismatic megafauna," Missy said.

"Excuse me?"

"All the big animals. Park staff call them charismatic megafauna." Missy smiled again and went off to service another guest at a nearby table.

Remarkable thing about Yellowstone, Clarence thought. The place was overrun with tourists, but nearly everyone stuck to the Grand Loop. Solitude could be found in the park—a visitor had only to park and walk a few steps away from the major attractions. Perhaps act a bit like Moran or Bierstadt and explore.

Before he could complete the mental transition from national park activist to art history lecturer, Nance entered the lobby. Thor accompanied her. Nance's brown eyes scanned the room. She threw him a quick wave of acknowledgment and then turned back to Thor. The blond man moved close to listen, too close for some people. Any closer and he might be standing behind her. Nance did not appear bothered by the violation of her personal space. She looked up at Thor, smiled at something he said. She fingered back an errant lock of her hair. They shook hands and parted.

Nance made her way across the crowded room. Clarence stood. He could be as gallant as any Norseman.

"I just ordered wine. I'll catch the waitress. What would you like?"

Nance checked her watch. "I'd like a beer. I'll have a coffee."

"French roast?"

"Large, to-go cup."

He walked to the bar, looking for Missy from Tucson. Instead, he found François from Montreal. He placed the order for the coffee and checked on his wine.

Nance sat with her head resting on the back of the chair, eyes closed. He said nothing and tried to slip quietly into his seat. Her eyes popped open, and she looked his way. "Your affidavit was skimpy."

Clarence nodded. "I left out the part about Wesley drawing his service weapon. I figured you had enough troubles."

Nance exhaled and made the slightest shake of her head. "Thanks for that. He is a new kid with potential. He overreacted. This is a big enough shitstorm already." She took a deep breath and closed her eyes again. "First chance I've had to sit down all day. Park superintendent's office, public information officer. They'd all like it solved fifteen minutes ago."

"Relax a minute, and listen to the music. I like this Bach piece. You can apologize after the drinks arrive."

Her eyes popped open again, and she sat up in her chair. "What makes you think I'm here to apologize?"

Clarence saw Missy making her way to their seats. He delayed answering until she had delivered the drinks and departed. Nance gripped her to-go cup in both hands, neither drinking nor speaking.

"You really should try the wine sometime. It's crisp."

Nance said nothing.

He took a sip before setting the glass down. "You know I didn't see anything. In the initial stages of a homicide investigation, you've got about a million and one things to do and forty-eight hours to get them accomplished. Yet here you are, spending some of that time with me. Even choosing me over Thor."

Her eyes widened.

Clarence cocked his head toward the lobby entrance. "The charismatic megafauna who went off for his romance novel cover shoot."

Nance nodded and tasted her coffee.

"You might want to take time out from your investigation for a quick ranger lecture on the art history of Yellowstone, but I think it's more likely that when you moved back the perimeter of the crime scene, you found something."

"I see a third possibility," Nance said.

"What's that?"

"I wanted to ask, are you always this charming?"

"I was raised by wolves. Left me without the usual human social graces. Probably explains why I like Yellowstone." Clarence reached for his wine. Pointedly, he kept his pinky extended as he took a drink. He held the glass back and studied it. Not the wine he ordered, he thought, then shrugged and took another sip. Adaptability was sometimes a key to survival in the wilderness.

Nance eyed him as she, likewise, drank from her cup. If she had expected to set him back on his heels a little with a blunt question, she'd be disappointed. Clarence remained unrepentant.

He felt her examination. "I give a good ranger lecture. Park visitors love me. You should catch it sometime. I really like finding answers. And I'm good at it." Clarence switched his gaze, looking for Missy. Failing to find her, he made eye contact with François, who busied himself cleaning a table near them. Clarence looked at Nance.

"Refill?"

She covered the top of the half-full cup with her hand. "Like you said, now I've got a million and two things to do."

He raised his glass toward François, who nodded and moved swiftly toward the bar.

Clarence looked back toward Nance and crossed his arms over his chest. He batted his eyes. "I'm sure you've gathered that beneath this square jaw and eyes like smoky quartz rests a cunning mind."

"Don't forget modest."

He gave a small smile. "I am the humblest man God ever created."

"So how did you know?"

"Elementary, my dear Watson. There was no spatter to be seen in the surrounding area. Your men were carefully picking their way about the rocks to avoid treading around the body. I saw no sign he had been dragged into that spot. Finally, the trailhead for the path taking anyone along the canyon floor is miles away. Those clothes of his did not bear the marks of hiking. He didn't walk there, wasn't dragged, and did not die on that spot. Therefore, the only reasonable possibility left..."

"He fell from above," Nance said.

"Like manna. After we reported the body, I assume that the park staff, highly trained emergency professionals, defaulted to a rescue. That's what the park does, they save wayward hikers. When someone discovered he was dead, they moved to default two, recovery. In the linear way that government works, no one paused to consider murder. And the need to think about crime scene," Johnson said.

"Pretty good for a summer ranger."

"The Park Service only hires crackerjack help."

Nance took another drink, larger this time. She turned away from him and gazed out over the lake. "Speed is critical in an investigation out here. The park gets two million visitors a year. They move through here and then drive someplace else. A large transient population makes swift action a priority. Every crime scene is outside. Rain, snow, heat, carnivores come along to degrade your location. We've got to get in and get it done. Fortunately, jurisdiction is clear on this one. Figuring out who runs the investigation can be a nightmare in cases near the boundaries of the park. This one happened squarely on national park property. It is federal jurisdiction." She paused and took a drink before continuing. Then, Nance turned to face him. "And don't get me started on the bureaucracy and the politics. Thank God he wasn't killed on top of Old Faithful. The superintendent would have given us ninety minutes to gather our evidence before he opened the site back up to tourists. Can't miss the eruption over something like a dead man."

Clarence waited for the rant to run its course. "What did you find?"

Nance shook her head and pursed her lips. "Oh, blood, hair, bits of brain and skull. He was shot up top and thrown over the side."

"Who was it?"

"Still trying to figure that one out. We get vandalism, poaching, and the kind of crimes that come when you give too many people alcohol. We don't get many murders. An FBI special agent is available to assist, but they come out of the Salt Lake City field office, and, well, time is pretty critical."

"But Thor got here quickly," Clarence said.

"Special Agent LaFleur isn't FBI."

"So, who does The Flower work for?"

Nance took another sip of her coffee and volunteered nothing.

François arrived with Johnson's wine.

"Let's talk about you," Nance said. "I don't meet many men under eighty named Clarence."

"Family name," he said. "Mom liked it."

"Philbrick up at Mammoth said you seemed to know your way around police procedure. I agree. What's your story?"

He, too, took another sip off his wine and volunteered nothing.

"Just when I was prepared to regret calling you charming." She picked up the empty wineglass at the base. "I'll just have to get this printed. Have the forensic guys rush it. I'll tell them I recovered it from the primary suspect."

Clarence held up his hands in mock surrender. Reaching across, he took the glass from Nance. She resisted only slightly before letting it go. François was cleaning a table nearby. Johnson added the wineglass to his collection and then returned to his seat.

"You know I don't have time for this. Don't make me take the wineglass away from the busboy."

He shrugged. "Retired Fort Worth PD. Used to do investigations."

Clarence felt her eyes search him.

"You don't look old enough to retire," she said.

"Medical retirement, long story. You don't have time right now to hear it."

He wondered if Nance would protest. Before she could, Thor came alongside her chair. He stood over her, shadowing Nance in blond hair and muscles. Clarence saw several pairs of eyes, men and women, turn to check out this physical specimen.

"We made an identification," he said. His eyes moved to Johnson.

"Sit down, have a drink, let's talk about it," Clarence said. "I hear the bar mixes a protein drink with vodka. They call it a Moscow Muscle." As he spoke, he flexed his biceps.

"Special Agent Tom LaFleur, this is Ranger Clarence Johnson."

They shook hands. Johnson made sure to clasp LaFleur's palm and not allow him to squeeze the fingers. Something might get broken.

"Johnson retired out of the Fort Worth Police Department."

"DEA," LaFleur said, "and you're an art teacher these days."

"Art history," Clarence corrected, "the key to understanding Western civilization. Like ancient Greek statues—big muscles, heads of stone."

"Guys, can you mark your territory some other time. I've got a murder here," Nance said. LaFleur's eyes moved between Nance and Johnson.

"He's a cop. He found the body," Nance said.

His eyes flicked back to Clarence, who gave him his warmest smile. LaFleur looked skeptical.

"You can talk in front of him." Nance's voice took on the edge of lead investigator whose patience was being tested.

Thor looked first to Nance and then to Clarence and paused before answering. "I got some results back on the fingerprints."

7

Paris, France
June 1795

Being above the Seine was far better than being below.

David walked across his new cell. A pair of double doors opened onto the balcony outside. They were locked. From his view, however, he could see grass and trees. Crude fences divided the former grounds of the estate into plots where people grew vegetables. He smelled dung and tilled earth. He could not be happier.

He had been moved to the third floor of the Luxembourg Palace. Light streamed through the windows of his sparsely furnished room. Standing against the glass, he felt the sun against his face. No longer did he suffer from the dampness through the stones. And when, on those occasions when he felt himself hot, he could open one small window and feel the cooling breeze.

Better to be above the Seine than below it.

Most of the furniture that once filled the room had been removed—and either burned or sold. A bed remained as well as a settee and a writing desk, little more. The small writing table would not be large enough for him to compose a work like *The Age of Reason*, as Thomas Paine had, but

David had no wish to write books. He had ample space to correspond with a few of his old students. A few more visited since he had been moved. He no longer felt dead and buried beneath the ground.

He turned and looked at himself in the small mirror that hung in the corner of the room. He traced the scar along his left cheek. His unkempt hair gave his face a triangular shape.

"You would think that such a thin face would make your mouth look bigger," the voice within his head said. His improved situation had not silenced his self-doubt.

He did not understand how it had all happened. The right word had been spoken to someone who undoubtedly spoke to another someone, and one day he had been lifted out of the pit and moved to this room.

He had been set free. Free from the aches brought about by the cold and wet, and free from the torment of Guinyard. The prisoners rumored that Guinyard had been transferred. David cared little for where the man was, only that his ill step and cruel manner did not occupy the third floor.

The hallway outside his door still retained a guard. The regular beat of the man's feet could be heard at night. The man treated him with respect, and David replied in kind. The guard imposed few limitations on his prisoner's activities. David imagined that his letters were read, although he said nothing worth censoring. Charlotte visited regularly, sometimes with guests. He requested the occasional book, usually Greek or Roman mythology, nothing radical or controversial. He knew that he was not free. He had not been allowed to roam at will as Thomas Paine had been. The restrictions mattered to him little. He had no wish to wander. David only had the desire to paint.

The emptiness in the room had become a blessing. He needed the vacant space to set up the enormous canvas that stretched more than twelve feet by seventeen feet.

He paused and redid his calculations. The canvas ran nearly 3.8 meters by 5.25 meters. Although difficult, he attempted to express himself in the measurements of the new order.

David walked along the length of the canvas. With each step, he pictured the creation that would occupy the space. He considered the colors, the action, each twist of the torso. Then, he stepped to the desk and reviewed the studies, the drawings outlining each section of the grand painting.

To the world, the painting would be a grand declaration in the Greek style. He would create a statement of the triumph of love over bloodshed, a cry for calm after the turbulent times through which all of France had just lived. The people, he knew, would flock to see a painting such as this. The public would need to feel that the virtues would ultimately prevail.

But there would be more.

The painting would be a banner to those who understood. After many visits and much time, trust had been rebuilt. Charlotte had shared most of her secret. He knew the great symbol existed. He knew enough to guess its location. Soon, he hoped to learn more.

With his knowledge, the Revolution could obtain this vestige of royal authority. He could bargain his way back to the forefront of politics with the information. His mind could not help but consider all the good he might accomplish should he restore himself. But he also knew that the Revolution must not be allowed to possess the scepter. They would destroy it, as they had so much already. David would not sacrifice art for politics. He had traded his wife and love once for a belief in the Revolution. He would not betray again. Never would he try to collect another thirty pieces of silver. Never again would he dabble in politics. He cared only for the art.

The people must be led, and to do so, they must have symbols before them. Moses had guided the Israelites with a pillar of fire. The ancient Greeks believed in the long scepter, crafted by Hephaestus, given to Zeus, and ultimately possessed by King Agamemnon. David would create the long painting. He would not draw a map to the scepter's location. He did not know where the royalists had hidden it, but he knew enough of the details to post a sign.

He dipped his hands into the basin and tried to wash the charcoal and coloring from them. David picked at a fingernail. His hands never came completely clean. As he dried them, he looked upon the crowded drawings, his eyes noting the buried symbols within his sketches. The centerpiece, of course, his most enduring symbol of royal authority he knew, dear Charlotte would stand front and center.

A turning key and a creaking door interrupted his meditations. Charlotte entered the room.

She blushed slightly. "I am sorry, dear husband, to have interrupted your work."

He liked the sound of the words. He raised his arms to embrace the room. "It is, after all, my jail. The doors should creak."

"The nobles kept the hinges better oiled."

"Enabling them to sneak about, undiscovered, for their assignations." David took her into his arms. "We of the Revolution believe in many virtues, including monogamy."

"It always appeared to me that the leaders of the Revolution were so painfully ugly that monogamy was the best they could hope for. Securing one woman would be a major accomplishment for most of them." The corners of her mouth upturned into a small smile.

Seeing the sparkle in her eyes, David laughed. "For every ugly man, there is an ugly woman. And these are men with great imaginations."

"Perhaps that is why revolutionaries make love in the dark."

He pulled her close to his chest. "I missed the gravity of our conversations."

"That is one of the things I missed."

He stood quietly, feeling her body pressed against his. Then, taking her hand, he guided her to the table. "I am nearly finished with my sketches. Let me show you."

His hands danced as he began explaining. The words came out faster and his pitch rose as he felt himself consumed by excitement over the work. "It shall be a grand battle, with kings in the foreground and soldiers all around. The kings shall have no clothes. Think of it, Charlotte. The women dressed, the men nude. Paris will have seen nothing like it." David paused for breath and touched his forehead with his fingertips. "The king has no clothes. It shall excite the passions of the public, and to those who know, it shall be a sign. We are declaring a private message."

"Perhaps a bit subtle," Charlotte said.

"This painting is not a map but rather a banner. We shall remind those who are with us that we have a great secret."

Charlotte's eyebrows drew together, the skin between them folded into a triangle. The corners of her mouth frowned.

"I have drawn a great ancient battle. Two armies battle for supremacy. Those of us who know see that the key lies with the woman standing alone in the middle. The raging warfare around shows the hardship that comes from ignoring the need to reconcile."

"Yes, yes, I see all of that," Charlotte said. "But where do the people find the message of the scepter?"

His fingers darted about the sketches. "I have been forced to be circumspect. You have given me so few details about where you have hidden it in the new world."

Charlotte turned away and looked at the floor. Her palm covered her mouth.

He gently touched her shoulder and turned her to face him. "I will bury more clues to the scepter's whereabouts when you trust me enough to confide in me."

"My husband, I cannot tell you."

"When, my Charlotte, will I have repented enough for the error of my past ways that you and your company will entrust me with the information? I can do little more with the painting than the vague hints I have put there."

Charlotte's eyes studied the drawings. Her lips pressed together so tightly they lost all color.

"How might I earn your trust?"

Charlotte drew a deep breath and exhaled forcefully. "My husband, I have been less than forthright with you."

He took a small step back.

She raised her eyes and met his gaze. "I can give you no more details for I do not know. I have told you where the scepter will be. As of yet, it is not there."

"The scepter is in transit?"

Charlotte shook her head. "The scepter remains hidden here. It has not left France."

"I'm such a fool!" His head sank and then snapped up to face her. Charlotte turned away, suddenly afraid. David's eyes blazed, and his face flushed. "I have been lied to this entire time." He waved his hands to the sketches and then toward the enormous canvas.

"Jacques-Louis, no...," Charlotte began.

"Am I some child whom you must keep entertained with fanciful stories?" He crumpled up one of the sketches and flung it toward the fireplace.

Charlotte dashed to the spot and recovered the drawing before he might kick it into the flames. Smoothing it against her dress, she returned the paper to the table.

He seized a knife. "And this enormous canvas. Let us slash it to pieces. Are not five small lies better than one great one? I shall create a series of little paintings, little stories so that all your circle can see how you kept me occupied. They shall all have a great laugh at my expense." He took a step forward.

Charlotte leapt in front of the easel. She grasped his wrist. "The man tasked to take it from the country was arrested. We have not moved the crown jewel for fear we have been infiltrated."

David stood still. His chest rose and fell. Gradually, his breathing slowed. He felt his heart rate slow and the heat from his face dissipate. Charlotte pried the knife from his fingers. It disappeared into the folds of her dress.

He looked at her. "All of France has ears. It will surely be found in time."

Charlotte balled her fists. Her jaw muscles knotted. "We are as paralyzed as we were before the Revolution. We cannot bring ourselves to act. We are fools with our feet stuck deeply in the mud. No wonder you divorced me."

He opened his mouth to remind her that she had divorced him but then stopped. Instead, he stood quietly. His eyes darted between his wife and the sketches. He stood again at a crossroads. Freedom, national acclaim, a return to the head of the national school of art, all the benefits of the Revolution could be delivered to him.

Charlotte seemed to read his thoughts. "Do you remember submitting paintings to the Salon?"

The question, posed at such a moment, surprised him. "Of course, but—"

She pressed a finger to his lips, quieting him. "You yearned to be recognized by the Salon, yet you always submitted your paintings late and of the wrong size for the exhibition space."

He looked down at the floor.

"You never fooled me that such mistakes were accidents. You think of yourself as a revolutionary, but you are not. You are a rebel. Against whom will you rebel?"

He stomped his foot. "We must stay with the plan regardless of the risks."

The firmness of his tone surprised them both.

"The risks of accidental discovery, a tongue loosened by drink, all manner of disaster awaits us if the scepter remains here on its native soil." As he spoke, David found himself talking faster and faster. His hands waved in the air; his enthusiasm built with each phrase. "Rousseau was right. We must get the pure thing away from the corruption of this society. The wild, among the savages in the state of nature, is the best and only safe place for us to hide it. We must move the thing to Louisiana and from there to the farthest corner of the frontier."

Charlotte nodded. "That has always been the plan. The fur traders tell of the place where even the savages fear to tread. They believe the place is haunted. Christian men swear that hell bubbles up there. All avoid the Devil's Land. The fur traders say that it runs along the banks of the river they call the Yellow Rock."

He nodded. "God will protect it even in hell. The location is perfect."

"But," Charlotte said, "we cannot trust anyone to move it. The man we entrusted sacrificed his head."

"But he did not talk?"

"He was willing to die for our cause."

"We will find new soldiers," David said.

"How will we know that the Revolution has not seeded itself among those we think we can trust?"

"They will not come from the fickles of politics, willing to change sides for the allure of money or power. We will take from those who are motivated to preserve a thing of beauty." He tapped the sketches with his index finger. "We will select new soldiers dedicated to art. Those who have betrayed will not know of their existence until the scepter is safely away."

"But who, husband, might we trust?"

"Artists. Students of mine committed to the preservation of art. Even those who have disagreed with me over the whisperings of the muse will help. They will not allow such a thing as the scepter to be melted down and scattered as some political statement."

She looked at him, eyes wide. He could tell that she desperately wanted to believe what he was telling her. Charlotte took his hands in hers. "Could it be possible?"

"Leave everything to me."

8

Lake Yellowstone Hotel
June 2nd

LaFleur waited to speak. Nance watched him. LaFleur, Clarence assumed, was used to having women look at him.

He lifted his glass. "I think I'll just drink wine until you let the tension build sufficiently."

LaFleur's eyes flicked to Clarence. His expression said, "Asshole."

It appeared to Clarence that a consensus was building among the feds about his character. Fortunately, he had the self-esteem not to curl up inside. He sipped his wine.

LaFleur returned his gaze to Nance. From his daypack he withdrew an electronic device. He showed it to her. "Digital fingerprint scanner. Useful for pinning down dope suspects in the field. Out there, names are commodities to be traded. I was able to make a positive proof of identity."

He paused again. Alison Nance smiled.

Johnson had to admire the man. "I've never seen someone use fingerprint ID as an aphrodisiac."

Nance laughed a little at that one. LaFleur's eyes flared at him again, sending the same message. Maybe "asshole" represented awakening self-awareness and not a criticism of him, Clarence thought.

LaFleur spoke directly to Nance, lowering his voice so that even sitting close, Clarence struggled to hear. "The dead guy's name is Phillip Ocone, associate professor out of Montana State University." LaFleur typed into his phone. He handed the phone to Nance, who studied the information. She returned the phone to LaFleur. He looked at Clarence with a small smile on his face. "Sorry, confidential federal material. You understand."

"What got his prints in the system?" Nance asked.

"Couple of priors. Prior drug conviction and trespassing on protected property. The prof got caught trying to steal buried artifacts."

"What did he teach?" Clarence asked.

LaFleur ignored the question until he saw that Nance awaited the answer as well. "History."

Nance turned slightly to look at Clarence. He smiled and shrugged. She turned back to LaFleur. "Tom, where did he live?"

"He rented a place in Bozeman. Don't know yet how long he has been here in Yellowstone. Or whether he was here vacationing or part of some research group."

Nance excused herself and walked toward the hotel check-in desk.

Clarence saw François hovering nearby, cleaning tables of empty glasses and plates. He handed over his empty wineglass. He turned back to the DEA agent. "Well, Tom, should we have a pushup contest?"

"You probably need to go get some rest," LaFleur said. "I'm sure you have a full day tomorrow handing out stickers and maps. Alison and I, meanwhile, have an investigation to conduct."

"You are pretty quick to dismiss stickers and their place in the overall mission of the National Park Service."

If Thor had anything cutting to say in reply, Nance's return denied him the opportunity. A man stood alongside her. His name tag said that he came from Oregon. He picked at the sleeve of his blazer.

"Hello, Robert," Clarence said.

The man stopped fidgeting and smiled. "Hey."

Nance's eyebrows raised briefly. "The reservation system can access all the park's hotels. Ocone stayed here at the Lake Yellowstone. The manager will get us into room 317."

"Follow me, please." Robert walked toward the elevator, followed by LaFleur. Nance took a step and then stopped. She turned back to face Clarence. "Come along."

"I don't think Tom would approve."

Nance rolled her eyes. "This is my case. The victim worked as a historian. I don't know if that's significant yet. But for the present time, you're my historical consultant, serving in an advisory capacity."

"I like it. Do I have time to get business cards printed?"

"Not if you want to see room 317."

The two of them walked toward the elevator, where Robert and Tom were waiting.

"How do you know Robert?"

Clarence shrugged. "I come here. His son expects to be varsity this year. We talk football."

"So, you can be friendly."

"I don't like to make a habit of it."

Outside the room, Nance handed them each a pair of latex gloves. When the three of them were ready, she nodded to the manager. He opened the door and stepped aside. Nance entered, followed by LaFleur. Clarence waited.

A bed and a pair of nightstands dominated the small room. The room had two chairs and a table arranged in one corner. A framed print depicting buffalo grazing hung above the table. Another print rested on the floor behind it. A luggage rack with a suitcase balanced on it stood against the wall where a television would normally sit in most hotel rooms. This, however, was a national park hotel; the room did not have a television.

Clarence moved to the far corner of the room.

"Good idea," LaFleur said. "Stay out of the way. And don't touch anything."

Clarence pointed at Alison. "I'm her historical consultant."

LaFleur ignored him and walked directly into the bathroom. "I'm starting in here."

"Something you ate?" Clarence asked.

LaFleur lifted the tank lid on the toilet. "Dopers always hide their stuff in the toilet. They never think we'll look there." He gazed down inside the tank, studied it for a moment, and then replaced the lid. LaFleur walked out and moved to the side of the bed.

Clarence looked out the window. Ocone's room faced the parking lot. He saw cars from many states and wondered which one belonged to Ocone. The window was well sealed to keep out the winter cold as well as noise. Clarence's eyes moved around the room, starting at the ceiling and working down the far wall before moving on to the next wall and repeating the process. "I'm not staying out of the way," he said. "I'm standing in a low-traffic area. I'm exploring the room in three dimensions before I start sloshing through the high-traffic areas, allowing my shoes to carry in hairs, fibers, and other contaminants from the lobby downstairs into the crime scene."

LaFleur cast a quick glance at his feet.

Clarence turned to Nance. "Locard's Principle."

LaFleur knelt beside the nightstand. Opening the drawer, he began to feel along the underside. His eyes narrowed, and his lips pressed together. He appeared totally focused on whatever he was trying to accomplish. Clarence again looked at Nance. She shrugged. They both watched LaFleur.

He felt the eyes on him and turned toward them. He spoke to Nance. "Hidey-hole for drugs."

Clarence lost interest and returned his attention to the room. Near his feet, the carpet bore two indentations, approximately a foot long, running parallel to one another. His eyes wandered up the wall, looking for irregularities. He found a faint black circular stain. Above the mark, Johnson located two small holes approximately three feet apart. With his cell phone, he snapped a picture of the carpet and the wall.

The pictures drew Nance to his side.

He shrugged. "You never know." He faced her. "I've got panoramas of your crowd from the crime scene, if you want them. They're on my computer at my place."

"Do women go for lines like that in Fort Worth?"

"I intended to email them to you if you'd like. But you're welcome to see my etchings and my rare books if Tom doesn't mind."

"Bingo," LaFleur said. He held up a baggie he had found taped to the underside of the nightstand. "Marijuana."

"You can't be serious," Clarence said. "We've got a weed smoker here in the national park?"

Nance took a step toward LaFleur and his evidence. She stepped forward and then backed up and looked at the carpet. "There's a pushpin lying here."

"A what?" LaFleur asked.

"Pushpin, for bulletin boards."

Clarence studied the floor, his eyes sweeping in circles. A spot of red just under the corner of the bed caught his eye. "I've got another one here."

Nance's eyes followed his pointing finger.

Clarence pointed to the wall behind him. "Something was pinned here."

Nance gestured to the black smudge. "Looks like something got circled with a black marker. The ink bled through the page."

"Whatever it was, somebody pulled it down in a hurry," Clarence said.

LaFleur raised the baggie. "Pulled down in a struggle with the dope dealer?"

Nance shook her head. "Nothing else seems disturbed."

"Crime scene will collect this?" Johnson said.

Nance snorted. "Sorry, city boy, but the Park Service doesn't have the resources. One crime, one investigator. I've got a friend trying to get down here to help."

They resumed the search, stepping carefully around the pins.

LaFleur picked up the desk chair and examined the underside for evidence. Satisfied that it was nothing more than a place to sit, he set it down in the middle of the room and climbed on it. He studied the light fixture. "Dopers love to hide stuff in these. Searchers always forget to look here."

Nance moved to the suitcase. Without moving any of the items, she peered into it.

Clarence searched the closet. He looked through the clothes that the dead professor had hung. Hotel management had painted the closet white, making it easier to see in the soft light. Johnson patted the pockets but felt nothing. He ran his hands down the length of each garment without success. Against the wall of the closet, an ironing board hung suspended from the wall. Johnson could see nothing out of place. He looked along the shelf of the closet but didn't find anything except an empty box for hiking boots.

LaFleur, meanwhile, climbed down from the chair. He wiped the dust from his boots off the chair, small bits clinging to the boot print left behind. "Nothing up here," LaFleur said.

Nance nodded her head in agreement. "Room looks pretty clean."

Clarence's eyes swept the room. "Anyone notice what's not here?"

LaFleur and Nance looked at him.

"What visitor comes to Yellowstone and doesn't bring a guidebook? Where are the tourist brochures you get when you come through the entrance to the park?"

"Likely in his backpack at the scene," LaFleur said.

Clarence looked at Nance. "You got the contents of the inventory?"

She pulled her phone and spent a moment waving it around. "Damn hard to get reliable reception here in the mountains. Hard to make a phone call, let alone download a file." Nance took a couple of steps toward the window. "What do you make of these carpet impressions?"

LaFleur pushed the chair back under the desk. Then, he leaned in to examine the impressions.

They studied a pair of short parallel lines.

LaFleur's chair gave Johnson a thought. He walked to the closet and recovered the ironing board. Opening it, he held the board over the impressions and then lowered it down slowly. He did not want to contact the carpet in case his assumption proved wrong.

The legs of the ironing board matched the lines on the floor.

Nance and LaFleur nodded. A little mystery had been solved. They moved away from the impressions, Nance back by the suitcase and LaFleur to the dresser. He began again, systematically checking the insides of the drawers.

"Good thing that the cleaning staff hasn't vacuumed since the body was found. Or we'd have lost the clue," Clarence said.

"What clue? The guy ironed his clothes," LaFleur said, barely looking up from his search.

"Check out the clothes he has hanging up," Johnson said. "Nothing is ironed. Besides, no man irons between the bed and the wall. There isn't room. Either he needed the extra light from the window for some delicate work, or..."

"Or what?" LaFleur asked.

"He needed the ironing board for something else."

Nance waved for both men to join her at the suitcase. "Check this out." Using the tip of her pen, she pushed aside the corner of a shirt, revealing the lower layer of the suitcase's contents.

"A power cord for a computer," LaFleur said.

"So, show me where the computer is," Nance said.

Three sets of eyes roamed the room, looking for something they knew wasn't there.

Clarence elected to state the obvious. "It's missing. We need to look at that inventory."

LaFleur faced him. "There is no 'we' here, Mr. Historical Consultant. I'm not finding anything calling for your expertise."

A knock at the door interrupted Clarence's crushing retort, or at least prevented him from punching a federal officer.

Nance opened the door. A woman stood outside, camera around her neck. At her feet was a hard-shell case.

"Hey, PPT," Nance said.

The woman greeted Nance.

Nance made the introductions. "This is Susan Shannon. She's a protection ranger working in the Tower region. She is also the best photographer in the Park Service. Unofficially, she is my crime scene officer. We call her PPT."

Shannon shrugged. "I make a good PowerPoint presentation. It's the federal government. Everyone gets a three-letter acronym."

They may call her PPT, but Johnson thought she ought to be nicknamed "Pockets." Like every crime scene officer he'd ever met, she had places to put gear stitched throughout her clothing. Her cargo pants had pockets running down the legs. Over her uniform blouse, she wore a vest that would make any fly fisherman proud. A 35mm camera hung from her neck and a daypack was strapped to her back.

Clarence stepped out into the hall to retrieve her gear case. François stood outside with a gray plastic tub. "You were down at the bar. What are you doing up here?"

François looked down at the tub and then up at Clarence. "The manager sent me to bus the floors. I'm gathering the dishes."

Clarence eyeballed him, but he saw no reason not to believe the young man. "Stay out of this area. We'll be moving back and forth for quite some time."

"Yes, sir," François said and hurried down the hall.

"Just a minute." He walked to where François stood. Nance and LaFleur came out into the hall. "Have you carried room service up to 317 before?"

François shook his head. "I don't usually do room service delivery. The manager sent me up here because we weren't too busy. The restaurant computer can tell you whether he ordered and who delivered it."

Clarence nodded and waved him on with his hand.

PPT had recovered her own materials. Her case sat open in the corner nearest the door. She stood still; her eyes studied the room in three dimensions.

Ranger Shannon faced the three of them. "Before I get started, tell me what you've already done to screw up my crime scene." Although her mouth was set firm, her voice had, Clarence hoped, a bit of a lilt to it.

He pointed at LaFleur. "He's been throwing his DNA all over. But I can't blame him. If I had hair like that, I'd want to brush it all the time too."

"Get a shower cap from housekeeping if you're going to stay here," PPT said.

LaFleur blushed.

Shannon's face broadened into a smile. "Gotcha."

Even Nance smiled at the exchange. Johnson loved working this room. He saw potential in teaming up with this crime scene officer. He was preparing his encore when Nance spoke up and outlined what they'd done. She pointed out the marijuana LaFleur had found as well as the pushpins and the holes in the wall.

Satisfied that any damage was not irreparable, PPT began sketching the crime scene. With a laser, she shot measurements, recording the information on a pad pulled from one of the vest pockets.

While PPT worked, Clarence leaned against the wall of room 317. His eyes studied the place. Something bothered him. Shoddy workmanship, he decided finally. While the room looked nice, it was clear that the painting crew had behaved like they were perpetuating a myth about government contractors. While most of the closet wall had been textured and painted, the area above the shelf had only been painted. The work crew had done a slapdash job, convinced no one would notice.

PPT stood on a ladder, checking the light fixture over the bed.

"Excuse me, Ranger Shannon," Clarence said. "May we look at something?"

She exhaled a long breath, the exasperated sound of someone interrupted in the middle of her work for someone else's priority. She climbed down from the ladder.

Clarence picked it up and carried it to the closet door. Taking a step up, he got to where he could comfortably examine the back wall of the closet. He turned to look at her. "Would you look at this, please."

They changed places. She needed to climb an extra step to study the back of the closet. She pushed against the wall with her thumb. "It's a piece of foam board that runs the length of the closet."

LaFleur, who had busied himself checking messages, pocketed his phone. "You've found the hidey-hole."

Clarence looked first to PPT before shifting his gaze to Nance. "Should we look behind the curtain?"

Nance nodded.

Standing on the desk chair, PPT slid the blade of a pocketknife between the wall and the edge of the foam board. Wiggling the blade gently, she worked the board away from the back wall. Clarence grabbed the board. He pulled it out of the closet and set it against the door. PPT climbed down, studied the board, frowned, and nodded.

Clarence stood beside PPT. "Well, we've learned something. The painter did remember to texture the entire closet." Then he flipped the board around to show Nance and LaFleur.

They looked at a copy of a painting.

9

Versailles, France
September-October 1795

David surveyed the assembled group. Four of Charlotte's most trusted aristocrats had arrived. Four of David's former students, passionately loyal to their old mentor, also waited. They each had confessed to him their private pain at seeing artistic creations become fuel for the fires of the Revolution. All gathered at a farmhouse outside of Versailles. Two of the artists brought attendants, men who in headier times had helped them tote stones for sculpting and carry easels and canvases. He had known these men for years. He trusted them.

They gathered in a barn, a host of men who had once been the leaders of France. Each man's lot had been better during the old regime. The scepter was a symbol of those lost days.

David had been released from prison in August. The most important painter of the Revolution retained a few influential friends who believed he had suffered enough. Although the last months of his incarceration had been easier, it had taken some time for him to fully recover. More weeks had been lost getting word to the assembled group. The utmost care had been taken to ensure that the notices could not be intercepted.

He spoke with each of them. As they talked, he searched their faces for signs of disloyalty. As an artist, he had studied physiognomy, revealing character through body poses and facial expressions. David employed all his learned skills. He found little reason for concern.

Two men came with their wives. None, fortunately, had brought children. Each was dressed as a peasant, although David could see that two had hidden swords beneath their clothing. He shook his head. The goal was not to battle the scepter out of France but rather to remove it by stealth.

They met at night, the barn lit by lanterns. The shed smelled heavily of farm animals. Outside, a group of stout men stood guard, allowing only the trusted to be admitted. Their eyes and ears sharp, watching and listening for the arrival of Republican forces.

When all who were to come had gathered, David pulled back on a tarpaulin. Straw bales banked the sides, hiding a tumbrel. He heard murmurs of surprise. Climbing onto the wagon bed, he looked out over desperate faces.

David could not tell the source of their discomfort. They might be worried about Republican troops. Others might simply be put off by the barn. Although all had found their station diminished since the Revolution, none had been reduced to living in a chilly cowshed with a floor caked in manure. Likely, they did not trust him to lead.

He scanned the assembled faces. "My brothers and sisters. Some of you do not know me. What you may have heard perhaps has not been favorable." The aristocrats, he knew, had come out of loyalty to Charlotte and to the cause, not to him.

"I am newly returned, but I swear by the blood that is within me, I shall not disappoint you."

These faces wanted to believe. He promised action, an opportunity to do something. He offered hope. Though their beards were less stylishly trimmed than in their former days, he saw himself surrounded by royals. "When I first learned that the treasure of Saint Denis, the Scepter of Dagobert, had been hidden here, so close to Versailles, I questioned the wisdom of those with whom I must place my trust and my life. But upon further reflection, I commend the plan for its brilliance. Only a fool would think that the thing would be hidden in the shadow of the palace of our departed king. Yet, here it is, surrounded by people who for generations have supported the Bourbons. Nowhere in France might this treasure be safer. The thanks of our nation go to those among you who have risked your lives to keep the scepter safe."

Smiles appeared on a few faces, nods and back pats given by other members of the audience.

"Much as we appreciate the sacrifice of those who have protected the relic since it was rescued from the Abbey of Saint-Denis, we know that it is no longer safe here. Each day, the desire within the Republican leadership grows to recover the last symbols of the monarchy so that they might be melted down and disappear forever."

The faces, smiling earlier, scowled. A rumble of anger rolled through the audience.

"It is true what he says," one of the aristocrats said. David recognized the man as Louis de Noaleste. "Someone heard a rumor in a tavern that I might have the scepter. Guards arrived at my home. They searched everywhere, throwing my scant belongings into the streets."

David nodded. "Here, we have temporary safety, but no enduring security. We will move the treasure outside the boundaries of our country, trading short-term risk for long-term protection."

He looked to the farmer standing to his left. "Guillame, if you will."

The man bowed and stepped into the small tack room off the main barn. He returned, carrying a lead tube. He set one end down at David's feet, holding it upright.

"Guillame Boucher has protected the scepter. His neck has been more imperiled than any other, yet he has remained steadfast. The man has earned his rest and our gratitude."

David twisted the tube's cap and worked it free. Reaching into the tube, he carefully withdrew an object sheathed in canvas. Slowly, he peeled back the cloth. Beneath the outer layer, an inner layer of velvet wrapped the object. As he removed this layer, his eyes watched the crowd.

The gasps told him that the object had been revealed. Many fell to their knees. He looked at the scepter. Rotating it slightly within his hand, he allowed all to see this symbol of divine power, the yellow light of the lanterns highlighting the filigreed and enameled gold.

Had he laid the scepter alongside his arm, he estimated that it would extend from his fingertips to his elbow. It had seemed larger when he had seen it in the hands of the king at Saint Denis, but such, he decided, is the nature of power. Above the rod, a golden hand held the world, long, thin fingers surrounding all the nations. Atop the world and upon a pedestal sat a statue, the oldest part of the mace, a woman sitting upon a great bird.

He held the scepter by the shaft. Even through the velvet, the object's power tingled. He sensed the kings and saints who had clutched it. He felt a commanding presence. This trip would be successful. David thrust out the scepter so that the audience might be an arm's length closer to its majesty.

He waited to speak until all had basked in its power. "This is our task, fellow lovers of France. We must preserve this piece until our nation sobers from this national drunkenness. We will hide this symbol until the country returns to its senses." With that, David again wrapped the scepter in its protective cloths and carefully returned it to the lead tube. Picking up the cap, he resealed the end.

"The question all ask, how are we to safely get this treasure to its new home?" With his boot heel, he stomped on the bed of the small tumbrel. "Monsieur Armand, one of the carriage makers to our king, worked to modify this old farm wagon. The bed is false, a hidden compartment lies beneath. He is a skilled craftsman; the cleverest eye will not see it." Taking a thin-bladed knife, David pried up one of the boards on the wagon bed. Reaching inside the hidden compartment, he situated the lead tube. He worked slowly; all present watched the theater. As he secured the scepter, he resumed his narration. "Armand prepared a special cradle within the compartment." He fixed the tube in place with ropes. "The lead pipe will remain fast even over the worst road."

Guillame helped him work the board back into its original place. With a small hammer, he tapped in nails marked by age and rust. "We will not be undone by shiny nails declaring our efforts."

David straightened and looked over the crowd. "The scepter is secure." He pointed with his finger, slowly sweeping the assembled crowd. "No one must ever again refer to the contents of this cart as a scepter. Alert ears are everywhere. If you must refer to the contents, call it a scythe. The success of the entire operation may depend upon your adherence to this rule." His eyes searched the crowd. He saw nods of understanding. Most had experience with court intrigue. They understood code words.

His tone relaxed. "Who stands ready to serve?"

Hands shot into the air.

He jumped down from the back of the wagon. "Then we must take turns. I only have three shovels."

The volunteers' eyes studied him, the shovels, the wagon, and each other.

He thrust shovels into the hands of the two men nearest him. "We must fill the wagon with manure. What would more likely dissuade a guard from searching?" He plunged his short-handled wooden shovel into the pile of dung and deposited the first scoopful into the back of the wagon.

Muttering complaints, the others joined the work. He made sure that all were provided an opportunity to assist in the important work of saving the crown jewel. When the manure pile heaped against the sides of the wagon bed, he called a halt.

"It is time to move to the next phase of the plan. We need men and women to escort the wagon to the coast. I have contracted with a ship to carry a small bit of cargo from Le Havre to an island in the Caribbean. For security, I will not name the ship or the island. We will move our wagonload of manure from here to Le Havre. I need two to drive the wagon and a pair of escorts out front as well as two more in the rear. All will be disguised as peasants, and all must act as if the wagon travels alone. The front and rear guards will be the eyes and ears of the wagon, but they must act in secret."

David culled those who did not raise their hands to volunteer. Raising his hand, he signaled to the guard stationed at the barn door. An elderly man and woman entered. Their patched clothing showed the marks of many repairs. They wandered among the crowd, occasionally pointing and whispering. Quietly, they studied everyone in the room. Some puffed their chests and protested, demanding to know the meaning. Others dropped their heads and appeared to hope that they may not be noticed. These, he assumed, had been questioned by Republican officials and feared the consequences of peasant identification. One man stood out to David. The couple, he saw, observed the man and then quickly moved on to the next. He motioned to the man. The man came, modestly, head bowed.

"Noaleste, you perform your part exceptionally well."

The man bobbed his head. "You are most kind, my lord. I wish only to serve France."

"You may well get that chance."

"Thank you," the man said before shuffling back to his place among the others.

After a few minutes, the couple approached the wagon. They spoke quietly.

David nodded, paused, and then gestured to a spot along the wall where they might stand.

He faced the crowd. "This is not a costumed ball to which we are attending. I have asked this couple, who have lived their entire lives as servants, to help me identify those who best resemble peasants."

"Ridiculous," one bull-chested man declared. "Foolishness that one must audition before risking one's life."

"Monsieur d'Aradon, those who travel will be responsible for carrying the treasure of France. Compared to that, your life and mine are irrelevant. As a teacher of artists, I can tell you that one with experience can tell at a glance whether one belongs in a costume. I have seen my students who aspire to paint that which they have not seen make the most ridiculous mistakes. Their minds do not conceive of things that we who have seen immediately identify. You would quickly lose your head, monsieur."

The man's face turned florid with rage.

David continued before the man could object. "That rage would reveal you. When confronted with authority, the peasants bow their heads. They may complain privately, but they bear their burden in silence. You would be revealed quickly and our mission ruined. You may storm, but you cannot escort this wagon."

The man's eyes roamed the room. Finding no support for his position, he stomped out of the barn.

David looked out across the crowd. "I have no wish to lose this treasure or to see brave patriots made martyrs." With that, he identified six individuals.

"It is not just your dressing but also your walk and your eyes." He beckoned the couple forward. The servants reluctantly stepped back into the center of the circle. "My friends will help you rehearse your demeanor as well as your attire. Study dutifully. Our success will depend upon your abilities."

The couple, clearly uncomfortable, began stammering out an introductory lesson.

Charlotte stepped forward and took her place among the six.

"Dearest Charlotte, may I see you for a moment?" David drew her away from the circle.

She looked at him, her face blank.

"This is not the place for you. Please allow these people to rehearse."

Charlotte's eyes narrowed to slits, her hands shaking. "You would still be imprisoned and this entire plan would not exist without me. And I am not to be a part of its execution?"

"My dear Charlotte, your great gift is your indomitable spirit, your refusal to compromise. I should have listened to the voice which comes with that iron will and never been foolish in the early days of the Revolution."

Charlotte's head snapped forward. She stabbed the air with her index finger.

He thrust his hand up in a halt sign. "But that spirit could not be contained or masked, my dear. This is not your role. Hiding your true nature—not a color you can paint." He crossed his arms over his chest and prepared to absorb Charlotte's verbal attack.

She grunted and marched out of the barn.

He stared at the door for a long time after she'd gone.

"This would be a good time for you to resume painting, Jacques-Louis. It appears that you will be a lonely man for quite some time," a man said.

Nervous laughter filled the barn.

Barges pushed up and down the Seine. The road from Versailles to Le Havre followed the river much of the way. Men working the barges called out to those driving the wagon. They returned the call with grunts and waves. The teamsters did their best to avoid speaking. Their rehearsals had shown how easily they might be revealed. Fortunately, they faced little challenge from fellow travelers along the way. David had deliberately departed on a warm day. Flies and the smell of manure kept most people at a distance.

At night, they stopped at cheap inns. The lead guards marked the inn with a small streamer of green cloth if they found it safe. David, posing as another traveler, spent the night as well. Although the guards, lead and rear, never acknowledged the wagon tenders, he could, on occasion, see his party exchanging discreet glances as if to say, "One day closer, brother." The team took turns keeping watch over the wagon until sunrise.

The cart moved slowly. They had learned never to hurry or to overtax their draught animal. Beasts could rarely be replaced on the meager earnings of teamsters. With endless long days of labor before them, actual peasants never dashed to finish the task. The royals were not traveling by post chaise on this trip. They did their best to look and to act the part of working men.

After two nights, David discreetly called together his band of travelers. While one acted as lookout, the rest crowded into a small room. The air in the room was thick and sour, each person bringing the stench of the manure cart, the soiled clothing from working under the full sun, and the sweat from the stress-filled days of watchfulness. David could not help but think how different the world had become for the assembled men and women. A few short years before, they would have called for perfumes and powders to mask the faintest unpleasantness. He must give them credit; they accepted their reduced station with equanimity.

He spoke, his voice barely above a whisper. He did not want a sound to escape the room, for information was a currency in troubled France. All heads pulled close to hear his words. "Late tomorrow, we should arrive in the port of Le Havre. This may be our most dangerous time. The manure, which has kept prying eyes at a distance, must be abandoned. No one would ship dung across the Atlantic. We must empty this cargo outside of town. An associate has delivered empty boxes to a small farmhouse. These we will use to fill the cart. Then we travel quayside. I shall ride with the driver and keep an eye alert for our man aboard ship. We will use the fading light to remove the scythe from its place in the wagon. The rest of you must take up positions as close as you can. Pick up something. Attempt to look as if you work there, but be ready to defend if you can. Tomorrow will be our most dangerous moment. I shall not breathe an easy breath until the ship sails from the harbor. Lay your heads tonight knowing that by this time tomorrow, we will have succeeded or be dead. Do not fail your comrades, yourselves, or France."

They left the room quickly and quietly.

The party set off early the next morning. Dark circles marked their eyes. No one had slept well. Stress and fatigue made them quarrelsome. As the sounds of seaside France replaced the rural noises of the country, petty disagreements were forgotten. The sense of danger replaced any personal divisions.

At the farmhouse, on the outskirts of town, the group unloaded the manure. Then, David pried up the floorboard. Everyone wanted to verify that the scepter had made the journey. The tube rested like a babe in a cradle. He nailed the board back into place. They filled the wagon with wooden crates, the sides picturing wine and foodstuffs. The men piled them atop one another. The tumbrel had high walls on the front and sides, and the back was open. The empty boxes loaded easily. They lashed the tarpaulin over their cargo.

David and the most skilled driver, a man named Aristede, rolled away from the farmhouse seated atop the wagon. David wore a broad-brimmed hat and a borrowed dirty gray cloak. Aristede dressed similarly, although the tattered clothes Aristede wore were his own. They would need to be, for Aristede was a large man. Two men rode ahead, scouting the way. The others trailed behind, hoping to delay any revolutionary forces. Despite the natural temptation to spur the draught horse forward, Aristede kept the pace steady as they had throughout the journey.

David remembered that Aristede had cut stone for the sculptor Pinot.

"And what do you do these days?"

"I hew rough stones. Many buildings need repair," Aristede said.

"A waste of your talents. You were married, as I recall. How is your wife?"

Aristede's eyes stayed focused on the leather reins. "Fever took her, sir."

"My sympathies."

They neared La Havre's harbor. The Revolution had fallen hard upon the city. Reduced shipping and commerce had taken a toll on the population. Still, a few ships prepared to depart. People milled about the waterfront. The wagon rolled quayside as the setting sun silhouetted the harbor, making it difficult to identify any craft. Aristede slowed the cart even further. He looked first to the water and then shifted his gaze to the crowded quay, blinking furiously to regain his vision after staring into the setting sun. David's gaze, meanwhile, never left the water's edge. He studied the craft, looking for a particular vessel.

He smiled. "Aristede, we are in luck."

"Stop that wagon!"

Aristede squeezed his eyes shut again. He quickly looked in both directions. The wharf was crowded. David saw that Aristede considered slapping the reins and seeking to dash. David placed a calming hand on his.

"Take a deep breath and relax. Remember to act like a peasant."

Revolutionary guards surrounded the cart. A stout soldier grabbed the horse. Pikes and muskets pointed at them. Fight or flight proved impossible. David inhaled and exhaled deeply, hoping to signal that Aristede should do the same. From the corner of his eye, he could see the driver's head wheel about, seeking escape. David patted him on the leg.

The officer pointed a pistol at Aristede. "Get down!"

David held up his hands in submission. He slowly descended, keeping his eyes upon the cobblestones, never looking the guard in the face. The man batted the back of his head. David's hat fell onto the cobblestones. He made no move to retrieve it.

He saw the heavy boots of the National Guard officer stepping closer, his foot scraping against the cobbles. The man crowded him, moving closer until the guard's toes nearly touched his feet.

"Look at me," the officer commanded.

David meekly shook his head, his eyes focused upon the street.

"I said look at me," the guard commanded. He grabbed David by the hair and forced his head upward.

His eyes were forced level with the man. David recognized the face. He looked upon Guinyard.

10

Lake Yellowstone Hotel
June 2nd

"Well, what is it?" LaFleur asked.

"An art poster mounted on foam board," Clarence said.

LaFleur snorted. "I hope the federal government isn't overpaying for your services."

Clarence shifted his gaze to PPT. "Okay with you if I put this down on the bed?"

The ranger nodded.

Longer than it was wide, the painting covered nearly the entire foot of the bed. He centered himself on the painting, the others crowded around.

"You are looking at a painting called *The Intervention of the Sabine Women* by Jacques-Louis David. He was a French neoclassical painter. If I knew I was giving a tutorial on eighteenth-century French painting, I'd have done a little research."

PPT pushed in front of them and began snapping pictures.

Nance looked out the window. "And you think he had this sitting on top of the ironing board?"

"Looks like he used it as an easel. It would block out the view of the parking lot."

She faced Clarence. "But, what's the point?"

He shrugged. "You're the investigator. I'm just a seasonal ranger. The idea behind the painting, as best I recall, is an ancient Roman legend. Rome in its early days found itself short of women. The Sabines were the tribes who surrounded the city. They refused to allow their women to marry into Rome. The Romans, led by Romulus, helped themselves by kidnapping a bunch of the women. Poussin painted the abduction in *The Rape of the Sabine Women*."

"You still haven't told us anything about this clue right here," LaFleur said.

Clarence held up his hand. "Patience. I want the government to get its money's worth." He looked at Nance; she made a circling motion with her hand.

"Romulus married the daughter of the Sabine king Tatius." Clarence pointed to a female dressed in white dominating the center of the painting. "This woman with her arms and legs outstretched is Hersilia, the wife of Romulus, the Roman king." He pointed to a figure with a raised spear. He then pointed to another man. "And the daughter of Tatius, the Sabine king. She is the star of the piece. The women get the men to stop fighting. The triumph of love over hate. David created the painting after the French Revolution. People saw it as a call for national unity."

"What's it got to do with us?" Nance asked.

Again, Clarence shrugged. "No idea. But I'll look the painting up in one of my rare books when I get home. You're welcome to come by and see them."

Nance slowly shook her head. "The invitation didn't work the first time, either. As tempting as it sounds, I've got work to do."

"I'll let you know what I find out."

PPT, who had begun crawling around on the floor, retrieved a plastic baggie and tweezers from her kit. She collected a small piece of white paper from under the bed and dropped it into the bag. She handed the small baggie over to Nance, who studied it for a moment, then passed it off to LaFleur, who barely glanced at it. Clarence took it from him.

He looked at a small torn triangle. Then, he walked over to PPT's crime scene kit. "Ranger Shannon, may I have a piece of butcher paper?"

"Find some trace that needs to be collected?" Crime scene officers used butcher paper to capture small particles that might fall off during evidence gathering.

"No," Clarence said as he tore off a piece. Walking to the wall where he'd earlier seen the pinholes, he held the paper up. "Too thick. I was hoping to trace these marks, but I can't see through."

"Newsprint," Nance said.

He looked at PPT, who shook her head.

Nance went out into the hallway. She returned with the weekly guide to Yellowstone activities and handed it to him. Through the stories outlining the schedule of events, he saw the black marks on the wall. He traced them onto the paper.

Nance watched him work. "What's the point?"

"I've got a hunch. I'll let you know if it works." He folded the page and stuck it into his back pocket.

"Take your Yellowstone guide and go before you screw up my crime scene any more." PPT's voice had none of its earlier lighthearted tone.

"I can take a hint," Clarence said. The others could as well. "Find me on the radio if you get anything," Nance said as she left.

In the lobby, Johnson surveyed the room. The musicians were taking a break, and the crowd had thinned. A few people loitered, admiring the beauty of the lake. He watched an elderly couple sharing tea. Another man drank beer from a bottle and performed an elaborate dance routine with his cell phone, twisting it about in search of better reception. A younger man pushed an older man across the lobby in a wheelchair. Both men dressed in black slacks and sweaters. Johnson recognized the older man from the crime scene.

He walked across the room and reached out his hand. "Clarence Johnson, Yellowstone Park Ranger."

The younger man moved to block Clarence's view of the older man, until he was stayed by a slight wave of the wrist.

"I know, I'm not wearing the uniform. But it's the sort of job where we're never off duty. Are you getting along okay here in the park?"

"We are well," the older man said. His dark eyes studied Clarence.

Clarence focused on the older man. He had a thin oval face and a thick shock of gray hair, neatly trimmed. His lips disappeared when he spoke. His sunken cheeks highlighted his eyes, made them more intense. He looked like a formerly robust man whose time in the wheelchair had withered him. Clarence felt sympathy. "Where are you visiting from? Yellowstone gets visitors from all fifty states as well as Canada each year. Though I sometimes wonder why. Banff is a great place to visit. The Canadian Yellowstone, some call it. Or maybe we're the American Banff."

"I like Yellowstone," the older man said. "The geysers and the paint pots, they intrigue me."

"I hope you are getting around easily enough. I saw you out on the trail today. The part we'd unfortunately had to close temporarily."

Looking behind him, the older man gestured to the younger man. He leaned down; the older man whispered something. Then, he turned his attention back to Clarence. "William helped me to see the Artist's Point. After viewing the falls, he noticed the barricade. William suggested that perhaps rangers had spotted a bear. We stopped to look. We would like to see Smokey."

"No, sadly, a man wandered too close to the canyon rim and fell. Nothing like a bear. Plenty exciting for him, though."

"And will the man recover?"

"Too early to tell exactly what will come of it. You know that the North Rim Road has some very fine turnouts that are wheelchair accessible."

"Thank you for the advice, Ranger Johnson. If you will excuse us, I must get to my room. The nature has left me tired."

"I didn't catch your name."

"Roger. Roger Barkley."

"Pleasure to meet you, Mr. Barkley. I hope you enjoy your stay and see your bear. From a safe distance, of course. Guest safety is a paramount concern here in the park." Clarence raised his gaze and looked to the man standing behind the wheelchair. He had a broad chest and a buzz cut. He looked, Clarence thought, like the villain in a James Bond movie. "And William, I'm sure all this chatting has left you tired as well. I hope you'll enjoy your stay. Don't go too near the canyon rim. Accidents can happen."

William narrowed his eyes and held the gaze before pushing the wheelchair past him. Clarence watched the two men roll to the elevator. Neither looked back.

He returned to Nance and LaFleur.

"What was that all about?" Nance asked.

"Recognized the wheelchair from the crime scene. Roger Barkley is the older man."

"A tourist stopping to look makes him a suspect?" LaFleur asked.

"Not necessarily. Just saw the man. Didn't hurt to get his name."

"I've got some hippie-dippy college professor murdered in the woods. I'm going to pursue the drug angle," LaFleur said.

Nance nodded before looking at Clarence. "See if you can tell me anything else about the picture."

"I'll be happy to. I'd also like to check out the contents of the backpack you recovered at the scene."

"I think the federal government has the resources—" LaFleur began.

"Come to the Mammoth station first thing. We'll get it out and look," Nance told him. "But be punctual. I can't wait on you."

"See you in the morning."

***

As Clarence drove toward Canyon Village, his thoughts alternated between the poster and Nance. He hadn't figured either one out before he got back to the RV. He paused outside. The RV's door banged gently in the weak breeze. Someone had been inside his house. Instinctively, Johnson's hand fell to his hip, reaching for his Glock. His hand came away empty. Johnson hurried to the Suburban and grabbed his flashlight. Crouching to lower his profile, he opened his door. As a cop, he had carried the flashlight in front of him, melded to his sidearm. He moved the light away from his body. If it drew fire, the bullets might pass wide. His hand gripped the light right behind the bulb. He hoped to club whoever might be inside.

Clarence popped his head into the room and quickly pulled it back. He sat outside, allowing his brain to process the information his eyes and ears had gathered. Nothing seemed out of the ordinary. He took both steps into the RV in a bound, making sure to land on his good leg. Switching on the RV's lights, his head flipped first in one direction and then the next. He felt both foolish and vulnerable. If an intruder remained, there was little he could do with his flashlight. Fortunately, he saw no one.

He also didn't see Tripod.

Clarence walked the floor of the RV. His computer had been taken. The dog bed had been overturned. He flipped it upright, hoping to find Tripod underneath. Clarence checked the bed and under the table. He saw no sign of his dog. Nothing else appeared out of the ordinary. He opened the drawer alongside his bed. Neither his handgun nor his guitar had been touched. He raked up bits of spilled dog food from the floor, using the time to think. As a cop, he'd learned that humans might do anything. Still, while computer theft might be the work of a common burglar, stealing a lame dog seemed unusual even by Clarence's cynical standards.

He again walked the length of the RV, down and back, confirming that nothing else had been disturbed. He opened the cabinet doors and the drawers. The burglar might have stashed the little dog into a cabinet to silence her while he worked. The burglary had the hallmarks of a smash-and-grab. Dash in, take the first valuable thing a thief could see, and get out before anyone would be aware. Under the circumstances, dealing with a barking but nonthreatening dog would only cause delay.

Clarence went outside. His flashlight beam swept across the RV park. He saw nothing. Switching off the light, he stood quietly for a moment, watching, and listening for the sound of a car or feet trying to escape.

Off to the left, he heard a noise. Spinning, he flicked on the flashlight and raised it to shoulder height. Ahead of him, low to the ground, a pair of glowing green dots looked back at him. He glanced to his chest to see if the laser sights marked him. The green spots might be the last thing he saw.

A rustling came through the tall grass.

He raised the flashlight. The two dots awkwardly moved toward him. He bent down as Tripod hobbled in his direction. The dog whimpered as Clarence collected her. He carried the small, frightened animal back inside the RV.

He examined the dog at the table. Tripod appeared to have been kicked or thrown out the door, likely landing heavily on her wounded side. Her fur was matted and dirty. In the kitchen sink, Clarence washed her clean, drying her gently with a towel. The dog whimpered again when he probed the side. Tripod seemed bruised and battered, but not seriously injured. Not nearly as injured as the guy who did this would be when Clarence found him.

He carried Tripod to her bed. The dog limped a circle before settling down and quickly closed her eyes. He watched the dog for a few minutes until he felt satisfied that Tripod was comfortable. In the morning, he'd report the burglary and swing by the stables near Canyon Village. A retired veterinarian worked there, tending to the horses. She might have some advice for treating a dog that had been mugged.

Clarence awoke bleary-eyed the following morning. Throughout the night he'd checked on Tripod. The dog never moved. Clarence listened to her steady breathing. The dog slept better than he had. Tripod struggled more than usual to get to her feet and ate less robustly than normal. At least, that was how it looked to Clarence. He took a moment to stretch out his leg, swinging it back and forth while supporting himself against the RV. Then, he made a makeshift bed on the passenger seat and got the dog settled in before driving down to the stables.

Carrying the dog under his arm like a football, Clarence walked to the corral looking for Kathy Carver. A stout woman with a bun of silver hair, she had spent her career in Bozeman working as a veterinarian. Mostly retired, she worked summers in Yellowstone, helping to maintain the horses used for trail rides.

Her eyes darkened as he explained what happened.

Dr. Carver studied the dog quietly before gently running her palms down her flanks. "I don't know if you've noticed, but your dog is not very symmetrical."

"I've been told that. She lost her leg in an accident. The Humane Society was going to have to put her down. Said she was unadoptable. I proved them wrong."

She probed the dog's sides with her fingertips.

"Did you know that the Humane Society charges full price even if you only get three-fourths of a dog?"

The doctor nodded before putting a stethoscope in her ears.

"So, I named her Tripod."

Dr. Carver removed the stethoscope and took her temperature. She glanced at the thermometer, then shifted her gaze, looking at him over the top of a pair of glasses.

Silver bun, half-moon glasses, Clarence felt he was being studied by an AARP ad.

"Your dog got her ass kicked. You ever been in a bar fight, Mr. Johnson?"

"Once or twice."

"Your dog has been in a brawl. She's taken some shots to the midsection. She's bruised and battered. If we were in Bozeman, I'd charge you for an X-ray. But I think she'll be fine in a few days."

Dr. Carver jotted down a list of symptoms to watch for. He tried to pay, but the offer was refused. She had a soft spot for three-legged dogs that still want to fight on occasion.

Clarence carried Tripod into the ranger station. He found his boss and explained the situation. Martinez slowly shook his head, his face a picture of bureaucrat resignation. Investigator Nance had already asked for and received permission to reassign Clarence for consultation. Martinez had adjusted the schedule accordingly. No front desk duty or ranger walks for the immediate future.

Martinez's face scowled. "I thought a cop would know enough to lock his doors."

Clarence held up the dog. "I had a security system."

Although he tried to resist, a smile broke on Martinez's face. He reached forward and scratched the small dog. Tripod turned her head to make the chore easier. "And what about that new talk? Was it..."

"Stored on the laptop," Clarence finished his sentence. "But your book is safe."

Martinez had loaned him a book on the history of Yellowstone. The two men had bonded over a shared love of the past. Martinez enjoyed telling stories about the park. Clarence liked to listen.

Today, however, Martinez muttered and shuffled off to his small office.

Clarence found an empty desk. Setting the dog on his lap, he called in a report to the law enforcement rangers. The woman on the phone made all the appropriate apologies for the government. Then, he logged on to the computer. He ran a search on *The Intervention of the Sabine Women*. Skimming articles, he tried to learn as much as he could quickly. He researched Jacques-Louis David. This was the work he had hoped to do last night, before he found his computer stolen. The study proved easier to do at the station due to the spotty reception in the mountains. He printed a copy of the picture, drew some circles, and scribbled down information in the margins. On his way out the door, he grabbed one of the maps the park rangers doled out to visitors. He had a couple of ideas he wanted to share with Nance.

11

Le Havre, France
October 1795

Guinyard looked at him. The small dark eyes studied his face. Then, Guinyard let go of his hair. David's head slumped. Guinyard's heavy boots stomped past him. He had almost forgotten the step-and-slide sound the man's feet made.

"I thought I recognized him, but I was mistaken," Guinyard said.

Head down, David cut his eyes toward Guinyard. Long, greasy hair still framed his small head. The man slowly stepped further and further away. Then, he spun on his boot heels. David watched him in profile. Guinyard raised his index finger and tapped his lips. Around them, David heard water lapping and sailors going about their business. Within his immediate circle, however, no one spoke.

Guinyard stopped tapping his lips. "Unless...I think, perhaps, I do recognize you." He turned and quickly walked back. He stood before David; his lips parted in the same cruel smile he had shown him at the palace. "I think it is just possible I do recognize you. You have certainly grown uglier. Your face almost serves as a disguise. But I think it is possible I have dealt with you before."

David kept his eyes on the cobblestones. He did his best to mumble a reply. "Pity, sir, I do not think so, sir."

"Do you call me a liar?"

David shook his head. Even with his body quaking with fear, he did his best to model the timid gestures of a peasant.

"Are you a smuggler, dog?"

Head bowed, he saw the other guards edge closer, the circle around him tightening like a noose. They, too, wanted to know what Guinyard might reveal.

Aristede pushed past the guard who had been standing in front of him. He ran up the quay. Two guards followed. Catching him, they threw him to the ground. David winced as he saw the wagon master's head strike the cobblestones. Aristede lay on the road. Both guards grabbed his arms and hoisted him to his feet. They half dragged him back to the wagon. In the fading light, David saw blood running down Aristede's forehead. His eyes looked dazed.

Guinyard caught David's chin. He felt the man's rough grip; the smell of dirt and blood filled his nose. Again, Guinyard tapped his lips with the index finger of his free hand. "Where was I? Ah yes, I thought I'd seen you before." He turned to face his fellow guards. "Have I told you, citizens, that before I was assigned here to the wharf, I worked as a guard in the prison at the Luxembourg Palace? I stood watch over some of the most villainous traitors to our country. I watched many loaded onto the tumbrel and carted off to the guillotine. A few, however, were spared. From them I learned to think like the enemy. That is why I am effective here at catching the smugglers. I know their simple minds."

He paused and slowly walked a semicircle around David, studying his face. He never released the tight grip on his chin. Guinyard pushed his finger into his cheek. "This man, I know. He is not a peasant but a notorious enemy of the Revolution. I once guarded this man. Before you, my brothers, stands the esteemed painter, Citizen David."

He heard no murmurs of recognition. He did not know whether to be disappointed or overjoyed that Guinyard's elaborate buildup had failed to elicit a response.

Guinyard stepped past David and grabbed the side of the wagon. "He would never be a simple teamster. He is smuggling. He will soon receive the reward that he deserves. Bind him."

Strong arms pulled his hands behind his back and lashed them together. They did the same with Aristede, although the effort appeared unnecessary. One guard put his hands against his chest and pushed hard. David quickstepped backward to keep his footing. He collided with the small crowd that had gathered to witness the arrest. No one made any effort to help him maintain his balance. He fell heavily to the ground. The crowd above him laughed and kicked at him.

Guinyard waved his hand over the loaded cargo. "What treasures does this small wagon hold?" Drawing his knife, he cut the rope holding the tarpaulin. Guards pulled down the canvas sheeting, piling it on the cobblestones.

David struggled to his feet. Although no one assisted, neither did they kick at him. Few seemed to notice, all attention focused upon the tumbrel.

Guinyard motioned for a guard to hold a lantern near the first crate. He ignored the writing, focusing on the picture drawn on the side. He picked up one of the boxes and paused. He frowned. Then his eyes widened, and his lips formed a thin smile. He looked at the crowd. "Who would like a case of wine?"

Every hand rose.

Looking at the nearest man, Guinyard tossed him the crate. The man caught the box, careful to avoid breaking any bottles. His face registered surprise. He shook the box. "It is empty, Citizen."

"What?" Guinyard said.

David heard the mock surprise in his voice.

"Smash the crate and let us see."

The man threw the box to the cobblestones and then stomped upon it. The crate flattened.

"Indeed, you are correct. It is empty. Why does the box proclaim wine when David fills the crate only with nothing?" Guinyard took another box from the cart. Raising it high above his head, he smashed it against the cobblestones as well. "For food, they eat and drink only air."

Guards with lanterns kicked at the broken remains, searching for any signs of contraband. They looked at Guinyard and shook their heads.

He smashed another against the paving stones. The guards again searched but found nothing. More crates were destroyed, kindling accumulated. They uncovered nothing.

The crowd grew restless. They had been led to believe that a traitor would be revealed. Instead, the port's guards had located fools who rode around with a cartload of empty boxes.

Guinyard stormed over to where David stood, his eyes mere slits. He snatched David's collar with his right hand, his left clenched into a fist. "What are you hiding?" Spittle flew from his mouth.

"Citizen Guinyard, I collect boxes for my artist friends. Few can make their living painting portraits in the new France. Old cases such as these allow them to cheaply store supplies. Although I paint little these days, I must earn a few sou to survive."

David heard the murmurs increase. He was winning the crowd. They could feel for a man whose livelihood had been smashed under the boot of a governmental tyrant.

Guinyard released his grip. He pushed David. The crowd behind him kept him from falling.

Guinyard walked slowly back to the wagon. "Your cart stinks."

"I rent it from a farmer who uses it to haul manure. It is what I can afford."

"Let the man be about his business," a voice in the crowd called. David heard murmurings of assent.

Guinyard held a lantern over the bed of the wagon. "And do your artist friends buy boxes that are stained with shit?"

"Release the man. You've ruined his business," another voice called.

"I wash the boxes before I sell them. Aristede helps me." He nodded to the man who had sagged to the cobblestones. "Your brutes might have killed him."

Guinyard's eyes panned the crowd. "An innocent man should not have run."

"We would all run," a voice said.

Aristede struggled to his feet. "If I lie down in the cart, will you drive, sir? I feel the need to rest." He moved unsteadily toward the cart.

As the driver shuffled by, David thought he saw a wink. A guard drew his knife and cut Aristede's bonds.

The wounded man flexed his hands and rubbed his chafed wrists. He turned to the guard. "Thank you for your kindness." By the pale light of Guinyard's lantern, he placed his hand upon the cart's bed, leaving small handprints of blood, summoning the strength to crawl inside. Aristede took two deep breaths. All, including Guinyard, watched the man's efforts.

"Wait!"

Guinyard pushed in front of Aristede, blocking him from the wagon. He drew close, the two men's noses nearly touching. "Are you a smuggler?"

"No," came the weak reply.

"If you are caught as a smuggler, you will know the guillotine. Do you wish to meet the guillotine?"

"No." The trembling word escaped from Aristede's mouth.

"If you confess, there is a chance, however slight, that you might live on in prison." Guinyard paused, letting silence fill the night. He raised the lantern; the light fell on Aristede's battered face. The squeaking of the lantern's handle marked the passing time.

Guinyard spun and raised the lantern, pressing it so close that David could feel its heat. "Do not tell me that you are a smuggler. I have waited too long to see you executed. Do not deny me a second chance to send you to the guillotine."

David said nothing.

Guinyard stepped back in front of Aristede and thrust him back. Putting his hand on the board where Aristede's hand had rested, he leaned on it. The board depressed. When he released the pressure, he felt the board return to its original position. He pressed again.

Guinyard slowly turned to David. The smirk returned to his face. "You almost succeeded."

Aristede's body shook. He dropped to his knees before David. "I am sorry. I have been foolish. I have revealed us." He began whimpering.

David patted his friend's hair, careful to avoid the bloody wound. Dirt, blood, saliva, tears, and sweat mixed on Aristede's face. "Do not fret, old friend." David's voice, however, barely exceeded a whisper.

Guinyard drew his knife. "Either this is the most poorly constructed cart in all of France, or a board has been removed and replaced. Let us see." He jammed his blade into the seam separating the board marked with Aristede's bloody print from the adjoining one. He worked his knife back and forth. The wood loosened. Another guard slid his blade beneath the board and pried. The nails came free. The guard pulled the board from the wagon bed and cast it upon the pile of shattered boxes.

Guinyard stared down into the hole he had created, his lantern held high. He turned and faced the group. "A babe wrapped in swaddling clothes. Shall we give birth?"

The crowd, whose anticipations had been raised and dashed, already responded weakly.

He reached into the hole. He grunted slightly as he cut through a binding. Guinyard then sheathed his knife, reached into the cavity, and grasped something with both hands. David saw that Guinyard held the lead tube.

Aristede made another whimpering noise.

"And behold what I have brought into the world?" Guinyard walked around, displaying the tube to his fellow guardsmen and the remaining crowd. He shook the tube. Whatever the tube held beat against both ends with a thud.

"Please be careful," David said. "It is...valuable."

Guinyard slammed the tube into his midsection. Air burst from his lungs. David doubled over and collapsed to his knees. He struggled to find breath. He vomited the remains of his midday meal onto the cobblestones.

"Valuables trapped below a dung cart. Perhaps I have done my highest duty rescuing them." Guinyard stepped close, passing the tube directly over David's bowed head. He braced himself to be clubbed. Then, Guinyard slid the tube in front of Aristede. "Perhaps you would like to see its contents?"

Aristede only whimpered. "I'm sorry, sir."

"Do not fear, Aristede," David said.

Guinyard spun on the balls of his feet. Wielding the tube like a club, he lashed at David, catching him on the shoulder. David collapsed onto the cobblestones. He lay dazed, vision blurred. He saw only the hazy outlines of boots. His cheek lay in the puddle of his vomit. His nostrils clotted with blood. He opened his mouth to breathe. His head rested on stone. The next blow would kill him.

"Yes, do not fear. We have this night freed a valuable thing for our new France. We shall all be witnesses." Guinyard stared down at the two men. David dared to raise his gaze. In the faint light of the lanterns, he saw Guinyard's triumphant face. "Even criminals may be witnesses." With that, he pried the cap from the lead tube. Directing one of his men to hold the tube, Guinyard worked the contents free. He held the wrapped bundle in his hands.

Running a finger over the bundle, he faced David. "Very nice cloth. Not coarse wrapping. The contents must be valuable."

He did not reply.

Guinyard lay the bundle on the quay. He unrolled slowly, allowing the crowd's tension to build. His smile remained broad. He clearly wished to enjoy his victory.

He gave the canvas bundle a last firm push and raised his arms triumphantly. The guards holding lanterns all leaned in to illuminate the contents. The flickering lights showed that Guinyard had uncovered a wooden rod.

Guinyard stomped across the canvas and snatched up the stick. Grabbing David's shirt collar with his other hand, he pulled him upright. He thrust the rod into David's face. "What the hell is this?"

David struggled to find his balance. Then, taking a pair of staggering steps, he gathered the canvas and did his best to rub the dirt from it. "This was perhaps your best idea. Unless you have ruined it."

Guinyard shook the rod, his face red with rage. "What are you talking about, fool?"

"When I was in prison, you told me that poor, desperate artists traveled to Louisiana. It occurred to me that they might need supplies for their portraits. Perhaps there was money to be made. I took my small savings and bought these quality canvases. I rolled them around that rod to keep them from becoming wrinkled. The lead protects them from salt water and sea air. All my efforts have been guided by your advice, Citizen Guinyard. Yet, you have ruined my boxes and my canvases. Who shall reimburse me for these damages?"

The soldiers backed away; the crowd tightened. One guard handed

David a coarse cloth. Nodding thanks, he wiped vomit from his hair and the blood from his nose.

"You have destroyed my livelihood," David repeated.

"See the courts," Guinyard said. He threw down the wooden rod; it clattered against the stones. He turned, followed closely by his troop. Pushing the crowd aside, they left the quay.

12

Grand Loop Road
June 3rd

The traffic moved steadily. Clarence almost made it to Mammoth Hot Springs. Almost.

South of Swan Lake, the cars slowed. Maybe bison in the road, he thought. They get the right-of-way in the park, not only because they are a protected species but also because they weigh more than some cars. His progress halted.

In a field near the lake stood a large wooden cross encircled by chairs. From a raised platform, a man stood, preaching to the assembled crowd. A good place for outdoor worship, Clarence thought, the pristine lake in the foreground. The Gallatin Range formed the backdrop. The organizers had wisely set up a flyleaf, protection in the event of a sudden storm coming off the mountains.

In the parking area, Clarence saw a van with a mechanical wheelchair lift. He turned into the lot and found one of the few remaining parking spots. He jotted down the license plate. Taking up his binoculars, he panned the crowd. Roger Barkley and William formed part of a small group behind the minister.

Barkley sat, head bowed. William, however, stood erect, eyes open. Clarence ran his field glasses over the rest of the dais. The woman to Barkley's left, he noted, did not seem to pray with the same intensity. Her head came up part way through, eyes open, and she, too, looked out over the crowd. She wore a stylish suit that stood out among the field jackets and hiking boots at the gathering. With his camera, Clarence took a picture of the group. William's eyes seemed to snap his way the moment the camera made its small click.

Returning to the binoculars, he scanned the group again, then widened his field of vision to encompass the lake and the surrounding area. Swan Lake had a reputation as a place to spot Yellowstone's wildlife. The morning revival had dissuaded most of the four-legged fauna.

At the edge of the crowd, he saw a familiar-looking young man. He tried to recall where he had seen him.

Clarence heard a small whimper. Tripod struggled to change her position in the passenger seat. Clarence crawled back into the SUV and returned to the road.

He pushed past the front desk, knowing from experience that the investigators gathered in the back. Outside the office, he stopped. Windows framed the door. Nance sat behind her desk. LaFleur perched on the corner of the desk, talking, his hands animating whatever story he told. LaFleur wore a tight-fitting shirt and jeans. He leaned close to Alison Nance. She did not seem to object. With her index finger, she teased her hair behind her ear.

The little wiggle of her finger, Clarence took that as the signal to come inside. He tapped on the door and pushed it open.

Nance slid her chair back slightly, widening the distance from LaFleur. Her hands dropped to her sides. "You're late."

"I went by the Boys' Department, trying to buy a shirt like that. They'd sold the last one. I had to try another store. It slowed me down."

LaFleur's look suggested he'd like to continue working alone. "We were discussing the results of the room search and looking at preliminary autopsy results." Here, he paused, unwilling to do more than just dangle information.

Nance shook her head. "Nothing final until the toxicology, but it appears that Ocone got shot and then pushed or fell off the side of the canyon. The medical examiner emailed photos as well as a copy of the report. No sign of a struggle."

"Ruined a Yellowstone vacation," Clarence said. He studied the pictures.

LaFleur pushed himself off the corner of the desk. "I think it was a work trip,"

"Historical research?" Clarence knew better than to dismiss any idea out of hand, and he hoped his expression and tone conveyed as much.

LaFleur shook his head. "Drug trade."

"Any reason?"

"Well, the prior conviction to begin with."

Clarence snorted. "A prior for weed possession hardly makes him a drug lord."

LaFleur narrowed his eyes. "I've got evidence to be suspicious."

Clarence strove to be conciliatory. "Maybe we'll find something in his backpack."

"We've already looked. Nothing in there," LaFleur said.

His eyes looked first to LaFleur and then quickly cut to Nance.

"We said we were going early. I guess ranch time is different than city time."

Clarence's eyes flared. "I got burglarized last night. They hurt my dog. It put me off my schedule."

Nance's look softened. "What happened? Did you report it?"

"Came home last night to find someone had forced my door. Took my computer. Kicked my dog. They got away. I stopped by Canyon Village and notified the rangers. The duty officer guaranteed that they would find the culprit. It seems they have a crack investigative unit here."

"Sounds like you got personal business to attend to," LaFleur said. "We got things covered at this end if you need to get back."

Clarence ignored him. "There is a revival of some sort going on at Swan Lake. Do those events have to register?"

Nance nodded. "Some groups do. It helps with traffic and facilities management. Others just agree on social media to meet in the park. We really don't have much control over it. This is public land."

Clarence stepped toward a map of Yellowstone mounted on the wall. He tapped the location. "They've put up a pretty big tent and erected a large cross. Seems like someone ought to know who they are."

"Why does it matter?" LaFleur asked.

"Barkley, the guy I met last night, attended. Just made me curious."

Nance turned to her computer and began scrolling. "I've got an email detailing usage today by a group called the Stauros Society. They obtained the required permit from the Special Park Uses office. Paid the fee. Don't know anything about them."

Clarence jotted down the name before pushing a piece of paper to Nance. "Can you check out this license plate?"

"Anything else?"

"It likely comes back to Barkley. Just wanted to see what we can learn."

Nance and LaFleur looked skeptical.

"You asked me to consult, I'm consulting."

Nance shrugged and began entering data.

"What did you find in the backpack?"

Nance's eyes did not leave the screen. "Not much. Protein bar and an apple. Pocketknife. Sketch pad, an assortment of pencils and charcoal. A couple of seven-point-fives." She read the confused looks on the faces of her audience. "That's what we call the topographic maps of Yellowstone—the ones hikers carry."

"Cell phone?" Clarence asked.

Nance shook her head.

"Who doesn't carry a phone?"

"A guy without friends," LaFleur said.

"Explains some of the trouble contacting next of kin," Nance said.

"Maybe your starving artist couldn't afford the cell bill. If only he had a second job. I hear there are openings in imports and exports," LaFleur said.

Clarence thumbed back through the autopsy pictures. "He had one. Ocone was a professor, remember. Did he have any drawings on the pad?"

Nance shook her head.

"We didn't find any sketches in the room. How long had he been staying in the park?"

"Six days," Nance said.

"And he couldn't find a subject worth drawing." Clarence pulled a picture and held it up. "Look at the hands. Not only are there no defensive wounds, there are also no color stains. You draw and shade, your hand gets dirty."

"So, you've proved he washed. Good for him," LaFleur said.

"You ever paint a house? It's hard to get all the paint off. Always finding one more spot. Same goes for artists."

"What's your point?" Nance asked.

"The pad and pencils, just a bluff. I think he had another purpose. Something he was searching for."

LaFleur clapped his hands. "Thanks for coming around to my way of thinking."

"I don't know if it was drugs."

Nance's eyes went back to the computer screen. "The license plate returns to a van rented out of Salt Lake."

Reaching into his back pocket, Johnson pulled out the tourist map of Yellowstone. "When PPT measured the pinholes in Ocone's room, the dimensions match someone tacking up one of these maps. The small scrap of paper we found on the floor is consistent with the map as well."

Nance's eyes looked at the map Clarence held. "So, he tacked up a map?"

"The black circle transferred through the paper to the wall. I think he was interested in this area." With his finger, Johnson traced an area just south of Swan Lake. This area of the park was lined with rivers and creeks.

Nance pulled a blue marker from the drawer. "Circle it."

He leaned over the map.

"Wait," Nance handed him a sheet of paper from the printer. "Put this underneath. I've got to work at this desk."

Clarence slid the protective sheet underneath and drew his circle.

LaFleur quickly took a picture of it with his phone. "I may have been wrong about you, Johnson. You've identified an area for some intense scrutiny."

"Looking for drugs?"

LaFleur blew an exasperated breath. "I know you want to make this something different, but look at the facts. The guy works in Montana, along one of the world's longest open borders. He could be part of an operation that smuggles drugs across the Canadian border." He looked to both Nance and Clarence. "Don't underestimate the amount of contraband coming through. Everyone thinks Mexico, but we've got a northern border problem as well. It is a short trip to mule drugs down to Swan Lake. Cars from all fifty states come to Yellowstone." He shifted his gaze to Johnson. "Let me ask you. If a local cop in Fort Worth saw cars from all over the country make short stops in a parking lot, would he be suspicious? Hell, yes. Here, it's touristy and it's natural. If you wanted to run a distribution network for the entire country, there are few better spots than right here."

"And the mastermind is a history teacher."

"No, I think he is some mid-level putz, smart enough to handle the details but not smart enough to avoid getting addicted. I think the prior for grave-robbing helped him capitalize his drug operations. But things have gotten out of hand for this Narc-eologist." LaFleur paused with a self-satisfied smirk. "My guess is that we'll find he was killed because he got greedy." LaFleur tapped the map. "But you've given me some ideas about where to look."

Nance looked to Clarence. "You don't agree?"

He put a finger to his lips and tapped them. LaFleur's theory felt more complete than anything he had. Still, something nagged at him. "It's plausible. But I don't know. The man had the Sabine Women picture alongside the map. I don't think he was drawing, and I can't make the picture fit with LaFleur's theory."

"Maybe he was promised the painting as payment for coordinating the delivery. Art guys like art," LaFleur said.

Clarence shook his head. "It's in the Louvre. Not likely to come to Bozeman anytime soon. He hid the picture, not the map."

"Explain the significance of the picture," Nance said.

He again shook his head. As Clarence spoke, he pulled up an image of the painting he had saved on his phone. "I can't. The painting is an anomaly. It depicts a Roman scene, but David painted it in a Greek style."

The comment elicited no reaction from either of them. Clarence showed them the image. LaFleur and Nance leaned in to see the picture. He moved the phone closer to Nance.

"The subject matter raises questions. The sunlight seems to come out of the west. Why would the Sabine women intervene after the battle had been raging rather than attempt to stop it in the morning? Yet, here stands Hersilia, the wife of the Roman ruler Romulus and the daughter of the Sabine king aglow in white. Even the Tarpeian rock is golden. Why did Ocone care?"

"The answers likely lie within his computer."

"Along with whatever else was pinned to the wall."

"You two have your art history class. I'm following up on the area below Swan Lake," LaFleur said. He took a step closer to Nance. Reaching out, he put a finger on her forearm. "We'll talk later and catch up on the details." Turning, he brushed past Clarence, the small smirk marking his lips. LaFleur pushed through the office door.

When he heard the door click closed, he looked up at Nance. Her cheeks looked slightly flushed. "Maybe now we can get some real work done."

"You don't buy the drug smuggling angle?"

He shook his head. "From my experience, it's not that hard to distribute drugs. I wouldn't do it from a place with a population density like Wyoming. The market is too small. Too many jurisdictions to get through."

"But you don't have a better idea."

He shook his head. "Not yet."

They both stood quietly in the office.

Nance looked at him. "Narc-eologist."

He nodded. "Little jealous of that one. Who knew Thor had a brain?"

Nance ignored the remark. "You want me to call the FBI down in Salt Lake and have them check out the rental car place?"

Clarence nodded. "And can you look up the Stauros Society?"

Nance climbed back into her chair and began typing. Clarence moved behind to read over her shoulder. Her hair had the sweet smell of cut grass. Before he could comment, the screen changed. Both began reading.

Nance's finger underlined the words on the screen. "An offshoot of

Roman Catholic faith espousing inerrancy of the Bible. The group also appeals to fundamentalist protestants. Members believe in personal spirituality and the ongoing intervention of God in the world through miracles and other forms. Organized groups can be found in the United States as well as Europe and South America."

"*Stauros* is the Greek word for cross," Clarence read. "I guess that explains it."

"Explains what?"

"Why they all lined up trying to part Swan Lake."

Nance rolled her eyes. "Don't criticize any park visitors who pay their fees and clean up after themselves."

He raised his hands in surrender. "Some folks call Fort Worth the buckle of the Bible Belt. These are my people. Most of them can even take a joke."

Nance nodded.

"I need to go check on my dog."

Nance followed him out of the office.

They walked over to the SUV. Johnson unlocked the passenger door. At the sound, Tripod began struggling to her feet. Clarence scooped the dog up in one hand and carried her over to the grass. The dog hobbled off, sniffing the grass.

"She usually moves fine. Laboring a bit today."

Nance watched the dog, then looked to Clarence, then back to the dog. "Did the vet mention that your dog only has three legs?"

Johnson put a finger to his lips. "Don't say anything. Tripod doesn't know."

"Tripod? You named the dog Tripod?"

"I know a guy who named his puppy Brownie because when you look at the dog, the first thing you see is brown fur. When you look at this dog, you see three legs. So, Tripod."

"But don't tell the dog," Nance said.

Clarence nodded. "We're both sensitive."

"I'll buy you a cup of coffee if you tell me the story," Nance said.

He looked at her. She cocked her head toward the Mammoth Hot Springs Lodge.

"They don't allow dogs in the restaurant. I figured we could talk without you-know-who hearing."

Johnson walked toward Tripod. The dog began running. Johnson saw that Nance's attention was focused on his dog's efforts. Tripod's initial steps had more hop than a four-legged dog. Once she settled into her stride, however, her motion smoothed. Nance smiled. Johnson picked Tripod up, scratched her ears, and settled her back on the car's seat.

"Guard the car. I'll be back in a few minutes," Johnson instructed before closing the door.

The seating at the restaurant proved awkward. They both defaulted to the chair facing the front door. After a moment's hesitation, they adjusted, settling into chairs angled toward the door, as if they expected the arrival of another couple. Both ordered coffees.

Nance tasted the coffee. "You think she can hear us?"

"She's a remarkable dog."

"What's her story?"

Clarence sipped. "I went into the Humane Society one day, and there she sat. The euphemism they use for a dog that has been mistreated is 'extra attention.' As in, this dog will need extra attention. They wouldn't keep her long because she was deemed unadoptable. But she looked like a fighter, and I needed a project."

"You like fighters?"

He took another sip. "I respect fighters."

Nance nodded. "Probably explains how you broke your nose."

"I did that myself. My agent told me I'd get more movie roles if I weren't so classically handsome." He tapped his nose. "This made me more relatable."

Alison Nance smiled. "Are you always full of shit?"

He nodded. "Mostly. The first time I broke it, a linebacker got his hand under my face mask in college. The second time, a drunk I arrested for public intoxication sucker-punched me. Should have seen them both coming."

"Saving things—that's why you became a cop?"

"Tripod and I sort of saved each other."

Nance's brown eyes studied him, waiting.

He took another sip. "And it will cost you more than a cup of coffee to pry the rest of the details. What about you? What brings you to the far corner of Wyoming?"

"I grew up not too far from here. My family raises cattle on a small ranch just over the border in Montana. Most feds want to be in big cities because that's where all the action is. But when I joined the park service, I never wanted to work anyplace but here in the West."

"You know, they say that Fort Worth is where the West begins."

"Well, don't try to peddle that up here."

Neither Clarence nor Nance spoke. Their server came and refilled the cups, then laid the bill on the table.

"Where do things go from here?" he asked.

"I'm going to follow up with the rental car because I said I would. Call the ME to confirm they didn't find any chalk or paint residue. I thought I'd arrange to search Ocone's office. Draft a warrant to look through his house if I can't get consent. You want to come?"

"Only if you promise not to start until I arrive."

"Early means early here in the West. Cows can't wait."

Clarence pulled out his phone and enlarged the picture he had taken at the revival. "If you locate this woman, see if you can get a name."

"What's her significance?"

"I don't know, but from the skirt and shoes, my guess is that she didn't come to Yellowstone for backwoods hiking."

13

Fécamp, France
October 1795

The reunion occurred in Fécamp.

Exchanging the wagon for mounts, David and Aristede rode through the night toward the fishing community along the La Manche, the sleeve of water some called the English Channel.

Initially, they rode a roundabout course. The other members of their party scattered in different directions. Satisfied that Guinyard had not followed, David straightened the course and pressed forward. They followed the coast road. At times, they were so near the water, he could hear the waves lapping the shoreline. Other times, the road turned inland. They passed fields and orchards.

"All will be explained soon," he said to Aristede, who rode quietly, confused and battered.

The morning sun had broken above the horizon when they descended the white cliffs framing Fécamp and reached the Hotel Rouge. David rested his weary mount. His body ached, but he did his best to ignore it. Looking to his left, he saw the sea. On his right, the town climbed up the hill. Ahead, across the Valmont River, the white cliffs resumed, culminating in the Cap

Fagnet. The light of morning bathed the hillside in a golden hue. The windows of the hotel remained shuttered to hold back the morning and to allow the hotel's guests more rest. The lower floors, still in shadows, showed brown and dirty. He looked longingly at the quiet rooms and dreamed of sleep.

When Charlotte emerged from the doorway, his fatigue disappeared. She wore her brown traveling dress. Although Charlotte struggled to mask her expression, a smile broke through like the rising sun. He needed no words to know that they had been successful. Forgetting the horses and Aristede, he ran to her and took her in his arms.

"You are magnificent," she said. They kissed in the morning light.

Louis de Noaleste emerged from the shadows of the hotel doorway. When David saw him, he released his grip on Charlotte and moved quickly to embrace the man.

"Well done, monsieur." He pounded Noaleste on the back.

The man beamed, accepting the congratulations.

Charlotte, meanwhile, walked to where Aristede stood. Her fingers lightly touched his injured face. His eyes remained fixed on the cobblestone street.

She turned and faced her husband. "Jacques-Louis, our friend Aristede is hungry. You have starved him of food and information. We must nourish this man."

"Of course, my dear. We must eat and talk. We all have stories to tell."

Charlotte led them to a table at the back of the hotel. Most of the dining room sat empty. The fishermen of Fécamp had already departed. The town's fashionable people were not yet ready to make their appearance. The server eyed them, his face pursed. He obviously noted their weathered clothing and the odd hour of their arrival.

David waved him to the table. "We require bread, wine, cheese."

The man nodded and turned to leave. David caught his sleeve and pressed coins into his hand. "And privacy."

The server glanced down. The money transformed his expression. He nodded smartly to the table. "Yes, sir." He scampered off with enthusiasm.

The couple chatted quietly until the server returned with the dishes. Aristede and Louis de Noaleste remained quiet.

"I have brought you some of the local herring. We smoke them," the server said, displaying a platter. "None better may be found in all of France."

"You are most kind," David said with a nod.

The server retreated to the far corner of the room.

Charlotte's eyes looked first to Aristede before flicking over to David. "Release this man from his prison of ignorance."

He turned to Aristede and nudged him with his elbow. "My friend, your performance exceeded all expectations."

Aristede's expression remained blank. "I saw you load the wagon with the scythe. I helped bury it beneath the manure. Then, I watched you display it upon reaching Le Havre."

The table grinned. He rested a hand upon the man's broad shoulder. "In painting, we have the trompe l'oeil, to deceive the eye. That is what we have employed throughout this journey. We have fooled the eye. And, in so doing, we have deceived those who could not be trusted."

Aristede's face did not change.

David rested his elbow on the table and held up one finger. "Monsieur Armand, the carriage maker, installed a hidden compartment within the tumbrel we have been riding. But a compartment need not only have one door. It might also have two." He raised the second finger. "Everyone in the barn that night saw me hide the scythe within the compartment. What they did not see was that I passed our holy relic through the compartment and laid it beneath the wagon. The manure masked any sound I might have made. I tied the tube of canvases into the compartment instead."

Aristede's eyes took on a look of recognition. "And we carried them all this way?"

David smiled. "We did not know who among the group might seek to betray us. We therefore elected to fool them all." Here, he paused and turned to his wife. "And you, my dear, your performance when I banned you was fit for the theater. I thought I had divorced myself again."

"Sometimes, my husband, it is not that difficult to remember how angry I have been with you. It is useful to let it out, like a belch after a fine meal."

His expression wavered. "You burped anger gloriously."

Charlotte bobbed her head in a quick nod. "Thank you, my husband."

David's eyes returned to Aristede. "Following our showy departure, we surrounded ourselves with escorts to ensure that everyone knew where the scythe was hidden. We pointed our tumbrel toward Le Havre, the seaport many use to depart for the new world. Then, once we were safely gone, my dear and courageous Charlotte emerged from her seclusion, climbed aboard the wagon containing the real scythe. She and Louis de Noaleste left quietly for Fécamp."

Charlotte picked up the story. "Once your boisterous party left Versailles, carrying not only yourselves but also the canvas and whatever spies lived among us, Monsieur de Noaleste and I rode rather anonymously and uneventfully here. We had no difficulties." She reached across the table and again lightly laid a finger upon Aristede's bruised face. "Unlike you, brave warrior."

Aristede blushed slightly. "This is nothing. The scythe remains safe?"

David smiled. "Fitting, don't you think. Fécamp, named for a miracle. Legend says that following Christ's crucifixion, Joseph of Arimathea collected up his sacred blood and preserved it. When Joseph died, a voice from heaven commanded his nephew, Isaac, to seal the blood and place it into a fig tree. The voice then told him to cast the tree into the ocean. The trunk of that tree washed ashore here. *Fécamp* means the field of the fig tree. The site immediately became a fountain of spouting blood."

David's head turned slowly, locking eyes with everyone at the table. "This town is famed for miracles and holy relics. Is it not right that our miraculous scythe should leave from here?"

"But how will it travel?" Aristede asked.

David put a finger to his lips. "In good time, all shall be revealed. But the fewer who know a secret, the better it is."

Aristede's lips downturned.

Again, David clapped him on the back. "Do not despair, my friend. Guinyard would not have been so easily persuaded if we had not been so thoroughly convincing in our portrayal of desperate pilgrims."

Noaleste pointed across the small table with a crust of bread. "And how did you know that Guinyard would be the officer?"

"I had no idea that La Havre was the place that pig had been assigned. When he failed to appear one morning at the jail, I felt I was through with him forever. I hoped his body had been tossed into the Seine by a former prisoner he had mistreated or a man he had cheated. You cannot imagine my surprise when I saw him standing in front of me, pulling my hair, demanding I look at him. Providence intervened. No man could have been more determined to reveal my plans than he. Guinyard knew I hid something in our old wagon, and he was correct."

Aristede joined in the hearty laughter around the table. When it subsided, he fixed David with his sad and puffy eyes. Then, he cast a glance to his left and right, reconfirming that they sat alone. "What happens to the scythe?"

David gestured toward the port. "Soon, it will leave for America. Louis has arranged passage. It will rest comfortably in the hold of a ship."

"May I not know?" Aristede asked.

"Although I trust you completely, the less said, the better."

"And shall you accompany it?"

"No," David said, "Louis de Noaleste has asked for and been given this honor."

Noaleste modestly studied his plate.

Aristede glanced his way and then, after a moment's hesitation, stood. "I request the honor of accompanying my comrade to America."

The table fell quiet. Noaleste narrowed his eyes and studied the man.

David broke the silence. "And why would you wish to abandon France to do such a thing?"

Aristede cleared his throat. "Jacques-Louis, there at the quay, I may have enhanced your deception, but I felt that I betrayed us all. I must atone for my wrongs, or I shall carry the burden of my cowardice around like a stone. I have no wife, no children. The Revolution took my family's small property. I leave behind little. And I stand to gain back much."

Louis de Noaleste's fists banged on the table.

Aristede looked at him. "I mean no disrespect, monsieur. This request is a personal crusade and does not reflect upon you."

"We should adhere to the plan," Noaleste said through clenched teeth.

David studied the two men. Charlotte leaned over and whispered into his ear. He nodded slowly but said nothing. The table watched him. Across the room, the server stood frozen in place as if he, too, were awaiting word.

Beginning with Charlotte, David's eyes circled the table. When he reached Aristede, he held his gaze. "I believe that you should go as well."

Aristede exhaled his breath. Noaleste stiffened slightly in his chair.

"The item will sail to New Orleans. The reports tell us that the town remains wild and untamed. Although we have French friends, Spain officially controls the area. Noaleste, you will need someone to watch your back. You may also have to evade the authorities."

"But he ran," Louis de Noaleste argued.

"A temporary failure of courage that shall not occur again." As David spoke, Aristede nodded enthusiastically.

Charlotte took her turn studying the group. "The entire undertaking has required a body of men and women working together. You two soldiers might help to realize the success of our mission. Can you join?"

Aristede solemnly nodded his head. "Yes, madame." He reached his open hand across the table toward Noaleste.

Louis de Noaleste glanced at the hand but made no movement toward it. As Charlotte opened her mouth, Noaleste's hand slid up the side of the table. He clasped Aristede's. His eyes looked at her. "Yes, madame."

"Excellent," David said, gathering up his glass. "Let us toast to your success."

The decision having been made, the tension evaporated. Each person seated at the table took up their cup and drank a hearty toast to the mission. They finished the meal, nearly returning to the conviviality they experienced prior to the discussion of travel plans.

"And now let us get you outfitted for the journey ahead." David stood, leaving additional money on the table.

Across the cobblestone street, masts of sailing ships floated like a forest in the water, the ships in the port soon bound for many distant destinations. The sleepy sea lapped against the pebbled shore. The waterfront remained quiet. Above David's head, seagulls circled, darted, and cried to one another. The air, sour with the waste of the harbored ships, pricked at his nose. David faced west, out into La Manche. He smiled. Tomorrow, the treasure, safely tucked into the hold, would leave. Only then would Noaleste and Aristede know the ship on which they sailed. Ahead stood the Church of Saint-Etienne. Shops nestled between the church and the hotel.

He pointed toward them. "Come, let us buy supplies and then pause to pray." He set off at a brisk pace, Charlotte at his side.

He saw Noaleste put a hand on Aristede's shoulder, slowing him. David could not hear what passed between the two men. Charlotte also saw the exchange. She looked to David. "Partnerships are an odd thing. One must wonder, will they enhance one another? Or wake up one morning to find the other's blood on their hands?"

14

———

Lake Yellowstone Hotel
June 3rd

Clarence returned to the RV and settled Tripod onto her bed. He drove to the Lake Yellowstone Hotel.

At the entrance, he studied the lobby. Several people sat by the great windows overlooking Lake Yellowstone, drinking coffee. He noticed the woman sitting alone, reading. She wore the same suit from this morning, her ankles delicately crossed, a pair of fit calves on display. A few employees swept and tidied, preparing the room for the crush of guests who would arrive in the afternoon. He spotted the young man he had hoped to find.

François sat at a small table. Clarence walked toward him, watching him pick at a sandwich, tearing off small pieces and bringing them to his mouth. He had his head up surveying the small early lunch crowd milling about the lobby. Clarence saw François's eyes register recognition before they passed over him. He stopped in front of the table.

"François, my favorite waiter."

The young man's eyes looked at him, his expression blank.

Clarence pointed to an area near the lobby. "You waited on me last night, right over there."

François studied his face and slowly nodded. "I'm sorry, sir. I see a ton of people."

"Hey, I understand. Besides, you don't get that much repeat business. You're not a particularly good waiter."

The young man looked at him. "What?"

"No, I think you heard me correctly." Clarence pulled out his wallet and dropped two dollars onto the table. "But no hard feelings. Here's a tip. I figure that you dropped your money in the collection plate this morning, a guy living on a waiter's salary might be broke."

"I don't understand?"

"Sure you do, François. You were at the revival at Swan Lake."

"Do you follow me?"

Clarence tapped his chest. "Me, stalker? No, I'm just a guy who notices things. Like how you kept cleaning the tables within earshot of our conversation last night. And how you delivered room service to the same floor where we were searching. And this morning, how you feel the need to get religion. Now you're here, monitoring the comings and goings in the hotel lobby."

François scoffed. "I am eating lunch. Waiters need to eat too. But we gotta do it when the paying customers don't."

Clarence nodded his head. He spread his fingers wide on the table. "Man has got to eat. Don't begrudge that. But it looks like you are keeping an eye on that woman." Clarence cocked his head toward a woman sitting alone. "She was at the revival this morning. I thought I'd warn her that she might be followed by an obsessed waiter."

"You have some strange fantasy about getting the summer help fired from their jobs. Had a bad experience at an Applebee's and you're taking it out on the rest of us?"

"I think you'll land on your feet. I'd bet my paycheck that you've got another job besides waiter." Clarence scribbled his number on a napkin. "If you feel like being honest, call me." He patted the table and turned away. "See you around, François."

Before François could reply, Clarence strode across the lobby to the chair where the woman sat, still reading. He noted the title, *Global Politics in an Information Age.*

"Beautiful," he said.

The woman's eyes did not leave the page. "Yes, the lake is beautiful."

Clarence sat down in the chair alongside. "The lake is always pretty. That's why they put the front of the hotel on this side. I meant your pendant."

Resting the book in her lap, she studied Clarence for a moment before glancing at her necklace.

"We don't get many women here wearing heirloom cameos."

Her eyes returned to Johnson. This time she held the look. Her eyes, the color of rich coffee, twinkled with amusement. She smiled, displaying, Johnson noticed, a small gap between her front teeth. It set her apart, made her unique. Not just a generic beautiful woman.

She closed the book, marking her place with her index finger. "You know much about women's jewelry?"

"Spent a lot of time in pawnshops." Before she could reply, he traced the outline of the pendant in the air with his index finger. "I like the elegant lines. It has the patina of age."

"How do you know it's not a knockoff?"

Johnson shook his head. "You don't look the knockoff type. I'm pretty certain it's authentic."

She nodded. "French, eighteenth century. My mother gave it to me. Her mother gave it to her. I'm sorry, but it's not for sale."

He held up his hands. "Couldn't afford it on a park ranger's salary. I just admire a work of art."

Her eyes studied him. "You know art?"

"A little. I can recommend some books on the art of the area. I mean, when you finish that light palate cleanser you've got there."

"Thank you."

"Or catch a ranger talk. There's one most evenings."

Her smile again, showing the gap in her teeth. "You are quite the salesman."

"No, ma'am, I'm a park ranger. The care of our park visitors ranks as our chief priority."

"I shall remember to fill out the comment card at the end of my stay."

He held out his hand. "Clarence Johnson, ma'am. If you could spell my name right, it might help earn me a promotion."

She took his hand and shook it. Johnson felt her warm, soft skin. The grip, however, suggested that she exercised regularly.

"Mr. Johnson, you're like a bad penny."

Clarence turned. Roger Barkley rolled up behind him. The man was dressed as he had been at the revival, in gray slacks and a blue shirt and blazer.

"Mr. Barkley, nice to see you again, sir."

Barkley's eyes focused on the woman. "I didn't realize that you two knew each other."

"I'd just introduced myself to Ms....?"

The woman looked to him. The amusement, Clarence noticed, had vanished from her eyes. "Noel. Noel Privé." She pronounced it *Pri-vay*.

"Roger, I just told Ms. Privé to be careful hiking in expensive jewelry. Wouldn't want to lose it on the trails."

"I shall keep all of your helpfulness in mind, Ranger Johnson."

"Please call me Clarence. Want me to spell that for the comment card?"

Roger Barkley rolled his wheelchair between the two of them. "If you will excuse us, Mr. Johnson. Madame Privé and I have some work we need to do."

"Then I won't disturb you." He took a couple of steps away from the table, then paused and turned back around to face them. "I saw you both up at Swan Lake this morning. Yellowstone can make a body feel close to God. I'm glad you're enjoying the scenery. Just remember to be careful."

"I shall keep that in mind, Ranger Johnson," Noel Privé said before dismissing him and turning her full attention to Barkley.

As he walked away, Clarence saw François bussing tables. He considered talking to the kid again but found that William blocked his path.

"Willy, I knew I'd find you around here somewhere."

William drew close, putting a shoulder into his chest. Clarence noted the faint smell of tobacco on the man's clothes. William's hard eyes tried to bore a hole into him. "It would be most unfortunate for a man to get too close to God out here."

. . .

He checked his phone. Nance had texted, LaFleur had news. Clarence started the Suburban and drove to Canyon Lodge to meet them. He found them together at the Geyser Grill, sitting at a small table away from other park visitors. As he came in, they were splitting an order of waffle fries.

"Be careful, old man," he said to LaFleur. "You know what those things can do to your waistline."

LaFleur's DEA T-shirt, like his other clothes, seemed to have been ironed and starched just before coming into the restaurant. LaFleur looked up at Johnson for a moment before studying the shirt. Its seams strained at the biceps. He patted his narrow waist. "I think I'm good, but thanks for the warning." With that he plunged a fry into the ranch dressing before popping it into his mouth, being careful not to dribble. He gave his trademark smirk.

Clarence pulled up a chair.

Nance opened her flipbook. "Tom's been outlining his theory."

LaFleur paused. He picked at a waffle fry and stirred the air with it, wielding it like a pointer. "You deserve the credit for this one."

"Thanks," Clarence said, waiting to see if he wanted the accolade.

"You got me thinking about that picture. This morning you told us about the gathering at Swan Lake. That got me thinking some more."

"You must be tired."

LaFleur ignored him. "I sent a couple of emails to the analysts in DC. They've confirmed my hunch." Here, he paused and drank from his glass.

Clarence had to give him credit for the buildup. He glanced at Nance. He couldn't tell if the theatrics were working with her.

LaFleur set his glass down and resumed. "Take the woman in white from the painting."

"Hersilia."

LaFleur waved away the interruption. "Sure. Overlay her outstretched arms and legs on the rivers and streams running south of Swan Lake." He reached into his pocket and pulled out a map of the region. With his finger he traced the blue lines on the map. "See how Obsidian Creek and Indian

Creek flare off the Gardner River. Approximates the stance she takes in the painting."

Johnson snorted. "If Hersilia were lying on her side rather than standing up."

"We don't know how the picture was hanging in his room. He mounted the picture on foam board. It could sit sideways as easily as the way it is supposed to hang."

"You found the picture in the closet," Nance said. "We have no idea how he displayed the picture."

"The wall showed evidence of a circle being drawn around this area." LaFleur stabbed the map with his finger. "The smart folks in DC confirm all of this."

"To what end?" Clarence asked.

LaFleur looked around, confirming that no one else was listening. "Here's my thought. If you ran a dope house in Fort Wayne—"

"Fort Worth," he corrected.

Again, LaFleur waved away the disruption. "Whatever. If you ran a dope house and cars stopped, hung around for a few minutes, and then drove off, you'd arouse the suspicions of the police. Here, it happens every day. We call it tourism." LaFleur began speaking faster. "Cars here from all fifty states. No one pays any attention to the national distribution here. Hell, cars come here from Canada, and we welcome them. Bring opioids across the border, ship them down to Yellowstone, and from here, they go everywhere."

"What's the painting got to do with this?"

LaFleur tapped his head. "Dopers are getting culture. Look. We collect cell phone data. Intercept phone calls. Monitor electronic traffic. We've got anti-encryption software. We can make it damn hard to send a message. But what if you didn't rely on a code? What if you found a piece of art that mapped out your distribution point? With a million paintings to choose from, one will match. Then that becomes the key to your communication. If it gets intercepted, law enforcement spends their time going over it, searching for a steganographic message hidden in the painting. We literally miss the big picture."

LaFleur sat back, undoubtedly awaiting a spontaneous outbreak of applause. Clarence shrugged.

Nance leaned forward. "A professor might be better suited to find the right map."

"A professor and doper," LaFleur added, "explains the absence of a phone."

Clarence looked at Nance. "We're still driving to Bozeman tomorrow, right? I mean, even though the case is solved."

"Pushing off at five a.m. Try to be on time."

Clarence ignored the jab.

"Joining us, Tom?" Nance asked.

"Love to, but I've got an eight a.m. conference call with DC to discuss this latest development." He shifted and looked directly at Nance. "Maybe we can meet when you get back, and you can brief me."

"I'll text you."

"I'll look forward to it." LaFleur smiled. Apparently, he reserved the smirk for Clarence.

Clarence had no doubt that this look had worked countless times over the years. "I hate to break things up, but I've got to get home to my dog." He stood up from the table. The rest followed.

Nance's cell phone vibrated. She looked at the number and sighed. She dismissed both men with a wave as she answered.

The two men cut across the lawn of the Geyser Grill to return to their cars. Near Clarence's SUV, LaFleur stepped in front and faced him. "You've been a big help in this federal investigation," he said, "but I think you've about done all you can. Maybe about time that you get back to your summer job, Intern."

Clarence shrugged. "I'm not a consultant for the DEA."

LaFleur smirked. "Just what are you the rest of the year? I mean when you're not busy with pamphlets and stickers. Do you serve a purpose in the fall and winter?"

Johnson stepped closer. A fraction of an inch separated the two men. "Sure seems important to you that I'm not around. You're not afraid of a little competition are you, Flower?"

LaFleur slowly raised his right hand and brushed a lock of his hair back behind his ear. "I think the lead investigator in this case has made her choices, don't you?"

Clarence shook his head. "I guess I'm just not as quick to decide these things as you are. But then, I'm not a fed. I work for a living."

LaFleur, hand at his ear, cocked his fist and threw a punch. Clarence slipped it, the fist passing in front of his jaw. Then, he buried his own fist in LaFleur's stomach. He heard the eruption of breath, saw the man's eyes bulge. Grabbing his shoulder, he tossed LaFleur to the ground.

"You telegraphed your punch," he said. "Too bad the DEA doesn't make you spend time as a patrol officer. You could learn a little about street fighting." He moved to step over the fallen man. "Sorry if I messed up your good T-shirt."

LaFleur threw a palm strike into his right knee. Pain exploded up his leg as he buckled. His face struck the ground. LaFleur pulled himself to a sitting position and then stood.

LaFleur stepped over him and walked to his car. "Sorry if I messed up your good T-shirt. Oh, and maybe your Smokey the Bear hat can hide the bruise you'll have by your eye."

15

Lake Yellowstone Hotel
June 3rd

François finished typing the secure email. He proofread it before hitting send. His uncle, a meticulous man, tended to pounce on small errors or imprecise wording.

Re: Ongoing Efforts

Barkley met Privé twice today. This morning they gathered at a religious rally at Swan Lake, Yellowstone, NP. Although together on the dignitary's platform, no obvious communication. Speaker condemned liberal sinners watering down holy Scripture. Advocated faith and discipline, not lukewarm 'Cafeteria Christianity' where everyone finds something they like without effort. Also condemned threats from Islamic madaris/madrasas? raising generations of youth against true virtues. Called for strong, reliable power centers. Praised Stauros Society for funding Western values in Holy Land, spec. schools in Jeru and Bethl.

Second meeting in Lake Yellowstone restaurant this PM. Attempted to bus nearby tables. Limited success. Talk of upcoming French elections. Believe Barkley funneling money through intermediaries to support Privé husband and party. She reports Cy will enhance national pride and deliver conservative vote. Will attempt to identify Cy.

Unable to learn more at meeting. Barkley saw me in vicinity. I offered to take order and was dismissed. No concerns that I'm compromised. A local ranger has begun to harass. I have a plan in place to deal with him.

    F.

16

Fécamp, France
November 1795

They rowed to a small ship before the first light of the morning, guided by the lanterns hung fore and aft. As they neared *Le Pinson*, a sailor tossed them a line. Aristede caught it and pulled them alongside.

The captain looked over the rail. "Are you ready? We must leave with the first light."

By the flickering lanterns, David strained to look at Noaleste and Aristede. Both men nodded. David's eyes shifted to the man at the rail. "Permission to come aboard?"

"Yes," the captain said before disappearing out of view.

David kept his voice at a whisper. "Good luck, our brothers. You carry a powerful symbol of French rebirth with you." He reached out and shook each man's hand.

Noaleste grabbed the rope ladder and began climbing on board the ship. Once safely on deck, he picked up a lantern. Turning, he looked over to the side. His face fully illuminated, he saluted them. "Farewell, monsieur and madame."

Charlotte kissed the cross she wore around her neck. "Our prayers are with you."

David watched the arc of the lantern as Noaleste surveyed his new home.

The captain seemed to hear his thoughts. "*Le Pinson*, she is small, but she is seaworthy. We routinely sail to the Grand Banks to catch cod. Fear not, my friend. You will safely reach land, and we shall pocket the wealth of a full hold."

"Yes, Captain," Noaleste said.

David marveled at the man's ability to swallow any doubts he might feel.

The captain turned his attention to the rowboat. "Worry not for the welfare of your companions. We shall leave the harbor and sail out into La Manche. We remain within sight of the French coast until we resupply in Brest. Should we encounter difficulties, your friends could easily float to shore."

"Thank you for your kind words, Captain. They set my mind at ease." In truth, they heightened his anxiety. The scepter would be at risk to even the smallest French patrol boat during the entire length of the coastal journey.

"My husband, some things are beyond our control."

Bowing to his wife's wisdom, he gave a Gallic shrug of acceptance. Then, he turned his attention to Aristede. He pressed a haversack into Aristede's hands. "We gathered a few things for your journey. Safe travels, my friend."

In the weak light of the lanterns, he could not tell where Aristede looked.

Aristede mumbled a reply. David felt a flutter of panic. He reached into his coat pocket. "My friend. I commission you to be our emissary. Deliver our hopes safely to the new world so that it might help to reestablish the old order." He handed Aristede a gold medal, an eight-pointed star fastened to a red satin ribbon. "The king himself gave this to me."

Aristede made a small intake of breath. He leaned forward and kissed David's hand. "I shall not fail you."

The captain's head reappeared over the side. "We must depart."

David looked. The east showed the first slivers of a carnation morning sky.

Aristede seized the rope and stood. He crawled up the side of *Le Pinson*.

"Aristede," David called. The man looked back down into the small boat. "Perhaps you should take this with you." He extended his arms and handed Aristede the lead tube.

"It has been on this boat?" Aristede asked. Even in the meager light, Jacques-Louis saw the man's wide eyes.

"I could not risk the boat leaving with it until I knew you two were on board to safeguard our dreams."

Aristede accepted the package and quickly stuffed it into the sack. He clutched the bundle to his chest like his first-born son or the Christ child. He hauled himself aboard *Le Pinson*.

David untied the line binding them to the larger boat. The captain pulled it back aboard. He asked no questions about the contents of Aristede's package.

"Farewell." David waved one last time. Then, taking the oars, he rowed back. Neither he nor Charlotte spoke. From *Le Pinson*, he could hear the activity as the boat made final preparations to get underway. The breeze still blew faintly, the sails fluttered lazily. The captain had assured him that they had enough wind to depart.

The bottom of the rowboat scraped against the rocky sea bottom. A local in a broad-brimmed hat waded into the shallow water and pulled them onto shore. David stepped out and carried Charlotte to the shore. Turning, he handed the man a coin. Wordlessly, the man resumed his slow walk down the beach. David and Charlotte stood at the water's edge. The boat slowly sailed out of the Fécamp harbor.

Charlotte looked at her husband. "Where did you get the medallion?"

He shrugged. "Robespierre gave it to me at the beginning. I thought Aristede's courage needed some bolstering."

"A revolutionary medal in support of a royal mission. You create illusions, my artist husband."

They walked down the beach following the craft.

Charlotte looked into David's eyes. "You should rest. The journey has taken a toll on you."

He nodded. With the responsibility lifted, he felt intense fatigue. "Wise you are."

Charlotte squeezed his hand and then, dropping it, turned and walked toward the town. "Go to the room and rest. I shall stop by the church to pray for their safe travels. Then, I shall join you."

He watched her leave. On impulse, he stripped his shoes and waded into the ocean. As the water splashed against his ankles, he watched the ship grow smaller in the distance.

A coarse hand grabbed his collar. Before he could turn to look, David felt himself pulled backward. He tripped and fell. He struggled to stand. A shadow stood over him and punched him once in the jaw. David rolled to escape, soaking his clothes, making every movement heavy and slow. The hand again clutched his shirt and dragged him several steps further into the water. The waves washed across his chest. The man pushed him down. David struggled to hold his head out of the water.

"I think I shall drown you and let your wife find your body."

David recognized Guinyard's voice.

With his free hand, Guinyard drew a knife. "Or perhaps I will cut your traitorous throat and let the fish have your remains."

A wave washed across his face. David sputtered to breathe. Hair washed into his eyes.

Guinyard slid the blade back into its scabbard. Then he pushed David's face beneath the water.

David flailed, but he could find nothing firm against which to push. His head pounded.

Guinyard snatched him from the water. He gasped for air.

Bending low, Guinyard drew close to David. "I do not think I will kill you. After the patrols seize that pathetic little ship, after you have seen your dreams fail, then I will watch you die. I will spend my reward, and you will burn in hell knowing that you have failed." Guinyard pulled him closer to his stained and broken teeth. "You shamed me in Le Havre. I knew you were up to something. I left my post and have hunted for you. I shall have my revenge."

The only air he could draw held the stench of Guinyard's stale breath. David closed his eyes. Perhaps it would be better to drown.

A heavy thud, followed by the release of Guinyard's grip, opened his eyes. Above him, Guinyard took a wobbly half step before collapsing into the water on top of him. The weight of the man pushed him down. David's face submerged. He rolled and freed himself. He struggled to his feet.

Alongside him, Charlotte dropped to her knees on Guinyard's back. Pressing the man underwater, she clasped her hands together and began praying. David reached for her arm, but she shook him away. "This must be done," she said through clenched teeth. "You will never be free. He comes from the Devil."

David looked toward Fécamp. No one ran in their direction. He dropped to his knees beside her. Beneath his knee, he felt the man's arm. It pawed weakly at the sand. David tasted sourness at the back of his throat. He spit into the water.

"Pray, husband," Charlotte said. "This prayer will be answered soon."

David pinched his eyes. He could think of nothing.

Aboard *Le Pinson*, a crew member showed Noaleste and Aristede their berths. He then disappeared back on deck. The craft slowly sailed away from the harbor. Aristede looked at his companion, who pointed to the lower bed. Nodding, Aristede crawled onto the top bunk. From his seabag, he withdrew a piece of rope. "Help me, please."

Louis de Noaleste held the lead pipe against one of the beams as Aristede looped the rope several times before pulling it tight. Then, he tied a series of knots, securing the scepter to the crosspiece.

"Why?" Noaleste asked.

Aristede kept his eyes on his work. "One of us should always remain with the scythe. Should we need to step away, I want to know that it cannot be quickly stolen."

"A moment, monsieur." Noaleste's hands disappeared into his own bag, returning with sealing wax. "Put a bit of this on the cap. That we might know if it has been tampered with."

Aristede nodded. "Good thinking."

The boat rose and fell. Aristede's eyes showed alarm.

Noaleste smiled. "Ah, we are out in La Manche. We are truly underway."

Aristede frowned. "I have traveled little by boat."

Again, the boat pitched. Aristede's eyes darted about the small space they had been assigned below deck. "Will that happen often?"

Noaleste laughed. "Only when we are moving."

Aristede swallowed hard and closed his eyes.

"Let us go onto the deck. The fresh air might help you. You can see the waves and know that there is nothing to fear." He led the way up the ladder. Aristede followed tentatively.

The crew worked busily, tightening lines to maximize the efficiency of the boat. No one on board seemed to take any notice of the creaking timbers or the rocking of the boat. Aristede felt the wind at his back and turned toward the stern. The captain stood, observing the water as well as the efforts of the small crew. He called out occasionally, but the men were experienced and went about their tasks with little direction.

Although the wind struck him squarely in the face, Aristede could feel sweat beads gather on his forehead. He spread his legs slightly further apart and bent his knees, modeling the stance of the captain. He hoped the position might help him to relax. He felt no better.

Noaleste appeared at his shoulder. "Sailing on the ocean is not quite like a raft on the local rivers. You will become acquainted with the ocean's rhythms. By tomorrow you will not notice the up and down, up and down. I promise you."

Perhaps that would be the case, Aristede thought. But for the moment, the mere mention of up and down aggravated what his stomach felt. He breathed deeply through his nose, pushing great amounts of air into his lungs, seeking to hold everything else still.

"Up and down," Noaleste repeated.

Aristede's eyes widened. He rushed to the side of the boat and threw his head out over the water. The smoked herring quickly returned to the ocean waters along with all the other contents of his stomach. Behind him, he heard a chorus of laughter. Aristede wished to turn and face them, but the boat rocked, and another wave of nausea overcame him.

One of the men shouted, "Looking down, the view never changes."

Aristede grimaced and pushed himself upright. Once again, however, seasickness struck. The vomiting seemed to bring no relief to his suffering.

Eventually, the captain stood by his side. He handed him a cup. "Drink some water," he said. But as soon as the water touched his stomach, it was hurled out again.

When Aristede forced himself upright, he felt so weak that he wondered if he could remain standing. His legs felt wobbly, and his hands quivered.

Noaleste joined him. "Go lie down. Guard the scythe. I shall remain on the deck."

Aristede shuffled forward. The hatch seemed to dance and move as he approached it.

Noaleste caught his arm and pressed an empty bucket into his hand. "Do try to hit this. We must breathe down there."

Aristede nodded before continuing his feeble walk across the deck. He extended his free hand to find the doorway.

With effort, he crawled into the upper berth. He lay miserably, listening to the groans and creaks of the wooden craft. His only solace was that he had nothing left to purge. His stomach still tried. But mostly, he lay on his bunk and moaned, his only companions the ship rats he could hear pattering around him. Up top, Noaleste called and laughed with the sailors. Aristede lost track of time. He drifted in and out of sleep, at times aware of near total darkness. He heard rhythmic footsteps above him as a sailor kept watch on deck. Aristede made several attempts to stand only to watch the small cabin spin whenever he tried. At times, he saw that Noaleste had brought bread and water. Eating, however, proved unsuccessful. Aristede felt death was certain. He had been a fool to volunteer for this expedition. From his seabag, he withdrew the medal Jacques had given him. He soured into melancholy. He had failed on the quay at Le Havre and again here aboard *Le Pinson*. He lay back on his bunk.

Awaking from a fitful rest, Aristede saw that light filtered in from above. He crawled down from his berth and pulled himself up onto the deck. He looked upon a gray morning.

One of the fishermen stood beside him. "You have the mal-de-mer bad."

Aristede realized that he had not had the chance to learn any of their names. "What is the remedy to make it go away?"

The man shrugged. "Land."

Aristede pinched his eyes shut, but the rocking only felt more pronounced. He opened his eyes and began walking slowly along the deck of the fishing vessel.

"Where do you go?" the fisherman asked.

"I shall make myself better," Aristede said. Keeping a firm grip on the rail, he walked down to the stern and then reversed course until he reached the bow. He repeated the trek. If the crew noticed, he could not tell. He did not take his eyes off his task.

After three trips he leaned against the rail. He felt exhausted.

"You've done well," the fisherman said. "We were watching. The captain barked at us to pay more attention to our tasks. The Brittany waters are tricky."

Aristede glanced up only briefly to notice that the setting sun lay more toward the middle of the boat. They sailed southwest. He nodded to the fisherman, then struggled back to his berth.

He awoke after again sleeping fitfully. Aware of some small bit of light, Aristede sought to gauge the time. He heard scraping noises at the foot of his bunk. The ever-hungry rats chewing. He closed his eyes, and then they popped open wide. Louis de Noaleste stood near the foot of his bed. With his knife, he sawed upon the bindings holding the lead pipe.

Aristede weakly raised his arm. "What are you doing?"

"Pity I awakened you," Louis de Noaleste said. "What does it look like I'm doing?"

"You're cutting the ropes to the scythe."

Noaleste nodded in the pale light of the lantern. "We are sailing into Brest for more supplies. The entire crew knows something is tied to your bed. I want to hide it before it is stolen."

Aristede nodded and lay back. "That makes sense."

"Rest, my friend. I shall take care of the scepter."

Aristede sat up in his bunk, nearly striking his head. His suspicions suddenly aroused. They had never referred to the scythe by name since they boarded the craft. If the goal was to fool the crew, they must not cut the lead tube free. Hide the scythe but leave the tube in its original position. That is what David did, the trompe l'oeil. With effort, he rolled from the bunk, landing heavily on the deck. "No, you mustn't."

Noaleste cut through the last rope. He held the knife in one hand and the lead tube in the other. He spoke in a warm voice. "I will keep it safe, my friend."

He had never called Aristede his friend. "You mustn't." He faced Noaleste.

"But I must. Look at what we must protect." Carefully, Noaleste put his knife back into the scabbard. Then, he twisted the cap on the lead tube. Small bits of sealing wax broke off and fell to the deck. He set the cap on Aristede's bunk. Delicately, he reached his fingers into the tube and slowly withdrew the scepter. He unrolled the velvet cloth, exposing the globe at the top of the scepter.

For the second time in his life, Aristede saw the shaft once held by kings. He felt his breath catch.

"Look at it." Noaleste's words were unnecessary, for Aristede could not look anywhere else. "See how the light dances off the delicate gold."

Noaleste's foot lashed out, kicking Aristede just below the knee. He collapsed to the deck. Noaleste came and stood over him. Holding the scepter like the king himself, he tossed the tube onto the upper bunk. "The mace is worth a fortune. Its value will help me to regain all that my family has lost."

Aristede's heartache exceeded the pain in his leg. "You betray us."

Noaleste gave him a thin smile. "I believe that history will show you betrayed us. Who will the world believe, the known coward or the distinguished head of the Noaleste family? Do not fret, my friend, the Englishman who has agreed to pay handsomely for the French crown jewel will circulate your description. Remain on this boat. Mal-de-mer is far preferable to the alternative. You have all been fools. This boat sails for the cold North Atlantic to fish for cod. It would never take us to Spanish Louisiana. Stay aboard. Become a fisherman." Noaleste tucked the scepter beneath his cloak and stepped over the prone man.

Aristede grabbed his leg and pulled it. Noaleste stumbled, then attempted to kick free, but Aristede held on with all his remaining strength. Noaleste lost his balance and fell.

Aristede rolled from under him. He crawled to his feet and positioned himself in front of the hatch. "You may not leave with it."

Noaleste lay the scepter on his bunk. He withdrew his knife. "The plan shall change to account for your body. Pity." Raising his hand shoulder high, Noaleste waggled the knife slowly, snakelike.

He made a quick stab, and Aristede jumped away from the knife's path. He felt fatigued. He knew he could not resist for long. Looking into Noaleste's face, he saw that the other man knew it too. Aristede felt prepared to die. He had disappointed those who had trusted him too many times already. Death would free him from his deep personal failure.

"It shall all be ended soon, my friend." Noaleste lunged with the blade.

Aristede sidestepped to avoid the blade. He stumbled and fell to his knee. His hand came down on Noaleste's bunk, his palm atop the Scepter of Dagobert. His entire body suddenly felt ablaze. Aristede looked to see if he had been stabbed. Noaleste's knife had missed.

He shot to his feet, holding the scepter.

Noaleste's eyes darted between his prize and Aristede's face. "Put that down, monsieur. Neither of us wishes to see it come to harm."

Aristede nodded and slowly, watchfully, moved to lay the scepter on his own bunk. His glance shifted only briefly to ensure that the precious cargo was safe. In that moment, Noaleste struck.

The knife pierced his side. Aristede, strangely, felt no pain. With one hand, he grabbed his foe's wrist. With the other, he clasped the lead tube. Wielding it like a club, he smashed down on the elbow of Noaleste's knife arm. Before the man could cry out in pain, Aristede twisted free of the knife point and guided the blade between Noaleste's ribs. The man's eyes widened. He tried to raise his ruined arm to remove the blade. Then he took a feeble step before collapsing to his knees. He fell face forward onto the deck.

Although wounded and bleeding, Aristede felt no pain in either his side or his knee. He did, however, have a problem. The body of his comrade lay on the floor.

He knew what Noaleste intended for him. Carrying the man over his shoulder, he struggled up the ladder to the deck. The watchman on duty stood at the stern. The brief scuffle had not alerted his attention. He slid Noaleste's body to the bow, tied a weight to his midsection, and, as quietly as possible, lowered him into the water. When he finished, he looked back. The watchman studied the sails, unaware.

Below deck, Aristede tore his bloodstained shirt into strips, then bound his wound with the cleanest parts. Shirtless, he cleaned the blood from the deck as best he could. Finding some bread and water, he ate quickly, then he bent over the bloodstain. Forcing his fingers down his throat, he purged the stomach contents. He dressed in his other shirt. Finally, he returned the scythe to its lead sheath.

He arose before first light. Last night had proved sleepless. The captain carefully guided the fishing vessel into the harbor at Brest.

"We shall resupply here before departing," the captain said, never taking his eyes off the approaching harbor.

"And then you sail for the northern seas?"

"The Grand Banks are where the cod swim."

"Then here I shall depart. My destination is further south."

The captain adjusted his course slightly. "And what of your friend?"

"My traveling companion has, I believe, already left your boat. Perhaps he feared the authorities."

The captain grunted. His eyes flicked away from the harbor long enough to look at Aristede. If he saw the blood seeping through Aristede's shirt, he made no mention of it. "You look healthier this morning. I hope that you remain free of the mal-de-mer for the remainder of your voyage."

Aristede nodded. "I believe I shall. My recovery has been miraculous."

17

Bozeman, Montana
June 4th

The sun had yet to make an appearance when Clarence rolled into the parking lot of the Mammoth station. He hoped that the darkness would hide the limp. His leg had throbbed all night, and he had slept little.

He found Nance studying her computer. Within the darkened office, the monitor's light bathed her high features in gray. Johnson stood outside and waved, trying to keep his movements to a minimum. He gestured to the two travel mugs he held. She acknowledged with a nod before returning to the screen. After a moment she stood, picked up the computer, and walked out into the narrow hallway.

She moved toward him. "Timely, I see."

Clarence made a sweeping motion for her to lead. "Timeliness, next to godliness, that's me."

Nance grunted and headed to the door.

Once Clarence got moving, he felt he walked almost normally. He hoped to be at speed before Nance turned around.

He wore khaki pants, this time with a golf shirt and hiking boots. Around here, hiking boots seemed to go with everything. Nance dressed in gray dungarees and the black windbreaker with "Police Special Agent" labeled in yellow. She also wore hiking boots.

Nance pushed the door to the station open with one hand. With the other, she reached back to take the travel mug of coffee.

Clarence handed her the cup. "How far to Bozeman?"

"About an hour and a half at the speed limit. But it's Montana, no one drives the speed limit."

She climbed into her SUV. Nothing identified it as a government vehicle. Clarence gritted his teeth, planted his leg, and swung into the seat, attempting to make the process look as effortless as possible. If Nance noticed, she said nothing.

She drove to the North Entrance Road. At this hour, few other vehicles were on the road. Nance said little, alert for foraging animals. As they passed through Gardiner, she turned and faced him. "Hungry?"

Clarence shook his head. "I'm good."

Nance glanced down at his leg. "If you don't want to get out of the car, we can do drive-through."

His face flushed. Clarence felt glad for the privacy of the predawn morning. "Either way, it's just the first couple of steps until I get up to speed."

"What happened?"

He studied his leg for a moment. "Want the long or the short version?"

Nance waved her arm at the front windshield. "It's Montana."

"Do you like oatmeal cookies?"

Even by dashboard light, Clarence saw Nance's scrunched face and raised eyebrow. Then, she shrugged and pulled beside a small restaurant with large well-lit windows. She kept the SUV's motor running. "Sit tight," she said, and hurried inside. Minutes later she returned carrying a white sack and two Styrofoam cups. Clarence watched as the morning breeze feathered Nance's hair.

She handed him the coffee and sack. "No oatmeal cookies, but the best cinnamon rolls in western Montana." She emptied the travel mugs onto the parking lot. "And your coffee sucks."

"Costa Rican breakfast blend, freshly ground this morning," Clarence said.

"Folgers, already ground, hot, fresh, and plentiful. Rancher coffee." Nance steered back onto the highway as she bit into her cinnamon roll, leaving a trace of frosting on her upper lip. "What do oatmeal cookies have to do with anything?"

"I like them. More importantly for this story, I like to bake them. Works as a stress reliever."

Nance nodded. She took another bite and, with the back of her hand, wiped her upper lip.

Johnson bit into the cinnamon roll. He chewed slowly, judging the flavors. Maybe a hint of cardamom in the dough, he thought. Nance watched out of the corner of her eye.

He gave her a thumbs-up sign. "The oatmeal cookie recipe I like, my mama's, calls for vegetable oil. One night, I had a hankering to make some, but I didn't have any oil. I drove to the grocery store. I also got some red wine because nothing pairs with an oatmeal cookie like a nice Syrah. Though some people prefer a hearty Cabernet." Clarence paused.

Nance offered no opinion.

He took a sip of coffee before continuing. "I am walking back to my car when, I'll be damned, some doper is robbing the cell phone store next door. I drew my off-duty weapon, taking up my shooting stance. I am pinching my groceries with my left elbow against my chest, trying to poke buttons on my cell phone with my thumb so that I can call it in. The bad guy steps outside. And, about that time, the grocer's security guard comes flying around the corner, yelling for the guy to 'freeze.' He's wearing his blue security guard uniform and looks, at first blush, like a Fort Worth cop. Well, the bad guy panics and fires. The shot grazes my leg. I drop the sack with the oil and wine." Clarence shook his head, recalling the episode. "Don't know why I held onto them. We don't run an active-shooter-with-groceries scenario in the academy. Both bottles broke. I got a shot off, hitting the bad guy. He starts crawling away. The security guard ran to me, pursuing the robber. By that time, my broken bottles of oil and wine have mixed all over the sidewalk. He sees a big pool of oily red liquid and thinks blood. He vomits right in the middle of it. Then, he slips on the oil, and his feet go right out from under him. Hits the sidewalk and knocks himself out cold."

"Nobody thought to call for a cleanup on aisle two."

Clarence nodded in agreement. "One plastic yellow sign and all this trouble could have been avoided."

"So that explains the limp?"

Clarence shook his head. "That, as they say in the movies, was only a flesh wound. I'm struggling to get up before the bad guy can get away or hurt anyone else. At about that time, a squad car from Fort Worth comes blaring onto the scene. A rookie officer jumps out and starts yelling his head off. He sees me, gun in hand, getting to my feet. Alongside is the unconscious security guard dressed like a cop. He is lying in the middle of a big pool of red wine and canola oil. The whole scene smells like stomach. The kid, convinced I've just gunned down one of Fort Worth's finest, draws his weapon. Shots start flying. One of his rounds hits my leg squarely. No way am I getting up after that one."

Nance glanced at the leg.

"Want to hear the strange part?"

"It gets more bizarre?"

"The rookie answering the call was the chief's son, fresh off his supervised time with a field training officer. He'd only been alone on patrol for two weeks. The department wanted to avoid the publicity of the chief's kid shooting an off-duty detective who broke up an armed robbery. They offered a pretty good settlement for me to medically retire. The package included an understanding that I would stay out of town for a while and not give interviews. That's why I took the seasonal job up here." Clarence paused for a moment and took a breath. "These days, some parts of me wake up faster than other parts, especially on cool days."

Nance stared straight ahead, watching the road. Her brow furrowed. Johnson ordinarily declined any invitation to tell that story, but he liked talking with her here in the pale light of a Montana morning.

Nance broke the silence. "That explains why they were pretty tight-lipped when I called Fort Worth."

Clarence nodded. "Probably. You checked up on me?"

"Federal government does not hire consultants without proper vetting." Nance's face studied him.

Clarence's fingers wiggled at the front windshield. "The road is that way."

"There's something you're not telling."

"I never baked the cookies."

"I'm serious," Nance said. "You're holding something back."

Clarence turned and looked out the window. He needed to decide. After three miles of silence, he kept his eyes straight ahead and spoke. "The security guard."

"The one who slipped?"

Clarence nodded in the dim morning. "Retired cop from one of the local suburbs. Making a few extra bucks to supplement his pension. Hit his head on the sidewalk. Died of a subdural hematoma."

Nance inhaled sharply. She pulled the truck over to the side of the road and faced him. "Clarence, that wasn't your fault."

He kept his eyes on the mile marker in front of the truck. "Maybe, maybe not. But you make the decision to engage, especially off duty, and you own all the consequences."

"The department must have therapists..."

"I can tell you all the lingo. That doesn't mean it's not still part of who I am."

"I'm so sorry."

Clarence stared at the mile marker, then he turned and faced Nance. "Thank you. But don't think your sympathy will cut you a discount. We've never discussed my compensation package."

Nance looked surprised. Then she dipped her chin and stared down at the cinnamon roll. She waggled the pastry.

"That'll cover the trip to Bozeman, but the rest of my fee is still subject to negotiation."

"Fair enough, but I may have to fire you anyway," Nance said.

He arched an eyebrow.

"I got a call yesterday from the Lake Yellowstone Hotel. François, that kid you hassled when we searched Ocone's room. He called to say you bothered him again."

Clarence snorted. "He's a crappy waiter with a very low pain threshold if he calls what I did harassment."

"Just leave the kid alone."

He looked over at her. Her eyes studied the road. The morning sun had begun to show, illuminating the eastern sky with a pink hue. The rose color illuminated Nance's cheeks. "You know something."

Nance held her gaze on the road and remained quiet.

"C'mon, you know something about François."

"Just leave the kid alone. He wants to talk to me when we get back. He said that he has information."

"If he tells you how to pick a wine, forget it. He doesn't know crap."

She ignored the comment. "Leave François alone. I'll talk with him."

"Why did he call you?"

"I think he has ties to the RCMP."

Clarence felt he should know what she referred to.

"The Royal Canadian Mounted Police, Canada's national police."

He nodded. "Not much contact with Mounties along the southern border."

She looked across the seat. "I doubt he's actually an officer. My guess is a snitch. But I think he has information that fits with LaFleur's theory. He dropped a sergeant's name. I left a message."

Nance pulled her cell phone and scrolled through voicemail messages. "François called me again later. Left a message. Tell me what you hear."

Johnson heard mostly broken fragments of sentences. He recognized François's voice. "It sounds like the young man wants to meet with you to talk about a dog."

Nance nodded. "I heard the word 'dog' and what sounded like 'allegiance,' but not much more."

"Cell phone reception sucks up here. François is hitting on you. Classic pick-up strategy. Bring a puppy to the park and women flock."

Nance grunted. "I think he is saying that if you come along, he'll sic the dogs on you. Leave the kid alone. I'll talk with him." The SUV rolled back onto the road.

Johnson let a mile pass before speaking. "You don't really believe that Yellowstone acts as a big narcotics distribution center."

"I don't think we can dismiss it just because you don't like the source."

Clarence rubbed his sore leg. "I got nothing against Thor. He is a brother officer."

Nance snorted.

"But," he continued, "I think LaFleur proves the admonition that if you're a hammer, you see the world as a nail."

"Meaning?"

"Meaning, Yellowstone is too far from anywhere. Distribution costs are too high. Too many states to pass through for interdiction. Running drugs in Dallas-Fort Worth is not that hard. No one needs to be this elaborate. I think a DEA guy finds himself predisposed to see overwrought schemes."

Nance quietly kept her eyes on the road.

"And this latest twist. If you take an eighteenth-century painting and turn it on its side, it might resemble a map of a river confluence. With data encryption, communications do not have to be that complicated. That's twisting facts to support a conclusion."

"And what's your explanation?"

Clarence turned and watched the scenery fly past. The morning sun had risen high enough to chase the darkness from most of the surrounding countryside. "I don't know." He took a drink of lukewarm coffee and returned to looking out the window. "I'm hoping to have a better idea after our field trip today."

Signs began to announce Bozeman.

"Do you know what the earliest French fur traders called this area?" Johnson asked.

Nance shook her head.

"They took the Native American name for the river and converted it to French. They called the river and the land alongside it *Roche Jaune*."

"I don't speak French," Nance said.

"I don't either, but I can do an internet search. It means 'yellow rock.'"

Nance's eyes looked at him. "That's your big clue? This area is named Yellowstone?"

"I'm not saying it's a clue. For as long as Europeans have been talking about this area along the river, they have called it Yellowstone. Even when the thermal features of the area had people believing that the area was a gate to hell, they called the land Yellowstone. I just think it is interesting."

Nance waggled her index finger at him. "I'm sticking with LaFleur's theory for the time being. We'll see what his beltway experts in Washington have to say."

"Think what you want. I just think his theory would make more sense if they had originally called this the Opioid River, then he'd have some merit. Maybe the feds' research will show that early French fur trappers called one of those streams 'Snort a Line of Cocaine Creek.' Trust me, I'll be the first to admit to Thor that I was wrong."

A throat-clearing sound escaped from Nance.

"You almost laughed," Clarence said.

"We all make mistakes."

They entered the Bozeman city limits.

After miles of country driving, Clarence found himself sitting at a traffic light. Stores, gas stations, and homes dotted the landscape. He found the congestion irritating.

Just before the light changed, Nance looked over. "What happened to the kid?"

"Who?"

"The chief's kid who shot you. What happened to him?"

"He resigned from the police force. I'm told he went to law school."

Nance grunted. "Perfect."

Clarence nodded. "He'll make a rich living suing clowns like himself."

They checked in with the campus police for Montana State University. The chief escorted them to Wilson Hall, a square, flat-roofed, brown brick building of late modern style. Clarence felt disappointed. Grand architectural structures appeared across campus, but the history department was not housed in one of them. The building did have a nice courtyard with trees. The chair of the department, Dr. Bill Jeffrey, met them at Ocone's office. The police chief opened the door.

"Lock it when they're finished," the chief said to Dr. Jeffrey.

The three stood in the doorway. Kilos of illegal drugs were not immediately available.

Nance looked at Clarence. "Without PPT, we're on our own."

"Appears so."

She stepped inside. A small window illuminated the office with a mix of grays and shadows. Johnson flipped the wall switch; fluorescent light flooded the room.

Dr. Jeffrey waited in the doorway, twisting at his bow tie. "You don't think you'll find anything that might embarrass the university?"

"If we run across evidence that he belongs to the Flat Earth Society or denies evolution, we'll make sure to keep it out of our official reports," Clarence said.

A short, pear-shaped man, Jeffrey continued strangling his tie. "I know this may seem funny to you. But we took a chance on Ocone. He had solid academic credentials and a good mind, but he came with...baggage. He had been involved in some scandalous behavior."

"Tell me about this baggage," Nance said.

Jeffrey looked down at his feet, then angled his eyes toward a bookshelf. "He got arrested. He trespassed on federal lands. He collected some native artifacts. He was naïve."

"And the drugs?" Nance moved slightly to see Jeffrey's eyes.

"He had some marijuana. All the kids do. Some in the administration wanted to let him go, but he was young. Termination would ruin him. I fought for him. I encouraged him to work hard to earn back the trust of the administration. If the academic community thought that we endorsed any dishonesty..."

Nance had moved to the desk and was opening drawers. She looked up from her exploration. "I'm sure Professor Ocone appreciated your support. We will let you know anything we can."

"Thank you," Jeffrey said. His hands slipped off the tie and clasped his belt.

Clarence studied the bookshelf. "What can you tell us about his trip to Yellowstone?"

Jeffrey's hands smoothed his unkempt beard. "Nothing at all. He was single and liked to explore. We are on summer schedule here at the university. He had no classes to teach. I don't know that I'd seen him since class let out. A bit of vacation in America's best idea, I suppose, to paraphrase Wallace Stegner."

Clarence's index finger traced the spines of books along the shelves. "What was his research interest?"

Jeffrey's hand moved back up to the bow tie. "He'd been specializing in Native American antiquities until that unfortunate business. Lately, he'd been struggling to find something...safer."

"The books seem arranged."

Jeffrey nodded. "Yes, Professor Ocone had an organized mind. He had the capacity for outstanding research. But brash, too quick to want to get to the conclusion. Academic writing, you know, requires one to be more pedantic, despite what Plato said."

Clarence made his most learned nod. He pointed to a stack of books at the end of the lower shelf. "Two art history books, a biography of Jacques-Louis David, *The Iliad*, the *Journals of Lewis and Clark*, along with a history of Wyoming. Any clue why all these are out of order?"

Jeffrey canted his neck to read the titles before shaking his head. "No idea."

"Where else did he go?" Nance asked.

Jeffrey looked at her. "Pardon?"

"You said Ocone liked to travel. Where else had he gone?"

His eyes drifted to the ceiling. "Two years ago, Greece. He spent a portion of last summer in France."

Nance pulled a pair of satellite photos from the desk drawer. "These are Yellowstone pictures. Any idea what he looked for?"

Jeffrey's hands returned to his beard. His eyes darted between the stack of books and the photographs. "I'm sorry, I don't know."

From the same drawer, Nance produced a plastic baggie containing marijuana. She dropped it on top of the photographs.

"Oh dear," Jeffrey said.

Nance lifted the baggie and looked at the professor. Small beads of sweat formed along his brow. "Any idea about this?"

"That's hardly the sort of thing he would discuss with the chair of his department."

"I'll be taking this with me," Nance said.

He nodded. "Of course."

"I also want his computer for a forensic analysis."

"And these books," Johnson said, pointing to the loose books stacked on the lower shelf.

Jeffrey puffed his chest. "The computer and books are university property. I don't think I can allow..."

Nance leaned over the desk, closing the distance to the professor. "What I don't think you can allow is to conceal evidence of a major drug-smuggling operation." She looked to her left and right. "I'm breaching classified information here to tell you that the DEA has reason to believe cartel operations are occurring within Yellowstone Park." She pointed to the small baggie of marijuana. "If this university or this department is believed to be implicated as co-conspirators, we're talking RICO, we're talking indictments..."

"We're talking the loss of all federal research money," Clarence said. "The university can turn a blind eye to potential drug running, but the United States government cannot."

"You're not suggesting the university played any part in..."

Nance leveled her stare at Dr. Jeffrey. "I'm suggesting that you're deliberately obstructing a federal investigation through your refusal to provide the most basic cooperation."

Clarence held up his hands, palms outward. "Look, let's not be overly dramatic here. I don't think Investigator Nance really means you'd be indicted for misprision. I think the chances are slim. Even slimmer that you'd do any serious time for it. Unless, of course, you got the wrong officer preparing the sentencing guidelines. But that's the nice thing about a doctorate in history. You might be able to keep researching in a federal facility, unlike the biologists or the chemists." He chuckled. "Hard to win the Nobel Prize surrounded by barbed wire."

Clarence wondered if he needed to grab Dr. Jeffrey a chair. The professor looked pale and weak-kneed. When he finally spoke, his voice emerged in a hoarse whisper. "And what could the university do?"

"For the time being, consent to the removal of the computers, books, photographs, and the weed. Then the reports would have to reflect your cooperation."

Nance kept her stare locked on Jeffrey as she produced a release form. "And call us if you run across any additional information."

He nodded while signing.

Nance made the short drive over to the apartment Ocone rented. The landlady studied them quizzically, looking through her thick glasses.

"I'm Special Agent Nance. I called earlier."

The elderly woman's face lit up with recognition. She opened the door fully and allowed them to enter. Nance presented her the consent-to-search form. The woman held her eyes over it as Nance read it verbatim.

"He was a good boy," the landlady said as she signed, her face close to the page.

She could as easily have been describing a dog.

"Very quiet. Easy to rent to," she said, looking up from the paper.

Clarence looked down at the form. The landlady signed with the small, neat hand of someone who cared about her penmanship. She reminded him a little of his mother.

Nance gathered up the consent. The landlady walked them to the rear of the house and pointed to the garage apartment. She handed a key to Nance. "He lived back there. I don't know if you'll find much. I've already had a neighbor girl over to do some cleaning."

She had accurately assessed the situation, Johnson thought. The one-bedroom apartment, sparsely furnished, yielded nothing of interest.

When Nance returned the key, the landlady handed her a shoebox tied with brown twine. "When the girl cleaned up, she gathered up some family letters, documents, and a few pictures. If you see his family, they might like them back."

Nance accepted the package and returned to the SUV.

"RICO," Clarence said, when they turned onto the highway leading back to Yellowstone. On his lap rode one of the art books as well as *The Iliad*. "You don't think you were a little heavy-handed?"

Nance shrugged. "Well, you know what Plato said."

Clarence laughed.

"And you didn't hold back, yourself. Where does a state cop get words like 'misprision,' anyway?"

"I heard some feds say the word on television. Been dying to use it. I think you owe the professor for a bow tie."

Nance shrugged again. "I didn't want to sit there all day. He'd call the dean. The dean would call the president. The president would call the lawyer. We've got work to do. I'll write a letter to the dean praising the history department's full cooperation in this affair."

Clarence nodded. He opened *The Iliad* and flipped until he found a dog-eared page. His eyes scanned the text.

Nance stole the occasional glance.

He pointed to a bit of underlined text. "*The Iliad*, Book Two. In the middle of this speech by Agamemnon, Homer takes a pause to give his audience a history lesson on the king's scepter."

"Sounds fascinating."

"Why was it sitting on the shelf with the history of Wyoming?"

"Too stoned to put it away, I'd guess," Nance said.

He read from the text. "Leaning then on his scepter, he addressed the Argives."

"I've slept since high school lit. What are Argives?"

Clarence's face bore a satisfied smile. "Good thing you've got a consultant. It's a poetic way to say Greeks. Agamemnon was talking to his troops before the siege of Troy."

"What does it mean for us?"

"Consultants don't work that fast. Not when we're on a per diem."

"After I talk to François, I might not need a consultant."

He looked out the window at the mountains. "Do you ever get tired of seeing them?"

"He who climbs upon the highest mountains laughs at all tragedies, real or imaginary."

He looked at her.

"Friedrich Nietzsche said it first."

"And I thought I was showing off with *The Iliad*."

"They let ranch girls into college too."

Alison Nance kept her eyes on the road. "Getting shot must have been hard on your girlfriend?"

"She agreed. Liz found that living with a homicide cop was not conducive to long relationships or reliable mealtimes."

"Try being female," Nance said.

They fell back into quiet. Near the northern entrance to Yellowstone, Nance slowed. "I'm going to call François."

"Want me to come along?"

Nance shook her head. "And scare him off, no thanks." She pulled off the road. Clarence listened as she left François a voicemail. Nance then scrolled through her list of contacts. She tapped the screen and put the phone back to her ear. Clarence opened the door and used the time to stretch his legs. He returned just as Nance was setting the phone down. Nance's lips pressed together tightly, their normal full red color faint.

"I just called the restaurant at the Lake Yellowstone Hotel," she said. "François left work early yesterday. He didn't come back."

18

New Orleans, Louisiana
March 1796

The *Rosalie* made port. Aristede stood on the deck and looked across the water at the city.

"This is La Nouvelle-Orléans?" he asked the man alongside him.

"No, this is Nueva Orleans," the man corrected. "But the Spanish alcalde will be forgiving if you are prepared to leave money and not make trouble. He knows these days his city is called by many names."

Aristede studied the captain. The man had charged heavily to carry him without questions from Brest to this port in America, but he had been true to his word. "And what do you call this place?"

"I call it Nueva Orleans, for that is what the customs officials call it. I will call the city whatever they want to keep them happy and lazy."

"And I shall adopt your accommodating ways," Aristede said, "for I do not wish to make trouble for either of us."

Aristede looked toward the customs house. "And what exactly do these men typically do?"

The captain matched his gaze. "Oh, they look at my manifests. They wave their arms, and then they hold out their hands."

"And what have you found is their attitude toward visitors?"

"Nueva Orleans is a stew into which everything is thrown. Do not insult their flag, their *rey*, or their alcalde as you walk down the gangway, and you shall be welcomed into their city."

"I shall be the ideal guest."

"I can readily believe that," the captain said as he reached out to shake the man's hand. "And what will you do now that your voyage is complete?"

Aristede looked back across the waters, his eyes surveying the city before him. "I shall look for someone."

"Perhaps I can be of service. What is the name?"

Aristede shook his head. "I do not know, but I will know him when I see him."

The captain excused himself and disappeared below deck. After a few minutes, he returned. He gave Aristede a hat. "If you are to walk the streets aimlessly searching a man, you had best wear this. This sun is not like the sun of Paris. It will burn a man in no time."

Aristede nodded his appreciation. The morning sun already beat down hard. He placed the broad-brimmed hat upon his head. "How do I look?"

The captain grunted. "Like a man who will spend his nights alone." He pressed a letter in Aristede's hands. "Find Marie Gilbert. Her establishment is on the upriver end of Burgundy Street in the Vieux Carré. Give her this. If you seek men without names, she will be as likely to know them as anyone in Nueva Orleans."

Aristede smiled. The letter disappeared into his jacket. "When we see a king again, you shall be rewarded."

The captain shrugged his broad shoulders. "It was the least I could do. Few have paid so much to work so hard aboard my boat." He watched the men from the customs house make their way toward the *Rosalie*. He turned back to Aristede. "Now go, we both have work to do. You have your secrets to spread. And I have my friends to bribe."

Aristede hoisted his seabag onto his shoulder. Inside, hard against his ribs, he could feel the lead tube he had borne across the sea. He walked down the gangway, stumbling slightly as he sidestepped to avoid a group of new arrivals kneeling in prayer. The rolling gait he had developed on deck served him less well on the streets of La Nouvelle-Orléans. One of the customs men mocked his clumsiness. Aristede barely noticed. His eyes were looking for the upriver end of Burgundy Street.

From the docks, Aristede crossed the levee and made his way to the Place d'Armes. People milled about, paying no attention to another arrival in their city. Sweat trickled down his back. Yet, he dared not risk removing his coat. Aristede did not want to lose his letter of introduction. He ignored his discomfort and pushed ahead.

Across the Place stood the Cathedral of Saint Louis. Removing his hat, he entered and offered a brief prayer of thanks for his safe arrival in Spanish Louisiana. He asked God's blessing upon the remainder of his journey.

He passed the long row of arches of the Cabildo, the government hall. On board the *Rosalie*, he had sought out sailors who had visited La Nouvelle-Orléans. He learned all that he could. He knew that the Vieux Carré, this part of the city, had been laid out on a grid following in the style of a great French city. The sailors explained that many of the original structures had been burned when the city twice caught fire. The Spanish had taken over the French territories in America after the failures of the French and Indian War of the 1760s. The new government had insisted that the reconstructed buildings be made with brick, tile, and stucco rather than wood to make future fires less devastating. He saw all of that as he strode down straight but muddy avenues. Newly constructed buildings in the Spanish style stood alongside charred remains of burned wooden structures.

La Nouvelle-Orléans perplexed him. The city design may be in keeping with the great cities of France, but, as he slogged through the muddy and sewage-drenched streets, he found this outpost to be primitive. Yet around him in the passersby, he heard French and Spanish. In addition, he caught snatches of German, English, and the strange mixed local patois. Aristede imagined that if he closed his eyes, he might well think of himself back in Paris. He would, of course, need to stuff his nose as well.

Fortunately for Aristede, he did not close his eyes. As he made his way up Toulouse Street, two men locked in a brawl burst through a door. They fell into the mud, punching and kicking. A group of spectators gathered round, drinking and exhorting them. Aristede could hear wagers being placed. He shouldered his way through the crowd and continued to his destination.

A heavily painted woman blocked his path. "What's your hurry? We have other attractions besides fighting."

"I must pass. I am late for an appointment." Aristede lowered his head and continued onward.

The woman cackled, displaying stained teeth. "Celebrate today, for the miasma may get you tomorrow. Come inside, stranger. Only a few pesos."

Aristede quickened his pace to separate himself.

"Hurry to the church, priest," the woman called before cackling again.

Upon reaching Burgundy, he turned in the direction he believed was upriver. Aristede's pace slowed. He looked for some sign of a woman, of Marie Gilbert.

Ahead of him stood an ornate three-story building of rose-colored stucco. Porches wrapped around the upper two floors, protected by arabesque ironwork railings. The porches shadowed the lower floors, protecting them from the direct sunlight. Out front, a barefoot slave, wearing a loose-fitting linen shirt, pushed debris out the open front door with a broom.

Aristede approached him. "Where might I find Marie Gilbert?"

"We're closed," the sweeping man said.

The tone surprised Aristede. "Might you point me—" he began again.

"I tell you that we are closed. Come back when the sun goes down."

"But I must..."

The slave raised the broom handle as if to strike. "I tell you, man, we are closed. Come back this evening."

Aristede saw the taut muscles on the thin man.

From inside the building, he heard a voice. "What is that noise, Samuel?"

"I'm sorry, madame," the man said. He blocked the entrance with his thin body. Turning his head slightly, keeping one eye on Aristede, the man called into the building. "A stranger asking for you. I've told him to come back tonight."

"No one can sleep with you two bellowing back and forth. Show him in, and let us see what he wants."

Keeping the broom raised, Samuel took the smallest step to one side. Aristede squeezed through the narrow space, his body tense should the broom handle swing toward his body. He quickly stepped inside. He looked back. Samuel eyed him for a moment before lowering the broom and resuming his sweeping.

Tables dotted the room, and a long bar stood at the far end. Painted scenes decorated the walls. Below them, blue draperies hung. As Aristede studied the paintings, a woman emerged from behind the cloth. She wore an expensive dressing gown loosely belted; pale flesh showed when the front parted. She seemed unconcerned about what Aristede might see. She held a book in one hand and a smoking pipe in the other.

Her eyes scanned Aristede. "You're the cause of all the commotion."

"Excuse my interruption, but I was hoping to meet Marie Gilbert."

"Samuel is very protective of me," she said before clenching the pipe in her teeth.

Aristede nodded. "A valuable trait in a servant."

The woman chuckled; small clouds of smoke escaped. "You are new in town."

"Only just arrived this morning. I was told to look for you."

Before she could speak, Samuel entered the room. Aristede barely noticed. The man moved with a hunter's quiet.

The woman turned her attention to him. "He says you have the mark of a fine servant."

The man put the broom into a closet hidden behind another drape. "I'm sure I would." Then, without another glance at the pair, he disappeared through the same drapes from which the woman had emerged.

The woman stood and studied him. She seemed entirely unconcerned about receiving guests in a dressing gown. She took another draw on the pipe. "Well, you seem to know who I am," she said. "Tell me who you are."

Aristede quickly introduced himself and produced the letter from his jacket. He held it out. Aristede watched her eyes sweep over him. He felt like a horse being examined prior to purchase. She stepped forward to take the letter. As she did, her dressing gown pressed against his seabag. He saw her eyes widen briefly, then just as quickly return to normal. He glanced at her book, a work by Molière. She gathered a wine jug and two mugs from the bar. After handing them to Aristede, she gestured toward one of the tables. As he poured, she seated herself, unsealed the letter, then smoothed it with one hand. She read the document quickly.

Her eyes came up and studied him afresh. "Captain Joulon says that you are a man in possession of secrets."

Aristede felt his elbow squeeze his seabag more tightly against his chest. "To answer that would be to betray the lie..."

Gilbert held up a finger. "I find myself to be a reliable judge of mystery and motivation. What is it you seek?"

"I seek a man."

"Captain Joulon has indeed sent you to the right place. All the men of La Nouvelle-Orléans pass through these doors eventually."

"I need a man who will take me upriver."

"That is easy. Many along the waterfront may act as guides."

"Far upriver. To the parts of Louisiana few men have seen."

"Trade relations are difficult. The United States sells goods cheaply here. The Spanish government embargoes. The United States retaliates. Travel upriver is often monitored."

"Then I need someone who can be secretive as well."

Picking up her cup, she waited until he had done the same. She took a drink and looked at him across the top of her cup. "The alcalde frequents my establishment when he wishes relief from the pressures of governing this territory. Why should I jeopardize my relationship with the Spanish government by helping you to violate the embargo?"

Reaching into his pocket, Aristede produced a small bag. The coins inside clinked as they landed on the table. "I can pay."

With one swift motion, Gilbert's hand swept the bag from the table. It disappeared into her robe. "The alcalde pays. My relationship with him promises long-term benefits."

"When the king is restored, there will be long-term benefits to loyal service as well."

"You sit in Spanish territory. The king has never been deposed."

Aristede rolled his eyes and looked at her.

"I must think about all of this. In the meantime, your money shall pay for room and board."

Aristede gave a curt bow of his head. "*Merci.*"

"*De nada.*"

19

Lake Yellowstone Hotel
June 3rd

François asked himself whether his career would end before it even began. The assignment felt like a dead-end job with little chance of gathering any valuable intel. He could hear the growing sense of frustration when he talked with his uncle. François would summarize his reports, outline his contacts, and detail his plans for moving forward. His uncle would listen and offer up perfunctory acknowledgments. The questions had become fewer and fewer. He thought that soon his uncle might pull him from the assignment.

His uncle wasn't actually a relative but rather his handler from the narcotics group of the Royal Canadian Mounted Police. The man had plucked François from the Depot, the RCMP's police academy in Saskatchewan, and offered him the opportunity to work on this undercover assignment. François hadn't selected them; they had chosen him. "Voluntold," they called it. Initially, he'd been honored. He assumed that they'd chosen him because he had displayed some special aptitude at the Depot. François had always looked skinny and boyish; he didn't resemble a police officer. He had begun to wonder, however, whether he had been selected because they didn't want to waste an experienced officer on a foolish assignment.

He drained his beer and opened another. He checked the time on his phone. Soon he would meet a guy he had chatted up in the restaurant. Likely another waste of time, but that was the nature of the work.

He took another swig and turned his attention back to the email he was sending to Uncle.

Am meeting this PM with potential source. Will update following meeting. Monitored N. Privé. She went to Grand Teton Park for rock climbing. Although I have limited experience, she appears skilled. I did not see her speak with anyone besides hired guide. Later, I made contact. Told her that I had met a friend of hers, "Cy." NP appeared surprised at my mention of name but made no comment.

I have identified DEA agent. LaFleur. He recruited me as CI regarding conversations within restaurant. Can I keep money he pays? LOL.

Previous report detailed difficulties with local ranger—am following up with lead investigator tonight. Harassment claim should resolve.

F.

François took another swig and hit send. Although this job had drawbacks, he did get to work with alcohol on his breath.

His uncle had given him simple advice once he joined the narcotics group: to forget everything the Depot had taught him. Don't stand like a police officer, don't sit like one. He had been instructed to grow out his hair. François had spent time hanging at clubs. He'd taken a job at a Tim Horton's to get food service experience and to spend more time with civilians.

François's uncle had briefed him on the operation. The French police had picked up some internet chatter about an operation that concerned them. The discussion centered around "the mace." French intelligence had split on what the mace might refer to. François remembered the briefing. His uncle had thrown up his hands with exasperation. Some analysts speculated drugs. Others believed arms smuggling, the notion derived from the mace's use as a medieval weapon. One theory posited that "Mace" was an undercover operative within the intelligence service itself, a notion derived from a character in a *G.I. Joe* comic.

"Pick a theory," Uncle had grunted. "No one knows what the fuck they're talking about." He had flung a piece of paper at François. "Even a basic internet search revealed too many definitions for the word 'mace.'"

François scanned the list. It was broad. From an ornamental scepter carried by royalty to the English name for a Chinese measurement of weight.

His uncle shook his head and lit a cigarette. "Pick a definition, and we can craft a conspiracy to build around it." Uncle exhaled a cloud of tobacco smoke and answered François's unspoken question. "Because that's how intelligence works. We pluck at threads, hoping to see a tapestry. The bastards never send us a plan. We've always got to find bits and pieces."

François pulled on a Rush T-shirt, jeans, and a flannel work shirt. He knotted his hiking boots. To his daypack he added a water bottle and a camera. After he met the man, he might try to get in a quick hike. There was no reason this trip had to be all work.

The French had reached out to Canadian law enforcement when tentacles of the operation appeared to cross the Atlantic. The mace had been delivered to North America, French intel reported. Attempts to enlist the Americans had failed. The information had not been deemed high value, lacking sufficient corroboration. His uncle had directed him to cross the border anyway. He'd handle any resistance that might arise, he'd assured François. They needed to find out whether the investigation had merit and then either press forward or close shop.

François had taken an online course on wine. That and his experience at Tim Horton's had landed him a job working at the Lake Yellowstone Hotel. The RCMP's leads pointed them there. In the jargon of the narcotics division, he'd embedded himself within the restaurant of the hotel. François had imagined his undercover assignment to be an adrenaline-fueled rush, leading a double life. Mostly, he'd found himself bored. Other than potentially making a marijuana bust on the kitchen crew, he wondered what, if anything, he was accomplishing. François waited tables, took drink orders, and collected empty glasses and dirty plates. He listened to conversations and tried to chat up customers.

Roger Barkley, the industrialist, had taken the top floor of the lodge. François had volunteered to deliver room service every chance he could. It had proved easy to do; the billionaire's party were notoriously poor tippers.

He'd heard some nationalist rhetoric but nothing unexpected from the founder of the Stauros Society. He'd seen Barkley a couple of times around the lobby and on the wheelchair-accessible trails. François had never seen him without a pained scowl. Money, it seemed, couldn't buy health.

Barkley scowled even while visiting with Noel Privé. She was someone François would like to embed with. She smiled when she heard his accent, recognizing a compatriot. He found himself enamored by the small gap between her teeth. He'd returned the smile, but by then she had her head buried back in her work. She read a great deal for someone who wore designer clothes for a living. Yesterday, she'd gone climbing. He hadn't detailed his plans to resume the conversation about Cy. His uncle, the old monk, would accuse him of not being focused on his mission. His thin reports and lack of documented progress caused enough grumbling already.

He had served beer a couple of times to Professor Ocone. The guy typically left the lodge at sunrise to roam around Yellowstone. Ocone taught at a university nearby, François knew. Some days, Ocone didn't seem to leave his room. He'd call down for room service. François volunteered to deliver. He used another waiter's swipe card to leave no footprint. Ocone sat alone in his room, hunched over a computer. He would crack open the door, never allowing François to look inside. He always billed the food to his room. He added a generous tip, the reason the other waiter was happy to let François use his swipe card.

"Fantastic day to be outside," François would prod. "I can bring you something if you are not well."

"I'm fine. Just trying to get some work done."

"You are a scholar, no? Should you not be out observing?"

"I'm working on a theory." Ocone gave a guarded answer before pushing the door closed.

He had served Ocone at the hotel bar. He gave him the occasional free beer to win his trust. François discreetly followed Ocone. The man had poked around the northern boundary and traversed Blacktail Plateau Drive, following the old Bannock Trail, a Shoshone pathway to the buffalo hunting grounds further east. François had worked hard to remain unnoticed on the undulating, one-way dirt road. The man had dawdled among the new growth sprung among the charred remains of lodgepole pines, the burned shafts remaining from the great Yellowstone fire of 1988.

About the time that François had decided to dismiss the man, his occasional odd muttering written off as the ramblings of an academic, Ocone had been murdered. That data point had been impossible to ignore.

Ocone's death had brought out the local authorities. François hurried to the scene and watched as law enforcement personnel scrambled up and down the rocky cliffside. It had reminded him of a training exercise on the PT course at the Depot. In the middle of his surveillance, a park ranger had taken pictures of him. He felt foolish to be identified so quickly. He had learned the ranger's name, Clarence Johnson. Johnson's interest in him seemed to wane. Then, it flared again. The rangers searched Ocone's hotel room. Johnson caught him eavesdropping on their investigation. François reported back that the park rangers, the DEA, and an outside consultant had formed a task force to delve into the Ocone murder. Uncle pressed for more information. The emails had grown increasingly pointed.

Uncle had been even more direct in his phone call. "Find out what they know."

"They didn't cover computer hacking at the Depot."

François could hear the slow exhale of breath over the phone. His uncle spoke very slowly. "Those who seek information often reveal what they know by the questions they ask and how they ask them. Dangle something. Listen when they speak. Do not be obtuse. Is this possible?"

François nodded to himself. He knew he had been thought a fool. His first posting might easily be his last.

The last time he'd seen Ocone, the professor had been in the Yellowstone lobby. François was about to strike up a conversation when Ocone had been joined by another man. That man's features looked familiar, although François could not place him. François had picked up a bar towel and begun wiping down tables, working his way closer to where they sat.

They kept their voices low, barely above a whisper. Ocone, however, moved his hands excitedly, nearly knocking over a glass. François prayed he would. It would give him the opportunity to move closer.

"Dagobert, I know it's here," Ocone said. From out of the whispers, the word seemed almost shouted.

François had no idea what the word meant. He cleaned the table along-side, picking up an empty glass.

"Allegiance," he heard. The remainder of the sentence was muffled. He turned and cocked his head, edging his ear closer.

"We're fine, thank you," the other man said, staring directly at François. He had ventured too close. François apologized for any interruption. Before leaving, he looked down at the table. The other man's eyes held him. François saw no expression behind the cold gray eyes.

François had arrived at an elegant solution to his problems. He had called Investigator Nance and dangled the useless tidbits of conversation gathered from Ocone's table. He would listen to the questions she asked. François would complain about Johnson's harassment and force the investigator to intervene. Then, he would visit Privé. She would ask questions about Cy. Finally, he would let LaFleur debrief him. His next report to Uncle would prove that he could listen.

Today, he'd seen the man again, the one who had met Ocone. François had spotted him back in the lobby of the lodge. François apologized again for interrupting him the last time and offered the guy a cold beer on the house. The guy had originally scowled and refused, but then as François cleaned the surrounding tables and kept at his good-humored banter, he'd broken through with the guy. He'd steered the conversation to Ocone a couple of times before changing tactics. The guy, he learned, had a day job, but his real passion was being a modern-day prospector. With a wink, he made clear that he didn't search for precious metals inside the park; that would violate federal law. When François showed interest, he offered to teach him a little about the business. They agreed to meet after François's shift.

He'd left work during his break. François had walked down to the lake. With the privacy of the surrounding water, he had called Investigator Nance. He left a message, mentioning Ocone and Dagobert and his allegiance. He had also told her about Johnson's attempts to bully him. François had been proud of his use of the word "bully," a hot-button word around workplaces. François closed by suggesting they talk in person. Well handled, he thought to himself.

Checking the time, he closed the lid on his computer.

He met the guy in the parking lot. François asked his name, but the guy batted the question away. "We stay away from names in the prospecting business, dates to when men with all kinds of trouble lit out for the gold fields to escape the law. Helps these days if you want to shade a bit on your taxes. Call me Bud."

Bud showed him the truck. They climbed in and rumbled up north along the Grand Loop.

"Where we heading?"

"Just outside the north entrance I've got a claim. Can't do any mining inside the park. But I'm just over the line."

"Professor Ocone help you find any gold?"

Bud looked across the seat at him and shook his head. "Just another thirsty tourist."

François nodded, making mental notes.

"Smell that, son? Always know when you're by the Mud Volcano because of that rotten-egg stink."

Outside his passenger window, François could hear the Yellowstone River. He listened to the night. "What sort of equipment do you use on your claim?"

In the darkened cab of the truck, Bud nodded. "I use a highbanker for most of my river work. Tonight, I'll use some of my hand tools to show you a little about my operation."

François smiled. "Don't want to reveal all your secrets."

Bud nodded. "Something like that."

He pulled off the road at the north end of the Hayden Valley, a wide, sub-alpine, grassy expanse bisected by the Yellowstone River. Bud pulled through the small, graveled parking turnout, positioning his truck within a small copse of trees, a rarity in the valley.

François looked over at the driver. "This won't be a shortcut. We'll likely get stuck. Pretty marshy country here."

Bud didn't respond. His eyes peered forward as he navigated through the trees.

"I thought we were going off property?"

"Quick stop," Bud said. "Call of nature."

François felt his palms begin to sweat. He glanced down at the locked door. For the first time, he felt the seat belt tight around his waist.

Bud unclicked his seat belt. François looked over at him as Bud drove the stun gun into his body. François didn't feel the small prick as the barbs struck him in the stomach. Suddenly every muscle of his body stiffened as if he had a massive cramp from head to toe. His arms and legs went rigid, every limb locked in place. His bladder voided. François groaned, unable to move his jaw muscles to utter a cry or a plea. He couldn't think.

Bud walked around to the passenger side of the truck and opened the door. He stuffed a cloth in François's mouth and fixed it in place with duct tape. Unfastening François's seat belt, he forced his body forward and quickly bound François's hands behind his back.

He turned his attention from François and rifled through the daypack. He ran his hands along the seams, feeling carefully for any anomalies. He shook his head. "Nothing here." He returned his attention to François. "You pissed on my seat." Bud's only commentary before dropping a bag over François's head.

He hoisted the young man onto his shoulder and easily carried him into the trees. Slowly, feeling returned to François's limbs. He scraped against branches. He knew Bud carried a bag hanging from his other shoulder. The swinging satchel occasionally contacted his leg.

Bud whistled softly.

He dropped François heavily to the ground. Grabbing his shirt at the shoulders, Bud pressed him roughly against a tree. François kicked with his legs, trying to stand, but Bud stepped down on his midsection, pinning him in place. He heard two popping noises behind him. Although Bud lifted his foot, François remained unable to stand. Only then did he feel the tight pressure of the rope across his chest, biting into his skin.

Bud snatched the hood from his head.

François's wide eyes darted about in the darkness as he tried to understand his situation.

Bud grunted. "You've seen my stun gun. I need to send a message to whoever sent you here. When I want to send a message, I do something dramatic."

He stepped away from François and unzipped the satchel he had carried into the grove. Bud kept his back to François, his voice low. "Ocone, the professor, he'd have understood. Likely, the folks who send shits like you out here, they'll figure it out."

Perspiration dripped from François. He blinked his eyes to keep them clear. He twisted, trying to loosen the rope binding him to the tree, but the rope wouldn't move.

"See the horse path over there?" Then, Bud shook his head. "No, you won't get it." He turned back to François. With a knife, he quickly cut away François's pant leg. François's appeals, through the gag, came delivered as grunts.

"You talk too much, kid. Too much to too many people." Bud tossed the cloth to one side and returned the knife to his pocket. He brought out a strap and wrapped it around François's leg just above the knee.

François recognized the combat tourniquet. They had studied their one-handed application in his emergency medical training class. He knew that they could mean the difference between life and death. Bud began twisting; François felt the pressure and the pinch. He looked at Bud.

"You recognize it, do you?" He locked the windlass in place. "You'll understand in a moment." Bud turned away and reached back into the satchel. He faced François, holding a small, battery-operated chainsaw. He wore a plastic face shield.

François made a bleating noise. Bud flicked the start switch, and the saw drowned out François's appeal. Even his muted scream couldn't be heard.

Somewhere during the process, François lapsed into unconsciousness.

When François came to, darkness still surrounded him. As his head cleared, his mind flooded with everything he had endured. He flailed in wild panic but found that he was still trapped against the trunk of the tree. He remembered the lessons of the Depot. François took several deep breaths to calm himself. He studied the darkness, attempting to assess his situation. He could see the stump of his lower leg lying beside him. There was no sign of his tormentor. Bud had cut his leg off just below the knee.

He hadn't interrogated François; he had merely tortured him. François didn't understand. What was important, however, was that he had survived.

He could see the first streaks of morning, pink fingers in the sky. They gave him hope. He knew that he was in bad shape, but Hayden Valley was a popular spot for tourists. Visitors traveled the Great Loop and scanned the valley with binoculars looking for wildlife. His leg hadn't bled much; he'd survived the worst of it. If he could remain calm, he felt confident that he'd be found.

As if on command, he heard the deep-throated breathing and grunting of his rescuer. He couldn't see him yet in the limited light, but he could hear him, heavy-footed and panting, making his way toward him. François made vigorous grunting noises, hoping the sounds could be heard over the man's own loud breathing. He prayed he wouldn't pass close by without noticing. He saw the tall grass ahead begin to shake. François's heart leapt at the impending arrival of his asthmatic rescuer.

The bear entered the small stand of trees.

20

New Orleans, Louisiana
March 1796

Marie Gilbert led him up the stairs and ushered him into a small room. "I hope that this will be satisfactory."

Aristede set his seabag down on the bed. "I have been aboard a ship for many weeks. I will be quite comfortable."

"Then I shall leave you. I have affairs to attend to," Marie Gilbert said. The door, Aristede noted, opened noiselessly. She pulled it shut as she left.

The room's furnishings were sparse. Besides the bed, it held a washbasin and stand. A mirror hung next to the door. Exposed joists ran the length of the ceiling. A lantern hung from one. Candleholders with tapers sat on either side of the washbasin. Clearly, this room did not typically serve as long-term accommodation. Wine-colored draperies bordered the window. They smelled heavily of tobacco and mildew and were tied back with a black cord. Small, fat angels painted on the ceiling looked down on him. Aristede recognized the rococo style. He moved to the lone window and gained a clear view of Burgundy Street. Stepping away, he lit the lantern and then untied the cords, allowing the draperies to block any attempts to spy into the room.

He looked for any place to hide his precious scythe. He did not trust his hostess. Aristede walked the floor, listening for loose floorboards. The ceilings and walls offered no niche. He sat on the bed, his eyes searching the room. After diligent study, he surrendered. His answer, he knew, must be outside.

He dripped candle wax around the caps of the lead tube. He rubbed the hot wax around, sealing the pipe. Then, Aristede pulled his shirt over his head. Looping the drapery cord around him, he bound the pipe to the small of his back. The rope pinched at his sides and irritated his stab wound. Putting his shirt back on, he checked his appearance in the mirror. Beneath his blousy shirt, the rope appeared invisible. Aristede hung his seabag from his shoulder and slipped out into the hallway. Rugs muffled the sounds of his footfalls. Gilbert's establishment seemed designed for people wishing to enter and leave anonymously. He slipped downstairs and out the still open door. He saw neither Marie Gilbert nor Samuel.

Following a zigzag course, he confirmed that he had not been followed. The path risked getting him lost. He had no feel for Nouvelle-Orléans. The grid pattern of the streets made it easy, however, to go a block up Burgundy, down Bienville. He walked down Dauphine, then skipped over to St. Louis. He tried to vary his pace, pausing to look around. Each street seemed crowded with sin, stench, and standing water. Eventually, he came to Maines and hurried back to the wharves.

He ducked behind a building just off the street and watched. Satisfied that he was alone, Aristede untied the rope and secured one end to the lead tube. He pressed the pipe against his stomach and held it in place with his hands clasped in prayer. Aristede then walked out onto the gangway and, finding another group of fresh arrivals, knelt among them in their worship of thanksgiving.

Moving slowly so as not to attract attention, he slid the pipe into the Mississippi River. It disappeared beneath the murky water. Bending so low in prayer that his forehead nearly touched the gangway, Aristede tied a one-handed knot, lashing the drapery cord to the underside of the gangway. He paused briefly to utter a prayer of gratitude that his time working with the sailors had greatly improved his skills with ropes and knots.

Glancing down one last time to satisfy himself that the scythe was as safe as he could make it, he uttered an audible "amen" and stood.

"I watched you pray, señor," a voice beside him said.

Aristede turned and saw a man dressed like a Spanish sailor. His deeply tanned face wore a thick moustache. Aristede eyed him cautiously.

"You bent so low, I thought you prayed in the style of the Mohammedans. Then, I realized you were facing north." Here, he made an open-mouthed laugh. He was missing several teeth. "I decided that you were either a bad Mohammedan or a very grateful Christian."

"The latter," Aristede said, laughing himself. "I had a very trying voyage."

The Spaniard slapped him on the back. "Relish your time on dry land. And spend all the money you can. My wife works in the El Toro Tavern. You must go there. They do not water their drinks nearly as much as some of the other places. It will help a man forget his troubles at sea."

"Thank you, my friend," Aristede said as he pulled away.

"El Toro," the sailor repeated. Aristede waved over his shoulder.

Back on land, he slipped into the shadows of a building and watched to see if anyone moved to reclaim what he had hidden. Satisfied, he walked back toward Marie Gilbert's establishment.

Aristede allowed his pace to match the pedestrians around him. He felt no need for evasive tactics. If he was being followed, he wanted his opponents drawn away from the river's edge. He continued up Maines Street. The crowds dissipated the further he walked. To his left, he heard activity. He pivoted and walked toward the noise.

Shouts in several languages, the squawks of chickens, conversations, and music all filled the air, growing louder as he moved closer.

He found an open area crowded with Africans. He did not make the mistake of assuming, as he had with Samuel, that all Africans were slaves. Among the crowd, he saw some men and women dressed in simple hand-made clothing; others dressed more extravagantly. Past the group lay a cemetery. All those gathered seemed oblivious to the dead. Instead, they concentrated on all manners of commerce.

He heard a man speaking French, but a French language uttered by a drunkard recently escaped from an asylum. The patois contained a great many non-French words. Aristede could barely make out the content.

He approached the man. "What is this place?"

The man's eyes widened as he, too, struggled to make sense of Aristede's question. Finally, he spoke. "This is the Place des Nègres."

"And why is everyone gathered?"

"They come to buy, sell, sing, dance. It is a day that the slaves are freed from their duties."

Aristede panned the area with his arm. "All here are slaves?"

The man shook his head, all the while keeping his eyes on the vendors and alert. "No, many freedmen come to sell their wares as well. And many more come to buy. When you have nothing, you ask little for what you have."

Aristede's face remained blank.

"Slaves are not allowed to own property. Excuse me a moment."

The man walked quickly among the crowd to a seller seated on a blanket. He negotiated briefly before handing over some coins. He accepted a chicken pulled from a handmade wooden pen. The man walked back carrying the bird. "When they scrounge berries or nuts or raise a chicken, they bring it here to sell."

"And the music?" Aristede raised his voice to be heard over the protesting chicken.

"After the sales have ceased, dancing will begin. Even a slave is free to dance his own steps. The musicians are preparing."

Aristede saw all manner of musical instruments, drums, gourds, homemade stringed instruments and flutes. Around them, colorfully dressed dancers waited for the business of the Place to die down.

Aristede pointed to a man selling long stalks. "What is that?"

The man followed his arm. "That is sugarcane. Have you never tasted it?"

Shaking his head, Aristede stepped toward the stack of long stalks. The man to whom he was speaking put a hand to his chest, stopping him.

"Allow me to go to him, my friend. He will be suspicious of a white stranger. I doubt he will understand your speech. He will certainly overcharge you."

Aristede studied the man. His expression conveyed no dishonesty. Aristede described the length and width he desired. The man whispered the price he expected to pay. Aristede handed over the money.

"Hold my chicken," the man said and disappeared into the crowd.

About the time Aristede wondered if he had been cheated, the man returned. They traded the chicken for a piece of sugarcane. The piece he had purchased was far too short and thin.

The man's eyes looked downcast. "Pardon my misunderstanding." Then, he produced a knife. "At least taste what you have bought. I think you will find it far superior. The thickness you seek would be past its prime."

Working with the knife, the man quickly sliced between the thick joints of the cane, cutting a piece approximately the length of Aristede's hand. Setting the cane on the hard, trampled dirt, he trimmed the outer bark, exposing the white, fibrous interior. Finally, he lopped a small bit off the end that had sat in the dirt. He handed the prepared piece to Aristede.

"What do I do with it?" Aristede asked.

A deep belly laugh rolled out of the man. He then took back the cane and cut off a piece slightly thicker than a pair of stacked coins. This he popped into his mouth. "You chew it."

Aristede popped the cane between his teeth. He tasted the delicious sweetness. He nodded with satisfaction.

The man smiled. "I told you, my friend."

Aristede spat out the fibrous remains of the sugarcane. "I need a bigger piece." He again showed with his arm the length and desired thickness.

The man shook his head. "That piece will not be as good."

"This is the size I need."

The man sighed and bowed his head. He accepted the money from Aristede and handed it to the sugarcane merchant. Aristede pressed close to make sure this time he received a proper piece. He felt certain that the negotiator was taking a percentage for his translation, but he did not care. The man returned with a cane the desired size. He handed it to Aristede with a slow shake of his head. "We are in agreement that this piece will not be to your liking."

"It is not for eating, my friend," Aristede said. He put the piece in his seabag and returned the bag to his shoulder. The cane was not as smooth as the pipe, but it was hard and mimicked the shape. He stood alongside the freedman and listened to the music. The dancers were beginning to move about the Place des Nègres.

"I must take my leave," Aristede said. He shook hands with the freedman and departed. He popped another piece of sugarcane into his mouth and chewed as he walked back to Marie Gilbert's.

Aristede went straight to his room and hung his bag upon a hook. Then, he made his way downstairs. Gilbert's establishment began to fill with people. A tinkling piano played in the corner. Samuel moved silently around the perimeter of the room. Waiters offered drinks on trays. He made eye contact with Marie Gilbert. She glided to where he stood, looking immaculate in a high-necked sapphire gown.

"I feel underdressed," he said as he surveyed the crowd.

"Because you are," she said. Marie gestured with her chin to a waiter. She took two glasses of wine and whispered to the boy. He disappeared and returned shortly with a jacket. "This should be your size," she said.

Aristede slipped into the coat and accepted the wineglass. He chatted briefly with Marie Gilbert until her roving eyes spotted an arriving man in an expensive suit. She excused herself and quickly moved to greet him.

Aristede turned and studied the painting behind him. He recognized the Place d'Armes, although just barely. Where he had seen a field of over-grown grass, the artist had envisioned a park with ornate hedges and stat-ues. The painting displayed grand buildings. Stylish pedestrians walking the clean streets of Nouvelle-Orléans. He gazed upon a representation of an idealized city.

He moved slowly about the room, gazing at the other paintings. In a quiet corner, away from the hub of the men, Aristede was drawn to a scene he recognized from Plutarch. Romulus directed the establishment of Rome. Having stood in the presence of David's paintings of ancient Romans, Aristede saw that this painter's work proved clearly inferior. His characters appeared far less lifelike, the passions contrived. The coloring missed a subtlety that David brought to his heroic paintings. Even the characters' noses lacked the aquiline shape of the noble Romans. In the background, however, the artist had painted a she-wolf. Her realism gripped Aristede.

She held him with piercing eyes. He could feel the beast's menacing power, even from the legendary nursemaid of Rome.

"Do you like the painting?"

Aristede turned to see Marie Gilbert. She gnawed on a short piece of sugarcane.

"I am captivated by—"

Before he could complete the answer, her hand shot out and grabbed his crotch. His eyes widened.

She spoke slowly and quietly, never relaxing the firm hold she had upon him. "I have in my day gathered great experience touching pipes. I feel I am most skilled in evaluating them, both large and small." Here, she paused and allowed Aristede to consider the statement. "This morning, I rubbed against a tube in your bag." She held up the stalk of sugarcane. "This was not what I felt. I do not like to be played for a fool." Gilbert pushed him back away from her. Aristede bent at the waist and covered himself with his hands. Gilbert grunted a laugh. "And you, sir, must not only learn who you might trust but also that you are not as clever as you believe yourself to be." She spun on her heels. Aristede watched the back of her blue dress swish into the crowd of men in her establishment.

He stood, folded in the middle, trying to slow his breathing and to think through everything she had said. Panic rose within him. He needed to confirm that the scythe remained secure. He checked for Marie Gilbert. She stood in the far corner, gaily laughing at something a uniformed man said, seemingly unaware any longer of Aristede's presence in the room. He raced out the door and flew down the street, making no attempt at secrecy. Dodging animals and pedestrians, forcing himself through crowds, he ran toward the riverbank. His chest pounded. Sweat poured from his forehead and ran into his eyes. Using the sleeve of the borrowed coat, he wiped it away and hurried forward.

At the river, he slowed his pace. He searched for any sign of pursuit but saw nothing. He stood on the gangway. He studied the area. No one knelt in prayer at this hour. His fear overcame him. He hurried to the edge of the gangway and lowered himself to his knees. He looked down into the brown water of the Mississippi. His rope floated lazily upon the water's surface.

He felt as if he had been stabbed. His throat seized, and his breath would only come in short gasps. Aristede snatched up the drapery rope and squeezed it. Brown water ran down his fingers. The scythe must have come untied.

Aristede rolled into the Mississippi. He kicked his legs and swung his arms, diving down into the water. He plunged his hand into the muddy bottom, feeling for the pipe. He stayed down as long as he could, blindly feeling, trying to recover what he had lost. When his body screamed for air, he rose to the surface and, grabbing a quick breath, dived back down. Aristede had never learned to swim, but that did not matter. He groped in the blackness trying to recover the scythe. Again, his need for air drove him to the surface. When he emerged from the waters, strong hands grabbed him and hoisted him from the river. They dropped him onto the gangway.

"No," he shouted and rolled back toward the edge.

"Fool, she is not worth it," a man screamed into his face and fell upon his chest, holding him fast upon the deck. "No woman is worth this."

Aristede struggled to free himself, but others joined the pile, restraining his hands and his legs. Aristede thrashed without success before surrendering, his anguished sobs combined with great coughs of swallowed water.

The man straddling his chest looked at him. "This is the way to handle her loss. First you cry. Then, you get drunk. Then, you meet the next one to break your heart." He grabbed Aristede by the wet collar. "Are you finished with this foolishness, or must we tie you up?"

Aristede nodded weakly.

"Then, I will release you." The man stood.

Aristede rolled onto his side and moved slowly to the water's edge. Staring down into the brown water, he spat, forcing out the swallowed water. The crowd watched anxiously, prepared to pounce if he made any move to throw himself back into the river. With effort, he pushed himself to all fours, resting on his knees and palms. Then, he stood, swaying on the gangway.

The rescuer looked him in the eyes. "Forget about her. Another will come along."

Aristede closed his eyes and nodded. Reaching into his purse, he withdrew some money and pressed it into the man's hand. "Thank you, monsieur. You've been most kind to a stranger." He walked slowly back into Nouvelle-Orléans.

Oblivious to the route, Aristede found himself back outside the door of Marie Gilbert's. Inside, a piano tinkled a welcoming tune. The music was lost on Aristede. He entered and, leaving a trail of muddy water behind, wandered upstairs. Around him he heard a few voices, but nothing caught his attention. In a fog of loss, he climbed to his room. He closed the door. The faint light of a single lantern lit the room.

He took the remaining drapery tieback. He stood on the bed and worked the rope around the ceiling joist before tying it. Failure hung on him like the wet and silt-encrusted coat he wore. He made a noose from the free end of the cord. Aristede should write a note, apologizing to Jacques-Louis David and to all the others who had trusted him. Repeatedly, he had failed throughout this journey. Despite this, David and Charlotte continued to give him positions of responsibility. He slipped the loop over his head. He would not write the letter. Aristede could not bring himself to confess the shame. Allow the others to feel that their efforts had not been in vain, he reasoned. He drew the rope tight around his neck, feeling it pinch against his skin. Let his comrades live a happy dream. He could not share his private agony of failure with his friends or the snakes of Nouvelle-Orléans.

Aristede's wet hand grasped his wrist. He closed his eyes and said a prayer begging forgiveness from his God, his country, and his friends. Eyes closed, he stepped off the bed.

The cord tore into his neck. He felt his eyes bulge and his mouth open, his body desperate for air. He felt as he had when he was underwater but with searing pain in his neck. His ears seemed ready to burst. Aristede opened his eyes. Despite his efforts at self-control, his hands scratched at the rope, his legs began kicking backward, trying to find the bed. His body resisted the efforts at self-sacrifice. He felt regret, but the cause of the despair, his brain, was too breath-starved to recognize it. Clouds gathered around his eyes. His vision began to shrink. His hands clawed with less vigor, and his legs ceased the efforts. Aristede's head lolled to the side. His body twisted slowly in the pale light.

21

Yellowstone National Park
June 4th

Back at Mammoth Hot Springs, Clarence watched Nance log in the evidence. "Sign the books out to me."

She looked up from the chain-of-custody form.

"You're processing the computer. I curl up with a book. It's forensic analysis."

She slid him the page. He signed with a flourish. "You're sure you don't want me coming along on the hunt for François?"

"Be careful with my books."

It was early afternoon, the sun stood high in the sky, and the weather seemed perfect. He thought about suggesting they buy some sandwiches and find some mountain overlook to discuss the case. His thoughts lingered on Alison Nance. Then, Clarence swallowed the idea. She needed to locate François. He had a theory that had begun to niggle at the back of his mind. He wanted to think about it more before he shared.

"You look like you're about to say something."

Clarence shook his head. "No, we've got work to do."

They each got started down the Grand Loop Road. Nance led. At

Undine Falls, a recreational vehicle got between them. Their distance gradually widened as the RV slowed at every meadow. Through the smoked plexiglass of the RV's back window, Clarence could see arms pointing at wildlife. America discovering her park. His mind drifted. He thought about the ranger talks. He wanted to teach people like the RV occupants about the art of America's West. Clarence's thoughts returned to the ones he was developing on artists who had used these views for inspiration. And Nance. He spent some time on the drive back thinking about Nance. He pictured her in a dress, her long legs wrapped in something besides her jeans or the ISB uniform. He hadn't spent this much time thinking about a woman since the shooting. He had been single-minded on the rehab. Rehab was nothing but physical training, and he knew how to condition. Clarence treated each PT session like two-a-days. Even ex-ballplayers remembered those workouts. They demanded focus. Too much single-mindedness, his ex told him as she packed to leave. Clarence let her go. It hadn't been the time for them. He had training.

An ex-ballplayer, an ex-cop, an ex-boyfriend, maybe he spent too much time thinking about things he wasn't anymore. Maybe that was why LaFleur pissed him off, because LaFleur still played the game.

Clarence shook his head to clear his mind. Daydreams might run him up the tailpipe of the RV. Maybe he needed a couch and a trauma counselor rather than a steering wheel.

Still, he thought, Nance would look great in a dress.

Tripod bounded down the stairs to the RV as soon as the door cracked. The dog stood on her hind legs and scratched at his pants. Clearly, the dog felt better. He scooped up Tripod and deposited her in the tall grass. Clarence unloaded the books from the back seat and carried them inside. Tripod stayed close, hovering around his feet as if scraps might fall from the volumes.

Sitting at the RV's small table, Clarence opened the first book. He picked up his Strat and absently played a familiar blues riff. Clarence immediately regretted the decision to work in the RV. The day felt too ideal.

He returned the guitar to its stand and carted the books back outside, then gathered his notes for the new lecture. Tripod stood on the top step of the RV, eyes wide, tail wagging so vigorously her entire body shook. Clarence settled her into the passenger seat of the Suburban.

They stopped at Canyon Station. The visitor's center was clogged with people wanting to get directions, to purchase souvenirs, to ask advice, or to report bear sightings. The numbers overwhelmed the on-duty staff. Clarence stepped up to a young couple carrying daypacks and hiking sticks. After a moment's hesitation, they accepted that he was a ranger in disguise and sought his advice about hiking routes. He pointed to a map and began answering questions.

Martinez appeared briefly, watched the flurry of activity, and then disappeared. When the rush passed, Clarence made his way back to Martinez's office.

"Working undercover?" Martinez asked.

"Just stopped by to check in. Saw the crowd. Trying to help."

"You could help by getting back here. You're a seasonal ranger. This is the tourist season."

"Shouldn't be much longer. I think I've about worn out my welcome with the Investigative Services Branch."

"I'm not surprised." Martinez turned his head back to the paperwork across his desk.

As Clarence turned to leave, Martinez looked up from his desk. "How's the new talk progressing?"

"I was just thinking about Albert Bierstadt on the drive down."

Martinez leaned back and searched the ceiling as if looking for the place where he kept the trivia hidden. He came forward in his seat. "His paintings of Yellowstone geysers got President Chester Arthur to come out here for a visit. Did you know that, college boy?"

Clarence shook his head.

Martinez grunted and returned to his work.

He drove to the Lake Yellowstone Hotel. He wasn't backing up Nance or looking for François, but he and Tripod had research to do. It could just as easily be done outside on a sunny day. Balancing the dog on his lap, Clarence spread the books across the cedar bench with a lake view. He picked up the *Journals of Lewis and Clark*. The book fell open to the back cover. Pages had been printed and stuffed behind the dust jacket. He recognized them as the diary of Thomas Moran, notes jotted down during the Hayden Geological Survey of 1871. Moran's paintings and William Henry Jackson's photographs of the region helped spark the drive to preserve this area as a national park. Clarence had read through the fourteen pages many times as part of his research for the ranger talk. He leafed through them again, reminding himself that the diary seemed to begin on page two. It picked up in mid-sentence: "...*of the route lay through a magnificent forest of pines*..." The succeeding pages described Moran's exploration of the area until August 14th, when he noted they

camped at Bradleys Ranch on warm spring creek. gold.

The next day, August 15th, he journaled that they

camped on a small

Here, the text again disappeared. He looked out over the calm crystal water of the lake and wondered what might have been detailed either before or after. He thumbed through the Lewis and Clark journals looking for any highlights or underlines. A pencil-drawn asterisk in the margin near the back of the book made him pause. The explorer William Clark had added "notes of information I believe correct" to the end of the journals.

At the head of this river the natives give an account that there is frequently herd a loud noise, like Thunder, which makes the earth Tremble, they State that they seldom go there because their children Cannot sleep—and Conceive it possessed of spirits, who were averse that men Should be near them.

Clarence made a mental note to add the comment to his talk. Every tourist knew about Lewis and Clark; mentioning them always helped to pique interest. He continued flipping through the book but found nothing else.

He laid the book aside and picked up *The Art of Thomas Moran*. He owned this edition and felt familiar with it. He leafed through the pages, looking at plates of the Yellowstone paintings Moran had done following the 1871 Hayden expedition.

Tripod began to make a rumbling noise in her chest. Her front leg began to quiver. Clarence smiled; the dog was chasing rabbits in her sleep.

With his index finger, he gently stroked the place between her pointed ears. The quivering slowed and then ceased. The dog resumed her peaceful nap.

Clarence looked out over the lake. A few canoes splashed through the water. Vacationers banging their paddles against the sides of their craft. The noise carried across the lake's surface. Through the trees, he saw two men walking slowly along a path tracing the lakeshore. Clarence closed the book and focused. He wished he had binoculars. Special Agent LaFleur of the DEA was meeting with William, the wheelchair-pushing bodyguard for Roger Barkley.

He moved Tripod off his lap and laid her on the bench. The dog's eyes popped open, and she immediately jumped down. Clarence gathered her up and tried to hurry inside the lodge. He knew they kept a pair of binoculars behind the desk.

Clarence took an unsteady step and paused. His leg had stiffened and refused to cooperate with his attempts to race. He limped through the front door of the lodge.

"Ranger Johnson, a pleasant surprise."

Noel Privé faced him, her unique smile on brilliant display. Leather hiking boots showed from under a pair of jeans. The boots appeared clean and untested. She had an oversized blue chambray button-down shirt and a double-breasted blazer. She wore wine-red lipstick, and her hair looked freshly styled.

He nodded approvingly. "Nice boots. They are what all the fashion models on the Rocky Mountain runways are wearing this season. And still with the cameo."

"Ranger Johnson, you say the nicest things. Would you like a coffee?"

"Do you mind drinking it outside?" He raised his hand displaying Tripod. "They prefer we don't bring dogs in here."

Privé's face took on a look of confusion for a moment. "Pity." She turned her head and made eye contact with the waiter. "Two espressos outside, *s'il vous plaît*."

He led her back to his bench. Clarence piled his books to make room for them. Tripod rested on his lap.

The waiter appeared. On his tray were two paper cups. Thin trails of steam escaped through the drinking port in the plastic lids.

Privé fixed the waiter with a hard stare. "Espresso is not served in a paper cup."

The waiter's eyes widened. "I'm sorry, ma'am." He turned and scurried back inside the hotel.

"I am not the only reader, it appears," she said. With long fingers she studied the titles in the pile. "You are a man of varied interests, Ranger Johnson."

"I'm polishing a lecture on Thomas Moran."

"He idolized J.M.W. Turner," she said.

"I'm impressed. Perhaps you should deliver the talk. Yes, he went to England to view paintings in the National Gallery. I don't know if he ever made it to France."

She nodded. "And what are your conclusions?"

Before he could answer, the waiter returned with two cups of espresso in demitasse cups.

Privé accepted the cup without looking up from the books. "*Merci.*"

"I don't break new scholarly ground. I want visitors to understand the role Moran played in establishing this area as a national park. The first explorers to the region thought of this area as full of bad spirits, hell on earth. They claimed that the Native Americans did too." He pulled the Moran book from the stack and opened it, showing the paintings. "The Hayden survey and other explorations sparked interest in the region. But a dry governmental report cannot capture the place like the images Moran painted and Jackson photographed."

He looked over and found that Privé was studying him rather than the pages.

"Your face, it gets excited when you talk about such things," she said.

"I like the idea that I've helped people get a better appreciation of Yellowstone. It's not world politics, but I like to think it has some value."

"Managing world politics is less about the grand moves. More about the small plays. Proper use of pawns with less emphasis upon the movement of the king."

Through the trees he saw LaFleur returning from the lakeside path.

"Do you agree, Ranger Johnson?"

He turned away from LaFleur. When he glanced back, the man had disappeared. "I wouldn't know, Mademoiselle Privé. I'm just a humble park ranger."

She made a small, slow shake of her head. "I hardly think that is all you are, Ranger Johnson."

"What more do you think I am?"

Privé pursed her lips and narrowed her eyes. "I find you to be an excellent jewelry salesman."

"And what will you do with your hiking boots?"

"Ranger Johnson, what would you recommend for a woman who wanted some vigorous exercise?"

"I might suggest that you be very careful hiking with new boots. Until they are broken in, you can get some serious blisters."

Privé smiled. "Ranger Johnson, please know that I am an expert when it comes to wearing new shoes."

He sipped his espresso. "From your English, I would almost guess you were born here, Ms. Privé."

"I'm really just a small-town girl from Wyalusing, Pennsylvania. I fell in love with Paris and moved there right after high school." Privé tapped the other book in the stack. "And how will you fit David into all of this Yellowstone business?"

"I just like looking at pretty things," he said, turning to face her. "This one I look at when I need a study break."

"I don't think we should just look. Let's touch," she said. Privé pulled the book from the bottom of the stack and opened it. The book fell open to *The Intervention of the Sabine Women*. "This one is in the Louvre. My husband's committee oversees part of their budget. Come to Paris, I will show you."

Johnson picked the book from her lap and flipped the pages until he came to *The Anger of Achilles*. "This one is in the Kimbell. Come to Fort Worth, I will show you."

Her eyes widened and lingered over the painting of Agamemnon arguing with Achilles. In the foreground of the painting were the characters. Behind them, through open drapery, the viewer looked out over a Greek plain with mountains in the background. Privé's index finger traced the characters. "They are fighting over the girl, aren't they?"

"How can you tell?"

"Because that's how men look when they fight over women."

Before Johnson could reply, Nance burst through the doors of the hotel. She stopped for a moment. Her eyes passed over Clarence and stopped at Privé. The two women measured one another.

"Noel Privé, I'd like to introduce Investigator Nance."

Noel's eyes appraised Nance's clothing. She frowned before she extended her hand. "You look very formidable with your badge. It draws attention to your hips. I feel I should salute."

Nance took the hand. Clarence watched her resist the urge to crush it. "You look dressed for an outing in the park."

"The rough and the wild, it's so sensuous. Don't you agree, Investigator Nance?"

Nance opened her mouth to reply, then paused. She turned her attention to Clarence. "I wonder if I might steal you away. It's rather urgent."

Clarence turned to Noel. "*C'est la vie.*" He retrieved a pine needle from the ground and marked the page in Ocone's art book. Then, he picked up Tripod.

Noel quickly gathered the collection of books and pressed them into his other hand, allowing the contact to linger for just an extra moment. "Until next time."

"I'll be in the SUV," Nance said and walked back through the hotel.

Clarence gave Privé a last look. "Thank you for the coffee." With that, he followed Nance.

She sat in the SUV with the motor running. Clarence's feet were barely off the pavement when she put the vehicle in reverse. He tumbled into the passenger seat. Books spilled onto the seat and floor.

"Look," he said. "Be mad at me for whatever reason, but don't start throwing my dog and your evidence around the inside of the truck."

Nance slowed down and entered onto the Loop Road traveling north. She remained quiet, her eyes fixed on the gaps in the traffic.

Her eyes flicked down to where Tripod rested against Clarence's hip. His left hand held her in place. "Sorry."

He looked over at her. "That wasn't so hard."

"Formidable, she called me formidable."

"That sounds like a compliment."

"That sounds like she called me fat."

"Privé is a witness. She met with Barkley. I was sitting outside, reading your evidence. Conducting a little surveillance."

"I saw your surveillance."

"She walked up and started talking to me. What was I supposed to do?" He decided not to mention Agent LaFleur's nature walk with William.

"And what did you learn?"

"Not much. I'd just gotten started when you arrived."

Nance grunted.

"She knows about Jacques-Louis David and Thomas Moran."

"Oh, she's French and she knows about art. There's a cliché. Did you learn where she keeps the beret?"

"We hadn't got to the part where I search her."

He saw her eyes snap toward the passenger seat. He kept a tight-lipped smile on his face. As soon as the words came out, he'd known it was the wrong time. But he couldn't snatch them back. After a moment, her head shot back, focusing on the road.

"I'm sorry," he said.

Nance kept her eyes focused straight ahead. He saw her knuckles whiten on the steering wheel. Slowly she relaxed her grip. She took a series of calming breaths, air in through the nose and out through pursed lips. When her self-control had returned, she looked over. Clarence watched her, this time his expression showed only concern. She shook her head. "Forget it. I overreacted. I wanted to find you. Hikers made a report. They located another body. The decedent is described as male, late teens to early twenties."

"And you think it may be François?"

She nodded, her lips tightly pressed together, devoid of color.

"Damn," Clarence said as he turned and stared out the passenger window at the passing pines and spruce.

"There's one more thing," Nance said.

"What's that?"

"The witnesses think he was tortured."

22

New Orleans, Louisiana
March 1796

When Aristede opened his eyes, chubby cherubs looked down on him. He knew he was in heaven. Aristede lay dry, warm, and comfortable. He felt freshly washed. Gentle sunlight fell upon his bed. Heaven existed as he had imagined it. Tears formed. He closed his eyes. God had been merciful. Aristede had disappointed so many people, had failed in his last earthly mission, and then committed the final sin of suicide. Yet, Saint Peter had unlocked the gates of heaven and allowed him entry. He closed his eyes and prayed. A lump formed in his throat as he attempted to comprehend such compassion.

When he swallowed, he made a sharp cry of pain. His throat felt on fire.

Aristede's eyes widened; heaven seemed as fraught with contradiction as the earthly life he had shed. His hands moved to his throat. Loose fitting bandages wrapped his neck. He probed gingerly with his fingers and felt the sharp sting of injuries just below the cloth. He pinched his eyes shut. Perhaps this was hell, he pondered. A veneer of paradise slowly being stripped away, lost hope the first of his torments.

Aristede sat up in bed. His head spun, and a wave of nausea came over him. He braced himself to remain seated. Ignoring the pain, he swallowed hard, seeking to calm his churning insides.

The sickness faded. He studied his surroundings. Aristede sat in his room in Madame Gilbert's establishment.

The drapes hung slightly parted. Overhead, the drapery cord he had used still dangled, the noose sliced away. His clothing was nowhere to be seen.

The lead tube lay beside the bed. Aristede's heart filled with joy. He swung his legs over the side of the bed. With a shaky hand he picked up the tube. He turned it over in his hand, studying it. Mud still clung to the caps on each end.

He dreaded looking inside, fearing that the returned tube may be but an additional torment to highlight his failure.

Curiosity overwhelmed him. He exhaled audibly. He must know whether the scythe remained. With trembling fingers, his hand tightened around the end cap.

The door to his room swung open. He dropped the tube onto the bed and covered it with his blanket. Marie Gilbert entered the room, her pipe clenched between her teeth. Her eyes swept over the blankets, and she snorted, a puff of smoke escaping when she did. The gaze shifted to Aristede's. Reaching over, Marie threw back the blanket. "You believe you know more about bedroom games than I?" Before he could answer, she pressed forward. "You owe me, sir, for two drapery cords and a coat. When I loaned it to you, I did not give you permission to go swimming in my outer wear."

Aristede opened his mouth. Before he could answer, Gilbert waved her hands, silencing him. The questions came in bursts of tobacco smoke. "What were you thinking?" Do you know how much these cords cost me? Imagine if Samuel and I had not been passing by your room. What if a gentleman and one of my girls had found you? Do you realize what might happen to my reputation?"

"I am sorry," Aristede attempted to say. The words came out in a painful and hoarse whisper.

"Come downstairs, we must talk," Gilbert said. "You shall have wine. That will help." Before he could stand, she stopped him with the flat of her hand. She disappeared down the hall and returned moments later with a dressing gown. "Put this on. Unless you intend to go swimming again." With a last cloud of smoke, she disappeared.

Aristede's knees wobbled as he stood. He threaded his arms into the robe and belted it around his waist. He paused to wash his face and to check his appearance in the room's small mirror. The whites of his eyes looked pink. He blinked rapidly, hoping to rinse the color away. They remained blood spotted.

Downstairs, Marie Gilbert sat in a corner of the front room. On the table before her stood a clay pitcher and a mug. She sipped red wine from a stemmed wineglass. As he approached, she poured from the pitcher.

"I've heated your wine, slightly. I felt it might be medicinal."

He nodded and took the warm cup. Raising it to his lips, he swallowed. "Thank you." His voice, although still a whisper, sounded less pained.

Marie took another sip. "Samuel and I were passing by your room. I heard a noise of suffering. He pushed the door open, and we saw you hanging there, foolish man. I held your feet and he cut the rope. Samuel reliably carries a knife. I feared for a moment that we might be too late. Your eyes bugged out of your head, and your face looked ashen. I could not hear you make a sound. Then, you sputtered a breath, and began making regular rasping noises. We got those wet clothes off you and moved you over to the bed. That is what I know. Tell me what I do not." She relit her pipe and leaned back into her chair.

Aristede looked around the room. He again studied the pictures painted on the walls. He thought about what to do, how much to say. His eyes settled on Marie Gilbert. She watched him through a veil of smoke. She seemed to read his thoughts. He decided to speak the truth. His heart told him that she would quickly see through his deception.

"I have been tasked to guard something extremely valuable," he began. "It was a responsibility given to me on behalf of France. Despite your courtesy, I felt that my small room could not safely hide my responsibility." He paused and drank more of the warmed wine before resuming. "I hid it in a place I believed secure. I moved carefully to avoid being followed. Then, upon my return, I felt an overpowering need to check upon my responsibility. When I returned to where I had hidden it..."

"The river," Marie said.

Aristede's eyes fell to the table. He made a faint nod of his head. "When I returned to the river, I found that my sacred trust had been taken. I had failed my friends and my nation. I could not explain. I did the only thing I knew to do."

"Samuel," she called.

A moment later, the man emerged from the back, wiping his hands on a small towel.

"Samuel, how difficult was it to track Monsieur Aristede?"

Samuel nodded his head. "Very simple, madame. Although he traveled with all manner of evasion, it quickly became apparent the line he intended to follow. I easily sped ahead and positioned myself so that I might watch him. He continually looked behind him as he walked. I, however, stayed in front and watched him discreetly. At the water's edge, he made a grand show of kneeling in prayer. With his head bowed, however, it was difficult for him to see whether anyone observed his actions. I simply went out after Mr. Aristede had left and untied the line. I brought the package back here as you requested. I left the drapery cord behind. I felt it had become sodden and ruined in the Mississippi."

She waved away the concern. "Monsieur Aristede has agreed to replace it for me."

Aristede bowed his head. "Now you've seen why I have gone to such efforts to protect my responsibility."

Marie Gilbert puffed on her pipe. She spoke through a cloud of smoke. "I have no idea what is inside."

Aristede raised his head, his mouth hung open in confusion. "But surely..."

"I am a businesswoman. I like to make a profit. If I looked and found a great treasure, I might be sorely tempted to take whatever valuables I discovered. Far easier to imagine that your responsibility, as you call it, is some dried-out piece of rabbit fur, some memorabilia from your childhood, a personal trinket valuable only to you. This story easily explains your passion and my lack of concern." She met Aristede's gaze. "I have a successful life in Spanish Nueva Orleans. If I learned of something valuable to the Spanish government, good business practice would require me to tell the alcalde."

Aristede nodded his head. "I understand."

"Everyone in Nueva Orleans has a story. Some people are English who found themselves on the wrong side of the American Revolution. Some owned plantations in Saint-Domingue and fled the slave rebellion. Even layabout freedmen like Samuel here have a story. Don't you, Samuel?"

"Nothing worth telling, madame."

Marie Gilbert cocked her head toward Aristede. "Would you like to hear my story, monsieur?"

Aristede bowed his head respectfully. "I would be honored to listen."

"My grandmother came to Nouvelle-Orléans as a casket girl. Do you know the phrase 'casket girl'?"

Aristede shook his head. "I do not."

"Shortly after the city was founded, the absence of women quickly became apparent. The French government assembled a group of young girls, most taken from the orphanages run by French nuns. They were handpicked by the bishop for their virtue. My grandmother, I am told, came from a rougher life and had spent time on the streets of Paris. Yet, a government official who appreciated her charms recommended that she be included in the travels. So it was that she came to America. The church and the king supplied each girl with a small traveling case, a casquette in which to carry their few belongings. Over time, the people here have mangled the word 'casquette' into 'casket.'" Gilbert paused to sip more wine and to tamp the tobacco down in her pipe. "The travel proved hard. Imagine these young girls kept below decks to protect their virtue throughout the Atlantic voyage. Many became quite ill, breathing the stale air of the ship's hold."

Aristede nodded. "I can imagine such circumstances."

"My grandmother, hardier than most with her time on the streets, cared for the sickly girls during their transit. Along the way, she learned many things. The lessons gained from the convents and orphanages that the girls gave to her. She arrived in Nouvelle-Orléans as an educated woman."

"It seems then that you come by your kindness honestly."

Marie Gilbert grunted a laugh at the phrase before she continued. "The casket girls fared poorly upon their arrival in Nouvelle-Orléans. Imagine, they came off the ship pale and sickly, coughing blood, consumption having taken hold during the voyage. The men of the city caught sight of ghostlike waifs with bloodstained teeth. All manner of stories quickly grew up about them. Some said they were cursed by the Devil. It was whispered that they would drink the blood of their victims. As a result, many were shunned or mistreated, others married poorly. The girls did not fare as they had hoped. Word returned to France. The situation became so bad that the king called many of the girls home."

Aristede waved his hand. He wanted to listen obediently, and he did not want to speak, but he felt confused. "Yet here you are."

"I said many of the girls. My grandmother, as I mentioned, had not been as delicate as some of the others. She adapted more easily. Her skills learned on the streets of Paris coupled with the social graces the other girls had taught her allowed her to quickly succeed in this town. She employed some of the other casket girls, and soon her business was thriving. Imagine how alluring the combination—the skills of a Parisian whore, the education of a convent girl, and the mystique of a young woman who arrived as a spirit of darkness, a blood-sucking ghost. The combination, I'm told, proved a powerful aphrodisiac for the local men. Her business thrived."

"And you have built upon the success?"

"My mother was born in the business, as was I. We have expanded. But this," Gilbert raised her arms to embrace the building, "this remains at our core."

Aristede nodded and raised his cup. "My compliments." His wine, he noted, had gone cool.

Marie Gilbert accepted the toast and took another sip from her glass. "Through it all, I remain intensely loyal to France. If *grand-mère* had remained in Paris, she likely would have perished, and I would never have been born. The king allowed her to travel to America despite her liabilities and offered to return her to France when he learned of the mistreatment. The monarchy was always kind to my family. And I will assist anyone who truly desires to be of service to his majesty."

"Why do you tell me all of this?"

"I make my living judging men. I read your passion for a cause. You expect to be betrayed. I thought my story might lessen your concern."

Aristede closed his eyes. He felt Marie watching him. He pressed his lips tightly together. He needed to decide. Marie said nothing, waiting.

Aristede shifted away from Gilbert. Samuel still occupied the third seat at the table.

Gilbert read the flicker of his eyes. "Samuel is loyal to me. You may speak freely."

Aristede exhaled slowly. Although anxious, he felt a weight being lifted. He had not been able to share this burden since Louis de Noaleste betrayed him. "I have a valuable thing," he began, careful not to name the object. "A thing which would be important to the next king of France when the monarchy is restored. The forces who wish that a restoration never occur desperately seek it. We have been told that in the far north of the territory here in America, there exists the Devil's Land. A land so perforated with doorways to hell that even the natives do not travel there. I have been chosen to hide this thing within the Devil's Land. There it shall remain until our country is ready for the return of the king."

Marie Gilbert's eyes looked first to Aristede and then to Samuel, gauging the reaction of both men. "That would be a long and hazardous journey."

Aristede pushed back from his chair and stood. "I am not so naïve as to believe that this trek can be accomplished on my own. I need a man." He walked to the wall and pointed to the painting of Romulus and the founding of Rome. His hand panned the picture. "My friend, Jacques-Louis David, would have much to say about the figures in this painting. He would say much about what the artist has done to Romulus." Aristede's hand came to rest over the she-wolf. "But I believe I need such a man as this. He has seen wolves. He knows what they are like. My friend David could teach him much about painting ancient Rome and the heroic human form, but he could teach him nothing about capturing the ferocity of the wolf. I need a man who understands the message of art. Such a man would understand why I need to preserve this artifact for France. But I also need a man who knows the wilderness, who can help me reach my destination. Failure will not benefit France." Returning to his seat, he leaned across the table, drawing himself as close to Marie Gilbert as he could. "Please, help me to find such a man."

Marie Gilbert stood. "Your wine has gone cold. Allow me to warm it for you." She quickly gathered up the pitcher and left the room.

After she'd gone, the two men sat at the table. They looked at each other, saying nothing. Outside, Nouvelle-Orléans could be heard at work and play.

Samuel broke the silence. "You think that the artist needs to study more before drawing the human figure?"

Aristede tapped his finger to his lips as he tried to imagine David sitting there. "I believe the master would say that Romulus has been painted too straight. The artist needs to emphasize the curves and the angles within the human form. He has made Romulus too stiff. He must also concentrate more on the hands and feet. David would complain about the difficulties in capturing accurately the hands and the feet of his subjects."

Samuel studied the table. "I met your David. I asked him once about joining his atelier. He told me that France would never accept one such as me." Samuel made a small laugh. "He also told me to take more time with my hands and feet."

Aristede's eyes widened. "Monsieur, I beg your apologies—"

Samuel cut him off before he could get any further. "He told me that the Academy required paintings to look a certain way, but they also required painters to look a certain way."

"I'm sure he meant no offense, Monsieur Samuel."

Samuel shook his head. "He was correct. They did not have a place for me in their Academy. I found my way here. I thought I could make a living with my painting. Second-rank painters in Paris are first-rank artists here. Marie Gilbert has become my patron. I hoped to see some things that would allow me to show Paris something new." He threw out his arms. "What do you think? Will I be accepted?"

Aristede paused, searching for words.

Samuel frowned. "You have said enough."

"It is hard to say what France will recognize these days. We are a nation that expresses ideals of equality and fraternity but takes the heads of those with whom we disagree. We are puzzling."

Samuel nodded. "As I feared. Thus, I will remain here until the nation will accept me."

Aristede swallowed his private thoughts about this likelihood.

Samuel again broke the silence. "Why must you take this thing so far?"

Aristede clenched his fists and squeezed. He had not spoken of such things since he had left David. He took a deep breath. "In France, they want to melt down all remnants of the king. We must hide it where agents of the government will not even think to look. The River of the Yellow Rocks, we are told, is like hell. Even the natives avoid this place."

"I doubt that the natives are as superstitious as you believe," Samuel said. Then, he shrugged. "But there are so few reports of the place. How do you know it is not a figment of the imagination? A mythical land created to keep children awake at night?"

Aristede rubbed his hands. Words had never been his friend. He struggled to express himself. "Those who know of such things believe it. I have been saved many times to come this far. My fate is not for this to end as a ghost story."

Samuel angled his head toward the painting. His eyes took on an unfocused look. He spoke slowly. "We had banked our canoe along the river. We were below St. Louis. That night, I sat by the campfire, the flame burned low. Outside the circle of light, the night wrapped around me like a blanket. I had dozed. Suddenly, I awoke. The hairs on the back of my neck tingled. I searched the darkness but saw nothing alarming. Still, the sense that something stood just outside my vision was inescapable.

"About the time I had convinced myself that I had engaged in the same sort of foolishness as those men from New Orleans who created bloodsucking monsters out of orphan girls, I saw the wolf. I looked at my companion, but he was asleep across the campfire. I did not want to turn away to rouse him. The wolf stood just at the edge of the darkness. I felt he judged me, deciding whether I would become easy prey. He stepped closer. The long, lean snout emerged from the darkness. His eyes looked green in the flickering light. The sound he made, it was unlike any dog I've ever encountered. A rumbling growl from deep within his chest. I kicked some wood into the fire, hoping to build it back. Slowly, I withdrew my knife. I raised my musket. The two of us eyed one another for an eternity. I felt those green eyes search me. I did not want to fire and waste my shot. We were like two gamblers. Then, he decided that he did not like the odds. He disappeared into the night."

"The image has stayed with you."

Samuel shrugged. "Your journey will not be for the fainthearted."

"Would you consider guiding me?"

Samuel batted away the suggestion. "There are more experienced guides to be found. I merely traveled to embellish my art."

"And it is exactly your art which leads me to beg this of you. Look, over there." Aristede pointed to the painting depicting New Orleans. "It is an idealized New Orleans you show us. A New Orleans as the Paris of the new world. You still think of Paris. Help Paris to someday reclaim itself. Help Paris to become the king's home once again."

23

Hayden Valley
June 4th

Even Clarence, an experienced homicide detective, closed his eyes and took several deep breaths when he came upon the scene at the outer edge of the Hayden Valley. François's body sat at the base of a pine tree. A rope beneath his armpits secured him to the trunk. The rope's knot had been stapled to the back side of the tree. François could neither reach the knot nor work it around to his chest. He had been unable to free himself. He had also been gagged.

Clarence doubted that freedom from the ropes would have helped François. Escape seemed unlikely. His left leg had been cut off below the knee. The limb lay beside him on the ground.

The leg had been crudely removed. Clarence assumed that the assailant had used a chainsaw. A tourniquet had been applied before the leg had been sawn from his body. Blood loss had been minimal.

François hadn't died from the amputation. He had been killed when the animals came around.

The smell of blood hung heavy in the still air. François had been a staked goat for the carnivores of the park. The arms of his shirt were shredded. He was covered in dirt and hairs. François's remaining leg lay under a pile of sticks and long grass. Chunks of flesh were missing from his face and shoulders. His abdomen had been slashed, the organs devoured.

Nance and LaFleur stood alongside him. She held her camera. "I'm hoping PPT will get here before we lose the light. She's coming with the Bear Management Staff."

"Bear Management Staff?"

"Your police department has specialized units. The park staff does as well. One of our problems is bear management. We've got plenty of bear hair around the body." Nance walked up to the body and pointed at the opposite side. "See there, just beyond his right hip? Those are bear tracks. It looks like the bear headed out this way after taking what he wanted." Using her right hand as a pointer, she gestured down the trail. Then she grabbed Johnson's sleeve and pulled him around the tree and down the trail approximately ten yards. "Here, we've got bear scat. Easily identifiable if you know what to look for."

Johnson nodded. "I see that all the time off Hemphill Avenue."

Before any of them might say any more, a Park Service pickup truck arrived. It was scratched and dented, with heavy-duty tires and cages protecting the lights and grill. From the driver's door, a weathered man emerged, tan-faced, silver-haired, in need of a haircut. His mouth hidden somewhere behind a walrus moustache. He walked slowly toward them. On his hip he wore a holstered .44 Magnum revolver. His eyes met Nance's. He made a slow nod of his head.

She introduced Clarence and LaFleur to Dan Arvin from Bear Management. As the introductions finished, PPT walked up, still fastening on her gear. Her eyes quickly went to today's assignment.

"Hell," was all she said.

Arvin exhaled a breath. His moustache fluttered. "Well, it does none of us any good to stand here staring at the poor bastard."

PPT began pulling out her equipment. She walked off by herself, doing her best to walk a wide circle over the uneven ground.

Arvin led them toward the body.

"An outfitter leading a horseback tour of Yellowstone came upon him."

Nance paused and cautioned. "We don't want to contaminate the scene until PPT has had a chance to take some pictures."

"We don't need to get too close," Arvin said. "Looks pretty obvious what happened." From his pocket, he pulled a small but powerful flashlight. He illuminated François's body, focusing on the still-attached leg. "See how the brush and dirt have been scooped up and over the lower half of the body? The bear was caching food, burying a meal for later. They like the viscera, more nutritional value." He circled the body and shined his light on a bare patch of grass and torn earth. "The bear did the digging there." Circling back, he stopped beside a tree and shined his light on the ground.

"Bear scat," Clarence said.

Arvin looked at him, a flicker of surprise in his eyes. Again, he nodded slowly. "Keep your eye peeled. The old boy isn't likely to wander far from this much food. He might be back."

Finishing the circle, Arvin shined his light on the detached leg. "A bear's diet is sixty percent vegetarian. When they eat meat, they typically go for grubs, gophers, and fish. Something as large as a human is out of the ordinary. Without the powerful scent of blood and the immobility of your victim, this likely would never happen. Whoever did this was a cruel son of a bitch."

"Limited blood loss with the amputation," Clarence said.

Arvin's fingers formed a circle. "Have you seen a bear's face? It's about one-third nose. They have the most highly developed sense of smell of any animal on the planet." He waved his index finger over the crime scene. "Cops think bloodhounds are good for tracking. A bear's sense of smell is seven times better than a bloodhound's. The scent from what we've got here could be picked up by a bear more than twenty miles away."

Despite the gruesome scene, Clarence couldn't help but marvel at the trivia he learned on this job. "What happens now?"

"On the Bear Management side of things, I'll collect some of that bear scat. We'll usually find something in there to get a DNA profile of our attacking bear. When we confirm which one did this, we'll kill it." He shook his head. "Ain't really the bear's fault, given the circumstances. He was presented with overwhelming temptation. Still, we can't have a man-eater loose in the park." Arvin kicked at the ground with his boot toe. Then, silently, he wandered over to the tree, knelt, and began collecting his samples.

LaFleur, Nance, and Clarence helped PPT unload a portable generator and some light bars. The fading sunlight filtered through the pines dappling the ground. It would be easy to miss a subtle clue, although little about this scene felt nuanced.

Clarence took a knee. Resting his elbow on his leg, he cupped his chin in his hand and studied François's body. After the initial shock passed, this became another homicide, the corpse more gruesome, but nonetheless a homicide. He found himself able to block out the sensory assault and focus on searching for illuminating details.

"Look at his arms," he said. "They're shredded. He was awake. The kid fought the best he could." From the corner of his eye, he thought he saw Nance shudder. His gaze shifted to the severed leg.

"Fucking drug dealers," LaFleur said.

Clarence and Nance both turned to look at him.

LaFleur's eyes flickered between them both. "That's who it's got to be. These guys like to send messages. You ever heard of a Colombian necktie? Pablo Escobar would slash down a victim's throat and pull the tongue out to hang there." LaFleur traced down his neck with his index finger. "These guys sit around and dream up ways to be cruel, to spook the competition." He pointed to François's body. "The guy who did this will likely get to be the featured article in next month's *Drug Lord* magazine."

Clarence grunted his reply.

LaFleur eyed him. "Does that mean you're over the man crush you've had for me?"

"Had to since you've started taking long nature walks with William." He turned to Nance. "That's Barkley's bodyguard."

"Bullshit," LaFleur said. "Never happened."

"I watched you go, practically holding hands."

"Just proves how blind you are. The case is about drug running. Only you can't see it."

Clarence looked at him. "Still jumping to conclusions, aren't you, Thor?"

LaFleur's eyes flared momentarily before he regained control. "The drugs come across the Canadian border. They get distributed from here nationally. We get our first hint that the Canadians might be following a cross-border lead, and their boy gets whacked. He gets killed in a way designed to frighten people from doing any more looking around this case. I think we got pretty good circumstantial evidence." LaFleur took a step toward Johnson. His fists were clenched, and the muscles at the corners of his jaws throbbed. "Don't disregard the facts just because you don't like the source."

Clarence took a step toward him, refusing to back down. "What about the first victim, Ocone? He was mapping art on his walls. His office had books on David and local history. I think there is another explanation."

LaFleur scowled and pointed. "Does this look like some painting to you? You've got a bullshit opinion."

"I'm not finding my opinion and then looking for the facts."

LaFleur took another step toward him. "You need your ass kicked again?"

"Boys!" Nance stepped between them. Her sharp voice brooked no argument. "We've got a job to do here, and your testosterone display won't help. Pour your energy into something useful. Our vic deserves better."

LaFleur's look said that this conversation had not finished. He turned and walked back to his vehicle. Clarence saw him stabbing at numbers on his cell phone. He hoped the call got dropped.

"Kick your ass again," Nance said.

He turned to see her studying him. Nance's eyes moved from his face to his leg. He shrugged. "We were negotiating the details on this joint federal-state task force."

"Not on my time. I've got enough to do without refereeing this nonsense. You don't have to be here, you know."

Clarence held up his hands in surrender. "I'll behave. There is no I in team."

Nance grunted. She strode to the other end of the crime scene and began searching.

Clarence returned to the SUV and rescued the quivering Tripod. He held the dog in his hand, palm under the chest, fingers behind her foreleg. Tripod may not have a bear's nose, but hers was sensitive enough to smell death in this place. Clarence leaned against the door of the Bear Management pickup. With his free hand, he rubbed the small dog down her back. Arvin came alongside. Together, the three quietly watched the encroaching nightfall. The brightly lit crime scene highlighted the darkness everywhere else.

Arvin leaned against the front of the SUV, disgust marking his face. He held the back of his hand beneath Tripod's nose. The dog sniffed him and pronounced him worthy. With his index finger, he scratched the pup beneath her lower jaw. The dog lifted her head to make the task easier. Johnson and Arvin stood there in the dark, two men scratching one dog. After a time, Arvin spoke. "The first documented case in Yellowstone Park of death by grizzly bear occurred in 1916. Frank Welch worked as a laborer here in the park, building the roads. He ended up on the wrong side of a mean bear known as 'Old Two Toes.' Seems the bear got his leg caught in a trap and tore most of his foot off in the escape. Made him angry and mean. Welch's coworkers figured that Old Two Toes deserved the death penalty. The story goes that they piled up some tasty-smelling garbage out in the open. Beneath the garbage, they had a barrel of dynamite. Midway through Old Two Toes' snack, they set off the explosives and blew him to hell." Arvin paused and pawed the ground with his toe. Then, he raised his head and looked at Johnson. "The bear has got to die, but if you can figure out who did this, I'm not opposed to feeding that bastard to the bear before we put him down."

24

Mississippi River
May 1796

The river stretched ahead of him for as far as Aristede could see. When he turned and looked behind him, the water extended backward to the horizon. It seemed almost impossible for him to remember a time when he and Samuel had not been working their way up the Mississippi or the Missouri. From the view ahead, he did not believe that he would know a time when he was not on the river.

Still, he must concede that the travels up to this point had gone well. Samuel had proven to be more adept at his frontier skills than he had modestly claimed. Aristede had listened to the lithe man and endeavored to learn quickly. He tried to make a mistake only one time.

Following his agreement, Samuel had led him to the river and studied the boats available for purchase. "Too small," he said, brushing past the pirogues lining the bank. With a critical eye, he examined a bateau. He rejected several outright and paused only briefly before several more. With each rejection, the owners cajoled him to return. With a wave of his hand, he moved on down the riverbank.

Samuel came to an old man. He had a single boat resting on the water.

A small smile crossed Samuel's face before he walked to the water's edge. Here, Samuel studied the boat carefully. He spoke to the boat builder in low tones, using the French patois Aristede had heard in the Place des Nègres. He understood only a few of the phrases. Samuel broke away from the grizzled old man and came back nodding his head.

"This is our boat, monsieur." He walked Aristede alongside, pointing out details. "Oak framed, she is stout enough to make the difficult journey. He has added the cross piece for extra strength. Look at the sides, see how he has tapered the planks so that they overlap? This helps to keep the boat waterproof." Samuel ran his hands along the hull. "Notice the planks, built with cut cypress. When we go into the bayous, look. Cypress, she grows in the water. Water and cypress understand one another." He interlocked his fingers. "They are partners. This boat is like a work of art. See how she sits with the water; she does not bob on top like she fears getting wet. She does not lumber as if waiting to be swallowed. They have an agreement, the river and this boat. I will trust my life to this boat. We must have her."

Samuel went on to point out the sturdy oarlocks and to show Aristede where they might raise a small sail on days when the wind cooperated. Aristede handed over the money and then watched as Samuel returned to the man to negotiate the price.

He returned with a smile. "He gave us a good price, especially since he knew that I would buy the boat regardless. This is an honorable man."

A good price, perhaps, but Aristede could feel that his purse was considerably lighter than it had been.

The old man helped them pull the boat from the water. Together, they turned it over. Holding the money in one hand, the old man ran his other down the length of the boat. He seemed to weigh the thirty pieces of silver he had accepted for the betrayal.

Samuel took the purse and tasked Aristede with sealing the boat to make it as watertight as possible. He left to buy the supplies for the journey. Aristede painted throughout the day. Watching the dockworkers, he stripped off his shirt and worked under the sun. He saw new arrivals pause to kneel in prayer along the docks. He remembered his experience, his hand gingerly touching his neck. Then, he returned to his work, applying a thick coat of paint. The old man hung around the edges of his work.

Aristede understood some of his commentary. He seemed of the opinion that painting was unnecessary, but if Aristede insisted, he might apply more to this spot and smooth the paint over here. The old man gestured his suggestions.

As the shadows lengthened, Aristede began to feel anxious pangs in his stomach. He had given most of his remaining money to Samuel. Aristede fought his growing concerns. The man had the opportunity to steal the scythe and had not even opened the lead pipe. Like a wave lapping the bank, Aristede's fears would surge to the forefront of his consciousness, then fall back, but never completely disappear. As he resolved to race back to Marie Gilbert's, he saw Samuel pulling a handcart loaded with supplies.

Aristede had named the boat *Marie*. Samuel nodded.

Together they pulled the cart to the building on Burgundy. "If we leave our stores on board the boat, neither will be seen again."

Before they left Nueva Orleans, Samuel had taken Aristede downriver and taught him the skills necessary to survive a journey on the great river. Aristede had assumed that his time working on board the trans-Atlantic ship would have prepared him. He had been wrong. He felt clumsy and useless. Aristede nearly capsized the small craft on several occasions. When he did successfully board, he was at the mercy of the water, unable to control the direction against the slightest challenge from the river. His arms and shoulders ached from the strain.

Aristede watched Samuel pilot the craft, his cable-like muscles barely seeming to strain as he made the boat dance across the water's surface. He proved equally adept with a musket and with the skinning knife.

Months passed as Samuel made him practice again and again the rudimentary skills of being a woodsman. Aristede chafed at the delay. Both Marie and Samuel ignored his protests.

Finally, Samuel had pronounced him fit enough. "The rest you will learn along the way..." He left his thought seemingly incomplete.

"Is there more?"

"The rest you will learn along the way, or you will die," Samuel finished the thought. "We must leave before the cold of the north renders travel impossible."

They loaded the boat with their supplies. Aristede lashed the scythe to the crosspiece. He did not want the lead pipe falling into the muddy water of the big river. That night, he slept on the boat as protection. Marie Gilbert accompanied Samuel to the riverbank at first light. She clasped Aristede's hand and wished him a *bon voyage*. Marie then watched the boat row out into the river and begin the trek. If she noticed the name, she made no comment. Aristede watched her shrinking figure until she disappeared. She did not wave farewell.

Blessed with a southerly wind, the small sail pushed them up the river without undue exertion. When the wind died down or blew from the opposite direction, they lowered the sail and took shifts pulling on the oars.

The greatest risks came from logs floating just below the surface of the murky water. They rotated shifts as the helmsman, sitting in the rear and steering with a single oar, eyes alert for hidden debris.

By the time the craft reached St. Louis, Aristede could not recognize himself. Any semblance of the hair and beard he had worn when he assisted the artists of Paris had long disappeared. His hands, calloused from long hours at the oars, were indistinguishable from those of any farm worker. Never a small man, his arms and shoulders had new muscle as well as a deep tan. In his attempt to preserve the monarchy of France, he had become more of a common laborer than he had ever been.

They resupplied in St. Louis, cramming the small craft with ammunition, black powder, and foodstuffs as well as glass beads and velvet ribbon to use as trade goods with the natives. Samuel pushed them off at first light. A few miles upriver, the boat came to the confluence where the Missouri River joined the Mississippi. Aristede rowed the bateau up the Missouri.

They soon came to St. Charles. Many of the town's residents were French, driven to the territory following the British victories in the French and Indian War. Although the Spanish governed this area, unlike Nueva Orleans, their presence in this small outpost was nonexistent. Aristede wondered whether he could speak freely among these ex-patriots. Trust had only occasionally been rewarded. The citizens of St. Charles could not leave farms or families to assist. Aristede, therefore, held his tongue about the true purpose of the journey, allowing the people to think they were fur traders off to seek their fortune.

Leaving town, he and Samuel rowed west along the snaking river. A week later, they arrived at Charrette, a community of seven French families gathered under the protection of a small Spanish outpost. They pulled ashore and talked to the people. Aristede and Samuel stood upon the boundary of the frontier. From here, they were unlikely to see another town, even one as hardscrabble as this, for the duration of their journey. They accepted the townsfolk's gifts of farm produce, milk, and eggs as the last they would see for many months. In return, they supplied the news they'd gathered along the river.

Days further upriver, Aristede thought back upon those visits as he rhythmically pulled on the oars. Had he fully appreciated the vastness and the solitude he would experience, he'd have spent more time speaking to the citizens of Charrette. At least, he thought, he'd have eaten another chicken's egg.

Usually, they ate venison. Samuel reliably killed a deer as the animals came to the river's edge to drink. Aristede would skin the animal and fry chunks of the meat. Samuel taught him to cut thin strips of meat and hang them from racks. He called the dried, chewy meat "jerky." The process preserved the meat without salt and allowed them to eat during their travels without pausing to hunt.

Some days, they varied their meals by substituting a fish Samuel caught off a line he trailed behind the bateau. Other times, the hawk-eyed Samuel piloted them to shore, and they gathered small plums or choke cherries. On land, Samuel made sure that they always secured the boat and never strayed from their weapons.

Aristede and Samuel raised the sail whenever the wind pushed them forward. If the breeze proved an obstacle, they took turns pulling on the oars. The other man often walked the bank or in the shallows towing the boat, a long rope slung over one shoulder, a rifle over the other.

Along one stretch, the river had carved steep banked sides. Over the bank, a cherry bush hung. Samuel secured the craft so that they might harvest the ripe fruit. When Aristede stood, he looked across the countryside. He saw a mix of timber and prairie. Pockets of trees dotted the landscape. Prairie grasses grew close to the water.

He pulled up a handful of the rich black earth. "A man could be a king out here."

Samuel nodded before returning to the cherry bush. "If your field did not flood in the spring or fall victim to a late freeze or a summer hailstorm. Of course, the natives might kill you."

Aristede dropped the dirt and returned to the bush. Above him, an Indian studied them. Aristede snatched up his gun. Samuel swatted the barrel away before Aristede could point it. "If he'd wanted us dead, we'd be facedown in the water."

Samuel climbed the bank. With hand signs and a few broken words, he communicated with the horseman. To Aristede's ears, he spoke in grunts and swallows. The man answered back with gestures and bits of French. Samuel nodded solemnly. He sidestepped back to the bateau. Reaching under the canvas tarp, he collected a few of their glass beads. He handed them to the native. With a single nod of his head, the man clapped his knees to the side of his horse and rode across the prairie.

"He is of the Omaha people. He said we would find apples growing farther up the river. He warned me that the apple trees stand on the other side of rapids that we will soon encounter. The Omaha have a *ton-wa-tonga*, I take that to mean a village, just beyond the apples. He invited us to stay and trade. I paid him for his troubles."

"What do you think?" Aristede asked.

"I think I'd like to get an apple fried up with my venison. A fellow needs some variety."

Aristede's mouth watered at the thought. Samuel walked upstream to survey the stretch ahead. Aristede rowed toward the fruit. Tall yellow grasses lined the banks; the river's high sides trapped the air. The space felt heavy and still. Mosquitos, their constant companions, thrived in this environment. Aristede strained on the oars to push through the cloud of flying insects.

Samuel joined him in the boat. He described the upcoming water. A sand island narrowed the channel of the river, funneling the water. They could hear the crackling sound as the stream raced across the shallows. "We are about to skin the Devil's Rattlesnake," he said. "We must both pull on the oars to propel ourselves through." He sat beside Aristede and grabbed one oar with his weather-beaten hands. "We will surely earn those apples."

Aristede shook out his arms and then grasped his oar and nodded. They rowed ahead slowly, conserving their strength. Ahead, the water spilled over the shallows, rattling the rocky bottom. It indeed sounded like a rattlesnake.

Waves hit the bow and splashed up over the sides as they moved into the first line of rapids. Their rhythm increased, the two men pulling as one. They drove the boat forward. The bow rose and fell. They felt the scrape as the *Marie* struck bottom and bounced back. More water washed over the bow.

Samuel called instructions, using an economy of words to save his breath. "My side," he called when he wished to nudge the boat starboard to avoid grounding the craft.

As they had pulled to the midpoint of the island, Aristede's oar caught on a rock just below the surface and locked in place. The wood snapped. Aristede found himself holding a useless shaft. With only one oar for propulsion, the boat began to spin. Aristede lurched to the back of the boat to grab the steering oar. His quick movements upset the balance, the boat dipped precipitously, water rushed over the side. Aristede fell back heavily onto the seat, pain stabbing him in the back. The cargo shifted, and wooden chests began to tumble out of the boat and float downstream. The Marie spun around, the bow grinding into the rocks along the shallows. Aristede heard the crack of the cypress planking. Water began seeping into the craft. Sensing disaster, Samuel rolled over the side. Putting his shoulder into the pointed stern, he drove the boat up onto the small island. Shouting instructions to Aristede, he raced down the river to capture the flotsam.

Aristede threw himself over the side as well. Ignoring his injured back, he waded to the bow. Grabbing the rope, he pulled the bateau as far up onto the island as he could. He quickly checked that the scythe remained tied to the *Marie*. Then, exhausted from the battle with the river, he dropped heavily to the sand.

Samuel returned, carrying the items he had recovered. He flopped down beside Aristede. "The snake bit us."

Aristede nodded.

After they had rested, the men surveyed the damage. As Aristede stood, he winced, his hand massaging his back. Samuel's eyes watched, but he said nothing. Instead, he detailed the work ahead. "We must empty the boat and carry everything to that point bar. We cannot stay here. The danger that upstream water washes everything away is too great. Tonight, we make camp. Tomorrow, we must find driftwood stout enough to build a new oar and to repair the broken hull. We must walk the bank and search for the items that got away. Fortune smiled, however, and we did not lose the tools."

The work began in earnest the next day. Under the oversight of the occasional curious native, Aristede went downstream searching for the remaining lost packages. He looked among the piles of driftwood for pieces that might be shaped into either planks or oars. They worked in turns, one always remaining behind to guard their drying possessions. As he walked downriver, Aristede heard a shot. Returning to camp, he found that Samuel had again killed a deer. Later, when Samuel walked upriver, he returned with six apples in a bag he'd made from his shirt. Behind him floated a stout log.

Within days, they had hewn the wood down to planks and repaired the *Marie* and fashioned a new oar as well as a replacement. They had dried enough venison and apples to allow them to push forward. On one sojourn, Samuel killed a bear. He rendered the fat down to a grease.

"It is the best cure in nature," he assured Aristede. He smeared the salve on his partner's injured back. "It also waterproofs and helps make a delicious biscuit." They traded with the Indians for corn flour before renewing their journey.

Before leaving, they surveyed the repairs.

"*Marie* looks to have a bruise," Samuel commented.

Aristede twisted, stretching his injured back. "The trip has been hard on us all."

They bade farewell to the spot they had dubbed "Fort Rattlesnake" and pushed forward with renewed vigor. Winter would soon descend, and they felt the pressing need to get further upriver before ice blocked their passage.

The mornings grew increasingly colder. Thin crusts of ice formed along the smooth shallows of the river. The river bent increasingly west as they traveled. Samuel and Aristede found themselves in the company of a friendly and peaceful tribe who called themselves Mandan. They wintered in the shadows of a large Indian encampment, building a cabin big enough for both men and the *Marie*. Aristede hid the scythe next to his bed alongside his rifle.

When Samuel was gone, Aristede would sit alone. The land could be quiet. He found himself thinking about why they traveled so far. Men could not be trusted to keep the secret. They must hide the scythe far away. The leaders had chosen the River of the Yellow Rocks, the land of the Devil. No one would venture there to find the scythe until it was ready to be found.

He could not quit. Jacques-Louis David had begun painting the first sign into *The Intervention of the Sabine Women*. The artwork would soon be on display. David and the others trusted Aristede to complete his task. He could not change the plan even when the stillness of the northern plains made him consider it.

Aristede stood. Better to work rather than think. He went outside to dig holes in the frozen ground. They were surrounding the hut with a palisade of sharpened logs. Although he and Samuel enjoyed the company of their neighbors, they remembered the hard-learned lesson of the Devil's Rattlesnake. The world could quickly change from friend to foe.

25

Canyon Campground
June 5th

Clarence felt bleary-eyed and jittery. He hadn't slept well the previous evening. Every time he closed his eyes, visions of François's torn body floated into his dreams. He'd awaken with a start. A gentle breeze blew through the trees surrounding and secluding the RV park. The tree limbs rustled, and the trunks groaned. Ordinarily, Clarence found nature sounds soothing. Last night, the creaking noises sounded like pain in the woods. He listened to the suffering and found sleep getting further away with each passing minute. Eventually, he abandoned the effort and brewed a large pot of coffee. He sat down at his small table to study his notes and to think. He stacked Ocone's books alongside him.

Clarence picked at the Strat and tried to concentrate on the case. His thoughts drifted. He lacked the third-party perspective that allowed him to seek and, usually, to find order in the jumble of clues a case presented. He had made a successful career turning the animal desires of humans into intellectual exercises, yet this time he found no threads to grasp. What, he wondered, left him unequal to the task—the foreign environment, Nance, LaFleur, his own injury? Tripod sensed his unease. The dog paced the narrow hall of the RV, her toenails making the tap-tap-tap noise on the floor. When she passed by, Clarence laid aside the guitar, reached down, and picked the dog up, placing her in his lap. Tripod quickly settled down and slept while Clarence stroked the small space between her ears. He stared at the blank page on his notepad.

He could not dismiss Nance's or LaFleur's opinions; they were both seasoned cops, yet his instincts told him that they undervalued the significance of the painting. Ocone had died studying it.

From the stack of books, Clarence withdrew the oversized book of paintings. He wanted to look back at *The Intervention of the Sabine Women*. His finger found the pine needle he used as a bookmark. Had that been only yesterday?

The book opened to *The Anger of Achilles*. As he gazed at the picture, his mind returned to the park bench, before he'd seen François's mutilated body. He wondered if he'd associate the painting and the death forever. David's painting forecast death. Agamemnon held his long scepter, the symbol of his royal authority, and denied Achilles his daughter, Iphigenia. Instead, she was to be sacrificed to the goddess Artemis so that the deity might be appeased, and the Greek fleet could sail to wage war on Troy. Achilles' anger flared at the news. As he reached for his sword, he was stayed by the authority of the kingly Agamemnon.

Clarence flipped the pages to the picture Ocone had in his room. He studied the Sabine women. He focused his attention on Hersilia's heroic efforts to keep her beloved kings, father and husband, alive. She entreated Romulus not to throw his spear. Then, Clarence flipped back to the Achilles painting. Agamemnon stood holding his scepter, the shaft extending beyond the limits of the painting. Outside Agamemnon's walls, the dark gray storm clouds gathered over the mountains. He paused and remembered Noel Privé running her finger over the painting. He had the sunshine, his books, and an attractive audience to discuss them. Yesterday had been a nice day suddenly shot to hell.

He began jotting random notes down on his pad. Faint memories from art history lectures niggled at his memory. He flipped between the pages, the staffs, the kings, the mountains. He cautioned himself not to fall in love with a theory and then to subordinate facts to fit. Still,

Clarence could not deny that he saw similarities he had not previously noticed.

When he had filled a page with random notes, he returned Tripod to her bed. The dog's eyes opened briefly at the inconvenience before returning to sleep. Clarence poured the cold remains of his coffee cup down the drain. He needed no further stimulation. What he needed was the internet. He tried his phone without success. Clarence climbed into his Suburban and drove to Canyon Station. He locked the door behind him. The station would not open for hours, and he did not want to be disturbed.

He typed words into search engines and scribbled down more notes. Clarence raked through his ideas. Some showed promise while others revealed themselves as little more than the misfires of a sleep-deprived and over-caffeinated mind. When he felt like he had organized his thoughts, he called Nance.

She answered on the first ring.

"Light sleeper," he said.

"The case. I'll sleep later. Everyone wants an update. I got a call from the office of Wyoming's congressional rep." Nance exhaled. "They all say they're calling to help..."

"But they want to know what's taking so long. When can they hold a press conference and announce victory?"

"Something like that." Nance paused. "I found Ocone's passport in the documents from his landlady. He'd visited France last year."

He nodded on his end of the phone. "Meet me at Lake Yellowstone for a cup of coffee."

"The restaurant is not open yet."

"I'll bring the coffee. I need your help."

"What do you want?"

"I want to go to the hotel. I need you to find out which room Noel Privé has."

Nance's voice hardened. "I'm a cop, not a dating service. Goodbye, Johnson."

"Just meet me. I'll explain. I need to talk to her. And I need you to be there."

He heard a long, slow exhale of breath. "You'd better have damn good coffee."

"The best. And bring a laptop with some crime scene pictures."

Nance exhaled again. "Anything else?"

Clarence drove back to the trailer. Tripod looked up expectantly. He set out the dog's food bowl and from the cabinet over the refrigerator, he retrieved his French press. Clarence ground the last of his Kona coffee beans. He'd been saving them for a special occasion. Bribing a fellow cop seemed special enough.

They had agreed to meet at the ranger station. Hints of morning light showed as a faint lessening of the darkness. Tourists, anxious to be the first visitors to somewhere, carried sleepy children down to cars. He watched taillights leaving the parking lot. After a few minutes, a single set of headlights arrived.

He carried his bag of supplies, and Nance unlocked the door. Spreading his tools across one of the desks, Clarence set to work measuring grounds into the bottom of the press. "Anything new?" he asked while he worked.

"PPT checked François's quarters. Found a laptop. It looks to have sophisticated security protection. ISB tech agents are based out of Lake Mead. I'm shipping it to the cyber guys."

"Government security?"

Alison shrugged.

Clarence added water, heated in the microwave. He warmed two mugs while he allowed the brew to steep.

"PPT found a note by the trash. Here's a copy."

"These mugs are best for good coffee. The bowl shape acts like a brandy snifter. The aroma concentrates in the slight narrowing of the opening. People fail to appreciate how much of flavor comes through smell." He filled the cups two-thirds full and passed one to her. She traded the copy for the mug. Nance held her nose over the mug's rim and breathed in the aroma. He eyed her expectantly.

"Smells like coffee."

His chin dropped slightly. "A philistine."

Nance nodded in agreement. "But a philistine who has waited long enough. What am I doing out at this hour of the morning?"

Clarence didn't answer. Head bent, he read the note recovered from François's room.

Roger Barkley
—more money than God
Car wreck and spinal cord injury—needs a miracle
Likes to project FDR persona—indomitable will
Repeated violations—EPA, FLSA, ICE at his businesses
"Rules are for the other guys"
Wants to be a fucking Knight!!!
Secret meetings with NP—sex??? Lucky fucker
Maybe I need to get a wheelchair

He looked up. "You've got to tell me Privé's room number. And email me a couple of crime scene pictures. I want to rattle her cage a little."

She pointed at the note.

Clarence shook his head. "Not much here. Ramblings of a horny waiter."

"After you rattle her cage?"

"Then you follow where she leads."

Nance sipped her coffee. "And where is she going?"

"I won't know till she leaves. But I think I can panic her. Once I'm gone, she will lead you to the next link in the chain."

"You sound pretty confident."

"I'm going to do some fast talking and hurl some allegations her way. Why abandon a strategy that worked so well on the chair of the history department?"

Nance studied the last drops puddled in the bottom of her coffee cup. "And what silver bullets do you plan to fire?"

Clarence walked around to the opposite side of the desk, closing the distance between himself and Nance. "You won't like any of it."

He was right, she didn't. But the helpless feeling of seeing François's torn body haunted them both. He could see that Nance recognized the need to do something.

. . .

Clarence knocked on Noel Privé's door. Under his arm, he carried the laptop. If he had surprised her with his sudden appearance, she didn't show it. She wore a red satin dressing gown knotted at the waist. He had to admit she looked remarkably put together for the hour.

Clarence took her proffered hand and shook it. Her skin felt warm. She ushered him into her suite. He glanced toward the bedroom and found the door closed. The drapes on the windows were drawn back. She had a sweeping view of Lake Yellowstone, the full blue sky a shade lighter than the calm water. She padded to the telephone. With an upraised finger, she stayed any comments. Privé placed an order with room service for two coffees. She took the chair across from Clarence and eyed him. "Had I known you were coming, I'd have had the service prepared," she said, her voice judging and finding fault. "To what do I owe this unexpected and early arrival? Have you come to help me choose jewelry?"

"I hoped to continue our conversation from yesterday."

"You have more pictures you wish to show?"

"In a manner of speaking." He opened the laptop and spun the computer around to face her. He hadn't intended to lead with the pictures of François, but he felt the need to disorient her. His early arrival had not succeeded. "You might recognize the body as one of the waiters from the restaurant downstairs."

He didn't look at the screen. Clarence kept his eyes on Privé. It took a moment for her to realize what she saw. Then, her eyes widened, the color drained from her face.

Clarence pressed. "We believe he worked for the Canadian government. That's what got him murdered."

Privé's hand moved slowly up to cover her mouth. Her eyes flickered back and forth between Clarence's face and the picture displayed on the computer.

"I've spent most of the night on the computer. I've learned some things. When we looked at the paintings, you focused on Agamemnon holding his scepter."

She pulled her hand from her mouth and fluttered her fingers, careful to shield her eyes from the computer screen. "The painting was David. It is art."

He tapped the computer screen with his index finger, compelling her eyes back to the photograph. "Do you see that? Someone amputated the boy's leg with a chainsaw." He emphasized the word "boy" and then paused, allowing the image to hang. Privé looked quickly and then averted her eyes. "Do an internet search with the terms 'scepter' and 'amputated leg.' You get a hit. But I think you already knew that."

Privé slapped the lid of the computer closed. "Take it away. Why the fuck did you show me this?"

"Language. Your American is showing." Johnson didn't raise the lid. He didn't have to. The image would remain. "Do you know what the search shows?"

"*Quoi?*" Privé's voice sounded thin.

"Saint Eligius, the patron saint of veterinarians. Legend has it, he needed to shoe a demon-possessed horse. He cut the leg off, nailed on the horseshoe, and then miraculously reattached the leg." He paused. "That's the difference between saints and men. This piece of shit left François's leg lying beside him so that the blood would attract bears."

A soft knock at the door interrupted him. Privé sat frozen in her chair. Clarence walked to the door. He accepted a carafe from a waiter. He turned back to Privé. "Coffee?"

Instead, Privé poured a whiskey and tossed it down. She stood behind her chair, her knuckles whitening as she dug her fingers into the uphol-stery. "Why show me this, you bastard."

"Eligius is also the patron saint of goldsmiths. He created the Scepter of Dagobert, the oldest of the French crown jewels."

Her mask remained inscrutable.

Clarence poured himself a cup of coffee. "This rarest of relics has been lost since the French Revolution. Sounds like the stuff French children read books about in school." He tasted the coffee, paused, and then shrugged in judgment. "But you wouldn't necessarily know, would you? You told me yourself that you're just a small-town girl from Wyalusing, Pennsylvania, who grew up and moved to the big city."

He waited. Privé said nothing. He sipped some more coffee. "I can make you a better cup. By the way, I also searched Wyalusing. I learned that the area used to be called Azilum. Royalists escaping the French Revolution built the settlement. They had a cabin ready for Marie Antoinette. She never made it."

"Monsieur Johnson, you are a wonderful storyteller. Although I fear you spend too much time on your computer with so much beautiful nature all around you. You are like a teenager."

Although her voice had regained its normal timbre, he saw tension in the muscles of her jaw. Privé struggled to keep herself under control.

"I still love to get outside," he said. "Some of the things you find in the woods are truly amazing. Of course, I haven't pissed off anyone who'll feed me to the bears. That picture of François, well, you just can't unsee it."

"I have every confidence that you and your formidable Investigator Nance will quickly bring such a man to justice." Privé stepped toward the door.

"I don't recall saying that the killer was necessarily a man."

Privé's step paused momentarily.

"Help me out here, Noel. Help me stop this before it gets any worse."

She opened the door. "If you'll excuse me, I have a busy day ahead."

"Please, Noel."

Privé closed the door behind him. Clarence rode down to the lobby and walked outside to the lake's edge. He turned back, facing the lodge, and gave a single wave to Privé, who stood in the window. She did not wave back. He strode off down the lakeside path.

26

Missouri River
April 1797

Aristede paced the cabin like a high-strung cat. The winter had passed. Dawn arrived earlier. Mornings showed thin layers of ice, like fine glass still formed during the night cold, but the river channel ran free. Aristede felt the stirring to press forward.

Samuel urged caution. Ice and snow remained at the higher elevations. Spring runoff would make the most peaceful stream wild and unpassable. The delay, Samuel assured him, would save time during the ensuing trip. "Never forget the Rattlesnake, my friend."

They had done all they could to prepare. Aristede had sealed the *Marie* using pine pitch and bear grease. Throughout the winter, they had sewn moccasins, sharpened tools, and mended ropes. The months together had joined them; the two men rarely needed words to communicate. They had dried enough food to fill every spare space of the bateau. Each day, Aristede found it harder to resist the pull of the open water. He stood outside gazing westward, seeking some sign that the way ahead was accessible.

One evening in early April, the two men sat together quietly finishing their meal. Aristede had spitted a rabbit. Samuel leaned back from the eating board they balanced upon their legs. He held his cup of pine needle tea between his hands. "I believe we should pack tomorrow and plan to leave the following morning." He paused to take a sip. "That is, if you have no objection to continuing."

Although Aristede's heart leapt at the prospect, he did his best to match Samuel's matter-of-fact tone. He took a sip of his own beverage. "I could be persuaded to depart. You would not find it inconvenient?"

Samuel gave a quick shake of his head. "The Mandan have been most hospitable, but we should not overstay our welcome."

Aristede broke into a broad smile. "Then we are agreed."

The next day became a blur of activity. They carried the boat back to the water, carefully checking the *Marie* one last time for any defects. Samuel and Aristede loaded their gear and secured it beneath the mended tarp. They filled the crevices with dried food as well as the spare moccasins and clothing. Once all was in readiness, they walked to the Mandan camp. They thanked the chief for his hospitality and doled out gifts.

They alternated guard duty to protect their cargo. When Aristede saw the first glimmer of eastern light, he hurried to rouse his companion. Opening the door to the hut, he found Samuel awake and dressed. Aristede smiled to himself; the man was as eager to get underway as he. They shook hands at the palisade gate.

"Bon voyage, monsieur," Aristede said.

Samuel pushed the boat free from the bank, and then the lithe man leapt onto the craft, carefully keeping his foot out of the frigid water.

Mandans followed, watching the boat make its way upriver. Around them, light gradually illuminated the sandhills, changing the land's color from rose to amber.

Throughout the winter, they spent much time with the Mandan. Both Samuel and Aristede had gained a better understanding of the native language and as a result had been able to interview the elders. On a piece of buffalo hide they mapped what they learned. Over late-night fires, the Indians pointed and gestured, enhancing the map until the travelers felt they had an accurate guide to the river ahead.

Along the banks of the river, small spring flowers bloomed. Dots of yellow, red, and blue spackled their way. Prong-horned antelope bounded across the prairie, while the deer remained more discreet, sticking to the shadows of the woodlands. Looking at the early colors of spring, Aristede found his thoughts drifting back to Nueva Orleans and to Marie Gilbert.

Each night, they made camp. During the day, Samuel killed an animal for their dinner. The local antelope, Aristede noted, had a sage-infused flavor, likely a result of the grasses they ate. He preferred it to the venison. Perhaps, he thought, after the winter months in the small hut, he suffered from deer fatigue. Aristede laughed to himself. For months, he had eaten a steady diet of venison and prairie tubers from a shared board resting on his lap, while he worked to restore the *grand couvert*, the elaborate meal the French king and queen ate in a banquet hall before courtiers and family.

At night, they kept the carcass of Samuel's antelope far outside the camp, bringing in only what they could eat. They banked the fire. Beyond the light, wolves scavenged the antelope's remains. The beasts circled their encampment, staying just outside the light. Aristede heard their low, throaty growls and remembered Samuel's painting. He would always throw another log onto the fire, building it up before snuggling to sleep with his musket.

Aristede and Samuel passed the mouth of the river known as the Roche Jaune. They knew that following this path would lead them to the land of brimstone, the Devil's Land, where Aristede intended to hide the treasure. They resisted the allure of the river. The information gleaned from the Mandan taught them that continuing along the Missouri would be the better path.

He pointed ahead. "We must take the scythe—" Aristede caught himself. The time for trickery with this man had long passed. "We must take the scepter that way."

Samuel nodded and dipped his paddle back into the water.

They pushed toward the mountains. Standing on the high banks of the river, the two men glimpsed the lines of peaks arranged before them to the south and west, each range higher than the one in front. The sight brought joy and despair. Aristede knew that he could not reach the Devil's Land without passing through the mountains, yet the enormity of the task became clearer with each westward mile.

Nearing midday on one of the countless days upon the river, Samuel made a long pull on the oars, then looked to Aristede. "And how shall we have our next meal? Would you prefer to eat your antelope jerked, or shall I bring the boat to the bank and seek to find fresh meat?"

Aristede, who had been studying the river ahead intently, raised his hand to quiet him. "Listen."

Samuel ceased paddling. He angled his head and turned an ear upriver.

Aristede saw that his friend, too, could hear the faint rumbling of falling water. He smiled. "I think we should forego the meal until we can eat by the falls."

Samuel put his back into the oars and rowed with renewed vigor. Ahead, the spray rose like the plume of smoke that guided Moses to the Promised Land.

They pulled ashore. Separately, they scouted the land ahead. That night, over the evening meal, they compared what they had learned. Samuel frowned. "We have only one choice. We must abandon the *Marie*. You and I could not portage the bateau over these mountains and beyond the great falls. We must conceal her here and carry only the supplies we will need to complete this journey." He pointed to the difficult way ahead. "Once we are beyond the falls, we will make dugout canoes and paddle onward."

"No!" Aristede dismissed the idea out of hand. He stomped heavily away from the fire and down to the riverbank. He stood there in the cold night air, staring across the water. Only after he had stood alone, listening to the sounds of the falls ahead, did he slowly make his way back to the fire.

When Samuel spoke, his voice held no hint of victory. "To know the truth and to admit the truth are very different things."

Aristede pressed his lips tightly together and nodded. He must leave the *Marie* behind.

In the morning, they began unloading the boat. They separated their provisions into supplies they would need for the journey ahead and those they would stockpile for the return trip. They gathered the tools to hew new canoes, gunpowder, ammunition, and trade goods for the natives. They stowed the remainder aboard the Marie and did their best to conceal her. Then, they began the climb upriver, the crashing sounds of the falls never far away. Aristede fashioned a rope sling and tied it to each end of the tube. He carried the scepter strapped to his back, leaving his hands free for portaging supplies.

It took four trips to transport the necessary materials beyond the falls. They climbed the route they'd chosen again and again, depositing their stores in a small outcropping of rocks, concealing the ever-growing pile as best they could. As the two men returned with the final load, Aristede saw a deerskin-clad leg sticking out from the rocks. A blanket lay spread upon the ground with their provisions heaped on top. Aristede dropped the bundle he carried and sprinted to the scavenging native. The man turned at the sound of heavy footfalls and attempted to run. The native's steps were slow and clumsy. Aristede tackled him. They rolled on the ground. Pinning the man beneath him, Aristede raised a heavy rock and drew back his arm. The native shielded his head against the blow.

Samuel grabbed his arm.

Aristede turned on him. "The man is a thief."

Samuel shook his head. "He gathers. The items were here to be collected, like acorns."

"He steals our belongings."

"The natives see things differently."

"They were here in the woods to be gathered," the Indian said in French.

Aristede and Samuel stopped and looked at him.

"May I sit up?"

Aristede looked first to Samuel, who nodded agreement. He released the man, keeping the rock poised and ready.

The man slowly eased himself to a seated position. He had a strong face with a sharp jawline, a hawk nose, and pointed chin. His eyes darted between the two men, missing nothing. "I will not run. I am called 'Foot-Like-Wolf' of the Shoshone people."

A small smile appeared beneath Samuel's bearded face. "You know that my friend here wants to kill you?"

Foot-Like-Wolf's eyes quickly moved to Aristede. "Yes."

"I would prefer that you lead us to your village."

Foot-Like-Wolf's eyes lit up. "I can do that."

"Then let us go." Samuel stood.

Foot-Like-Wolf struggled to his feet, warily watching Aristede, concern plainly marking his face.

Aristede looked over the boxes. "Can we trust our supplies will remain untouched?"

"Many of my people are on the hunt. Few travel this far from the village," Foot-Like-Wolf said.

Aristede slung his musket over one shoulder and the pipe over the other. "I will shoot you if you run."

"Do not worry, I will not run." As Foot-Like-Wolf spoke, he took a heavy step forward. Aristede saw that although the man's chest and arms looked fit and strong, his left leg was locked stiff. The impairment rendered him incapable of flight. He swung it forward and balanced awkwardly upon it while stepping naturally with his right leg.

"I am called Foot-Like-Wolf because I was born with four toes, like the wolf. My foot is round. I cannot run. The hunting parties do not take me. I scavenge for the tribe. I am like the dog. I learn to speak to the trappers who walk these woods. I learn the language good. None speak the French better. That is why the tribe keeps me. Why do you wish to see the elders?"

"We would like to arrange a guide into the Devil's Land."

The native's eyes showed no recognition.

"The land along the Roche Jaune, the land that rumbles and smells of brimstone."

Foot-Like-Wolf shook his head vigorously. "The spirits are angry in that place. But I'm told that the hunting is good. My people will not betray that land."

Aristede's face fell.

"My people will not take you there, but I will." Foot-Like-Wolf stretched his arms. "I walk far and wide to gather for the tribe. I know the way to the Land of Angry Spirits. I will guide you. I will trade you guide for many things."

Samuel nodded his head. Aristede pushed himself between them. "How can we trust this man?"

"Monsieur, the negotiation with the tribe would all be done through me, unless either of you speak Shoshone." Aristede recognized the voice of a man who survived by his wits. "If you cannot trust me to guide, how can you trust me to negotiate on your behalf?"

"We have a map."

"Let me see this map," Foot-Like-Wolf said.

Samuel unrolled the buffalo skin on the ground. The Indian barely glanced at it. "Those who drew this are not Shoshone." He gestured toward the flowing water. "The river soon splits into three parts. Without a guide you will be left to search until the snow falls and the game becomes scarce."

Aristede could not argue. "I will sit in the back of the canoe. If you betray us, I will shoot you."

Foot-Like-Wolf smiled. "If you have canoes, we will travel much faster." He waggled his fingers before them. "I am not Hands-Like-Wolf."

Aristede and Samuel exchanged looks, the decision silently made. Samuel turned back to the rocks. "We have not dug the canoes out yet. But with three to labor, they will go much more quickly."

The ringing of the axe and the adze echoed through the woods as the three men transformed two tree trunks into dugout canoes. When they had prepared their boats, they repacked the supplies into the crafts. Samuel piloted one while Aristede and Foot-Like-Wolf occupied the other.

The journey upriver renewed in earnest. Aristede knew that Samuel keenly felt the delay while they had dug out the canoes. He paddled, anxious to make up the time. Aristede's strokes lacked the ease of the more experienced Foot-Like-Wolf. Instead, he channeled his anger at abandoning the *Marie* into his efforts. Paddling on flat water, with growing confidence that their Shoshone guide would not lead them astray, they navigated through the waters quickly, feeling their destination within reach.

They pushed the canoes past high mountains that fell directly to the water's edge. Rocky gray cliffs and Ponderosa pine trees surrounded them. They strained against the current, sometimes paddling and at other times walking ahead dragging towlines. They struggled forward until they found themselves at the site where three waterways converged.

Foot-Like-Wolf held up his hand signaling for them to stop. Both canoes paddled to the bank. They sat in the soft grass lining the river and rested.

Foot-Like-Wolf raised his hand, pinching his thumb and index finger together and splaying his other three fingers apart. He pointed in the direction of each of the tributaries before him. "From these three mothers, the great river is born."

Samuel and Aristede studied the headwaters of the river they had so long struggled to master. Aristede looked at him. "And which one do we follow?"

Foot-Like-Wolf shrugged. "Who knows?"

Aristede's eyes flared with anger. Foot-Like-Wolf laughed. "A good joke, no?" He pointed decisively to the southeastern tributary. "This one. We call it *Cut-tuh-o-gwa*."

Samuel reached over and patted Aristede's shoulder. "*Cut-tuh-o-gwa*, what does that mean?"

Foot-Like-Wolf looked skyward and thought. "Swift water."

Samuel exhaled as if he'd been punched in the stomach.

Aristede pulled himself to his feet. Although his frown was hidden behind a thick mask of untrimmed beard, his chin drooped, displaying his disappointment. "Then let us get started."

They pushed back into the water and followed the *Cut-tuh-o-gwa* upriver. The river ran slow and smooth, the valley wide, lined with cottonwoods. The men made good progress, and their sense of enthusiasm for the trip returned.

For the next several days, they paddled easily. Their chief obstacles were the flies and mosquitos that fed along the still river.

Over the campfire, Samuel looked at Foot-Like-Wolf. "Swift water, your people call it. Shows that the natives have a sense of humor."

Foot-Like-Wolf shrugged. "At least you can laugh. Your friend here rarely even smiles."

They both looked to Aristede, who leaned over the fire, stirring the venison stew he had prepared. A rich aroma rose from the pot, enhanced by the tubers and herbs Foot-Like-Wolf had helped them collect.

Aristede glanced up. His eyes roamed both men, hardening when he looked upon Foot-Like-Wolf. "I'll smile when our job is done." He adjusted the lead pipe that lay across his back. He had taken to wearing the sling day and night.

The next day, the wide valley floor began to narrow. The mountains drew closer to the river. Here, the river made its way through a series of tight canyons. Snowmelt from the higher elevations kept the water level high. The water ran faster, sluicing through the riverine boulders.

The canoes pulled alongside.

"*Cut-tuh-o-gwa*," Samuel said.

Aristede nodded. "Swift water."

Samuel exhaled. "We must portage."

Aristede glanced down at Foot-Like-Wolf's foot. He pointed at a spot beyond the first boulder. "See the eddy. The water calms behind that outcropping. Let us put ashore there." Before the others could argue, he dug deeply into the water and pushed the canoe forward.

They battled the falling water. Although they had paddled for countless days and the muscles of his back and shoulders had grown thick and strong, Aristede felt the strain as he attempted to move the craft upstream. They slid past the first boulder and aimed to thread between two others. The white water splashed off the rocks, drenching them. Aristede struggled to shake the water from his face and to keep his vision on the destination, drawing incrementally closer.

As they passed a large rock, the water boiled up, lifting and twisting the canoe. Aristede felt himself flung into the air. He splashed into the icy water. The driving stream spun him, the lead pipe strapped to his back dragging him down. He flailed wildly, attempting to reach the surface. The twisting and turning left him unable to discern up from down. He hit a boulder hard with his back, driving any remaining air from his lungs. Then, his head struck another rock. The world disappeared.

.   .   .

He opened his eyes to thick, cloudy smoke. Darkness lay all around him. This time, no angels looked down. Surely, if he was dead, then this was hell. He took a breath and felt a sharp pain at his side. Aristede knew that he was alive, that this was not eternal torment but rather the pain of a broken rib. He tried to sit up but felt himself spinning. He surrendered back to the ground.

A circle of light fell into the dark space. He recognized Samuel's voice. "You aren't dead, after all."

"And you are not an angel, unless the cathedral's images are wrong, and angels hide their wings behind beards."

Samuel grunted a laugh. "I am not your angel. Foot-Like-Wolf pulled you from your watery grave."

Aristede's eyes widened. Ignoring the pain, he sat up and began padding the ground around him.

"Is this what you seek?" Samuel held up the lead pipe.

"Thanks be to God." Aristede hugged the scepter's case to his bare chest. He unscrewed the cap and looked inside.

Samuel nodded. "It is safe. Foot-Like-Wolf rescued it from the water."

"And my clothes?"

"Ruined in your wrestling match with the rocks. We have repaired them as best we could."

"Where am I?" Through the campfire smoke, Aristede's eyes roamed the structure of sticks and rushes.

"Foot-Like-Wolf knew of this abandoned wickiup. He carried you here while I gathered our supplies. The man walks slow, but he is strong like the ox."

Foot-Like-Wolf crawled through the opening of the wickiup.

Before he could settle, Aristede spoke. "Were you able to find the small black box?"

The native nodded. "It remains protected by the chest in which you packed it."

"Will you bring it to me?"

Foot-Like-Wolf nodded and disappeared outside. He returned with the black case under his arm. Aristede took it.

He rested his weight on an elbow. Aristede spoke in short bursts, ignoring the pain in his ribs. "You have been kinder to me than I have deserved." He opened the black case. "The man who sent me on this quest, gave me this." He removed from the box the medal, the gold eight-pointed star hanging from a red satin ribbon. "Please accept my apologies and my gratitude. I should like to declare that you are a full-fledged brother of the king's expedition."

Foot-Like-Wolf's eyes widened. He bowed his head so that Aristede could place the medal around his neck. The Shoshone straightened up, his fingers lightly touching the gold medallion. His shining eyes flickered between the medal and the two smiling men.

His face broke into a broad grin. "Merci, monsieur. I have always been the dog. Today, I am a warrior."

27

Lake Yellowstone Hotel
June 5th

Clarence continued down the lakeside path until the bends of the trail left him out of sight of the hotel. He knew he had not been followed. He worked his way through the undergrowth back toward the hotel. He was glad he walked the lake path first to loosen up his leg, as the fallen limbs and brambles made this trek difficult.

Clarence came to the edge of the tree line. The Park Service kept the area around the lodge open for clear viewing. He hoped that Noel had left her window perch. With the next step, he would be exposed. He hesitated.

In that moment, he saw LaFleur studying the front of the lodge.

He pressed himself against a lodgepole pine and watched the DEA agent. Nance, he decided, must have called him in to help with surveillance. Made sense, he thought. Still, he did not reveal himself to LaFleur. Clarence tried to watch both Noel Privé's window and Agent LaFleur.

A flutter of the drapes drew Clarence's attention to the window. Had he seen movement, he wondered. He could not tell for sure. When he looked back to LaFleur's location, the agent had disappeared. Johnson studied the empty space and waited for the man to return. Nothing happened. Clarence hurried to the lodge.

As he entered, he cursed to himself. He had never learned where the security office was located. He stepped over to the front desk. Ahead of him in line, a mother held her young daughter. The woman asked about workmen outside the lodge interfering with nap time. Assured that no maintenance work was being done to the walls of the building, the mother left. Robert worked the front desk. He gave Clarence directions.

He entered the small office. A hotel security guard in a blazer sat before a bank of monitors. Behind him, Nance stood. The expression on her face made him wish that he had gotten directions to the bar. "What took you so damn long?"

"Trying to be covert. Didn't want to return too quickly. What did I miss?" Clarence studied the monitor covering Privé's hallway.

"Nothing. She hasn't moved. You didn't do a thing."

"I rattled her."

"Clearly you don't know much about women."

Clarence understood Nance's frustration. With the body count rising, they had pinned their hopes on this gamble. He had spent many long hours sitting on a suspect, waiting for something to happen. He knew how to manage his emotions.

"She's moving," the security guard said.

All eyes saw the figure stride down the hall. There could be no mistake. Privé walked straight into the camera, head held high, elegant attire swaying as she walked.

"No missing that," the security guard said.

"She is giving us her catwalk strut," Nance said.

Clarence studied the walk. Privé had slightly lengthened her stride, placing one foot directly in front of the other as if she were walking on a line. The foot placement caused her hips naturally to sway with each step. "You know about modeling."

Nance made no response. She kept her eyes focused on the monitor.

They watched Privé pause at the end of the hall, standing calmly awaiting the elevator. The guard adjusted the monitor and captured her walking toward the restaurant.

Hotel management had placed the camera for the restaurant on the ceiling. It provided a panoramic view of the dining area. The resolution did not allow security to focus tightly on any particular table.

Neither of them needed high resolution to follow the action. Privé sat alone near the windows. She ordered breakfast and read a book. Occasionally, she lifted her head to peer out the window. Privé seemed content to spend the morning in solitude.

"Any other ideas?" Nance asked, frowning.

Before he could answer, her cell phone buzzed. Nance glanced at the number and answered. She listened quietly. The frown deepened. Clarence found himself leaning closer, hoping to catch a word. "I'm in the hotel already. I'll be right there," she said.

She looked at him. "Housekeeping found a body in one of the guest rooms. The room is registered to Roger Barkley."

28

Cut-tuh-o-gwa River
August 1797

They walked slowly, cutting a narrow path between the raging Cut-tuh-o-gwa and the steep canyon walls. Foot-Like-Wolf assured them that the boulder-strewn rapids did not last long. They would soon find themselves back in tranquil waters. Trusting their partner, they portaged the dugout canoes rather than abandoning them to make new ones on the other side of the rapids.

Foot-Like-Wolf and Samuel carried first one canoe and then the other. The distances magnified when the path needed to be covered multiple times. Aristede, loaded with as much baggage as he could carry and supporting himself with a walking stick, did his best not to slow the traveling party. They trudged forward, saying little. The sounds of rushing water echoed off the canyon walls.

After three days of slow travel, Foot-Like-Wolf studied the landscape and announced that they had passed the most difficult stretch of river. The churning water, however, still proved too rough to resume paddling. The level ground widened, permitting them to fashion rollers for the canoes. Although this lessened the strain on the men, each night still found all three collapsing to the ground, exhausted from the day's labors. At the break of each new day, they struggled forward. Tributaries branched off from the Cut-tuh-o-gwa. It seemed impossible to tell which stream represented the main channel. Foot-Like-Wolf, however, remained ever confident, and with sharp gestures, he blazed their trail. Aristede privately reserved any doubts, particularly when Foot-Like-Wolf chose a path seemingly away from their destination. They had cast their lot with him.

Increasingly, however, Aristede began to worry that their native guide had lost his bearings. The Shoshone's scouting forays took longer each day. Although Foot-Like-Wolf's confidence remained undimmed, Aristede could not shake his growing concern that the stoic demeanor masked the native's fears.

At noon break after a difficult morning climb, Aristede's concerns bubbled to the surface. "This land we seek, is it not the home of bad spirits, the place to be avoided?"

Foot-Like-Wolf nodded. "White hunters say it is so." He chewed slowly on the small noonday meal Aristede had prepared. The fatigue brought about by the increased workload made it difficult to hunt for game.

"If it is a place your people do not travel, then can you really be sure that you know where it is?"

Foot-Like-Wolf looked at him. "You think I have led you without purpose?"

"We cross many streams, some thick and wide, others meager. You choose, we follow. From the three forks where the great river began, the land we seek lay to the east, toward the morning sun. Yet, the streams seem to lead us south and on occasion west. The snow will return before we can retrace our steps if you have chosen incorrectly."

Foot-Like-Wolf set down his food, stood, and wordlessly walked away. He disappeared through the lodgepole pines and spruce trees surrounding them. Aristede looked at Samuel, who could only shrug. Samuel sat back, leaning against a rock, and waited.

The two men spent the afternoon sitting and waiting. Samuel disappeared briefly. Aristede heard a shot. Samuel returned, carrying a rabbit. Both exhausted men appreciated the rest, yet both felt the need to push forward. They had traveled so long, the idleness felt like imprisonment.

Later, Samuel shot another rabbit. Aristede cleaned and prepared them. The work dulled the growing sense of unease. Aristede wondered whether Foot-Like-Wolf had abandoned them in the wilderness of the far-north Spanish territory.

As the sun hung just above the western mountain peaks, Foot-Like-Wolf returned. He walked between Samuel and Aristede. Without speaking, he opened the bag hanging from his waist and poured out tubers he had gathered. On top of these, he laid green marsh reeds. Wordlessly, he settled himself back in his place, completing the triangle among the men. He picked up the food he had set down earlier and resumed eating. His face, however, held a look of satisfaction, a small upturn of a smile that did not disappear even when he chewed on the jerky.

Samuel gestured toward the reeds. "Gone a long time to search for a few stew vegetables?"

Foot-Like-Wolf's smile disappeared, and his brow furrowed. After a moment's thought, his eyes widened. "You make joke. These are not for dinner. They are reeds."

"Yes, they are," Aristede agreed.

Foot-Like-Wolf's eyes scanned his audience. He saw no signs of recognition. "They grow in still water. Less than a half day's walk ahead, they can be found."

He smiled again, this time joined by the others. This difficult leg of the journey might soon be behind them.

Foot-Like-Wolf lacked the French words to explain the route he had followed. With a series of increasingly frantic hand gestures, he conveyed the geography ahead, the widening of the fields, the lessening of the slope. Samuel began to nod rapidly. Even though Aristede did not understand all the details, he became caught up with the enthusiasm of his traveling companions.

They stewed the rabbits and added the tubers, ignoring the reeds. They bedded down early that night.

The next morning, Aristede and Samuel discovered the flat, smooth water of the Cut-tuh-o-gwa nearby. They happily wetted their canoes and resumed paddling upriver, the stream following a wide, meandering course toward the east. They paddled easily along the snake-like path of the river.

Their spirits were high, the paddles bit deeply into the clear, cold water. The men covered many miles. Aristede, nearly recovered, took his turn driving the canoe toward the destination.

As the sun nearly crested overhead, Foot-Like-Wolf held up his hand. Both canoes pulled together. He gestured with a sweeping hand across the round, smooth-edged lake before them. "We are at the mother of the Cut-tuh-o-gwa."

Samuel and Aristede took the news with satisfied nods and then resumed paddling. They crossed to the east side of the lake. There, they beached their canoes.

Aristede stood on the small beach and studied the land. A verdant meadow lay in front of him, tree-lined ridges rose in the distance. He looked across the blue lake they had just traversed, the cottony clouds reflected in the calm water. He breathed deeply for the first time since his rib injury. The air smelled faintly of wildflowers. He thought of Marie. He looked at Foot-Like-Wolf. "This is the land of evil spirits?"

Before Foot-Like-Wolf could answer, a rumbling could be heard in the distance. Foot-Like-Wolf angled his head toward the sound. "My people do not fear this place." He paused, searching for a word. "We respect it. Have you seen the banded snake? It has attractive colors, pleasing to the eye. Until it bites you with its venom."

"Which way do we go?" Samuel asked.

Foot-Like-Wolf shrugged. "I know little beyond here. I have never traveled this far."

Aristede pointed in the direction of the rumbling noise. "That way."

Samuel looked at him. "Divine inspiration, my friend?"

Aristede shook his head. "The eastern mountains look steep. I am tired of going uphill."

They set off through the tall grass of the meadow. The pipe slung across Aristede's back while his rifle hung from his right shoulder. Hugging the ridge, they climbed steadily, the terrain easy. The path they chose led to a break between the high summits. They followed the faint remains of a native trail through the pass. On either side, the mountains rose up, sharp, pointed peaks off their right shoulders, high, table-like peaks off the left. They rested that night along the shore of another small lake. The night closed in dark, the surrounding mountains blocking the light from all but the circle of stars overhead. Aristede fell asleep listening to the groans and rumbles of the earth.

At first light, they followed the course of a small stream. They traveled northeast. Samuel and Aristede required regular breaks. After so long in the canoe, their legs were not prepared for extended hiking. Buffalo and elk proved plentiful. The men ate meat-filled diets. They also saw the largest bears they had ever encountered. Samuel raised his musket to fire upon one of the great beasts, but Foot-Like-Wolf quietly pushed the barrel down.

"*Wid-dah*," he said, curving his fingers to simulate powerful claws.

The men slept far from the remains of any animal they killed.

Keeping to the meadows and walking north and east, they came to a series of terraced rock formations. Steaming water ran across many of them, the air fouled with a smell that alternated between acidic and sulfurous depending on the wind direction.

Samuel looked at Aristede. "I think we've found the border of hell."

Aristede nodded. "Then let us cross the River Styx."

The earth occasionally rumbled. They gazed upon colored pools of hot, reeking water. Rock formations of polished cones dotted the landscape. Dead trees stood beside some of the pools, the water proving fatal rather than life-sustaining.

When asked for details, Foot-Like-Wolf could only shrug and apologize. His tribe had never ventured to this area. The buffalo avoided the area. There was little grass for grazing or water for drinking.

They established camp and spent the next days working in slow circles, exploring the area, widening the circumference of their knowledge until they might locate the appropriate reliquary. The first day, they traveled together. To the marvels they had witnessed, they saw plumes of hot water shooting high into the air.

That night, by common consent, they elected to travel separate directions the next day, allowing them to expand their range.

"Tell me again what I will be looking for?" Foot-Like-Wolf asked as they bedded down.

"We will know when we find it," Aristede said. Without further explanation, he rolled over and fell asleep.

They each set off early the next morning. After several hours of walking, Aristede returned to camp. Foot-Like-Wolf knelt over a small fire, cooking a midday meal. He looked at Aristede. Then, his eyes studied the stew. When he spoke, frustration marked his voice. "This is the sort of riddle my white brothers engage in, search for the place which will be known when they reach it."

He looked up. A broad grin marked Aristede's face. "You have found something?"

"We must eat and then wait for Samuel."

Samuel returned. Both he and Foot-Like-Wolf ate quickly, anxious to see the spot Aristede had found. He led them north, hugging the edge of the terraces.

Aristede paused and pointed to the mountain before them. "It reminds me of a burial crypt, don't you agree, Samuel?"

"My friend, I have seen too many mountains to become poetic about them today. Is that what we've come to see?"

Aristede shook his head. "Merely a landmark." He led them through a small break in the trees. He pointed to a rock formation. "This is the start of the trail. I am reminded of the liberty cap worn by the revolutionaries back in France."

Samuel arched his head to study the cone-shaped rock formation before him. "I have struggled to be an artist, but I do not see a liberty cap. I see a penis."

Aristede laughed. "That is because you have been an artist in a brothel. I see a liberty cap. If you are correct, then we have the ideal commentary on what the Revolution has done for our country. I hope that all who follow will call this the liberty cap."

"The formation stands the height of six or seven men. A penis the length of seven men will certainly get remembered," Samuel said.

Aristede doubled over, grabbing his belly. He straightened and wiped his eyes with his sleeve. "And that it is just the first of many treasures we will find." He set off walking briskly south and west. Foot-Like-Wolf struggled to maintain his pace. Along the way, they passed small springs of vibrant colors. Heat radiated off the water. They rounded a bend and stood over a series of terraces, many of the rocks polished white.

Aristede looked at Samuel. "Notice the color. I carried alabaster stones for Pinot. They were not this pure. I am reminded of the finest linen death shroud." Water trickled down across the smooth, flat surfaces, making them glisten. Aristede led them along the path and then up a steep incline until they overlooked a large spring. "I think that this will keep any who believe in an afterlife away."

Samuel looked at the water, deep blue and boiling as if the bottom of the spring provided a hole into hell. He looked at Foot-Like-Wolf. The native had taken a step back away from the devilish pond. All faiths shared a repugnance to the prospect of hell.

The water escaping from the spring flowed down the hillside to the east and trickled over another set of terraces. Aristede, however, led his small party further west and south. They walked through a natural amphitheater of rocks. Trees, stunted perhaps by the foul air, struggled to grow among the stones. Aristede kept an additional set of terraces on his left shoulder until he turned sharply to the right. A few traces of his earlier passage marked the only evidence of human activity. They passed through a narrow gulch before climbing up to a flat spot of land barely wide enough to accommodate them. Here, Aristede halted. He stood next to a dark teardrop-shaped crack in the rocky ground. He lay on his stomach at the middle of the crack and peered inside the hole. Pulling his head up, he looked to his comrades. "Gaze into hell, if you dare."

Both men accepted the challenge. Samuel lay down at the far end of the crack while Foot-Like-Wolf settled at the high round end. They all looked inside. Aristede felt the dank and warm air rising and pressing against his cheeks. He saw skeletal remains of small birds on the floor of the cave perhaps fifty feet below him. Water pooled at the side of the cave. Aristede's head began to pound, and it seemed like his eyes started to lose focus. He blinked his eyes to clear his head. He felt as if he were tumbling down inside, even though he knew his chest and body lay solidly upon the rocks. Aristede pushed himself over onto his back and stared upward at the great sky. He breathed deeply; gradually his head cleared.

Foot-Like-Wolf watched him. "This is a bad place."

Aristede nodded excitedly. "No one will voluntarily come here. I think it is the perfect spot. Don't you agree, Samuel?"

Samuel continued to stare down into the hole.

"Samuel, you agree, my friend."

He did not reply.

Aristede moved to where his friend lay. "Have you spent so much time among the Spanish that you have adopted the midday nap?" He thumped his friend upon the shoulder. When there was no response, he rolled him over. Samuel's face was pale, his breathing shallow and his lips blue. Aristede pushed down upon his chest, driving out bad air, and then raised his arms to help new air flow. He repeated the process, calling for Foot-Like-Wolf. After several more pumps, Samuel began to cough violently. Then, he began to breathe on his own. Gradually, his color returned. Samuel opened his eyes, then closed them again.

"You have returned," Aristede said.

Samuel gently massaged his brow. "My head is pounding."

"There is a miasma within this crack. The air is better at the high end."

Samuel dragged himself to a seated position and buried his head in his palms. After several minutes, he pulled his face from his hands. He massaged the sides of his head and pinched his eyes shut. Opening them, he nodded. "This will be the spot. If the effort does not kill us."

"Did you see all the dead birds?" Foot-Like-Wolf asked.

"Satan keeps his larder here," Samuel said. His face remained pale.

Aristede and Foot-Like-Wolf moved their camp near the rock they had begun to call the Liberty Cap. With some practice, Aristede found that he could say the name without smiling. Samuel, meanwhile, hunted for buffalo. He brought sheets of hide back to the new camp. Aristede cut the hide into strips and began plaiting a great coil of leather rope. While he worked on the project, Samuel dried meat, and Foot-Like-Wolf foraged for roots, berries, and nuts, stockpiling provisions for the return trip.

When Aristede had enough rope, he shaved a stout pine limb until it was round and smooth. Then, he led the party back to The Devil's Kitchen, the name he had given to the crack in the earth.

"I should like to be lowered down," he said as he outlined his plan. He thrust out a palm, silencing Samuel before he could object. "The miasma accumulates on the low side. I will enter from here. You will lower me down." He laid the pine bough across the opening. "This limb should prevent wear on the rope. Once on the cave floor, I will hide the scepter from all prying eyes. I will keep the rope taut throughout my efforts. Should the rope go slack, you will know that I have succumbed to the bad air. Pull me out should that happen."

Foot-Like-Wolf nodded. After a moment, Samuel gave a single dip of his chin.

Aristede tied the rope around his waist, knotting it in the front. After clasping hands with Foot-Like-Wolf and then Samuel, he carefully climbed over the lip of The Devil's Kitchen. The walls curved outward. Climbing proved impossible. He released his grip and swung back and forth like a pendulum as the other two lowered him to the cave's floor.

He paused for a moment to find his footing on the uneven surface. Aristede could not recall ever having stood in a gloomier place; he found the sense of mortality pervasive. Dead birds littered the ground. The creatures had sought shelter and been overcome by the miasma. The dark gray walls added to the gloom. The only light came from the small oculus through which he had descended.

Aristede felt a quick tug on the rope. He had forgotten to keep it taut. With his left hand, he pulled any slack out of the ascending rope. He began to walk slowly toward the pool of water. His eyes slowly adjusted to the meager light. The pool, shaped like a water droplet, sat angled to the oculus. Light from above bisected the pool. He had seen only a portion of it from above. The round end of the pool slowly bubbled. The bubbles must be the source of the miasma. He ranged widely to the narrowest part of the drop, stepping carefully and keeping himself away from the gas. Water trickled down the rock wall and ran across the cave floor to the pond. In the pale light, Aristede saw marks on the cave walls. The water at times must run higher. He moved to cross the small stream and explore the far side. He saw a small outcropping of rock. From where he stood, it looked to be an ideal spot to hide the tube. He felt the long journey nearing its climax. With equal measures of excitement and relief, he stepped forward.

He stopped. The buffalo thong was fully extended. By venturing wide of the pond, he had exhausted his rope supply. Aristede must hide the scepter here on this side. He pulled on the buffalo hide line, yet the rope remained taut. Each tug received an answering pull.

He could go no further. But he must.

Aristede grabbed a deep breath of the air around him. Then, slipping his knife blade between his chest and the loop, he sliced himself free from the safety rope.

"Aristede!" He heard Samuel's panicked voice call.

The rope shot backward and disappeared up the hole. They had followed his plan and yanked him skyward. He could not waste breath explaining or apologizing. Aristede stood alone on the cave floor. He drew a deep breath and held it.

Stepping over a bird's skeleton, he walked deeper into The Devil's Kitchen.

29

Lake Yellowstone Hotel
June 5th

Clarence looked at Barkley's dead body. Then, he began his private dance. He took a step and then paused, allowing his eyes to roam in three dimensions, attempting to take everything in before stepping again and repeating. He carefully avoided allowing his eyes to drift outside. The room had the hotel's best view of Lake Yellowstone. The water sparkled with sunshine.

He avoided letting his mind focus on the body lying facedown on the table. There would be time. The body would be studied in detail, stripped, washed, and examined fully. This moment was the only time to see it in the context of its location, Barkley's final environment.

Although he had his mind open to possibilities, it wasn't hard to guess what happened. Barkley had a plastic bag over his head, and his wheelchair had been pressed hard against the table. With his arms trapped, someone had suffocated the man.

With Barkley paralyzed, it wouldn't take the strength of a bull. But a pair of strong legs to keep the chair pinned against the table would help. Water dripped from the table. Two water bottles lay on the floor.

He took a step. "Who found the body?"

One of the rangers glanced down at his notes. "Wilma, one of the maids here at the hotel. She came by late to make up the bed. She knocked and, when she didn't get an answer, let herself inside."

Nance stepped forward. "Where is she now?"

The ranger's eyes shifted. "We stashed her in one of the vacant rooms. She is spooked."

"Someone with her?"

The ranger nodded.

"Who last saw him?"

"Room service delivered dinner last night. They came inside to collect the dishes after he'd eaten."

"And when was that?"

The ranger glanced down again at the notes. "They collected the dishes about ten p.m. last night. Wiped down the counters and table before they cleared the room."

"Anyone account for William, his assistant?" Nance asked.

"Left the park." He cocked his head toward Barkley's body. "He needed something from Salt Lake City."

"When did he leave?"

"Yesterday," Clarence said.

Nance looked at him.

"The dishes. If William were here for dinner, a private guy like Barkley would have had him set the dishes outside."

Nance nodded.

PPT pointed to the floor. "The water bottles can be tested for finger-prints in no time. Comparing them to latents always depends on the quality. DNA takes longer."

"And when do we start?" Clarence asked.

"We start when we finish processing this crime scene." PPT's voice lacked any of her usual good humor. "City Boy, in this little department, 'we' means me."

"I know you'll get to them as quickly as possible," Nance said, her voice calm.

Clarence respected her handling of the situation. He knew that nerves frayed with each death.

"I can almost guarantee some comparable fingerprints," PPT said.

Nance and Johnson looked at her. Her index finger beckoned them to the small refrigerator in the room. "See the counter."

"A fingerprint in white dust," Nance said.

"Like someone wanted us to know they were here," Johnson said.

"Maybe," PPT said. "Or maybe God just felt sorry for you and Yellowstone."

"Is it Barkley's?" Nance asked.

"Can't say for sure, but I think it's unlikely. It's chalk. Unless Barkley climbed rocks, shot pool, or taught third grade, I don't think he'd have chalk on his fingertips."

"Weight lifting?" Clarence said. "Does he rehab here?"

PPT nodded. "I'll process it and let you know."

Nance knelt before the water bottles. "Look at this."

She pointed; a bit of red stained the mouth of one bottle. "Recognize the shade?"

Clarence did. He walked to the refrigerator and snapped a picture with his cell phone. He collected a quart-sized plastic baggie, a blank ten-print card, and a DNA collection kit from PPT's evidence kit. "C'mon," he said to Nance.

"Mind telling me where we're going?"

"To shake things up."

He led her down to the room where the ranger had put Wilma. Clarence walked to the mini fridge and grabbed a bottle of water, ignoring the frightened maid. He emptied it into the sink before smearing soap onto the surface, leaving behind a white, sticky film. He dropped the bottle into the baggie.

The lobby was quiet. Few visitors remained inside on this bright morning. Just as well, Clarence thought, he may have run through them in his purposeful stride toward the lone woman sitting at the table.

Privé looked up as they came to the table, a broad smile across her face.

She stood and extended a hand to him. "Ranger Johnson, what a pleasant surprise to see you again so soon."

He grabbed the outstretched hand. Clarence smelled fresh lavender. He felt slight bumps of scraped skin along the pads of her fingers.

Privé pulled back her hand. Her eyes narrowed.

"I'd like you to come with us," Clarence said. "I need to ask you some questions."

Privé's eyes flashed irritation. "At what point does this become harassment?"

"After this, I think that there will be only one more visit. Both will be brief. I'd like you to consent to giving a DNA sample and a set of fingerprints."

Privé took a small step backward. "*Pourquoi?*"

"Exclusion samples. Strictly routine."

"I don't understand. What are you excluding?"

"You, Ms. Privé. There has been another murder, and we need to exclude everyone we can as a suspect."

Noel Privé stepped back, separating herself from them. An armchair stopped her. Her chest rose and fell in short bursts. She spoke in a whisper. "Who?"

"Your associate, Mr. Barkley. But this time, there appears to be a treasure trove of forensic evidence left behind." Clarence pulled the plastic bag holding the water bottle. He watched Privé's eyes widen in surprise before she regained control. He rolled the bottle displaying the cloudy surfaces. "We've already collected the evidence." Clarence's eyes shifted to Nance. "I love the speed of these federal investigations."

"When I want something done, they say I can be formidable," Nance said. "If we can just get the quick reference samples, we'll leave you to enjoy this beautiful day in Yellowstone."

Privé's eyes stayed focused on the bottle. "And that came from Barkley's room."

Nance nodded. "Criminals are a damned funny lot. Snuck in without anyone seeing and then forgot to take the water bottle. You wouldn't believe the other evidence she left behind. I guess the stress of a cold-blooded murder makes people careless."

Privé slowly sank down into the chair. Her hand shook.

"If we might just get your samples, we'll be on our way. It is, I don't suppose you'd be surprised, a busy time for us."

Clarence knelt beside the armchair. "This might be easier if we did this at the table. There is some paperwork to go through. You know, lawyer stuff. Need to make sure that it is all admissible in court."

Privé did not reply.

Clarence sat down. Taking a pen, he began filling in the basic information on the fingerprint card. "I'll just get the paperwork started. We've got a lot to do. It seems a witness saw someone on the outside of the building climbing up to Barkley's floor. We're hoping to get reference samples from everyone having access to a window on this side of the building." Bending over the card, he wrote some more before looking up again. "Makes me sorry we wasted the resources watching you. If we'd have had even one person surveilling the outside of the building, we could have caught the person in the act." Checking his watch, Clarence noted the date and time on the card. "Can't understand why someone would climb out the window to get there. Seems much easier to take the stairs or the elevator. Unless you thought you were being watched, I suppose."

He looked to Nance, who merely shrugged. "It is a mystery."

"And that's what we get paid for. Well, you, anyway. Me, I'm just a tour guide. Ms. Privé, I'm ready if you are." With an open hand, Clarence gestured toward the other chair.

Privé stood, one hand still on the armrest of the chair. She looked pale.

"Are you all right, Ms. Privé? You don't look so good," Nance said.

"No."

"No what, Ms. Privé?" Clarence asked.

"This can't be."

"What can't be, Ms. Privé?" This time, Nance asked.

"Barkley, I just saw him. He was fine."

Clarence slowly shook his head. "The tragedy of murder. You never know when you might see someone for the last time."

"I mean...I was there...in his room." As Noel Privé spoke, she slipped back into the armchair. The energy seemed to have drained from her.

"When were you there?" His voice had a hard edge to it.

"This morning, after you left my room."

"But we had it under surveillance."

Privé answered in an emotionless monotone. "As you said, I went out the window. A trick I learned, climbing in the Pyrenees."

"But why?" Nance asked.

Privé exhaled a short, humorless laugh. "Because I knew you were watching. It was fun."

"Why did you go?"

"To tell him what you'd reported. Things were getting out of control." Privé brought her arms across her chest and clutched her shoulders.

"And you left fingerprints behind," Clarence said.

"Doesn't that prove I had nothing to do with this?" Privé said. "I use the chalk to climb, all climbers do. You think I would scale a wall with a chalk bag and forget to wash my hands?"

"I never said anything about chalk." He leaned into Privé, eyes narrowed, jaw firm. He could feel the anger smoldering within him.

"What things were getting out of control, Noel?" Nance's voice, by contrast, sounded soothing. Slowly, she twirled her finger, encouraging Privé to continue.

"The search for the scepter. To begin with, it was merely a crazy idea batted about among conspiracy theorists, the *fou*, lunatics. To my husband and me, it was little more than a dream. Then, Barkley got behind the idea. Hired Ocone, the researcher."

"And what was Barkley's interest?"

Noel Privé pinched her eyes tightly closed. "Barkley believes in an international federation of American conservative beliefs. A sort of Knights Templar for the modern era. That is his Stauros Society. More than that... he is...was hoping for a miracle. He believes that the scepter might possess a cure."

Johnson cocked his head. "For paralysis?"

"It is the handiwork of a saint, blessed by God."

Nance's eyes widened at this declaration. "And you, what is your interest?"

"To bring back to Paris this symbol of French aristocracy. It would empower my husband's political party in the next election for the

National Assembly. With enough seats, we can return France to its true path."

Clarence's eyes studied her face. "And where is your husband while you search for this artifact?"

"I am from America. I can move freely. He would attract attention." Privé closed her mouth tightly, pressing her lips together. She scanned their faces. "He has done much. Arranged for Ocone to be a recognized researcher at the Louvre. He made possible for David's painting to be X-rayed and studied."

Clarence slid forward on his chair, narrowing the distance separating them. "There is something more. What is it?"

They watched the struggle behind her eyes. After a moment, Privé's head bowed. "Stories say that my family was once known as Noaleste. Generations ago, my forefather betrayed France and his people, motivated by greed. We sought to hide our shame by changing our name to Privé. It is French for 'private.' We have lived with this stain ever since. That is how I knew of the authenticity of the claim to the scepter's existence. I have it verified by an independent source, my own life story."

"And have you found it?" Nance asked.

"Not yet, but we are close. I can feel it in my heart."

"And where do you think it is?"

Noel shook her head. "I don't know. That is why Barkley was using his... influence to get information from the government, satellite images, ground-penetrating radar. The tools to allow us to finish." Head bowed, she stared down at her hands, still quivering in her lap.

Clarence slid off his chair and knelt in front of her. "Who is doing this?"

He watched as she slowly shook her head. "I don't know Barkley's man."

Nance spoke sharply. "Who said it had to be a man?"

Noel Privé looked at her, eyes narrow. "I don't know Barkley's person. I never asked. It seemed best not to know. As I left, he promised to arrange a meeting. We had both become concerned about..." Privé looked directly at Nance before continuing. "We had both become concerned about that person's increasing use of violence."

Clarence rocked back on his heels and stood up. Briefly losing his balance, he quickstepped sideways and grabbed for the chair to catch himself. Both women looked at him in surprise. After a moment, he waved away their concerns. "Squatting too long."

Nance looked back to Privé. "What made you think you could pull this off?"

Privé stiffened and said nothing.

"C'mon, Noel, help us understand. Nobody looks good in prison clothes," Clarence said.

The French woman slumped forward and chewed on her bottom lip.

Clarence watched the debate inside her. "Help us."

She sat up straighter. "I'm playing a game where I have ends beyond your small imagination. I don't want to look at pictures of the famous and powerful. I want to be the famous and the powerful." She paused for a moment. She gave him a broad smile. Raising her forearm, her forefinger followed a serpentine route before pointing to her mouth. "Do you see this gap between my front teeth? Dentists call it diastema. Did you ever wonder how a girl from Pennsylvania with an oddly shaped mouth could become a model in Paris? She does it by setting a goal and allowing nothing to stand in her way. I want to be famous and powerful. Not so that I can be looked at and adored. I've done that, Mr. Johnson. I've been the hanger for clothes created by the world's top designers. I want to be powerful because that is the way to get things done."

Clarence wondered who the true power of her husband's political party really was. "And who is Cyrus?"

Privé looked confused.

"Don't stop now, Noel. You've been overheard talking about Cy. Who is he?"

Her mouth pursed into a small pout. She thought without saying a word. Then, she laughed. "You know so little."

"Enlighten us," Nance said.

"When they smuggled the scepter to America, they referred to it as a scythe. The scythe is not a person, it is the thing. The thing we must have."

"And you won't let a small thing like murder stand in your way."

Privé shook her head. Her eyes dipped; the moment of rebellion had passed. "I did not kill him. We needed him, and he needed us. I don't know where I go or what I do. As I told you, Barkley had asserted control. He had the resources."

Nance spoke. "What you won't do is go anywhere. Not until we get a handle on this."

Privé looked at her briefly before breaking off and studying the floor. "*Oui*, Inspector."

Nance kept her eyes locked on the top of Privé's bowed head. Despite the circumstances, Clarence could not help but smile.

———————

"I thought you might arrest her," he said as they walked back to Barkley's room.

"Still might," Nance said. "But I believe her."

"And it might create a helluva international incident."

Nance nodded. "There is that."

Arriving back at the room, they found LaFleur standing by the mini fridge reviewing photos on a computer.

Clarence pushed through the taped-off barricade and snatched the computer off the island, snapping the lid shut. "Who authorized this man to enter the crime scene?"

"Need I remind you, Ranger, that I'm a federal agent," LaFleur said.

"A DEA officer. There is nothing in this investigation to suggest drug involvement. So you are merely an unauthorized person polluting this crime scene."

LaFleur's face reddened. Before speaking, he turned to Nance.

Nance stepped close and spoke softly. "We've got to keep the people down. You know the drill."

LaFleur's eyes remained on her. Nance's face never wavered. He shot a quick glance at Clarence and then stepped toward the door.

"Just a moment," Clarence said, moving to block the door. "Where have you been in this room?"

"I went to the bar and looked at the photos."

"Anywhere else?"

"No," LaFleur's barely contained rage apparent in his tone.

Clarence's eyes quickly went to PPT, who nodded. "All right," he said and took a step away from the exit path.

LaFleur mumbled something and began walking.

"Wait," Clarence said again.

LaFleur exhaled audibly. "What now?"

"Where have you been this morning?"

LaFleur looked at him, his eyes narrowing to slits. "Are you accusing me?" His fists clenched and unclenched. The veins on his neck throbbed.

"Simple question, LaFleur."

"Federal business, possible drug involvement, above your pay grade." He snapped his head away from Clarence and marched out of the room.

30

Roche Jaune
August 1797

Aristede's eyes focused on the dark corner of the cave. He saw the place where he must hide the tube. If anyone peered into the cave and did not succumb to the miasma billowing up from hell, they would still see nothing. A searcher must crawl down inside the cave to find the thing. Even on the brightest day, the crevice would remain in darkness. This must be the location.

He picked his way carefully across the rough cave floor. He felt his heart beating faster. From above he heard the panicked shouts of his comrades. He stepped over the thin trickle of water, treading carefully so as not to fall. He had a headache. Against the far wall, he wedged the tube behind a rock outcropping. Using the palm of his hand, he hammered it into the crevice. His lungs felt tight, and his eyes burned. He smeared moist earth across the tube, wiping it flat with his hand to further disguise it. He wanted to do more, but his body screamed for air. He blinked rapidly, willing himself to return. Aristede quickened his pace back to the cave opening. He stepped on a slippery rock and fell. The breath exploded from his lungs. He inhaled and exhaled, his body desperate for air. The pain in his head intensified. He wanted to lie down for just a moment. He saw the sleeping birds. They looked at peace.

Aristede heard a voice from above. He could not make out the words. He smiled. God spoke to him. He had completed his mission. Aristede could rest. He knelt to pray.

A leather rope dangled beside him, striking him in the face. He had expected more. God told him to tie the braid around his waist. The Church's description had been so wrong, he thought. He looped the cord around his stomach as God instructed and made a simple knot. He felt himself pulled to heaven.

Aristede stared into the intense sunlight. The light of heaven burned so brightly it hurt his eyes. He squeezed them shut. He felt hands pushing down on his chest, forcing him to take deep breaths.

With slow dawning, Aristede realized that he was not in heaven. Samuel knelt over his face, berating him for his foolhardy and dangerous choices. He shouted to every tree and rock that he should leave Aristede down there in the cave, his skeleton a signpost of stupidity and a further discouragement to all who might pass this way from exploring The Devil's Kitchen.

When Aristede's head cleared, they made their way back to the campsite. Samuel did not say much that night or the next day, clearly still angry at Aristede's foolhardiness. Aristede bided his time. In his heart, he knew that he had chosen the best location to safeguard that which they had carried so far.

31

Lake Yellowstone Hotel
June 5th

Nance turned on him as soon as LaFleur left the room. "Why do you have to be such an asshole?"

"I saw him lurking outside. I asked a logical question."

"He's DEA, his job description includes lurking."

"Or maybe he's working both sides and you just can't see it," Clarence said.

Nance bit her bottom lip.

"And he was contaminating the crime scene—Locard's Principle."

After a moment, Nance shook her head. "We're done here. Go back to your desk and hand out your brochures. Just get the hell out of my crime scene." With special emphasis on the word "my," she thrust an arm toward the door and then stomped past him, following LaFleur's path.

Clarence stood in place, his eyes watching her until she disappeared down the hall. He looked over to PPT, who briefly met his eyes before looking back down at her camera viewfinder. "Is there a reason you've got a hair up your ass about that guy?"

"Can't put my finger on it. My instincts tell me not to trust him."

PPT made a noise Clarence thought was a laugh. "Need me to draw you a picture?"

He stepped to the window and looked out across the idyllic scenery. "Did you ever think that a national park is the only place in America where everyone can walk around with surveillance gear, and no one thinks anything about it?"

PPT grunted.

"I mean it," he continued. "A guy walks around with a pair of binoculars or a parabolic microphone and headset. We just assume he's a bird watcher from Michigan or Iowa. I can never shake the feeling that the surveillance is being conducted on us."

PPT looked up from her work. "And I can't shake the feeling you know why you don't like LaFleur."

He paused and then shook his head. "It's not Nance." He paused again. "Not completely, anyway. He's waving his hands at the drug angle like he desperately wants us to look over there. Makes me suspicious."

"That's why I like physical evidence," she said as she snapped a picture, the bright pop of the flash acting like a punctuation mark. "You don't have to figure out where you stand with evidence." Another flash followed.

"Sounds pretty attractive right about now," Clarence said, glancing back down the hallway. "Think I could make it as a crime scene officer?"

PPT looked at him, a thin line traced around her right eye from contacting the viewfinder. "I don't know," she said. "I do know that you'll have to find someplace else to practice because the lead detective has ordered you out of this crime scene." She turned away and resumed her work.

He exhaled a long, slow breath and walked out the door.

32

New Orleans, Louisiana
July 1804

Aristede watched them raise the flag at the opposite end of the Square. The morning felt steamy, heavy with the humidity, it clung to him like a wet shirt. Today would be another hot day. He watched the flag lay listless against the pole, neither stars nor stripes clearly visible.

He felt the perspiration trickle down from his brow. He mopped his face. He turned to his companion sitting to his left. "So many times during my travels I felt cold. Cold water, cold snow, cold ice, the cold seemed to seep into my bones, and I thought I might never feel warm again. Sitting here, stewing in my own juices, I wonder if I would not trade."

Marie Gilbert looked at him from beneath her parasol and smiled. "Perhaps you are never happy unless you are someplace else."

"Perhaps that is why I returned to New Orleans. Here, I can always be someplace else without the effort of paddling upstream."

She raised a questioning eyebrow.

"I left France for this Spanish city that had once been French." He paused and pointed with his chin toward the flag. "It became French once again. Then after I return, the city becomes American. It seems that I continue to move all the while sitting still."

Marie shook her head slightly beneath the shade of the parasol. "You remain the same stupid boy you were when you first washed up on these shores. They may raise and lower different flags whenever they like. They do not change Nouvelle-Orléans. It will always be French."

The nod he gave in reply was little more than a dip of the chin and a blink of both eyes. The less he moved, the less Aristede felt the oppressive heat. "You are, as ever, correct. The officials give their edicts in English. The city, however, remains the same."

"The city has improved. You have returned and stayed," Marie said.

Aristede smiled and patted her wrist.

Pulling away, she switched the parasol to her right hand so that he might not take it again. "I am not in the business of sentimentality."

Aristede looked at her. He could not keep the small smile from showing at the corners of his mouth or hide the twinkle in his eyes. "Why, then, have you allowed me to stay at your establishment all this time?"

Marie used her left hand to sweep away his question. "I need a man about the business to help with the chores. You filled the position I generously held open for Samuel."

"He asked me to convey his regrets."

She grunted by way of reply. "That layabout artist never did an honest day's work, anyway."

"You are again correct," he said, nodding. "Foraging for food and shelter among hostile natives provides far more opportunities for napping than sweeping and washing dishes in a brothel."

"I'm glad you have come around to my way of thinking. Let us return. You have chores to do."

Aristede stood and offered his hand. Placing her hand in his outstretched palm, she stood. This time, she did not release her grip. Together they walked slowly back toward the business on Burgundy.

Aristede took little notice of the passing buildings. Instead, his mind returned to his friend. Samuel initially had been furious with him for untying the rope and venturing into The Devil's Kitchen to hide the scepter.

Gradually, his anger subsided. Aristede knew that it would. Risk had lived with them for the entire journey. They wore it like clothing.

Following their success, the trio had retraced their original line. They had parted from Foot-Like-Wolf at the confluence where the Cut-tuh-o-gwa rejoined her sisters to form the Missouri River. Foot-Like-Wolf wore his medal and promised them that he would speak of them around the fires of his people as long as there remained breath in his lungs. Never, he assured them, would he betray their mission. To safeguard the secret, he pledged his sacred honor. Following his final words, he limped off down the trail, swinging his deformed foot before him as he had on the first day they had met. He disappeared into the trees.

Aristede and Samuel paddled their hewn canoes downstream. They pulled them ashore and camped for many days near the spot where they had originally entered the water above the great falls. Restored and strengthened, they hiked back down the trail until they located the *Marie*.

Here, Samuel announced his intention to remain. "I did not tell you earlier," he said, "for I did not want to give you time to dissuade me. I grew fond of you, once you became a useful part of this expedition."

Aristede swallowed the lump he felt in his throat. "And I thought you might return to Nueva Orleans with fresh pictures to draw."

Samuel gave a thin smile. "You have put your finger on it. I have decided to remain here rather than to return and live in that in-between world of one who is neither a slave nor free."

If the journey had taught Aristede anything, it was to recognize determination. He gazed into Samuel's eyes, then nodded and held out his hand. "I will miss you, my brother."

Samuel shook his head. "No, you won't." His smile broadened. "Without me around, you might actually make some progress with that woman you desire."

Although daylight remained, the two made camp. They sat by the fire talking over the great adventure they had shared. In the morning, Samuel helped Aristede push the bateau out into the water. Aristede watched his friend grow smaller on the riverbank. He turned to look at the river ahead and map his course. When Aristede looked back, Samuel had disappeared.

Aristede spent another winter with the Mandan, renewing friendships among people whom he knew he would never see again. In the spring, he moved quickly downstream, the water pushing him forward rather than pulling him back.

Marie's tug on his sleeve brought him back to the present. "And where is your head this day?"

He faced her. With his eyes, he traced her profile before speaking. "Wondering whether Samuel is looking upon anything so lovely this morning."

Marie's mouth formed into a small smile. "He is undoubtedly lying beneath a buffalo hide with the homeliest native in the tribe and trying to persuade her that he can draw." Aristede saw that the compliment pleased her.

Aristede had not been able to argue with Samuel, for he knew exactly how his friend felt. Somewhere along the solitary expanse of river, he concluded that he could not go back to France. His life had changed, and he had no reason to return. He could not resume being someone else's man back on his native soil. He would stay here and build something for himself. He had finished his task, closed this chapter of his life. He must begin a new one.

And now, he walked the streets of New Orleans with Marie by his side. This was the place where he needed to be, even if he occasionally must sweat more than he wanted.

He had written a long letter to Jacques-Louis David describing some of the wonders he had seen on his journey into Louisiana. He told of storms on the prairie where the wind roared like a mighty dragon. He had sketched the outlines of a mountain with a snow cap summit that he had named for his friend. He apologized profusely for the poor quality of the drawing. Aristede had outlined the miles traversed and the difficulties and the astounding sights he had beheld. Finally, Aristede had explained that he would not be returning to France, his life was to be found here in America. He hoped, however, that his friend would remember all the moments they had together. For his part, Aristede would cherish the times and remember them like a priceless jewel. He poured his heart into what might very well be his final communication with his old comrade. Aristede closed by professing his deep affection.

And it was all a cipher.

Around the table at Fécamp, before boarding *Le Pinson*, David had established the code. It must be easily communicated. David could not be sure that the authorities would arrest those who remained in France. The cipher must be easy to explain. If the authorities caught wind of their secret, no amount of cleverness would help them to escape. David was certain that the entire French navy would be deployed to arrest them and to recover the scepter. If, as David hoped, the revolutionary authorities had no idea about the true purpose for this small band of royalist warriors, then no one would attempt to decipher a letter to an aging artist from a long-time friend. Aristede frowned as he recalled the final meal in Fécamp. All seated at the table had assumed that Noaleste would be the letter writer and Aristede the dutiful assistant.

Aristede, however, knew the cipher. The overlay letter described in detail his time in America while the secret letter relied upon every third word to convey the message's true purpose. He told of the secret cave that might be described as The Devil's Kitchen. He told of the path, beginning at the rock formation he had dubbed the Liberty Cap, although it looked more like a man's penis than a head covering. He hoped David would appreciate the humor. Aristede had also described the mountain that looked like a burial shroud.

He led Marie to the water's edge. They had to be careful to avoid being run over by men scurrying back and forth offloading cargo from an arriving ship. He remembered watching *The Sparrow* sail away. She was bound for France and carried his letter to Jacques-Louis David.

Aristede saw the clean, fresh wood of a new pier. The Americans had built more of them. With the settling of hostilities among the great powers of Europe and the consolidation of the new American empire, commerce had flourished. More space had been needed to bring ashore the trade goods and to load exports. These were prosperous times to be in Nouvelle-Orléans. With the letter's departure, he had been freed of his last bond to the old world. Aristede turned his full attention to succeeding in this new land.

Marie interrupted his reverie and leaned close. "Do you know another way to defeat the heat of Louisiana?"

Aristede looked at her and shrugged.

She pulled his hand gently in the direction of Burgundy Street. "Don't wear clothes."

33

Canyon Campground
June 5th

Clarence stared at the pages spread across the small dining table. Tripod lounged in his lap, his index finger scratching softly between the dog's ears. With his other hand, he swirled the beer in the bottle before taking a swallow. Perhaps he needed a higher blood alcohol level, he thought. Linear thinking wasn't getting him anywhere.

His eyes flicked back and forth between prints of *The Intervention of the Sabine Women* and *The Anger of Achilles*. He studied the warriors and geography, hunting for an elusive clue. The art presented the only place he could search since he'd gotten himself banned from the crime scene. His instincts told him that something lay there, waiting to be found. He studied Achilles, looked into the anger of his eyes. He opened Ocone's copy of *The Iliad* and refreshed his memory of the opening line:

Sing, Goddess, Achilles' rage, black and murderous that cost the Greeks incalculable pain, pitched countless souls of heroes into Hades' dark...

Achilles, that greatest of warriors, had been consumed with rage and pride. He allowed himself to be controlled by emotions that were themselves reactions to the feelings of others.

Clarence shook his head to clear his mind. He didn't need to write a term paper on Achilles, he needed to figure out what role, if any, the painting played in the hidden scepter.

He refocused his attention on Agamemnon. He, after all, held the scepter. It was Agamemnon who would sacrifice Iphigenia to Artemis so that the fleet might sail. Agamemnon stood before the tent opening with the mountain in the background. Could he recognize the geography? Clarence studied the mountain, thinking back upon the views he had seen. Picking up the paper, he rotated his wrist, foreshortening and lengthening his view of the mountain. He quickly abandoned the effort and flung the paper back to the table. David had never been here, never seen these peaks. His drawing would be an approximation at best. He took another pull from his bottle. He closed his eyes, scratched his dog, and thought about what he might be missing.

Setting his empty bottle alongside the others, Clarence gently shifted the dog off his lap and onto the bench. He limped toward the refrigerator and grabbed another beer. Twisting off the cap, he placed the fresh beer on the table. Then he opened the folder containing all the biographical information he could find on David. Clarence picked up his guitar. He silently fingered chords and slowly reviewed the information. David had been imprisoned when Robespierre fell from power. He had later regained influence by aligning himself with Napoleon after being released from custody. After Napoleon had fallen, the Bourbon household had briefly been reinstalled in power. He had exiled himself to Brussels. David died an expatriate.

Clarence took another drink before returning to his seat. Tripod briefly raised her head and shifted her weight, then settled back down, her head supported by Clarence's thigh. David had fostered a great many pupils, and as a result, his influence persisted. Even those who ultimately departed from his style recognized the role he played in their artistic development.

He fanned the printed pages across the table, looking for his list of pupils. He scanned the list. He recognized some of the names and stared blankly at others before settling on Jean-Auguste-Dominique Ingres.

Some long-ago memory picked at his brain. Ingres's paintings had distorted shapes and spaces and, as such, made him a forefather to the modern art of Picasso. Yet, he had always thought of himself as a history painter carrying on the tradition of his teacher, David. They had gone their separate ways yet shared a connection. What, he wondered, was he not remembering? He tried without success to access the internet from the RV. He considered briefly driving to the ranger station to boot up the computer but discarded the idea. He had drunk too much beer to be out on the road.

Clarence opened one of the art books and flipped through the pages until he found the works of Ingres. Achilles seated before craggy mountains, behaving as a king, Oedipus in the mountains riddling with the Sphynx at the entrance to his cave, Napoleon on his imperial throne holding his scepter—each might be a clue. He pushed back against the seat and forced himself to pause. He felt himself on the brink of the investigator's worst mistake, allowing the conclusion to influence his evaluation of the evidence. Still, his mind swirled. There were strands of a solution tantalizing him, he could feel it. He closed his eyes and breathed deeply.

He opened them and punched buttons on his phone.

"What," Nance said, answering immediately.

"Let's fight tomorrow. Tonight, do me a favor and search the internet, would you?"

"Why?"

"Because my computer got stolen, and I'm too drunk to drive."

Nothing but silence came through the phone.

"What do you need?" Nance asked.

"Search for Jean Ingres's connection to other painters of the era."

"You do know I'm in the middle of a few things," she said.

Clarence heard the fatigue in her voice. "You're keeping yourself from getting bogged down with the arrest paperwork for a DWI this way," he said. "Besides, crazy as it sounds, I think that the solution to this case lies in researching a bunch of old Frenchmen." He paused. Clarence could hear the clicks of a keyboard through the phone.

He twisted the cap off another beer.

"This does not give you license to keep drinking," Nance said.

"Give me something to do," Clarence said before taking a swig. He listened to her breathing and fought the temptation to interrupt.

"I'm looking. Ingres lived in France...spent time in Italy...Rome. Studied old masters. Sat at the feet of Raphael."

"Work with anyone alive at the time?"

"Had students he shepherded. Spent time with the English painter J.M.W. Turner in Rome. Some of the students went on to be famous. I've got a partial listing."

He set down the beer. "Go back to Turner." Clarence heard Nance's fingers clicking on the keyboard.

"Both stayed at the Villa Gregoriana in Rome. Studied landscape painting. Not finding any information about what they talked about. No journals or diaries. Want to hear the list of students?"

His eyes roamed the books on his table. "Sure, print a copy. I'd like to look at it later."

"You don't sound like you're paying attention. Better pour your drunk self to bed."

"You're probably right. I'll talk to you tomorrow," he said, suddenly anxious to get off the line.

"What are you thinking?" Nance asked.

"Disjointed thoughts of a drinking man."

"So, you're going to leave the lead investigator hanging?"

"Let me see if it sounds intelligent when I'm sober."

Nance snorted. "There's advice we could all use." She hung up the phone.

The last comment invited follow-up questions. He resisted the temptation to call back. Instead, he set water on the stove to boil. Clarence had an idea he wanted to pursue. He might be drunk, but he needed to be a wide-awake drunk until he had run this down.

The next morning, Clarence sat outside the ISB office waiting for Nance's SUV to arrive. He had a mild headache and a burst of enthusiasm. He approached her from the side as she was unlocking the door to the office. His leg skittered across the ground.

Nance jumped back from the door and assumed a fighting stance, her face alert for danger. "Oh, it's you," she said, relaxing.

"Expecting someone else?"

"Long night," she said by way of explanation.

He nodded.

Nance pushed open the door and stepped back. He walked into the office carrying a brown paper sack, a folder, and a pair of books marked with torn scraps of an envelope. Nance followed behind, flicking on the lights.

Clarence pulled a small bag from the sack. "I brought coffee."

"We have some here," she said, pointing to the can.

"No, you don't. I'll get this started. You turn on your computer."

She nodded and walked to her desk. "And then you can tell me about last night's big mystery."

Clarence took a chair opposite her. She tapped at the computer. He listened to the gurgle of the coffeemaker as the scent of fresh brew filled the office. She looked up at him, dark circles beneath her eyes.

"Well?" Nance prodded.

He opened the art book to a bookmarked page and laid it on the table. "I think that there is a thin line tracing from David to Thomas Moran. I think the pictures and descriptions give us clues to the location of the scepter."

"And why Moran?" Nance asked, her eyes studying the pictures on her desk.

"He was the chief artist for *Scribner's Monthly*, a magazine devoted to art and science. He got included on the expedition to Yellowstone. Protecting this scepter, whether it is a holy relic, French royalty, or just a rare and priceless piece of art, was the legacy of these artists. Moran picked up the cause from Turner, and the line traces back to David."

"And they kept it a secret—this society of artists?"

"Almost." Clarence leaned into the desk and opened the Wyoming history book they'd found in Ocone's office. "Moran couldn't quite help himself. His journal from the Yellowstone expedition mentions gold on August fourteenth near the northern boundary of the park." He flipped to the entry and pointed to the page.

Nance read the cryptic entry before looking back at him.

"Another thing," he said, his words flowing faster. "In an interview with the *Helena Herald* newspaper, he reported that they discovered many curiosities not previously observed."

Nance frowned. "And he couldn't possibly have been referring to geysers or waterfalls."

"I'm not saying he was explicit. It is, after all, hidden treasure."

"So, what did he do with it?"

Clarence shook his head. "I don't think he did anything. They are the guardians of the treasure. The hiding place had worked for years."

"And where is the hiding place?"

He shrugged, his lips pressed together. "That remains a mystery." He tapped at the picture of *The Anger of Achilles*. "Agamemnon stands before a mountain in the painting. I don't know which one. If we could find a cave, black and murderous, the passageway to Hades."

Nance's head popped up at this. "Why do you think that?"

He shrugged again. "Opening lines from *The Iliad*, Achilles and Agamemnon's relationship."

Nance studied *The Anger of Achilles*. After a moment, she tapped the mountain. "We're looking at Sepulcher Mountain up by the Mammoth Hot Springs." She paused and angled the paper slightly. "We should be able to see the Liberty Cap. I can't explain why it's not visible." She looked at Clarence, the corners of her mouth forming a small smile.

"You seem pretty confident. I applaud your eye for artistic detail."

Nance shook her head, but the small smile remained. "It doesn't look much like Sepulcher Mountain, but the guy who described it wasn't much of an artist."

"Now who's keeping whom dangling?"

34

Brussels, Belgium
May 1819

David stood in front of the easel, wiping the paint from his hands. He pinched his eyes tightly. His head ached this morning, a stabbing pain above his left eye. He angled his body away from any direct sunlight. David swallowed and did his best to ignore the headache. He had nearly completed the painting; today would be the day. He massaged his temples and waited for the pain to pass. The pressure he felt to complete the painting had taken a toll on his health.

He studied the men portrayed on the canvas. Achilles' face flushes with anger. David felt satisfied that he had accurately captured the rage. Achilles' eyes, however, remain calm, the look of a seasoned killer. For the painting to succeed, he must show controlled fury. Agamemnon, the Greek king, has just revealed to Achilles that Iphigenia may not marry. Rather, she is to be sacrificed to the goddess Artemis so that the Greek fleet might sail to Troy. Achilles reaches for his sword, intent on murder at the betrayal.

David's eyes shifted to Agamemnon. He dabbed paint at one of the folds in the king's robe, enhancing the shadow.

Achilles' sword never leaves the scabbard, his arm stayed by the authoritative presence of Agamemnon. The king's facial expression projects calm facing this attack. With a single finger, he commands Achilles to cease. The other hand holds the scepter, the symbol of royal authority.

And here, for David, was where the painting began.

He confirmed that his hands were free of paint. David carefully picked up the old letter and studied it. He hardly needed to look at the document, for he had read Aristede's letter so often that the words were written on his heart. The man described the voyage to America with only the briefest allusion to the treachery of Noaleste. Aristede reported on the hazardous journey into the heartland of America as he delivered the scepter to the most secretive place any man could imagine. David read again about the assistance of Samuel, David's former student, in the quest. He closed his eyes and concentrated, trying to remember the man. Although he had so many students over the years, there had been few Black painters. Surely, one day Samuel's face would float into his memory. The headache, however, acted like a thick fog at sea, obscuring the details. The man remained only a shadow in his mind.

Thought of Aristede brought a smile to David's face. Pinot's former assistant had proven surpassingly loyal. He could not imagine the hardships the man had endured in his quest to place the scepter. The letter had been vague, speaking only of "often cold" and "difficult." Aristede provided little imagery to sate the reader's appetite for knowledge.

David blew out a long, slow breath. He had arrived at the cruel irony of this quest. The journey would not have been successful without the tenacity of Aristede, a common man made uncommon. A lesser man would not have persevered, David felt certain. He knew Noaleste had crumbled under the temptation of carrying the royal relic. Upon reading Aristede's report, David had quietly whispered Noaleste's name within the circle of those who still dreamed of the return of a king. All had been made aware of his betrayal. That family name would be forever stained.

Without Aristede's practicality, the journey would not have succeeded. His single-mindedness of purpose, however, denied him artistic imagination. David had done his best to capture the mountain Aristede outlined, although the details were sparse. He hoped that he had portrayed the peak with reasonable accuracy. The cruelty, David thought, for the very skills

Aristede needed to complete his portion of the task, his raw-boned, rough workman's character rendered his descriptions so incomplete as to frustrate David's efforts to portray an accurate map within his painting.

David returned his attention to the letter. Aristede had provided two details. He related to David the stone formation that served as the signpost for the path. Aristede wrote that he considered calling it Scepter Rock, for it rose straight, but he found it looked more like a penis than a scepter. He had named it the Liberty Cap, a mocking reference to the revolutionaries.

The other description was of the cave itself. Aristede had described The Devil's Kitchen. Here was imagery he might create.

For long years he had considered this question. He had hoped for Aristede's return. He wished to reward the man for his loyal service and, more importantly, to question him for details. David felt desperate for words he might turn into images. Aristede, however, had elected to stay. He had made his home in Nouvelle-Orléans. Samuel had not returned either. A pity, David thought, the eye of a painter could be his salvation.

Neither man could be blamed for remaining outside of France. The Revolution had eaten the soul of his country. The Reign of Terror and David's own imprisonment had caused him to reconsider the true worth of the cause. Then, democracy had been replaced by the Emperor Napoleon I. David's career had experienced a rebirth. He had fallen under the spell of Napoleon. David had considered calling for the return of the Scepter of Dagobert and placing it in the hands of the emperor. He, however, had sat upon the throne too briefly for there to be any agreement about his rightful place. Then, Napoleon had been exiled by the European armies. During his reign, he had sold Louisiana to the United States. The scepter now lay beneath foreign soil. After his final defeat, a weak Bourbon king had been reestablished by the victors. All with eyes could see that Louis the 18th was not worthy to hold the staff created by God's own Saint Eligius.

David found himself shunned by the new Bourbon king. He and Charlotte had crossed the border and moved to Belgium. Here, he painted and corresponded with his far-flung students. They dreamed of days when a worthy king might return to France.

But now, by 1819, he wondered whether that day would occur within his lifetime. David felt tired, a bone-weary ache. Charlotte encouraged him to rest. Some days, he found it difficult to muster the energy to paint. Still, he must complete this task. He must pass along the secret information that Aristede had delivered to him. David considered his painting from a different angle. Frowning, he added a small stroke of black paint. The subject matter perplexed him. David had once considered painting himself as Moses, standing atop Mount Nebo. There, he glimpsed the Promised Land, the place he would not live long enough to enter. He had put aside the idea and returned to his favorite theme, the classical Greeks. He painted the great king Agamemnon and behind him the secrets to the Scepter of Dagobert's location.

He returned to the decoded letter; each movement of his head aggravated the pain above his eye. David read of the loyal native, Foot-Like-Wolf, who, despite the hardships, had remained faithful to the task. Aristede had not provided a physical description of the warrior. David had chosen, therefore, to capture Foot-Like-Wolf's spirit in tribute. He had painted Clytemnestra, the mother of Iphigenia. Despite the pain at the sacrifice of her daughter, she remains obedient to the king. She sacrifices for the greater good. David reread the letter detailing how Aristede and Samuel had ushered Foot-Like-Wolf into the band of men committed to protecting the scepter. They had bestowed the medal of merit. Aristede noted the native's pride. David had originally painted a small red daub onto Clytemnestra's gown, representative of the medal. Later, he painted over it. He never thought it looked right. Occasionally, history must give way to art.

Charlotte appeared in the doorway. She carried a small plate of food. Silently, she set the plate down on a table and stood beside him, studying the painting. Her eyes looked critically upon the canvas. "You are nearly complete?"

"On the plains, over Agamemnon's right shoulder, I believe I shall paint a small shaft of rock. To the unaware, it will appear to be Greek statuary, but to our brothers and sisters to come, it will be the Liberty Cap to which Aristede referred."

Charlotte's head bobbed in agreement. "And what of the cave?"

David gestured with his paintbrush to the distant mountains. "A thin plume of smoke, perhaps, representative of the Devil's breath oozing out of

The Devil's Kitchen." He paused before exhaling slowly. "Had I painted the Old Testament scene, it would have been easier to place the Devil."

She smiled, then turned and faced him. This conversation had occurred many times. Despite the success and the legion of students who were indebted to Jacques-Louis David, the self-doubt never fully extinguished. "But you paint the classics. That is what you do. That is what you have always done." Her eyes looked at him, searching his face. Her smile faded. "You look so tired, my husband. You must rest."

He looked back, his eyes holding hers. Then, a fresh pain made him pinch his eyes shut.

"Come lie down," she said. "Rest, and then eat a bite. The painting will be here."

"They are but a few swipes with the brush."

She pulled her head back, the concern in her eyes momentarily replaced by skepticism. "You are Jacques-Louis David. There are no swipes of paint. You think and plan and change. If you painted faster, we would be richer."

"And if you did not think of money like water to be poured from a jug."

Concern furrowed her brow. "I promise that I will buy nothing while you rest."

He nodded slightly. "You are my wise physician." He moved to set the brush down but found that he had difficulty releasing his grip. David felt a tingling sensation in his fingers. His hand trembled, spraying paint droplets over part of Aristede's letter. Charlotte, seeing the difficulty, pulled the brush free. She took his arm and began guiding him out of the room.

"That brush must be cleaned," he said.

"I will see that it is done. I once lived with a painter." Charlotte helped him shuffle out the door of the studio. They walked slowly down the hallway.

"And this painter you kept, what was he like?"

"A horrible lover whose breath frequently smelled of garlic and fish. He had the conversational skills of an African baboon." She guided him into the bedroom.

"And why, do tell, did you keep such a man?"

She turned David around and slowly helped him lower himself until he was seated on the side of the bed. "I found that when I wanted to apply cosmetics, he proved helpful to have around the house."

"Then you should go to him."

"I likely will. But in good time, for I have no need of cosmetics at this moment."

David thought of a clever retort. He looked at her. Then, he cried out in pain. It felt as if someone had placed a burning ember on his forehead. He fell backward onto the bed, eyes wide, staring at the ceiling. The right side of his face drooped. His fingers closed inward. His right arm began to spasm. David turned his head to the left and right, looking for his wife. His eyes had become cloudy, and he had difficulty seeing. He cried out again.

Charlotte screamed. Splashing water into a basin, she pressed a cold cloth against his forehead. Then, she ran from the room, begging for someone to come to their aid. Finding the maid hanging laundry, she begged her inside. Charlotte raced back toward the bedroom.

David exhaled a slow, labored breath as she passed by the studio.

35

Mammoth Hot Springs Station
June 6th

Nance clearly enjoyed this moment of superior knowledge. The fatigue Clarence had seen in her eyes moments before disappeared. Her smile beamed. He read it as a victory smile. She waited for him to ask, her finger tracing the rim of her coffee cup.

Clarence closed his books, pushing his loose pages into a single pile. "Shall I email you the research, or do you want the hard copies?"

Nance's smile broadened; a line of straight teeth brightened the room. "Don't pout," she said. "It's unbecoming for a man of your stature. You're being churlish."

"Churlish," Clarence repeated. "Quite a word for a Montana farm girl."

"It's a ranch, and you're being condescending. Hardly the way to behave when I have information that we both know you want."

He angled his head toward the coffeemaker. "I brewed good coffee. That's got to be worth something."

Nance's finger made another slow lap around the rim of her mug. The smile disappeared, the lips set in a level, contemplative frown. "I'm thinking."

"I could tell by the frown."

Nance shook her head. "Churlish and condescending...still not working. But good coffee is worth something." Nance paused a moment before continuing. He leaned forward in his chair, closing the distance between them. She swept her hands over the art history books on the table. "You actually worked harder on this than I have. I got lucky. And I owe you for putting me on to it. Yesterday, you said that you thought that the answer lay with the old. You meant the paintings, but it got me thinking. I pulled those letters of Ocone's, the shoebox his landlady gave us, the lady who was nearly blind."

Clarence nodded. He remembered the house in Bozeman.

"Well, the letters consisted of a birthday and a Christmas card, a couple of emails he'd printed off, and a photocopy of a letter from a man named Aristede to Jacques-Louis David. Aristede detailed for David the trip to bring the scepter to America and hiding it up here at the far end of the French territory. Of course, about the time Aristede got back to New Orleans, Napoleon sold all the French holdings to the United States."

Clarence's eyes widened.

Nance nodded. Reaching into her folder, she withdrew several copied pages. "Ocone had a copy of the original letter. I stored his original in the evidence locker. But first I made a copy of my own." She laid the document on the table.

Clarence stared down at the letter. His fingers reached down and gently touched the corner. Carefully he turned to the second and then third page of the document.

"There are actually two documents. The first is a long and rambling letter from the frontier. Apparently coded. The second deciphers the code. It is incomplete. At least one page is missing."

Clarence looked down at the pages. He looked up at Nance. She retained the broad smile. "This letter is written in French."

"And that, sir, is why you are a detective." Nance pulled another document from her folder. With a flourish, she handed him a translation. "I only typed the second deciphered letter. My guess is that Ocone kept a hard copy because he needed to work on the translation."

Clarence's eyes darted back and forth between the two documents. He quietly read the English version. When he finished, Clarence looked up at Nance. "I'm impressed, translating two-hundred-year-old French handwriting. No wonder you look like you didn't sleep much. You never mentioned that you could read French."

Nance shook her head. "My language skills are limited to ordering French fries or French toast."

"So, Noel Privé helped you pound out this translation?"

"That would make sense," Nance said, nodding, "but I don't fully trust her. Remember the spider act she did on the side of the hotel? She is also related to one of the actors."

Johnson tapped on the art book. "Her husband's political connections made this possible."

"Don't forget, her great-great-grandfather or whatever may have been the first person to try to steal the Scepter of Dagobert. Didn't want to give her a clue to the relic's location. Thievery may be genetic."

Clarence leaned across the table. "You're determined to keep me hanging on all of this. You didn't have time to type each word into a translation program. I can't imagine that the Park Service has the sophisticated software it would take to make a translation out of a scanned handwritten copy."

Nance nodded. "You're overlooking the obvious clues. Our crime-fighting task force has a French speaker. You should listen to him order a bottle of wine."

Clarence's eyes narrowed. "LaFleur translated this?"

Nance nodded.

"You let that son of a bitch get first look at the letter? How do you know he gave you a legit translation?"

"He's DEA." Nance's voice sounded crisp and hard. "You may not like him, but he has the skills we need. His grandmother spoke French when he grew up. He studied it for four years in college."

"He showed you his college transcript. What else?"

Nance rolled her eyes. "I don't have time for this petty crap." She moved to gather her papers.

Clarence slapped his hand down on the translation. "Where is LaFleur now?"

"How the hell should I know?" Nance tugged at the translation, but he refused to relax his grip.

"Where is LaFleur?"

Nance looked at him, eyes ablaze. "Likely you'll find him in his room sleeping. LaFleur stayed up all night translating French from two centuries ago to help us out. He didn't have to do that." She pulled again on the translation.

Clarence took back his hand. "Why did he, do you suppose? Why do you think the DEA lost a night's sleep wasting his time on a theory he'd already dismissed as bullshit?"

Nance stuffed the translation in her folder.

"I'm going to go ask." Snapping up his books, he marched to the door.

Nance stopped him in the middle of the parking lot. "Let's take my SUV."

He stood still, considering the offer.

Nance opened her arms, her eyes wide with exasperation. "I'm going. C'mon if you're coming." She climbed into the driver's side of the SUV.

Clarence walked to the passenger side. He dropped his books onto the back seat. Nance pulled out of the parking lot and pointed south down the Loop Road.

"He stays in Grant Village," Nance said as they neared the West Thumb of Lake Yellowstone.

Clarence considered asking how she knew about LaFleur's living situation. He swallowed the comments. Nothing would be gained by antagonizing her. Instead, he turned and faced the pines flying by outside his window. He tried to focus on assembling the bits and pieces of information scattered between the paintings and the letters. The sun shone through the window and warmed his face.

He snapped awake and looked around.

"You dozed," Nance said, her voice sounding amused. "Sunlight, no sleep, happens."

"Sorry," he said, as he wiped drool off his chin. He knew she hadn't slept last night either.

"Forget about it. I grabbed a nap on the drive down as well." When she looked at him, she smiled.

Her eyes did seem clear, Johnson thought. At least they had, for the moment, gotten past their feud in the parking lot. The ride to Grant Village remained quiet, but at least the tension from earlier was not suffocating in the SUV.

At the Village, they drove slowly through the parking lot before pulling into a spot reserved for the manager.

"Do you know the room number?"

Nance's eyes scanned the parking lot.

"Room number?"

"Two fourteen." Nance looked at him. "What are you going to do?"

"If I find him sitting at the breakfast bar, I'm going to order a cup of coffee and have a civilized chat about favorite hikes in Yellowstone. If I wake him up, I'll do the same." Clarence walked toward the lodge.

He took the stairs two at a time. Quietly, he moved down the carpeted hallway with Nance in pursuit. He stopped in front of LaFleur's room and stood just to the side of the doorway. He knocked hard. Nance stopped behind him, reached around, and added her own knock.

They waited. Nance looked at him. He gave a small shake of his head. "I don't hear anything." Johnson saw that Nance's hand covered her firearm.

He rapped again. Hearing nothing, he scanned the hall looking for someone from housekeeping. Then, he slammed his shoulder into the door. The wood cracked, and the door swung free.

"Johnson," Nance said.

"Charge the DEA for the damage," he said before stepping inside. Nance followed him. They quickly searched the room. She moved to the bathroom while he checked the closet. With the toe of his boot, he kicked beneath the bed. The frame was solid. No one hid beneath.

Nance pointed to the bathroom. "His stuff is still here."

"We know he didn't go far. LaFleur would never travel without beauty aids."

"Not the time, Johnson."

Clarence nodded. "I didn't see his car in the parking lot. But the closets look intact."

"I'll radio dispatch," Nance said. "If he is still in the park, we'll locate the car."

"Somebody will see him," Clarence said. "It's a Porsche, not an RV."

Neither of them spoke until they returned to the SUV. Nance leaned against the driver's door. "Back up to Mammoth Hot Springs. The clues we have begin at the Liberty Cap."

"But I need to make a stop at the Canyon Visitor's Center."

Nance narrowed her eyes.

"I've got an idea, but I need an expert."

"And you want to let your dog out before she soils your floor."

Clarence gave her a guilty smile. "Something like that."

"You could just try telling the truth."

Clarence placed his hand over his heart. "I did, mostly."

The itinerary resolved, they got into the SUV.

"You're welcome to come in. This will just take a moment," Clarence said as they parked in front of his RV.

Nance shook off the invitation. "I'll wait here."

Unlocking the door, he saw Tripod pacing back and forth across the threshold. Clarence held the door as the small dog jumped outside and headed off to the tall grass. He watched her for a moment before stepping into the bedroom and retrieving his handgun. He ejected the magazine and confirmed that it was loaded. He holstered the weapon and clipped it to the small of his back. Clarence adjusted his jacket to conceal the firearm. The entire process took less than a minute. He grabbed two bottles of water. Picking up Tripod, he scratched her ears and settled her back on the dog bed.

He rejoined Nance. "Thanks. We're both more comfortable."

"So transparent," Nance said.

Clarence called the Canyon Visitor's Center. He put the phone on speaker.

"Didn't you used to work here?" Martinez asked.

"And will again soon," Johnson said.

"Not likely. We've hired a drone to conduct your tours. The robot keeps more reliable hours."

"Help me get back to clean out my locker. Tell me where I might find a cave that historical types called 'The Devil's Kitchen'?"

The line went silent. Johnson could almost hear the old man thinking. "The early explorer Jim Bridger called this area 'the place where hell bubbled up.' We've got references to hell and the Devil everywhere."

"How about caves venting smoke?"

"Sounds like dragon's breath. We've got the Dragon's Mouth Springs and the Black Dragon Cauldron south on the Loop Road, near the Mud Volcano."

Nance pulled to the shoulder of the North Canyon Road and listened. If Martinez was right, they were driving in the wrong direction. "Nothing ever had that name on the early maps of the region. Most of the poetic names were coined after the railroad arrived. Helped lure tourists to this exotic region." He paused. "If you think that's a physical description, there's no telling where it might be. Dragon snout, jagged teeth both could be common rock formations, but snow and ice might easily have eroded a cave entrance from the early days. A dragon then could look completely different today."

"What about over by the Liberty Cap and Sepulcher Mountain?"

Johnson and Nance waited through another pause. "A small cave field where volcanic gases sometimes accumulate might fit your bill. We don't advertise the area. Suffocating tourists proves bad for the park's wholesome image."

Nance nodded her head enthusiastically.

"Can you describe the location for them?" Clarence asked. "I promise I won't tell anyone with Iowa license plates."

"Only so you'll get back to work," Martinez said. "These drones are keeping me up at night." He described the landmarks leading to the caves.

Nance watched as he ended the conversation with Martinez. "The Black Dragon Cauldron is back to the south."

"But that's not the right way," Clarence said.

"Agreed." She sped off toward Mammoth Hot Springs.

36

Nance slowed near the Mammoth Hot Springs parking area. She spotted LaFleur's Porsche sandwiched between a rented sedan and an RV. Few cars dotted the other parking lots for Mammoth, unusual for a June day. Clarence considered breaking the driver's side window and searching the car. That would likely set off the car alarm and might even distract the tourists. He settled for looking through the window. He saw nothing. Resting the back of his hand on the hood, the engine felt warm. "He hasn't been here long."

Nance, meanwhile, scanned the boardwalk and then the parking lot. She shook her head. "I don't see anything."

Clarence pointed across the Lower Terraces. "Then we hike."

"There is our first clue, the Liberty Cap."

"I still don't see a hat."

Nance checked her radio and handed him one. "Focus on the trail."

Clarence pulled his copy of the letter and *The Anger of Achilles* from his back pocket. He studied both one more time, committing the details to memory. He did not want to be distracted on the trail, flipping back and forth between his reference materials. After a final careful review, he nodded.

They walked single file. Nance led. Clarence glanced over his right shoulder at Sepulcher Mountain and compared it to the mountain portrayed in the painting. He saw little resemblance, but as Nance had noted, David relied upon the description of someone who did not paint to capture his imagery. Clarence gave the mountain a liberal interpretation before pressing forward toward an uncertain destination.

They kept to the established trails, making the interpretation of the route more difficult. The passing centuries had altered the landscape. Geological changes caused some springs to dry up while new ones formed. The water escaped through different fissures in the earth over time, changing the growth of these travertine rocks. Still, Clarence thought, Yellowstone was federally protected, so what few landmarks the clues provided were likely as intact as he would find anywhere.

As though attracted by a shiny bauble, Clarence couldn't help but have his attention drawn to the pools. The trail had been routed this way because the Park Service knew the thermal pools were eye-catching. He saw that despite a lifetime here, Nance also looked as she passed by the small round wells. The water bubbled up from deep below, heated by the magma beneath their feet. Around the edges, vivid streaks of color formed —browns, oranges, greens and red—bacteria living in the super-heated water. He watched them bubble quietly without the rumble and whoosh of the geysers down in the basin.

Together they worked their way through the Lower Terraces' elaborate limestone drapery. Clarence always liked this section of the park. While it lacked the combustion of the geysers, the terraces' sculpted quality appealed to him.

Nance stopped. He pulled up and scanned the area. Slowly he advanced and stood alongside her.

Nance looked at him. "Up or down? The trail separates."

He studied the choices. The main trail branched upward while a small trail led downhill. Clarence shrugged. "The letter doesn't give us a clue."

"Want to flip a coin?"

"Why choose? You go up, I'll take down."

"Splitting up is a bad idea."

"We can't let someone else find the scepter." He left unsaid who. Clarence tapped his belt. "We've got radios."

"Johnson, he is DEA."

"If you say so." He waggled his finger between the trail choices. "Up or down?"

"Up," Nance said, and hurried off without another word.

He pushed himself down the trail. His eyes swept the ground in front of him and to the rocks above, his gaze quickly settling into a triangle pattern. He slowed. Ahead, his trail passed through a natural amphitheater. The path ran through the center, splitting the bowl. Rocks rose all around. The land offered only small rocks and a few scrub trees, nearly devoid of cover, a perfect spot for an ambush. He looked up but could not see Nance. Her trail had taken her wide and around the amphitheater.

Clarence pressed his radio. "Nance, you see anything?"

"I got nothing so far. Moving forward, stay in contact."

He signed off and inched ahead, his eyes following the triangular search pattern. Overhead, a hawk soared, hunting for prey. Clarence saw nothing alarming, nothing out of the ordinary, yet he couldn't escape the tension he felt. He squatted down, lowering his profile, and shielded himself behind a small ponderosa pine. He had run enough search warrants to know that quiet did not necessarily mean safe. He had to move. Standing still, allowing his mind to imagine the worst, only made the next step harder. Clarence drew his gun, holding it by his hip. His eyes swept the amphitheater's walls one last time. He swallowed hard and stepped out from behind his cover. Keeping his eyes focused on the rock walls, he jogged through the amphitheater. On the other side, he paused, massaged his leg, and slowed his breathing. He pulled air slowly in through his nose and then exhaled fully, taking his time, lowering his heart rate.

His radio squawked. "Johnson, anything to report?"

"No, Nance, just living the dream."

He pushed ahead along the trail. Away from the open amphitheater, the trail narrowed, the walls of rock on both sides closing together. Scrub trees crowded the trail. A small bend limited his ability to see ahead.

Clarence paused and pressed himself against the rock face. Looking ahead, he saw nothing but the empty trail. Two strips of bright yellow National Park Service tape had been stretched between a pair of trees, blocking the path. A sign fastened to the barricade informed him that the trail was closed for maintenance.

He smiled and radioed Nance to tell her that the bad guys couldn't have come this way. The trail was closed. He got no response. The rock walls surrounding him limited his signal. He clipped the radio to his belt, knelt, and slipped under the barricade.

It made him feel rebellious.

The trail undulated ahead, the rough ground rising and falling. The trail widened and narrowed as the geography permitted. Away from the thermal features of Mammoth Hot Springs, few tourists ventured even this far. The flagship national park in America, and Clarence felt like he had the place to himself. He unclipped the radio and called for Nance again, without result.

Perhaps he did.

The trail narrowed and passed through a gap in the rocks. If Clarence reached out his hands, he could touch the walls on either side of the trail. Up ahead, the trail curved and bent back. He could only see that the trail climbed.

The radio squawked again. He glanced down, hearing fragments of sentences. "Nance, say again."

The rock above him shattered. Shards scratched his face and clouded his vision. Clarence threw himself against the rocks, trying to shield himself. He heard what sounded like a burst of high-pressure gas escaping. Fragments flew. A tourist might think that the gas sound was the brief eruption of a geyser. He knew better. Someone had fired a muffled rifle at him.

Another shot exploded overhead. He pushed himself back hard against the stony outcrop. A small thumb of rock jabbed his thigh, and he felt the leg give way. Clarence collapsed to the ground. He squirmed to pull his exposed limbs behind the limited shelter of the outcrop. He felt his leg. He'd not been hit; the old wound had picked this time to flare. He silently cursed the injury. Rage and a growing sense of panic rose within him. He silenced the distractions and focused on the problem. He was trapped. Ahead and behind, the trail curled back away from his hiding spot. If he moved either way, he'd be exposed. He couldn't look ahead to assess the situation. To do so would mean certain death.

Johnson tried the radio without success. He pulled his phone. He had no service. He activated the camera and set it to take a selfie. With one hand, he fired three shots blindly around the rock. He extended the camera, hoping to see something on the screen. The effort failed. He saw rock walls and a dirt trail. Another bullet slammed into the ground just in front of him. The shot forced him to pull back his hand. He fired two more shots in blind anger up the trail, hoping that the reports would get Nance's attention.

Clarence tried to climb to his feet, pushing up on the rocks with his hands while pawing to get his feet under him. His leg, however, would not support his weight. He sat back, feeling alone and helpless.

He heard the radio squawk static without words, the occasional broken syllable.

"Why don't you come out? Save us both a great deal of trouble," a voice said from somewhere up the narrow gulch.

Johnson couldn't get a fix on the position. The words bounced along the rock walls. The voice sounded familiar, but he could not immediately recognize the speaker.

"Throw out your gun," the voice said.

The location seemed different. Had the hunter moved, or were the echoes reverberating off different rocks?

"The cavalry cannot rescue you here. Do not allow your friend Nance to die needlessly for your mistakes."

"What do you want?"

"Please, Ranger Johnson, don't act stupid. I want to recover the scepter and leave. And you are in my way."

"Political fanatics never just leave," Johnson said.

"This isn't about politics," the voice said. "At least for me. It's only about the money. Do you have any idea what some would pay for a magic wand of historic gold?"

"You don't sound like a sincere believer."

"Oh, I'm a believer. I believe I'm about to become a very rich man."

The voice sounded closer. Clarence pushed against the rock wall, trying to get to his feet. He needed to move. He searched for options. He couldn't climb. The small rocky spur provided his only protection. Yet, his position was known, and he couldn't return fire. Retreat exposed him. With his free hand, he grabbed a clump of grass and tried to pull himself to his feet. The shallow roots pulled free of the ground, his back slamming against the rock. Clarence felt the air forced from his lungs. Dirt and sand rained down on him.

"Johnson, I heard shots," Nance's voice crackled over the radio.

The muffled pop of another shot followed instantly by exploding fragments of rock caused him to press more tightly against the outcrop.

Clarence made his best guess as to the sniper's position. He would roll and fire. He could not allow himself to let the shooter dictate all the terms of the battle.

He looked down and took three deep, calming breaths, centering himself for what he knew he had to do. When he raised his head, he saw someone behind him moving silently up the path. Clarence snapped his gun up and aimed. A quick hand gesture waved him off. He saw LaFleur. The DEA agent could have shot him if he'd wanted to. Instead, his focus was on the trail ahead. Clarence raised his hand in warning. He stabbed at the air to indicate his best guess of the gunman's position. LaFleur's eyes shifted in the direction he pointed. As if in slow motion, he saw the DEA agent's gun raise toward the spot. He heard the high-pressure gas sound, the muffled report of the assassin's rifle. Clarence pushed hard with his good leg and rolled to the middle of the path, his arms extended. In one smooth motion, he found his target partially exposed and distracted by LaFleur. Clarence fired three times. The rifle clattered against the rocks before landing on the trail.

Keeping his gun focused on the shooter, he skittered awkwardly ahead, propelling himself with one arm and his good leg. He came first to the rifle and hurled it behind him. Clarence kept his eyes on the enemy, prepared for a sudden attack. One of his bullets had torn through the man's throat. He saw no froth, no air escaping from the man's lungs. The man lay dead. He knew he recognized the voice. He looked down on William, Barkley's assistant.

Clarence holstered his weapon. Using the rocks like a ladder, he pulled himself to his feet. He hobbled back to the rifle. Stabbing the barrel into the ground, the stock became a crutch. He tested his bad leg and felt it holding his weight. The unreliable bastard was almost back to normal. He brushed his sleeve across his face to clear the accumulated sweat, blood, and dust. Clarence rubbed his ears to clear the ringing noise.

Keeping the rifle for support, he turned. Nance knelt over LaFleur. She was shouting into the radio, but he couldn't make out the words. Clarence limped in her direction, his pace quickening as his leg grew more confident. He cast aside the rifle and hobbled the last few steps before dropping to his knees alongside her. There LaFleur lay, a gunshot wound to his abdomen. Clarence's fingers probed his neck for a pulse. LaFleur's heart beat wildly. Nance called again into the radio, begging for assistance. Clarence tore off his jacket and shirt, wadded the clothing up, and pressed it atop the bullet wound. "We've got to stop the bleeding."

Nance pulled her shirt off and dropped it alongside LaFleur. A voice came over the radio. Nance yelled their location.

LaFleur took a gasping breath and then a long exhale.

Clarence grabbed Nance's hand and pressed it onto his blood-soaked shirt. "Pressure, here!" He flattened his hands above LaFleur, poised to start CPR.

37

Yellowstone National Park
June 6th

LaFleur took another breath, and then another. His respiration eased.

"I couldn't get here," Nance said. "I could hear the shots, but I couldn't do a damn thing about it."

They remained quiet. Clarence waved his hand over LaFleur, keeping the insects away. They shared a water bottle. He offered to relieve Nance, but she refused to budge. Her blood-stained hands kept direct pressure on the wound.

"He saved my life," Clarence said.

Nance nodded. "You know what we need to do."

The statement surprised him. He looked down at LaFleur.

"I got this," Nance said. "Now, climb that hill and find the damn scepter."

Johnson's eyebrows raised.

"We're doing everything we can for Tom. When the backup gets here, all hell is going to break loose. They are going to throw a wall around this spot and keep us so far away that we'll be lucky to read about it on the internet. No one is going to believe this story unless we bring them something tangible. I think the proof is up there." Her eyes fixed on LaFleur. "I think we owe it to him and to ourselves to finish this."

Clarence struggled to his feet. He took Nance's proffered flashlight. Then, he walked to the rifle and made it safe, ejecting the magazine and clearing the chamber. He looked back at Nance and LaFleur.

"Go," Nance said. "We need this."

He began walking.

"Johnson," Nance said.

He looked back.

"Fire three shots if you need help."

He looked at LaFleur. "And you'll do what?"

Nance didn't answer.

Near William's body, he found an earpiece.

Johnson struggled on the short, steep climb to the top of the hill. He rested most of his weight on his sound leg and pushed forward with the injured one, daring it to keep him from completing this last task.

He paused on the hilltop. William had a metal frame erected over a hole in the rocks. From the tripod, he had suspended a harness and rope attached to a pulley. Clarence saw a parabolic microphone pointed down the trail, next to a zippered green bag. He stepped over and studied the equipment. "That's how he knew I was coming," he said to no one. "He had the path under surveillance."

Clarence shined the flashlight to the cave floor and illuminated the remains of several dead birds. "Safe bet that carbon dioxide accumulates down there." The footing below looked wet and uneven.

Clarence searched the green bag and collected a cache bag, gloves, and a prospector's hammer. He sat on the rocks and started wiggling into the harness.

He strapped on a helmet William had left behind and confirmed that the lamp worked. Clarence shoved his own flashlight down into his pocket. Then he picked up the free end of the rope.

"Belay on," he said before swinging over the entrance to the cave. Slowly, he played out rope and lowered himself to the floor.

He looked around, illuminating the floor, walls, and ceiling of the cave. Clarence worked carefully, following a mental grid like he was working a crime scene.

He took a step and paused, surveying the cave, making sure that each grid overlapped the previous one. He assumed that Aristede had hidden the scepter high off the ground to avoid rising and falling water levels. Clarence was careful, however, to include the floor and the lower walls in his search.

He worked outward. To his side, he heard the faint bubbling of a pool. Ahead lay the far wall, the darkest corner of the cave. About chest height, he saw a small outcropping of rock, a small thumb of stone. From his vantage point, he couldn't see the walls on either side. Clarence stepped forward and studied the wall. Millennia of flowing water had worn the rock smooth. He moved to survey another spot. The gritty walls showed nothing, unchanged since the time of the dinosaurs.

Clarence felt tired. His head hurt. He wanted to sit down and rest. He shook his head, magnifying the pain. He needed to find Aristede's treasure and return to Nance.

He stepped back. Too smooth, he thought. His hand rubbed the rock wall above and below the spot that had caught his eye. Both felt different. With the hammer side of the prospector's tool, he scraped at the rock surface. Beneath the accumulated surface dirt, he saw the dark gray of lead.

Using the sharpened pick, he scratched the back wall of the cave, marking the smooth lines of a vessel the cave had long gripped. When Clarence felt confident that he had identified the edges, he worked the pick behind the back of the tube and pried. With a crack of resistance, it broke free from the cave wall.

Clarence held the pipe in both hands and carried it back to the cave opening. Despite everything that had happened, he could not help but smile.

He took a deep breath to clear his head. He felt dizzy. Clarence wondered if he could get himself up the rope. As he drew his gun, it clanged into the pipe.

His weapon dropped to the ground. He looked at it. The dirt spun. He knelt and grabbed at his firearm. He couldn't leave a handgun loose in a national park. His thoughts were muddled. Everything seemed to move in slow motion. He knew it was the air of The Devil's Kitchen. He had to get out of the hole.

Clarence dropped the pipe into the cache bag. He grabbed the rope with both hands. He tried to walk up the wall, use his legs to help him climb. He took a step; the rope pulled him back to the center. He swung like a pendulum, his shirtless back scraping against the rocks. He had to do this with arms alone.

He climbed, hauling his feet off the ground. He stretched out his arm and pulled himself upward. When his hands met, he repeated the process. After several pulls, he rested. His chest heaved, sweat ran off his brow. He wiped his face against his bare shoulder. He focused on a fixed point on the cave's entrance. He needed to keep himself oriented, even as his head spun.

When his head broke the surface, he hooked his leg over the lip. He pulled himself out and lay on his back. He breathed fresh air and stared at the high sky.

Clarence picked his way back down the hill. A pair of rescue workers treated LaFleur. As he neared, the pair lifted LaFleur and strapped him onto the back of a specially designed all-terrain vehicle. Clarence picked up his pace, but they disappeared down the trail before he could arrive.

"Freeze right there. Show me your hands."

Clarence stopped and turned. A uniformed officer, weapon drawn, eyed him.

"He's with me." Nance stepped between the two. "I...I told him to check the perimeter."

"Find anything?" the officer asked.

"No sign of anyone else," Clarence said. He cocked his head toward William's body. "He had a camp atop that hill. Some sort of apparatus for exploring the cave. I'm a city boy, I don't know what that's about."

Nance turned away from the officer. Despite everything, the corners of her mouth formed a small smile.

38

Billings, Montana
June 6th

Nance and Johnson raced to the trauma center in Billings, Montana. The responding ranger at the shooting scene had instructed them to remain, but they ignored him. The ranger didn't stop them. Apparently, he found it hard to argue with a special agent wearing only a sports bra and LaFleur's blood.

They stopped only briefly to allow Clarence to recover his cache bag. "I didn't want to carry it into the crime scene."

He withdrew the tube and tried to show it to Nance. She shook her head, keeping her eyes on the road. The SUV raced toward Billings. Radio traffic reported that LaFleur had been helicoptered there.

When they stopped for gas, Clarence bought two black T-shirts with buffalo silhouettes and "Big Sky Country" logos.

They arrived to find LaFleur in surgery.

The hospital gave them a room to wash off the blood. While Nance checked in, Clarence made a couple of phone calls. Martinez agreed to deliver Tripod to Dr. Carver. The vet would watch her until he could get back.

"Full fare even for three-fourths of a dog," was all she said.

A doctor found them in the waiting area and gave them a succinct report. The surgical team had removed part of LaFleur's small intestine and repaired some internal damage. Agent LaFleur should, however, make a full recovery. The doctor authorized them to go back to LaFleur's room.

They sat, keeping vigil, surrounded by tubes and monitors. Nurses came in occasionally. Mostly, they had the room to themselves.

With the emergency behind them, Clarence found himself increasingly curious about the contents of the pipe. He thought he saw Nance casting glances toward the cache bag.

LaFleur made a noise. Nance's head popped up. None of the hospital staff appeared alarmed.

"I think he's awake," Nance said.

Clarence thought he looked like Tripod chasing rabbits.

"Since he's awake," she continued, "I think we should open it. It would lift Tom's spirits to know what's inside."

"So, we should do it for LaFleur?"

Nance nodded.

Clarence undid the bag. He pulled out the pipe. He knelt.

"Just a minute." Nance gathered a blanket from the closet and spread it on the floor.

Clarence began cleaning the lead, working the dirt and calcium carbonate off the surface.

"Should we have a conservationist or some specialist for this?"

"Probably," Clarence said as he continued working.

She began cleaning the other end. Working together, they soon had the tube returned to a dark gray color. They stopped and looked at one another.

"You ready for this?" she asked.

He nodded. "For LaFleur. You?"

"Hell, yes," she said and handed it to him.

He twisted the cap. Nothing happened. He handed it back. "Looks like you need a man with muscles."

Nance stood and carried the tube into the bathroom. She wedged the tube firmly between the toilet and the sink. Clarence grabbed the cap and again pried on it.

Nothing happened.

"Don't suppose they have a prospector's hammer they'd let us borrow," Clarence said.

Nance drew her 9mm. She ejected the magazine and cleared the chamber. Returning the magazine for extra heft, she tapped the top and sides of the tube. She took hold of the pipe. Clarence grabbed the top. Gritting his teeth, he twisted the cap with all the strength he could muster. Nance turned the tube in the opposite direction. His eyes widened. He began to nod. He felt the smallest movement and heard a faint crackling noise. Pausing only long enough to shake out his arms, he tried again. The accumulated years of resistance began to give way. The lid slowly turned. He made one full rotation and then another. Then, he stopped and solemnly looked at Nance. "This should probably be the responsibility of a licensed federal official."

Nance smiled broadly and grabbed the cap. She carried it to LaFleur's bed. With a single half turn, it came free. Together, they looked down inside.

And saw nothing.

She shined her flashlight down the tube. "There is something gold down there." Nance turned the tube over and poured the contents onto LaFleur's bed.

A gold medal with a few remaining threads of a red satin ribbon lay on his blanket.

The only sound came from LaFleur's monitors.

39

Yellowstone Region
August 1871

Watching Owl stood hidden in the shadows and silently observed the blue-coated soldiers standing alongside the man they called Mo-Ran. Although not a soldier, Mo-Ran had been their traveling companion. He spent his days making small drawings. For nearly fourteen sunrises, these soldiers had explored the area of the Yellow Rocks. Watching Owl had been their constant although unseen shadow.

Yesterday, the party had chanced upon the rock formation. The chief of the soldiers and Man-Who-Draws-Pictures, as Watching Owl had come to call him, became very excited. Pressing as close as he dared, Watching Owl heard them discussing the Liberty Cap, the strange name that his father had taught him the white men called the rock.

This morning, Man-Who-Draws-Pictures had gathered up a sack of food and supplies and set out to explore the area. Watching Owl trailed him. He followed Mo-Ran up the hill to the small cave. Watching Owl had guarded this spot since inheriting the responsibility from his father, who had guarded it before him.

With rope, Man-Who-Draws-Pictures had lowered himself down into the cave. Watching Owl had considered cutting the rope and allowing him to die in the hole. He knew, however, that the soldiers would come looking. Watching Owl could not kill them all. Instead he had remained hidden until the man returned to the surface.

While Watching Owl waited, he thought of the day his father had first brought him to this site. His father had told him how his ancestor Foot-Like-Wolf had promised to guard that which the ground held for so long as the grass grew. His promise had been bound by a medal given to him by his ancestor's white brothers. Watching Owl's father had pinned the shiny gold medal with the worn red cloth to the bare skin of his chest, allowing the blood drops to moisten the ground. Watching Owl made his blood commitment to the task that had been his family's sacred responsibility for generations.

Watching Owl heard the creak of the rope as the man returned to the surface. Although his hands were empty, Watching Owl could tell by his expression that the man had found it. He had the face of a victorious warrior. Feeling his knife, Watching Owl considered killing him before Man-Who-Draws-Pictures could spoil the secret that he, his father before him, and his father's ancestors had so carefully guarded.

Before Watching Owl could attack, Man-Who-Draws-Pictures was joined by the leader of the blue coats. Armed with a long knife and pistol, Watching Owl deemed his chance of success too small. He would wait and kill Mo-Ran while he slept.

The guard had been too vigilant. Entry into the camp had proven impossible. Then, the next morning, much to Watching Owl's surprise, the men broke camp and left the Roche Jaune without recovering the object.

Watching Owl felt relief but also concern. It would, he knew, only be a matter of time before others would come back to take that which he had so long guarded. He knew what he must do. Once the blue coats were beyond the waters of the Roche Jaune, Watching Owl returned to the sacred hole in the ground. There, he had lowered his daughter down inside the cave. He had been training her since she was young to take over his task when his winters proved too many to uphold his responsibilities. She recovered the tube. From it, they had taken the golden stick of which his ancestors spoke. Into the tube, he had her place the medal that had been passed down for generations. Those who truly came looking for the golden stick would know whom to ask. Watching Owl instructed his daughter, Rising Sun, to hide the golden stick somewhere new and to tell no one, not even him, of its resting place. This way, he reasoned, the secret would not be revealed until those who were deemed worthy by the Great Spirit were brought forward.

Rising Sun disappeared into the woods. As the sun set, she returned empty-handed. Watching Owl never asked where she had gone. Instead, he knelt before her. Looking into her face, he could see that she was tired and dirty. She had, he knew, worked hard to hide the stick. He took each of her hands in his. He turned her first to face the setting sun, faint red rays behind the mountains. "That is the setting sun, the day which has been." He turned her to face the opposite direction. "That is where the day which shall be comes from. We look to the day which shall be." He turned her to face him. In her eyes he saw the commitment to her family's honor. "You will know when the time is right, my child," the father began. "Take your smartest and bravest child. Tell them the secret of the stick. Tell them to be a faithful watcher. And when the time is right, tell them to pass the secret on to their bravest and smartest child. We must guard the stick so long as the grass shall grow and the rivers shall run. Be faithful, my child."

Rising Sun nodded, a single bob of her head.

Watching Owl pulled back his shirt. "When my father passed the secret on to me, he pinned the medal to the skin of my chest as a sign of my commitment. We have left the medal behind for those who might follow." Watching Owl drew his knife. He made a quick slash across the palm of his left hand. The blood flowed. The knife lay in the flat of his right palm. Without hesitation, Rising Sun seized the blade with her left hand and squeezed it tightly. She bit her lip, but she did not cry out in pain.

Watching Owl took back the knife, then he took her hand in his. Rotating her wrist, he sat with her silently. He looked into his daughter's eyes.

"Together we have sealed our family's commitment."

Again, Rising Sun nodded. Drops of their mingled blood wetted the ground.

40

Yellowstone National Park
June 8th

Once the hospital confirmed that LaFleur's condition had stabilized, Nance and Johnson lost their refuge. Investigative Services personnel flew in from Washington to head up the inquiry. Additional personnel raced up from Grand Teton National Park.

The last two days had been a blur. A protection ranger escorted him to an empty room in the hospital. The lead investigator kept him separate from Nance. PPT arrived and photographed him. She swabbed his hands and shrugged when he said he'd already washed. She collected his phone. Clarence didn't mind letting it go; the damn thing never got reliable reception in these mountains, anyway. PPT asked if he needed anything. He told her that he didn't. He knew his dog was safe. PPT left. He sat alone in the room.

A ranger he'd never met drove him back to the Mammoth Hot Springs Station. The ranger deposited Clarence in the same room with the same affidavit forms he'd filled out previously. He again wrote out what he'd seen. He knew this was the beginning. The lead investigator arrived and interviewed him. Clarence assumed the investigator compared his story to Nance's. Then, the investigator returned and interviewed again. Clarence stood and stretched out his leg, massaging the muscles as best he could. The park service job ordinarily kept him active—hiking, teaching, explaining, and helping. The inactivity and stress had him wound tight.

When everyone seemed satisfied that he'd been recorded and sampled, Clarence was released. In the parking lot, he found Nance's vehicle. She sat behind the driver's seat, door open to the afternoon air. He walked up to her.

She cocked her head toward the passenger seat. "Get in."

Wordlessly, Nance drove south. She passed the Canyon Visitor's Center and followed the North Rim Drive. She pulled off the road, gathered up a small daypack, and led him to a trail.

"Are we going somewhere?" Johnson asked.

Nance gave him a look that said it was a stupid question. He had to admit it was, so he stayed quiet and walked. They hiked past Grand View. He saw a sign directing them to Lookout Point. Before they reached it, however, Nance veered off onto an overgrown patch of brush faintly resembling a trail. He struggled to stay with her through the terrain.

"Keep up," she said.

"I'm bigger. I run into more things."

He rounded a corner and found her sitting on a rock with a view overlooking the North Rim. The falls tumbled in the distance. From the daypack, she produced two paper cups. He found an adjoining rock and slowly lowered himself. He gestured toward the cups. "What's that?"

"It ain't coffee," she said, handing him one.

He sipped and felt the burn of bourbon as it slid down his throat. He looked at Nance.

"An old cop gave me a pint. She said there would be weeks like this."

Clarence took another sip. "A pint might not be enough for a week like this."

She spread her arm and traced the canyon rim. "Yellowstone can be a dangerous place to be drunk."

"Yellowstone can be a dangerous place sober."

Neither one of them said anything for a long time.

Nance looked at him. "Do you know where you are?"

Johnson shook his head.

"Moran Point. The Park Service no longer shows it on the map, but most believe that this is really the spot where Thomas Moran made the sketches for his paintings of the Yellowstone Canyon. The perspective is wrong from Artist's Point on the South Rim. I thought you might like to see it."

"How come nobody told me this before?"

"We don't tell rookies everything their first summer. Yellowstone doesn't give up all her secrets."

Clarence gave a little snort of laughter. Then, he gazed back across the expanse of rock walls and watched the Yellowstone River. "Thank you."

The distant sound of falling water mingled with quiet rustling in the surrounding trees.

Nance watched the gentle sway of the branches in a nearby lodgepole pine. "Do you think it was ever there?"

He didn't need to ask what she meant by "it." He nodded.

"What do you suppose happened to it?"

"Stolen?"

She shook her head. "I don't think a thief would put the lead pipe back."

"Nor leave the medal behind. That is antique French."

Nance nodded. "The letter..." She paused and swallowed before continuing. "The letter LaFleur translated told of a native guide named Foot-Like-Wolf. He guided the two French explorers to this spot. We didn't pay much attention to that portion at the time because we were busy deciphering the code to find the location."

He sipped his drink.

Nance studied the brown liquor in her cup. "The French author described a ceremony where they inducted the warrior into the Society of French Heroes. He writes that they gave him a medal."

Johnson raised his eyebrows and considered what she had told him. "You think maybe he moved the scepter after the others left for extra security."

Nance nodded. "Makes sense." She raised her cup to her lips and then paused. "The Shoshone people inhabited the area that Aristede described."

Johnson assumed she had said something important. "Any of them still around?"

Nance pointed to the southeast. "If you walk that way, the next protected land you come to is the Shoshone National Forest."

"If you hadn't noticed, I'm not from these parts."

"The Shoshone and the Arapaho live on the Wind River Reservation just on the other side of the forest. People from the tribes make their livings as outfitters and trail guides in this area."

Clarence took another sip. His eyes ran the length of the canyon. "So, it might still be out there somewhere."

Nance's eyes followed the same path. "Native Americans have been living on this land for at least eleven thousand years. If they want it hidden, I think the scepter's whereabouts will remain a mystery."

"Another Holy Grail, a mythical treasure out there somewhere."

"Until the worthy appear."

They sat silently, nursing the liquor in their paper cups. The setting sun threw orange and golden streaks across the sky extending down to the canyon walls. Clarence watched the deepening colors.

"You were right about the art," Nance said.

He nodded. "But I was wrong about LaFleur."

Nance nodded.

Clarence looked at her. In the fading light, he couldn't judge her expression.

"I called WASO. They're doing background work. They can't say anything," Nance said. The light, apparently, was not so bad that she couldn't read his confusion. "That's the Washington Support Office, the Park Service headquarters in DC."

"So what did they not tell you?" he asked.

"William used to attend engineering school. He quietly got expelled for selling drugs. Connected, East Coast family. No scandal."

Clarence nodded. He knew the situation. You didn't have to be an East Coast cop to deal with rich people who wanted concierge treatment through the criminal justice system.

"William had trouble finding a job worthy of his abilities. He bounced around, not exactly on a successful career path." Nance sipped her drink.

"A disappointment to the family name."

Nance nodded. "Then he fell in with Barkley. William had the patrician values of the Stauros Society and was whip-smart in science and engineering. Barkley used him as his man servant and bodyguard."

"Pretty demeaning for a guy with a good education and a blue-blood family background," Johnson said.

"Then, it seems, Barkley became obsessed with the quest for the Scepter of Dagobert. He needed a miracle to get out of his wheelchair. He already had art people, and it turned out that he had a strong science guy standing behind him."

"All William lacked was a moral compass."

"And then he got greedy," Nance said.

They sat in silence staring out across the nothingness beyond the canyon wall.

"I think," Nance continued, "that LaFleur figured out some of this about William. Saw him as a possible informant. Tried to work him. That's why you saw them together. You know how secretive cops can be about their snitches."

Clarence considered the possibility and nodded. "Smart guy, but LaFleur should have known who his friends were."

"Don't go there."

Clarence couldn't think of anything else to say. He knew she was right. Instead, he picked up the bottle and refreshed his cup. Nance extended her arm. He poured more bourbon into hers. "What happens now?"

Nance took a drink. "I get some paid administrative leave while the Bureau figures that out. Apparently, some don't approve of my lone-ranger actions."

Clarence shrugged. He knew the feeling.

She looked at him. "Who'd have thought that Wyoming wouldn't like a cowboy?"

"Careful," he said, "those sorts of comments might get you a reputation as a smart ass."

"I'll blame it on the people I hang out with."

"Hang out with?"

Nance looked at him, nodded, and smiled.

Clarence raised his cup in salute. He liked the sound of that.

The Hidden River: A Murder in the Everglades
Book #2 in the Johnson and Nance Mysteries

In the Everglades, a senseless murder unearths long-buried secrets.

When artist Hezekiah Freeman is found drowned in the shallow waters of Everglades National Park, Special Agent Alison Nance and Clarence Johnson are tasked with uncovering the truth behind his death. What initially seems like a tragic accident soon reveals itself to be part of a larger, more intricate conspiracy.

As they begin their investigation, Clarence and Alison discover that Hezekiah's artwork holds more than his artistic genius. Beneath layers of paint lay cryptic clues to a hidden history that some want to keep buried. The details suggest that Hezekiah was searching for something within the park, something that might have led to his untimely death.

With each step closer to finding answers, the danger intensifies, forcing Johnson and Nance to untangle the connections between the murder and stories that the Everglades have long held.

**Get your copy today at
severnriverbooks.com**

ACKNOWLEDGMENTS

I want to express my sincere gratitude to the many who helped launch the Johnson and Nance books. Thank you to the team at Severn River Publications, particularly Andrew Watts, Amber Hudock, and Cate Streissguth. I'd also like to recognize the efforts of my editor, Kate Schomaker. You were patient and kind.

I am grateful to Paula Munier, my agent at Talcott Notch. Thank you for sticking with this project.

Thank you to Steve Yu, retired National Park Service, Investigative Services Branch, and to Linda Veress, Public Information Officer at Yellowstone National Park, for technical assistance.

Thank you to the Arvin Family Nation for your unwavering support. Your belief in me and this project has been a source of inspiration. I also want to express my gratitude to the friends who encouraged me to keep at it. Special thanks to Jack Thielman, Sam Thielman, Richard Alpert, and Alison Trinkle.

The danger in expressing gratitude is that I will omit deserving names. As with the technical errors and geographic liberties, the fault lies with me.

ABOUT THE AUTHOR

Award-winning author Mark Thielman has published short stories and novellas in *Alfred Hitchcock's Mystery Magazine, Black Cat Weekly, and Mystery Magazine*, as well as numerous anthologies. He draws upon his career as both a criminal magistrate judge and as a prosecutor in his writings.

Sign up for Mark Thielman's reader list at
severnriverbooks.com

Printed in the United States
by Baker & Taylor Publisher Services